DONATION

HIDDEN PLACES

HIDDEN PLACES

MAINE WRITERS ON COASTAL VILLAGES, MILL TOWNS, AND THE NORTH COUNTRY

Joseph A. Conforti

Camden, Maine

Down East Books

Published by Down East Books
An imprint of The Rowman & Littlefield Publishing Group, Inc.
4501 Forbes Blvd., Ste. 200
Lanham, MD 20706
www.rowman.com

Distributed by NATIONAL BOOK NETWORK

British Library Cataloguing in Publication Information Available

Library of Congress Cataloging-in-Publication Data
Names: Conforti, Joseph A., author.
Title: Hidden places : Maine writers on coastal villages, mill towns, and
     the north country / Joseph A. Conforti.
Other titles: Maine writers on coastal villages, mill towns, and the north
     country
Description: Camden, Maine : Down East Books, An imprint of Globe Pequot ;
     Distributed by National Book Network, [2020.] | Includes bibliographical
     references. | Summary: "From the late nineteenth century to the present,
     Maine writers have explored the experiences of living in a variety of
     far-flung settings. Taken together, their body of work composes a
     remarkable literary map of a diverse and changing Maine. 'Hidden Places'
     explores the identity of Maine through its writers and the people and
     places they wrote of"— Provided by publisher.
Identifiers: LCCN 2019041837 (print) | LCCN 2019041838 (ebook) | ISBN
     9781608937288 (cloth) | ISBN 9781608937295 (epub)
Subjects: LCSH: American literature—Maine—History and criticism. |
     Authors, American—Homes and haunts—Maine. | Maine—In literature. |
     Maine—Social life and customs. | Maine—Intellectual life.
Classification: LCC PS253.M2 C66 2020 (print) | LCC PS253.M2 (ebook) |
     DDC 810.9/9741—dc23
LC record available at https://lccn.loc.gov/2019041837
LC ebook record available at https://lccn.loc.gov/2019041838

♾™ The paper used in this publication meets the minimum requirements of
American National Standard for Information Sciences—Permanence of Paper
for Printed Library Materials, ANSI/NISO Z39.48-1992.

For all the Mainers, natives and newcomers,
who have enriched my life.

CONTENTS

CONTENTS

ACKNOWLEDGMENTS

I have acquired a number of debts in the course of writing this book. Wes Mc-Nair offered crucial advice at the final stage of my work. He took time from his busy schedule as a nationally recognized poet to help me clarify what I wanted to say. He suggested a title in place of my clumsy effort. The final product incorporates his suggestions. Cathleen Miller, curator of the Maine Women Writers Collection at the University of New England, was generous with her time and help. She and her staff invariably responded collegially and quickly to my requests for material from the rich collection of writers' papers. Ron Formisano continually supported this project while he was busy writing the perceptive books on American politics for which he is so well known.

Former students and colleagues have had a hand in this book. Victoria Geibel gave chapters 2 and 3 a close reading and suggested ways to improve them. David Richards offered important advice when I was at an impasse early in this study. He also suggested that I should aim to get the book out by the bicentennial of Maine's statehood. Aran Shetterly proved a dependable source of encouragement when we were not talking about the Red Sox. Five friends and colleagues never failed to say positive things about the progress of my work. Thanks to Jim Leamon, Richard D'Abate, Richard Maiman, and Walter Christie. And to Oliver Woshinsky—you are dearly missed.

At Down East Books, I want to thank Editorial Director Michael Steere for his strong interest in this project from my initial inquiry. I appreciate his quick response to questions I had along the way, from acceptance of the manuscript to the publication of the book. At Rowman & Littlefield, I want to thank Senior Production Editor Patricia Stevenson for her help.

PROLOGUE

In the middle of the nineteenth century, Nathaniel Hawthorne took stock of America's expanding continental frontier. He lamented, "We have so much country that we have no country at all. New England is as large a lump of earth as my heart can readily take in."[1] Though he spent part of his youth in Raymond, near Sebago Lake, and graduated from Bowdoin, Hawthorne's "heart" failed to take imaginative possession of Maine, New England's vast northern frontier. Granted, a missing eighteenth-century map of a sweeping Maine proprietorship plays a role in *The House of the Seven Gables* (1851). Yet, despite his connections to the state, the geography of Hawthorne's literary imagination fixed on what represented the "real" New England to him—namely, Massachusetts. Perhaps he realized that Maine could accommodate within its borders most of the rest of New England. Even before the state finally settled its international boundary with Canada in 1842, Maine had become a geographical outlier within the region.

Today the state's northern Second Congressional District, at twenty-seven thousand square miles, ranks as the largest east of the Mississippi River. It is almost as if Maine belongs in a different part of the country. No wonder a distinguished Maine poet has dubbed the state the "Montana of New England."[2] Of course, Maine boasts thousands of miles of coast and scores of islands. Perhaps, then, the state is more aptly considered New England's Alaska. From mountains to dense forests to the sea, Maine represents a rich mosaic of physical and human landscapes that have changed over time.

Fortunately, across the decades, Maine has produced nationally recognized novelists who wrote place-based fiction. From the late nineteenth century to the present, or from Sarah Orne Jewett to Monica Wood, the writers who form this study's focus have emerged from the Canadian border to the New Hampshire state line and from Down East to the northwest hinterland. They have explored Mainers' lived experience in far-flung settings: island and coastal villages, northwoods lumbering communities, unincorporated townships, backcountry hamlets, and mill cities and towns. Taken together, their body of work composes a remarkable literary map of a diverse and changing Maine.

What, then, do I mean by Maine's *Hidden Places*? On one level, my title refers to remote and obscure corners of the state that leading writers present to a reading public, to a community of general readers, critics, and teachers. Consider the woodsy village of Allagash or unincorporated Enchanted Township, places so out of the way that the former merits barely a speck on the typical Maine map and the latter doesn't register at all. Sometimes my title alludes to places now obscured by the passage of time—historical moments, for instance, beautifully captured by Maine writers who tell stories about year-round life on small lobstering islands during the Depression or about Down East as it made the transition from seafaring to sardines and then to summer people.

But *Hidden Places* suggests something more. It refers to the way good writers provoke readers to see and understand seemingly familiar places with a new awareness. By "place," I mean shared public space. Physical geography, which includes climate and the historically layered, built environment, shapes our sense of place. Writers evoke these elements, often by creating composites of similar communities. Place-based writers frequently engage in a kind of "aboveground archeology." They deepen readers' local knowledge and broaden their understanding of the state in all of its diversity.

Writers "unearth" much more, for Maine is also a storied place. That is, the sense of place is a product of representations—of the concrete images and stories that structure how we perceive a particular locale and grasp its significance and distinctiveness. A community's historical works, literature, art, museums, and civic monuments tell stories and create a narrative sense of place. As one historian has put it, stories "give order, shape and a trajectory to the clutter of things."[3] With respect to my topic, Maine place-based literary fiction generates stories that help us understand where we are (or where we are from) and thus who we are. Writers construe place as both a territory on the ground and a country of their imaginations. The authors discussed in this study help insiders see more clearly what is distinctive about their communities and encourage outsiders to better understand what might seem quaint or "queer" about the state.

Maine-born and Maine-based writers have created a rich body of work about the Pine Tree State as a place. Thus I have chosen not to include poetry, which would have swelled this study's length. For similar reasons, I have decided not to incorporate Stephen King, whose work in its enormity serves as a kind of literary analog to Maine's vastness.

I focus on novelists starting with Jewett and the Maine coast and concluding with Wood and the western Maine mill town. In most cases, I suggest that though authors wrote passionately about Maine and with deep understanding of its people, the significance of their work extends beyond the state's borders. Many of the authors wrote multiple bestsellers. Two won Pulitzer Prizes. Three others received notable, though less well-known, awards for their writing. All published with prominent New York houses, except for Jewett, whose books were issued by Boston's leading press. Some of this study's authors successfully reached international audiences.

I concentrate on literary fiction, those writers who display the most skill and originality in the use of language and in their deployment or creative revision—in the case of Carolyn Chute—of the novel's conventions. I approach the authors' work from cultural, historical, and literary perspectives. Which is to say that I contextualize their novels to illuminate the importance of place in the best Maine fiction across a century and a half. This study employs a multitude of memoirs, histories, interviews, and letters; they frame settings for grappling with authors' writing lives and most important work. I also cite numerous national and regional reviews as well as bestseller lists to gauge the reception of writers' work and to reveal critics' perceptions of Maine. For one thing, by the 1930s and 1940s reviewers talked about the "Maine novel" as if it denoted a distinctive tradition within American literature.

The writers in *Hidden Places* mattered, in part, because Maine mattered. That is, over the decades examined in this book, Maine increasingly accrued cultural capital in the American imagination. Such currency arose from multiple sources: a widening awareness of Maine's majestic coastal beauty and its mountainous interior surrounded by lake-dappled, densely wooded terrain; the ongoing work of painters, who had been the first to introduce urban audiences to Down East's glories in the middle of the nineteenth century; summer vacationers, especially those who returned year after year to seasonal "camps"; notable people who became associated with the state, such as the Rockefellers, Winslow Homer, E. B. White, and May Sarton; back-to-the-landers and their famous gurus, Scott and Helen Nearing; the rise of L.L. Bean, with a brand that seemed to distill essential qualities of Maine and its people; and more.

My analysis of Maine novelists suggests a series of questions that, drawing on my chapter-by-chapter discussions, I will revisit in the epilogue. Is *The Country of the Pointed Firs* the "great" Maine novel, as even critics who judge it as a "major-minor" work of American literature acknowledge?[4] As the grande dame of Maine fiction, Jewett minted the term "imaginative realism" to describe her writing. Did she establish a tradition that subsequent writers carried on in their representations of Maine? Women overwhelmingly dominate the canon of writers who I consider created the best body of work about the state. Did women writers possess a special affinity for place, a distinctive sense of rootedness? Why have writers not produced a major novel that delves into the character of Portland as a place? This glaring gap in Maine place-based fiction remains puzzling in part because pre–Civil War Portland experienced a notable literary flowering.

When I began *Hidden Places*, I had no plan to divide the study into three parts. But after discussing the lives and work of Sarah Orne Jewett, Mary Ellen Chase, and Ruth Moore, I realized that they formed a coherent section, which I have titled simply "Coast and Islands." The second section shifts to "The North Country and Backcountry." I devote the last section to "Mill City and Mill Town." As these titles suggest, Maine's most important novelists have written about all of the state's representative landscapes (Portland excepted) and the people who have created and transformed them. Within my topical organization the chronology moves from writers of the past to those of the present. But the progression does not adhere to a tight linear timeline because of my thematic organization.

In a sense, this study of place-based literature is related to Delorme's *The Maine Atlas and Gazetteer*. In different ways and to different degrees, my work and the *Atlas* capture a diverse state at the granular level, one representation at a time. I have tried to make *Hidden Places* accessible to general readers. But I hope my work draws interest beyond my primary audience.

Some will question exclusions from the story I tell. I have tried to anticipate such objections. In some cases, I briefly discuss writers only to explain why my emphasis resides with a contemporary. Thus this study does not pretend to be a comprehensive literary history of Maine from Jewett to the present.

I

COAST AND ISLANDS

❶

COASTAL COMMUNITIES OF WOMEN

Sarah Orne Jewett

Sarah Orne Jewett abides as an icon of Maine letters. She is the only Maine-born-and-raised fiction writer who has achieved a place in the American literary canon. (Of course, Stephen King stands as one of the giants of American horror fiction.) Mary Ellen Chase, herself a prolific Maine writer and longtime professor of English, described in effusive prose her view of Jewett's standing among Maine writers. "All Maine writers, without exception, look upon the flawless work of Sarah Orne Jewett with an admiration approaching reverence," Chase claimed. "All of us realize only too keenly that at our best we are not worthy to unloose the latchet of her shoes."[1] Chase's rhetoric defied the understatement that was so emblematic of Jewett's work.

Jewett came from a well-off family in South Berwick, Maine, twelve miles west of Portsmouth, New Hampshire, and one mile north of the important waterpower at Salmon Falls. Jewett's paternal grandfather was a ship captain, merchant, and shipbuilder. He lived in a stately Georgian house in the center of South Berwick.

The town began to change with the War of 1812 and its aftermath. As the decline of trade and shipbuilding accelerated, commercial profits shifted into textile production. A woolen mill was constructed on one side of nearby Salmon Falls in 1822, a cotton mill on the opposite side a decade later. South Berwick's population surged by 40 percent in the 1830s. Sarah would grow up with mills, tenements, and Irish and French-Canadian immigrants almost at her doorstep. This world did not serve as the focus of her work, but she didn't completely ignore it, either. In fact, it has been argued, Jewett marks the first important American writer who sympathetically portrayed the Irish.[2]

Sarah's father, Theodore H. Jewett, graduated from Bowdoin College, studied medicine, and became a highly skilled surgeon. Nevertheless, he settled into a career as a country doctor, though he found opportunities to lecture and teach at the medical schools in Maine. Sarah's maternal grandfather, William Perry, was also a doctor, a prominent surgeon in Portsmouth, under whom Jewett's father studied. Perry's oldest daughter, Caroline, married Theodore Jewett in 1842.

Sarah was born in 1849. Perhaps her father wanted and anticipated a boy. They christened her Theodora Sarah Jewett. Apparently, her father faced disappointment two more times when the last of his children, Sarah's sisters, arrived. Still, she developed a special, close relationship with her father; in fact, she revered him. As a young girl Sarah often accompanied her father as he made house calls along the coast and throughout the farming backcountry. "I used to follow him about silently like an undemanding little dog, content to follow at his heels," she recalled in "Looking Back on Girlhood." She later considered becoming a doctor. Most important, she drew on her experience with her father in composing her important novel *A Country Doctor*.[3]

Jewett graduated from Berwick Academy in 1865. She published her first story two years later. Then in 1869 she placed the first of her many stories with the *Atlantic Monthly*, arguably the most prestigious literary and cultural journal of the time. She met its publisher, James T. Fields, and his wife, Annie Adams Fields. Through them she was introduced to such writers as Henry James, Longfellow, Lowell, Whittier, and Elizabeth Stuart Phelps.

When James Fields died in 1881, Jewett began an emotionally intimate lifelong relationship with Annie, who was fifteen years older. Jewett, who suffered from what we now call rheumatoid arthritis, spent upward of half the year (especially winter) with Annie. She also enjoyed Annie's company in summer at her home on Thunderbolt Point in fashionable Manchester-by-the-Sea. Then, too, they traveled extensively together, including four excursions to Europe, where they met the likes of Tennyson and Matthew Arnold. In other words, over the course of the 1880s and 1890s, Jewett became a prominent member of Boston's cultural elite. She possessed a comfortable income from her prolific, successful writing that augmented family wealth.[4] Jewett's relationship with Maine, though not her loyalty to the state, shifted. She flowered into something of a Maine outsider-insider, with implications for her writing.

Jewett's intimate relationship with Annie was known as a "Boston marriage." Her most thorough biographer describes their commitment "as a comprehensive and loving partnership offering mutual support . . . and entirely free of any assumptions of power common in traditional male-female marriage." No evidence has surfaced showing that the otherwise "passionate" Jewett-Fields bond involved physical intimacy.[5]

Over the last few decades, feminist critics have been principally responsible for Jewett's incorporation into the American literary canon, though not without dissent. They have challenged the judgment of mostly male scholars who have relegated Jewett, at best, to advanced placement in the late nineteenth-century school of local color writing. She worked on a small human canvas, the argument goes, mostly through short stories and books of "sketches," for lack of a better term.

Such criticism, feminists have argued, fails to acknowledge how Jewett deftly depicts a countercultural world in which widows and "spinsters" not only dominate demographically but also infuse small-town life with "female" virtues, not "self-assertive masculine individuality."[6] Major characters balance communalism and individualism. They combine pride and humility, self-reliance and social nurturance. Women characters are sometimes herbalists and healers in more than the medicinal sense. In sum, Jewett's women often embody a gendered Maine village ethos of fortitude and fellow feeling.[7]

As to the literary form of her work, Jewett does not follow the novel's conventions. Her sketchbooks, novellas, and novels typically have no or a slight plot, which in male works often follows a quest. Her focus is on character and, we should add, on the importance of place. Feminist critics argue for Jewett's writing as a gendered alternative to the dominant form of men's work.

My purpose is not to become embroiled in this debate over the merits of Jewett's literary standing. Yet one can't simply set it aside; gender provides thematic substance and shape to much of her work. Nevertheless, my focus is on how Jewett imagined Maine, how she created characters, represented communities, depicted seascapes and landscapes—all of which were grounded in the real Maine of her experience. But Jewett's Maine was also a product of her imagination. Still, in Jewett's Maine, place and gender intersect, especially in her best work.

Jewett's writing life was severely limited after an accident in 1902. She was thrown from a carriage and suffered a spinal concussion. Her literary output plummeted. She wrote stories sporadically before she died of a stroke in 1909.

Over the course of her writing life Jewett published approximately one hundred and fifty stories, two books of sketches, and three novels, excluding her children's work.[8] Any assessment of her achievement rests on her best work: *Deephaven* (1877), *A Country Doctor* (1884), *The Country of the Pointed Firs* (1896), and the choicest of her short stories, whose number will vary depending on the critic/reader.

I have chosen to exclude *A Country Doctor* from my analysis. In many respects, it is the least evocative of Maine among Jewett's major works identified above. To be sure, she portrays a small group of Maine people, principally the humane, scholarly Dr. John Leslie, who, like Jewett's father, chooses a country practice over more prestigious, lucrative opportunities, and his young guardian who becomes the feminist Dr. Nan Prince. Among other things, as the doctor and the young Nan visit patients along the coast and throughout the countryside, Maine's seascape and landscape are only faintly evoked. *A Country Doctor* is essentially a dual character study of Drs. Leslie and Prince.

When she was a budding writer, Jewett's father offered his daughter advice that proved to be influential. He told her to write about what she knew best. As she later described it, her principal subject matter consisted of "simple country people" and the "trivialities and common places of life."[9] When Jewett was twenty-two years old she recorded in her diary something else Dr. Jewett told her: "Father said one day 'A story should be managed so that it should *suggest* interesting things to the reader instead of doing all the thinking for him, and setting it before him in black and white.'" Reinforcing such a literary realism is what Jewett drew from Flaubert—namely, that a writer needs to make the reader "dream."[10]

Jewett described her writing in 1894 as "imaginative realism,"[11] though she left the term unexplained. She writes about common country people and everyday life where nothing seems to happen. Yet Jewett shows the human drama that takes place among ordinary people in daily life. Her realistic facts are deployed to stir the reader's imagination. A character, a relationship, or especially, concrete images of nature in Maine, might all suggest a transcendent moral and spiritual domain beyond our tangible one. Jewett typically doesn't preach. She intimates; she implies; she gestures. Jewett developed her imaginative realism over many years. *Deephaven*, her first book, and *The Country of the Pointed Firs*, her finest work, harness the elements of imaginative realism to far different degrees. This is not to suggest that *Deephaven* simply transcribes common life and lacks an artistry of its own. It is to propose, however, that *Deephaven* has elements of an artless artistry. For all their stylistic differences, *Pointed Firs* and *Deephaven* revolve around similar themes: summer visitors discovering the beauty of the Maine coast and coming to grips with the hardships and humanity of its people as well as the quiet heroism of their daily lives.

DEEPHAVEN AND THE POST-HEROIC SOUTH COAST

Between 1873 and 1876 Jewett published three stories in the *Atlantic* that were set in the fictional fishing-farming village of Deephaven. The York, Maine, seascape was readily recognizable to any reader familiar with this alluring stretch of the south coast. Yet in her Deephaven stories Jewett recast a real place into an imagined one.

Novelist William Dean Howells, editor of the *Atlantic*, suggested that Jewett develop her stories into a book. He was especially impressed with her ability to capture realistic Maine speech—indigenous folks' diction, often awash with references to the sea; their distinctive pronunciation of words; and their lilt, when the narrator and her companion elicit long stories from even the most reticent Deephaven fisherman. Jewett worked almost to the point of nervous exhaustion revising and adding stories to her three published sketches.[12] *Deephaven* appeared in April 1877. Twenty-three editions were published over the next two decades.[13]

In the book's preface, Jewett cautioned readers not to identify *Deephaven* with a specific locale. She also claimed "the characters will in almost every case be looked for in vain."[14] Jewett shaped some fictional folk into composites drawn from many she knew. Through the alchemy of her imagination and artistic purpose she invented other individuals, who were still informed by types that were familiar to her. Only one Deephavener was a real person and drawn to full scale. She is also perhaps the grimmest character: a senile, mad former member of the gentry whose brother committed suicide almost at her feet.

In several places, Jewett outlined one of the realities of late nineteenth-century Maine coastal life that animated her writing. Beginning around the age of fifteen she had witnessed "'city dwellers' make their appearance near Berwick." She was appalled at the way they "misconstrued the country people and made game of their peculiarities." Summer visitors roused Jewett to portray how, far from "awkward, ignorant" people, most country folk led "grand simple lives."[15]

Jewett was also outraged by the popular depiction of the New England Yankee in mid-nineteenth-century American culture. The rustic rube with an accent as thick as molasses who blunders into the city entertained audiences from the stage to fiction. Even Harriet Beecher capitalized on this cliché in her Sam Lawson stories and in her novel *Oldtown Folks* (1869). Since summer people had been fed a cultural diet of Yankee caricature, Jewett feared "that townspeople and country people would never understand one another, or learn to profit by their new relationship" in Maine.[16]

Jewett's comments about country people and the Yankee character help clarify her principal audience. In *Deephaven*, the narrator refers in passing to two women characters who read the "new magazine," as they called the *Atlantic*. But people in Maine fishing and farming villages were not the prime audience for either the *Atlantic* or Jewett's writing. Rather, urbanites in the Northeast of the middle to upper-middle classes formed the bulk of the *Atlantic*'s readers.[17] Jewett branched out to other first-rate periodicals such as *Century, Harper's*, and *Scribner's*, whose readers were precisely the kind of people who were increasingly drawn to Maine.

For urbanites seeking a summer respite from their rapidly growing industrial, immigrant, and crowded surroundings, the Maine coast was appealing on several levels. From vibrant trading ports engaged in international trade, places like Deephaven had long been reduced to gray fishing villages that modernity seemed to have passed by. Seemingly frozen in time and radiating characteristics of an appealing "unmodern picturesque"[18] world, Maine's Deephavens increasingly drew summer people with money to spend. "Old salts"—retired, rheumatic ship captains, and not a few people who were perceived as "queer folk"—added color to the local scene. Deephaven's rocky seascape and pine-studded landscape and their interplay with natural light formed what Jewett later described as a distinctive "northern look."[19]

Deephaven is a series of loose-jointed character sketches and "as told to" stories. It is not a novel; there is no plot propelling the action and providing the book with a narrative spine. *Deephaven* evokes the village's seascape and landscape with descriptions that help pace the reader through the torrent of spoken works for which the visiting Bostonians serve as an audience of two.

Deephaven opens in Boston. Kate Lancaster and Helen Innis, two twenty-four-year-old single women, become the visitors or protagonists, if one may appropriate that novelistic convention. Helen, who serves as the narrator, is far less privileged than her wealthy friend. Kate forgoes an affluent summer vacation for a change. Her family scatters to fashionable Newport, Rhode Island, and Lenox, in Massachusetts's Berkshire Hills, as well as to Lake Superior. Kate invites Helen to spend the summer with her in Deephaven, accompanied by two family servants. The other two have been dispatched to Newport. Kate's recently deceased great-aunt, Katharine Brandon, has bequeathed a stately old house to her mother. "The town," Kate tells Helen, "is a quaint old place which has seen better days. There are high rocks at the shore, and there is a beach and there are woods inland, and hills, and there is the sea." Helen reflects that a summer in Deephaven might unwind as a dull affair "for two young ladies who were fond of gay society and dependent upon excitement." They pack plenty of books. But the human drama and the natural beauty of Deephaven will supplant a reading holiday.

The outsiders' acceptance into Deephaven society begins even before they arrive. On the stagecoach from the train depot, twelve miles from the town, Kate and Helen meet Mrs. Kew, wife of the lighthouse keeper, herself an enlightened person—an outsider from the hills of Vermont. Kate exchanges seats with Mrs. Kew so that the latter can sit facing forward. Mrs. Kew is nearly overwhelmed by this act of kindness from a Boston lady. The coach ride and conversation mark the start of a friendship; the Bostonians visit Mrs. Kew often in the lighthouse.

Kate secures entrée into Deephaven life in part because she is a descendant of the much-respected and charitable deceased Miss Brandon, who emerges, even in death, as the community's benevolent matriarch. As her gesture on the stage-coach suggests, Kate embodies the generosity of spirit of her great-aunt, after whom she is named. Helen, in turn, profits from her association with Kate. The encounter with Mrs. Kew establishes that Kate is "polite," "kind," and devoid of "condescension," as Helen describes her. The young women's reputation circulates via the web of Deephaven's communal ties. "They don't put on no airs," the briny Captain Sands says of Kate and Helen.

Shortly after their arrival in Deephaven, the friends visit Mrs. Kew and expe-rience the therapeutic natural splendor of the village's setting. After supper, they mount the lighthouse steps and watch the interplay of clouds and sun over the ocean at day's end: "There was a little black boat in the distance drifting slowly, climbing one white wave after another. . . . But presently the sun came from behind the clouds and the dazzling golden light changed the look of everything . . . one could only keep very still, and watch the boat, and wonder if heaven would not be somehow like that far, faint color, which was neither sea nor sky." Jewett offers an early example of imaginative realism, though she tells rather more than she suggests.

On visits to the lighthouse, the Bostonians "twice . . . saw a yacht squadron like a flock of great white birds." It is a compelling image of summer people invading Maine coastal waters and a striking contrast between leisure craft and Deephaven's weathered working vessels: dories, lobster smacks, and deep-sea fishing ships. Yachting only became a major recreational activity of the well heeled at midcentury. They established clubs along the coast and competi-tive racing. Over the course of the summer, Kate's friends moor their yachts at Deephaven to visit her—another reminder, if Deephaveners need one, of the well-off world to which she belongs. No one in Deephaven appears troubled by Kate's privilege and the community's poverty. Jewett portrays Mainers who are too proud to ask for help and who accept the world as it is and make do.

Mrs. Judith Patton is one of those proud Deephaveners. Kate and Helen meet her soon after they arrive. She is a widow, like so many other local women, many of whom have lost men at sea. Mrs. Patton was a neighbor of Kate's great-aunt. The widow fell into crippling poverty and poor health. She was too proud to ask for help from the town—to "go on the town," in the common parlance for local welfare. Katharine Brandon discovered her plight and "scolded" her for not asking for help. She bought Mrs. Patton food, sent her to the doctor, and directed her servants to assist the unfortunate neighbor. Miss Brandon includes Judith in her will, putting her "beyond the fear of want" in old age. Kate draws on the social capital—the mutual trust—in the community that her great-aunt generated over her lifetime.

In her own way, Mrs. Patton is another woman who nurtures the community. She knows everybody's secrets, but "she told them judiciously if at all." Mrs. Patton is the one who attends to neighbors who are ill. Like other Jewett women, she is a healer with special knowledge. A skilled herbalist, she knows how to brew "every variety of herb tea." And when she loses a patient, she takes responsibility and becomes "commander in chief at the funeral."

If Mrs. Patton is a kind of repository for all the community's secrets, she keeps in confidence the dark side of her marriage. It is another neighbor who tells Kate and Helen that her husband was "shif'less and drunk all the time." He died young and left her impoverished. "Noticed that dent in the side of her forehead, I s'pose?" the neighbor asks. "That's where he liked to have her killed; slung a stone bottle at her." It is too much for the genteel Bostonians. "'What!' said Kate and I, very much shocked." There are more jolts to come as Deephaveners tell of life's hardships. *Deephaven* is an oral book, but not, in the main, dialogue driven. Kate and Helen mostly listen. Jewett is a kind of literary anthropologist, a cultural go-between who explains a "remote" tribal world to outsiders—that is, to summer visitors, among others. Thus she lets the natives speak for themselves, in their own tongue. Indeed, at one point Helen makes an acute observation on the sort of anthropological design of *Deephaven*. As to transposing speech, "It loses a great deal in being written, for the old sailor's voice and gestures and thorough earnestness all carried no little persuasion."

One thing not lost in translation, however, is Jewett's superb rendering of common Maine coastal dialect in the late nineteenth century. The pronunciation of words is rich and vibrant, captured from a kind of documentary point of view, without a hint of caricature. A former captain describes a crafty merchant as "ter'ble perlite." Deephaveners liberally use adverbs such as "p'r'aps" and "al'ays." They employ expressions like "land o' compassion," and "so's to be contented." They suffer from "narves" and their always "re'clectin'" or "re'flectin'" for their visitors. They enjoy things like wild "rosbry." Kate's last name is "Lank'ster" to Deephaveners. Moreover, the sea pervades their language. Old salts are "condemned as unseaworthy," to quote Captain Jacob Lent. Or perhaps the rheumatic captains are akin to the storm-tossed shipwrecks in Deephaven's harbor, of the kind that were all too common along the nineteenth-century Maine coast, adding to the "romance" of the sea for outsiders and artists.

Maine's distinctive coastal dialect emerges in all its resonance from the detailed stories Deephaveners tell about their lives. A surprising number of these accounts, like Judith Patton's story of domestic violence and drunkenness, darken the two Bostonians' understanding of Deephaven. In fact, for readers only familiar with *The Country of the Pointed Firs*, *Deephaven* may prove unsettling.

Kate and Helen befriend some leathery-faced old salts who often congregate in the morning, "sunning themselves like turtles," on one of the wharves. They hear stories of adventures at sea and of Deephaven's prosperous days. They become interested in a reticent, lame fisherman who they frequently see around one of those vernacular Maine fish houses that straggle along the coast. Helen offers a detailed description of the "workshop" where tight-lipped Danny spends so much time: "In there was a seine or part of one, festooned among the cross-beams overhead, and there were snarled fishing-lines, and barrows to carry fish in, like wheelbarrows without wheels; there were the queer round lobster-nets and 'kits' of salt mackerel, tubs of bait, and piles of clams; and some queer bones, and parts of remarkable fish, and lobster-claws of surprising size fastened on the walls for ornament." The double use of "queer" only serves to underscore how exotic the interior of the fish house appears through the eyes of city visitors. It also suggests the seeming oddity of Danny, who is silently at ease among the artifacts of his existence.

The Bostonians engage Danny in a brief exchange about fish, a subject that is his lifeblood and about which he is surefooted. Danny begins to relax his guardedness; his shyness and reticence have been like an inactive volcano that suddenly erupts and pours out words and stories. He rescued a cat from drowning or worse at Charlestown Bridge, presumably in Massachusetts. The cat was "screeching real pitiful" and clinging to a pier. Boys were hurling rocks at her. Danny nursed the injured, starving creature back to health. "I don' know as I ever had anything like me as much as she did," the fisherman confesses.

Then Danny's ease with the two young women grows; they mostly listen. He turns more personal, disclosing the trajectory of his early life. Orphaned at the age of nine, he was "bound out to a man in the tanning trade." Hating the work, he ran away to sea when he was "a little bigger." He fell from the "topsail," crashing to the deck and suffering permanent injury. Danny recovered in a Catholic hospital, which he calls "about the best place I ever was." He was impressed with the Catholic nuns: "they were real ladies." Danny's out-of-character confessional mode then becomes clearer; Kate and Helen are "real ladies," though Danny never actually describes them that way. He doesn't have to. He has seen them along the waterfront regularly. In other words, on one level, Kate and Helen remind him of the nuns.

For the rest of the summer, Danny says nothing about himself to Kate and Helen. He seems embarrassed by how much he has revealed already. He reverts to a closemouthed fisherman. Then, on the day of their departure, the visitors appear on the shore to say good-bye to people. Danny does speak, however tersely: "Goin', are ye? Well, I'm sorry; ye've treated me first-rate; the Lord bless ye." Then he flees. One can imagine these were the same simple words of Danny's good-bye to the nuns.

At the end of their stay, the most sorrowful story begins to unwind. It is perhaps a good example of imaginative realism. On a scintillating July day, when coastal Maine is a tonic recalled in the dark of winter, Kate and Helen travel with Mr. Dockum "four miles from Deephaven." The seascape changes abruptly: "The shore was so rocky that there were almost no places where a boat could put in, so there were no fishermen in the region, and the farms were scattered wide apart; the land was so poor that even the trees looked hungry."

They tie their horse at "a little house by the sea," and Mr. Dockum walks off inland to meet a man. The young women explore the rockbound coastline. "It was a delightful day to spend out of doors," Helen recalls. The description of nature once again suggests the hardscrabble life of the local Mainers they are soon to encounter. Kate and Helen climb the highest rocks and stare down at the rolling, rhythmic sea "dashing its white spray high over the ledges." Helen asks herself, "What could it be [like] in winter when there was a storm and the great waves come thundering in?" The friends then seek the shade of some "gnarled pitch-pine" that "looked like a band of outlaws; they were such wild-looking trees." Perhaps, Helen reflects, "their savage fight with winter had made them hard-hearted."

They return to the house and wait for Mr. Dockum. Kate and Helen make friends with "thin and pitiful" children, giving them candy and part of their lunch. The father appears and they generously pay him a dollar for taking care of their horse. He is grateful: "I never earned any money as easy as this before." Their kindness opens the floodgates of the family's ordeal, which apparently goes unacknowledged in the "distant" Deephaven community.

"I'm willin' and my woman is," the man, who remains nameless, says in tears. "It looks sometimes as if the Lord had forgot us," which upsets his wife, who considers it near blasphemy. They both suffer from poor health; he can't "foller" deep-sea fishing. Moreover, his trade as a boatbuilder has become all but useless: "folks buys 'em second-hand nowadays, and you can't make nothing." His farmland is unproductive. The family seems to subsist on money their son sends periodically from his job in a Boston shop.

After the visit, Kate and Helen think and talk often of the family. When they meet "Andrew" in town one day, they give him things for his family, urging him to visit them whenever he is in Deephaven. Though they never saw him again, "they made many plans" to visit the family. They don't return until late October, just before their departure for Boston. On a "perfect autumn day" the oldest Dockum boy drives them. "The air was warm, and sweet with the smell of bayberry bushes and pitch-pines and the delicious saltiness of the sea." But this reminder of their uplifting summer holiday on the coast only serves as a prelude to their discovery that the parents have succumbed to life's undertow. The mother died first, and then the still nameless man drank himself to death. The four children are being separated. Two orphans are bound out to another family. A half sister of the deceased man reluctantly takes custody of the other two. She resents the burden since she has just finished raising her own children. Someone among the men waiting at the house with the family praises "Andrew" and gives his life an appropriate epitaph: "He was a real willin' honest man." Kate and Helen witness their first walking country funeral.

One does not have to be steeped in Jewett's literary investment in the tension between individualism and communalism to surmise what might have happened to Andrew and his family. Suppose they lived in Deephaven or very nearby, or suppose they were part of Deephaven's "imagined" community that was defined not by geography but by relationships. Would the community have let them perish? Like great-aunt Brandon's assistance to Judith Patton, Deephaveners, particularly village women, would surely have staved off the family's tragedy.

Jewett was only twenty-eight years old when *Deephaven* was published. The book has shortcomings, including some preachiness and an assertion of free will, as the Bostonians are pleased with themselves for "choosing" to have an enjoyable summer. Still, whatever its flaws, *Deephaven* represents an important accomplishment. It successfully, and sometimes beautifully, evokes the Maine coast in summer (and once in autumn). It offers a diverse gallery of distinctive Maine coastal people, who are not stick figures or simply typecast, but real flesh and bone and blood believable characters. It captures common coastal Maine speech at a moment in time and resists lapsing into entertaining Yankee caricature. *Deephaven* also initiates Jewett's focus on women.

The collection was a popular success but received more mixed reviews from critics. William Dean Howells praised the book in the *Atlantic* and understandably perhaps made no mention of Jewett's still underdeveloped imaginative realism.

The sketches were devoid of "every trick of exaggeration." They possessed "the very tint and form of reality; we could not express too strongly the sense of conscientious fidelity which the art of the book gives." Other critics made the point more baldly, and perhaps unfairly. *Deephaven* was portrayed as a kind of local color looking-glass realism. The *New York Times* was downright dismissive. *Deephaven* "if condensed considerably . . . would read well in letters . . . [and] it is by some mistake, doubtless, that it got into print at all." However, John Greenleaf Whittier, though he belonged to a different era, wrote Jewett that he had read *Deephaven* three times and had bought copies for friends.[20]

THE COUNTRY OF THE POINTED FIRS: WOMEN AND PLACE

In the nearly two decades between Deephaven's appearance and the publication of *The Country of the Pointed Firs* (1896), Jewett's familiar southern Maine coast continued to change. Consider faded York. By the 1890s, summer people took imaginative possession of the original center of the town and hastened its transformation into "Old York," an authentic embodiment of unmodernized, picturesque Old New England. They preserved or renovated old houses, repaired the Congregational church, and spiffed up the town green. Jewett approved of such developments. She felt less urgency to serve as a literary mediator between local and summer people, though she didn't forsake this literary stance in *Pointed Firs*. Also by the 1890s, she was more inclined to accept factory workers who took up residence in South Berwick.[21]

Jewett had changed in other ways as well. She now had lived among the Boston literati for months at a time for more than fifteen years. The small-town author of *Deephaven* had matured into a sophisticated international traveler who had also journeyed as far south as Florida and as far west as St. Louis. Though she always returned to South Berwick, her relationship to Maine shifted. By the time *Pointed Firs* was published, she remained an outsider-insider, but her cultural distance from Maine had widened. Yet Jewett believed that her travels in particular gave depth to her perspective on Maine. As she wrote to Willa Cather, "One must know the world so well before one can know the parish."[22]

Jewett planted her *Pointed Firs* "parish" somewhere along Maine's midcoast. Dunnett Landing is an out-of-the-way, obscure village unspoiled by summer visitors. Only the yachting crowd occasionally intrudes on the life of the Landing's "authentic" Maine folk. Though Jewett claimed to have shed the role of cultural go-between, the urbanites who consumed her scores of stories in highbrow magazines were free to receive *Pointed Firs* as an introduction and enticement to another real and imagined uncolonized nook of coastal Maine.

Dunnett Landing is a kind of mosaic of locations that Jewett visited in August and September 1895 whose beauty and tranquility took hold of her imagination. Jewett and a friend stayed on Islesboro, off the coast of Camden. She sailed around the island "all among the 'pointed firs.'"[23] To the west she could see the rolling Camden Hills, which descended almost down to the water's edge. Annie Fields joined Sarah on Islesboro, and they traveled by steamer back to the mainland. For a month they took up residence in Martinsville, a slight village with a handful of families near Port Clyde. Jewett wrote to a friend in Boston how the house she occupied with Annie had "a green field that slopes down to the sea." From the window in her bedroom, she observed "a potato field, where the figures . . . work all day against . . . a background . . . of the pointed firs that belong to Maine, like the grey ledges they are rooted in." Sarah and Annie came to know the families of Martinsville. Jewett spent hours "under a spruce tree" lost in thought or absorbed in reading.[24]

Shortly after her stay in Martinsville, Jewett began work on what would become *The Country of the Pointed Firs*. The stories that would appear as chapters were first serialized in the *Atlantic Monthly* in January, March, July, and September 1896. Jewett returned to Martinsville during the summer before finishing the final chapters. The book was published in November 1896 with no revisions.[25] It was printed and reprinted with exceptionally wide margins on all sides of the pages to make the stories seem to constitute a longer book. This original edition was significantly altered after Jewett's death. Fifty pages were added to the original text. Two "Dunnett Landing" stories, one of which ("William's Wedding") Jewett left unfinished, were included in 1910. A third was added in 1919. Then Willa Cather rearranged the order of these posthumous alterations in 1925.[26] For this book, I have chosen to use Jewett's original text.

The Country of the Pointed Firs reveals how Jewett had changed as a writer since *Deephaven*. The book has more unity. The visitor-narrator grows over the course of the summer. She is not just an observer of Maine life, as were Kate and Helen. She participates in the course of Dunnett Landing's mostly small events, becoming something of an adopted daughter. *Pointed Firs* is less of a talkative book than *Deephaven*—that is, less of a collection of "as told to" stories. *Pointed Firs* displays Jewett's cosmopolitan sensibility, acquired over two decades of living comfortably in Boston and traveling the world. She often reaches for the universal, humanistic meaning in the parish particulars of Dunnett Landing. Jewett's prose is spare but also more lyrical than *Deephaven*.

Pointed Firs is a more powerfully visual work than *Deephaven*. It has drawn parallels to Winslow Homer's Maine marines of the same period. But there are crucial differences. Homer was a naturalist, more interested in the study of the sea. Unlike Jewett, people or houses are often missing from his panoramas. Then, too, there is nothing in Jewett comparable to Homer's close-ups of the sea or his winter marines.[27]

The nameless narrator first visited Dunnett Landing briefly while yachting along the Maine coast a few years earlier. It amounted to a tourist encounter. The village's "quaintness" and seemingly unchanging character charms the urbanite. Despite its remoteness, the people of Dunnett Landing cling to the "childish" belief that somehow their village resides at the "centre of civilization." The narrator returns in late June, intending to complete a long writing assignment in a place without distractions, a village where supposedly nothing happens.

We might pause to reflect on how Jewett privileges summer (and fall, to a lesser extent) in her work. It is as if Maine is more "Maine" during the summer months, whether or not she writes with an audience of tourists in mind. To be sure, Jewett does use winter settings, as in the minor sketch "A Winter Drive" (1893) or the story "Aunt Cynthy Dallett" (1896). But she is far less invested in the Maine of winter as literary subject matter. As she wrote to a correspondent in the winter of 1895, "Sir, when you have seen one snowfield you have seen all snowfields."[28] Apparently newly fallen snow against a background of deep green pointed firs failed to redeem the Maine landscape in winter or sufficiently stir Jewett's literary imagination.

Dunnett Landing has no summer hotels, so the visitor arranges to board with a sixty-seven-year-old childless widow, Almira Todd. Summer boarding became a common practice in northern New England in the late nineteenth century. It offered country folk an opportunity to earn badly needed money. In turn, urbanites expected country hospitality and good homemade food, along with clean air and natural beauty.[29] Mrs. Todd's boarder reaps far more than she envisioned.

Almira Todd is a large woman, tallish and heavyset. She also cuts an outsized figure in Dunnett Landing. "Almiry," as she is known, lost her husband at sea, like so many women in the community. Other men perished in the Civil War or sought their fortunes in the west or in cities. Thus the demographics of Dunnett Landing, like so many late nineteenth-century Maine coastal villages, are skewed. It is a matriarchy; older women form the fabric of community. Almiry Todd is peerless in this process. She not only makes and sells popular spruce beer but also forages in the countryside for herbs. Mrs. Todd maintains a "queer" herb garden. She knows when and how to combine herbs for particular ailments. From her house she runs a "rustic pharmacopoeia" with a steady flow of townspeople to her door. Like Jewett's father, she knows when to minister to emotional ills; she is not above deploying what we would call a placebo. Mrs. Todd is also a rustic philosopher: "I must say I like variety myself," she tells her boarder; "some folks washes Monday and irons Tuesday the whole year round, even if the circus is goin' by."

Perhaps Mrs. Todd's character may be traced back to Harriet Beecher Stowe's *The Pearl of Orr's Island* (1862). Thirteen-year-old Jewett read the newly published novel and fell in love with it, though she later came to recognize its literary limitations. Yet Stowe depicted women who serve as kind of progenitors for Mrs. Todd. Stowe described a "class of females who might be denominated, in the Old Testament language, 'cunning women,'—that is, gifted with an infinite practical 'faculty' which made them an essential requisite in every family for miles and miles around."

Mrs. Todd and other Dunnett Landing natives speak with a distinctive diction. But their Maine coastal dialect is not as thick as Deephaveners' speech or that of Stowe's Orr's Islanders. A few fishermen are the exception in Dunnett Landing. To be sure, Jewett repeats striking localisms such as "sleeving," or walking arm in arm with someone. She also introduces new idiomatic pronunciations: "sca'ce" (scarce) and "holt" (hold), for example. Yet peculiar expression is not as common in *Pointed Firs* as in *Deephaven*. In the former, folk mainly drop the letter *g* from words ending with *ing* and *f* from *of*. In other words, through her representation of Maine speech, Jewett preserves local color while simultaneously striving to modulate it, to resist deploying it for entertainment value as Stowe did.

Mrs. Todd puts her boarder in charge of dispensing herbal remedies while she is away from home. The callers constantly disrupt the writer, who then rents the empty schoolhouse for the peace and quiet she requires. "Well, dear," Mrs. Todd confesses, "I've took great advantage o' you bein' here. I ain't had such a season for years, but I never had nobody I could trust." The landlady has begun to form a bond with her boarder.

The visitor retreats to the schoolhouse, but it affords no relief from the village life, where nothing is supposed to complicate its tranquil surface simplicity. The schoolhouse provides a window onto Dunnett Landing. After attending the church service for a deceased woman she had come to know, the narrator withdraws to the schoolhouse. As in a painting, the schoolhouse window frames the woman's walking funeral against a sweeping backdrop: "The bay-sheltered islands and the great sea beyond stretched away to the far horizon southward and eastward; the little procession in the foreground looked futile and helpless on the edge of the rocky shore. It was a glorious day in early July, with a clear, high sky; there were no clouds; there was no noise of the sea." The narrator tempers the sad scene of death at high noon on a stunning Maine coastal day. Her realism pivots to the imaginative. The sparrows sing happily as the coffin progresses toward the cemetery. They celebrate "with joyous knowledge of immortality, and contempt for those who could so pettily concern themselves with death."

Among the funeral walkers, the narrator spies a man who looks like "an aged grasshopper." It is Captain Littlepage, who soon appears at the schoolhouse window. The narrator welcomes the visit. Already she hungers "for news from the outer world"—that is, from Dunnett Landing. The captain is one of the community's eccentrics, their queer folk. He is obsessed with his long-ago experience in the Arctic. Shipwrecked, he learned about what he considers "a kind of waiting-place between this world an' the next." It is a zone that looks like a town in the sea but disappears as soon as someone comes ashore, where strange men beat back visitors.

The captain's story goes on too long. Nevertheless, he does say something important about Dunnett Landing's, and coastal Maine's, nineteenth-century seafaring history: "In the old days, a good part o' the best men knew a hundred ports and something of the way folks lived in them . . . [they] could see outside the battle for town clerk here in Dunnett." The town is now at "low-tide," culturally speaking. "Shipping's a terrible loss to this part o' New England from a social point of view, ma'am." In other words, the captain's experience of the world instilled in him a kind of cosmopolitanism provincialism; it gave him something of a new perspective on the "parish." The urban, cultured, well-traveled narrator reverses the captain's odyssey. She progresses from urbane tourist outsider to knowledgeable "insider" of Dunnett Landing parish. Her summer will alter her view of the world she has left behind. All human drama does not reside in the city.

The narrator leaves Captain Littlepage and chances upon Mrs. Todd, who has observed their conversation. "Funerals always sets him goin'," she explains. Almost in a heartbeat, the gray sky is set ablaze like a luminist painting: "[a] gleam of golden sunshine struck the outer islands, and one of them shone out clear in the light, and revealed itself in a compelling way to our eyes." It is Green Island, where Mrs. Todd grew up. Her eighty-six-year-old mother, Mrs. Blackett, and her sixty-year-old brother, William, still live there. He is another of Dunnett Island's odd folk. A kind of disabling engrained childish shyness afflicts William. The visitor and Mrs. Todd make plans to visit Green Island.

A beautiful summer day arrives, and Mrs. Todd decides it's time to make their journey, simply using a dory! Johnny Bowden, one of the scarce young people in Dunnett Landing, who is Mrs. Todd's cousin, accompanies the two women. He and the narrator row until a sail is lofted to carry them to their destination. Mrs. Todd skillfully steers the dory through perils, displaying mariner abilities, which the narrator adds to her herbalist and rustic philosopher talents.

As they approach the island, Mrs. Todd offers a piece of her wisdom: "You never get over bein' a child long's you have a mother to go to." The octogenarian is a small sprightly woman who greets them with warmth. She speaks in a heavier dialect than her daughter. She has passed her adult life isolated on the island, though she remains connected to Dunnett Landing. Jewett's persistent literary stake in the relationship between the individual and the community furnishes a thematic scaffold for *Pointed Firs*'s sketches.

William remains tending his fish weirs rather than coming to greet the visitors. The narrator leaves the house to enjoy the weather and the setting, hoping to encounter William. When he does appear, she sees a slight, slender figure with round shoulders who resembles his mother in every physical respect. Though he does speak first, the narrator recognizes that it is starting conversation that paralyzes him. He invites her to take in the view from the great ledge, which the place-bound islander describes to the widely traveled visitor as the grandest "view in the world." The narrator offers another sweeping painterly visual of the Maine coast, this time facing westward: "There above the circle of pointed firs we could look down over all the islands, and could see the ocean that circled this and a hundred other bits of island around the mainland shore, and all the far horizon. It gave a sudden sense of space, for nothing stopped the eye or hedged one in."

For Mrs. Todd, Green Island possesses strata of experience, memory, and regret. She and the narrator go for a walk, ostensibly to pick the special pennyroyal that thrives on the island. It is found in a location that is "sainted" to Mrs. Todd, and only her mother knows about it. Almiry and her husband used to retreat to this spot. He perished near Green Island directly in front of this site consecrated by lament. The secret place leads to the sorrowful recesses of Mrs. Todd's heart. She confesses that she loved someone else, not Nathan. She married him, though she only liked rather than loved him. Nathan's death preempted his inevitable knowledge of Almira's secret. She never married again and thus remains childless.

The narrator turns lyrical, universalizing Mrs. Todd beyond the story of a simple, though gifted, Maine figure: "An absolute archaic grief possessed this country-woman; she seemed like a renewal of some historic soul, with her sorrows and the remoteness of a daily life busied with rustic simplicities and the scents of primeval herbs." The two women leave the island with a transformed relationship; they share something of a mother-daughter emotional compact.

With the trip to Green Island, *Pointed Firs* strays toward Hawthornean terrain and themes of secret guilt and moral irony. "Poor Joanna," the story that follows, involves an extreme individual and the "unpardonable sin" that descends directly from Hawthorne's moral universe.

Mrs. Susan Fosdick, a friend, comes to visit with Almira. One night they are discussing the peculiar people who once resided at Dunnett Landing in larger numbers. Mrs. Fosdick refers to poor Joanna and her self-imposed exile on Shell-heap Island, once a Native American settlement. The narrator expresses an interest in hearing the story. Mrs. Todd responds sharply, "I never want to hear Joanna laughed about." Not only was the woman, who had been deceased for twenty-two years, the cousin of Mrs. Todd's late husband, but the herbalist and the island hermit also shared a moral identity, as both were unable to marry the men they loved. Joanna's response to her predicament, however, was very different from Almira Todd's and may have been more honest.

The story unfolds as Mrs. Fosdick and Almira carefully relate the details and Dunnett Landing's reactions. Joanna was engaged to a man who jilted her one month before their wedding, married a woman from further up the coast, and left for Massachusetts. In Joanna's fury and depression, her "thoughts was so wicked towards God," as she told Mrs. Todd, "that I can't expect to be forgiven." She believed that she had committed the unpardonable sin. Jewett, unlike Hawthorne, doesn't ruminate over what, if anything, constitutes an unpardonable sin. She lived in a post-Calvinist world. A Puritan shadow didn't hang over her Maine. She made an easy transition from the family Congregational Church to Boston Episcopalianism.[30]

Perhaps the story of poor Joanna is sufficiently dark and tragic. Her blasphemy is serious enough. Yet maybe Joanna was wrong and her unpardonable sin is constituted differently. It is not her blasphemy but her belief that she is beyond God's mercy and forgiveness that constitutes her unpardonable sin. Joanna, ironically, thereby elevates herself above God.

Joanna gives her comfortable wealth away, never sees the mainland again, and lives out her days in a two-room cabin that her father had built before he married. Mrs. Todd goes out to visit her with the pharisaical minister, whose book knowledge and shallow personal religious experience Joanna respectfully ignores. Mrs. Todd feels rage toward the seminary minister and his incapacity to grasp the depth of Joanna's torment. She pleads with Joanna to come back to Dunnett Landing and live near her, or at least spend winter with Mrs. Blackett on Green Island. Joanna declines and prevails on Mrs. Todd never to ask her again to leave the island. Almiry then pulls out a coral pin that Nathan brought back from the Mediterranean for Joanna. She, in turn, says, "I want you to have it, Almiry, an' wear it for love o' both o' us."

Yet the community won't simply leave this "isolato," to use Melville's term, abandoned and forgotten. Folks leave packages for her on Shell-heap's shore; Mrs. Blackett visits Joanna and gets her to promise that she will signal over to Green Island if she needs help; William brings fresh farm items to her; and Joanna sees "one or two . . . old folks." When she dies, boats along twenty miles of coast arrive at Shell-heap, mostly out of respect for the hermit.

Significantly, the story of poor Joanna is positioned almost precisely at the center of *Pointed Firs*. The Hawthornean type of tragedy gives some shadow to the sun-drenched summery quality of the book. The narrator's visit to Shell-heap Island undergirds the centrality of poor Joanna's story to *Pointed Firs*. She captures the late summer's alterations to the island's landscape. "The fresh green of June" has given way "to a sun burnt brown that made [the islands] look like stone, except where the dark green of the spruces and fir balsam kept the tint that even winter storms might deepen, but not fade." There is a residue of life on Shell-heap, ruins that form a "shrine" to what we might call the uncompromising eccentricity of Maine's monastic nun.

The narrator finds a well-trodden path of "pilgrims" who knew Joanna and young people who learned of her. Joanna has become both a curiosity and something of a saintly figure, only lacking miraculous cures to her credit. All that remains of her simple dwelling is its foundation. The mainland "lay dim and dreamlike in the August haze." The narrator is provoked to reflect with an arresting tide of images that capture the universal element she extracts from poor Joanna's life: "In the life of each of us I said to myself, there is a place remote and islanded and given to endless regret or secret happiness; we are each the un-companioned hermit and recluse of an hour or a day; we understand our fellows of the cell to whatever age of history they may belong."

Then the narrator hears merriment from a boat. She ponders the many times Joanna must have heard laughter from partying boaters. She wonders how the hermit of Shell-heap might have felt when the sounds of such worldliness punctuated her cloistered life.

"Poor Joanna" is a powerful, distinctive story in *Pointed Firs*. It displays a range of emotions; it is laced with irony and shows how Jewett has mastered her craft since *Deephaven*. Appropriately, the "Bowden Family Reunion," the longest and most affirmative section of *Pointed Firs*, immediately follows Joanna's story.

The reunion marks summer's social high point and something of the season's culmination, as shorter days and cooler evenings portend fall's arrival. For the narrator, who has all but forsaken the schoolhouse and her writing assignment for immersion in Dunnett Landing's life, the reunion represents her rite of passage and initiation into communal membership. She becomes the daughter that Mrs. Todd never had and is symbolically ushered into the Bowden family.

The reunion underscores the inbreeding that occurs in a diminished coastal community where demographics have gone haywire. As Mrs. Todd observes, "When you call upon the Bowdens you may expect most families to rise up between the Landing and the far end of the Back Cove. Those that aren't kin by blood are kin by marriage." Boats and carriages stream toward the Bowden Place. It is a "northern sort" of morning, "sunshiny air . . . with a cool freshness as if it came over new-fallen snow." The "fragrance of fir balsam" mingled with the "faintest flavor of seaweed from the ledges, bare and brown at low tide in the little harbor."

Along the way to the reunion, Mrs. Todd and her mother are greeted as local luminaries, hailed by people in dooryards and extended warm wishes. They reaffirm how Mrs. Blackett's "far island and these scattered farms [are linked] into a golden chain of love and dependence." The warm exchange with the local doctor serves as a reminder of how he and the herbalist are "partners." It is all rather too mawkish and reminds one that what is missing from *Pointed Firs*, as has been much commented on, is any semblance of conflict, whether between the backcountry and the coast or the old entitled captain-gentry and Dunnett Landing's fishermen. The most we encounter is Mrs. Todd's bad blood with Mari' Harris. "I hate her just as I always did," Mrs. Todd uncharacteristically erupts against her late husband's cousin. We are offered no explanation. (It won't come until four years later in a related story, which will be discussed.) The comment stuns the narrator; yet it serves to humanize Mrs. Todd.

Another character describes Mari' Harris as looking like a "Chinee." This comment represents a rare occasion when Jewett's work expresses anything like an ethnic slur. Her Boston was a hothouse of nativism. The Immigration Restriction League was founded in the city in 1894. Yet, as already noted, Jewett wrote sympathetically about Irish and French-Canadian immigrant workers. The use of "Chinee" at the Bowden family reunion appears to be an accurate recording of what Jewett heard in Maine. It is similar to the slur "Portagee" for Portuguese, which formed part of the coast's vernacular.

The Bowden Place is five generations old. The dwelling "stood, low-storied and broad-roofed, in its green field as if it were a motherly brown hen waiting for the flock that came straying toward it from every direction." The striking image of how reunion day pulses with people and emotions is offset by the family cemetery, which inscribes the history of coastal Maine in the second half of the nineteenth century. Women are primarily interred in the walled burial lot. Men often met their end at sea.

The festivities begin with an organized march into a cleared grove. The narrator has grown more ruminative. At least for a summer, thanks largely to Mrs. Todd, she has formed a thread in the tapestry of life in Dunnett Landing. Shifting to the collective *we*, the narrator frames the Bowden reunion in broad humanistic terms that transcend the parish setting: "The sky, the sea, have watched poor humanity at its rites so long; we were no more a New England family celebrating its own existence and simple progress; we carried the tokens and inheritance of all such households from which this had descended, and were only the latest of our line." Such framing and the narrator's learned references to "ancient Greeks" and their mythology (for example, Antigone and Persephone) enables *Pointed Firs* to gesture beyond the parish folk and their experience in a way *Deephaven* doesn't.

Near the end of the reunion, Mrs. Todd and the narrator consummate the latter's incorporation into Dunnett Landing's community. They share an "early apple" pie with the frosted words "Bowden Reunion." Mrs. Todd gives the narrator the piece with the family name while she consumes "Reunion." This completes the progress of the summer visitor toward "going native," so to speak. The consumption of lived experience at Dunnett Landing and its islands apparently displaces the narrator's pursuit of her written work—and, ironically, gives her more material for future writing.

Something alarming occurs, however, at the communion table. There is a large replica of the Bowden House, which collapses "into ruin at the feast's end." We know that the farewells until next year are fraught with the sadness of the fleeting summer and advancing mortality. The heavy foot of time on life's treadle means that many of the feasters will come to grief before the next reunion.

Jewett might have ended *Pointed Firs* with the evocative, richly textured story of the reunion and moved directly to the brief account of the narrator's painful departure. But she wrote in installments for the *Atlantic* with no expectation of publishing a book. Thus, she introduces an aged fisherman, an unsociable figure. Elijah "'Lijah" Tilley is another of Dunnett Landing's odd folk. He recalls reticent Danny of *Deephaven*.

Elijah is "small, elderly, gaunt-shaped" and a very accomplished fisherman, judging by his haul. "He appeared to regard a stranger with scornful indifference." The narrator has gained entrée to so much of Dunnett Landing's community, and she would like to tug on the thread of this remote fisherman's personal story. She comes face-to-face with him on the waterfront. He is carrying a haddock and shifts it from one hand to the other to prevent it from soiling her dress. She reads this as a signal that "my company was accepted." Tilley invites her to his home later that day, and his peculiarities and the narrator's pathos emerge.

In his domesticated setting, Tilley discovers his voice. It's a monotone, however. He continues obsessively to mourn the death of his devoted wife, now gone nearly eight years. He doesn't refer to her by name but as "poor dear." His domestic life has slipped its mooring. Tilley regrets the anxiety-laden existence that his poor dear endured while he pursued deep-sea fishing. She constantly watched out to sea for signs of his return, acquiring that faraway gaze that, Jewett claimed, was a distinctive mark of fishermen and their families. Poor dear "use to say the time seemed long to her, but I've found all about it now. I use to be dreadful thoughtless when I was a young man and the fish was bitin' well," he continues. "I'd stay out late some o' them days, an' I expect she'd watch an' watch an' lose heart a-waiting." He swims in regret and guilt. He leads a rudderless life in a house without his wife.

'Lijah keeps the house precisely as poor dear left it. The interior serves as a memorial to her. She used to boast of the complete set of "chiny" that he bought for her in Bordeau. When neighbors went to serve tea after the funeral, they discovered a broken cup that poor dear had wrapped in paper and pushed to the back of the cupboard so he wouldn't see it and be disappointed. 'Lijah spends the winter, when he doesn't fish, sitting in poor dear's chair, knitting socks and staring out at the sea.

The narrator later discusses her visit to 'Lijah's home with Mrs. Todd. "There's some folks you miss and some folks you don't, when they're gone," she reflects, "but there ain't hardly a day I don't think o' dear Sarah Tilley." Death brackets *Pointed Firs*, as do Jewett's strong women.

The end of summer makes Mrs. Todd's house "cool and damp in the morning." Now the "light seemed to come through green leaves." The narrator knows that "the sunshine of a northern summer was coming to its lovely end." She must return to her urban world. She carries with her a new knowledge of a Maine parish where "nothing" ever happens: "there were many delightful things to be done and done again, as if I were in London." *Pointed Firs* is more than a picturesque novella about coastal Maine. It is also a humanistic acknowledgment that life's drama takes place anywhere and everywhere.

The leave-taking is painful for both the visitor and her host, the cosmopolitan and the parish priestess. Mrs. Todd hardly talks to her guest on the day of her departure. She prepares a basket for the visitor and then leaves, claiming that she has to visit a neighbor who has had her third stroke. The narrator runs after her, but Mrs. Todd waves her off. The summer visitor finds small packages on the kitchen table, including a West Indian basket she had admired, food for the trip, and a little "old leather box." It contains the coral pin that poor Joanna would not accept from Mrs. Todd.

The narrator leaves on a small steamer. She watches the shore disappear with one final striking mirage-like image. "Presently the wind began to blow, and we struck out seaward to double the long sheltering headland of the cape, and when I looked back again, the islands and the headland had run together and Dunnett Landing and all its coasts were loss to sight."

Pointed Firs won "universal acclaim" after it was published.[31] Not surprisingly, the *Atlantic Monthly* swelled with plaudits for Jewett's accomplishment. *Pointed Firs* revealed a "light thread of identity of place and character on which the stories are strung." Jewett had managed to make "a seacoast of her own . . . lifted just above the horizon of actual land." Other reviewers spoke of the book in terms of a kind of restorative summer vacation. *The Bookman* noted that *Pointed Firs* "is a story of wholesome, simple, rural life, with the sea for tonic and the sunshine of summer for warmth." As Jewett's book *The Independent* stressed, "One feels the sea air and smells the pine breath. It is a summer outing among good, honest folk, a free and easy exploration of a neighborhood, of a region where conservatism is truly provincial and rural honesty stoutly prevails."[32]

Though not without flaws, *Pointed Firs* is certainly the most polished, engaging piece of writing on the Maine coast at least until the 1930s and 1940s, and perhaps beyond. Jewett was surprised by the response to her work. She had written the *Atlantic* installments facilely, unaware that she was creating her most enduring work. In her literary modesty, contemporary critics would see that she had produced an unpretentious masterpiece. However, they would miss the point that modesty, then and now, represents a character trait of many Mainers.

"THE FOREIGNER": A WOMAN OUT OF PLACE

"The Foreigner" (1900) is the only one of Jewett's four Dunnett Landing stories that was not posthumously inserted into *Pointed Firs*. It is arguably the finest of the lot, as well as the longest (which may explain why Willa Cather left it out). "The Foreigner" imparts some balance to Jewett's generally uplifting and sometimes glowing representation of community in Dunnett Landing.

"The Foreigner" is a story about the failure of community, which Mrs. Todd partly shares. In fact, as the story progresses, the narrative becomes as much about Mrs. Todd as the foreigner. Among other things, we learn more about the herbalist through her relationship to the foreigner. Thus, though the story may be read on its own, "The Foreigner" acquires more meaning in the context of *Pointed Firs*. It could have been stitched seamlessly near the center of *Pointed Firs*, thereby augmenting Jewett's literary achievement.

The narrative unspools one night in late August that reminds Mrs. Todd's guest that summer's end draws near on the Maine coast. Rain pelts Mrs. Todd's house, and the gales make the structure "rock and . . . creak as if it were a ship." The summer visitor sits in her room by a comforting fire. She hears Mrs. Todd's cough outside her door, the equivalent of "a plain New England knock." The visitor invites Mrs. Todd to join her. Readers of *Pointed Firs* know how companionable, even intimate, they have become over the summer.

Mrs. Todd sits down with the cat on her lap and her fidgety hands fumbling over her knitting. It is the kind of night when ships are lost at sea. The restive Mrs. Todd is worried about her mother and brother out on Green Island. More acutely than the summer guest, she hears the roaring breakers. "How they pound! . . . I always run of an idea that the sea knows anger these nights and gets full o' fight," she observes. "I can hear the rote o' them old black ledges." She recalls that this was the kind of night when "old Mis' Cap'n Tolland died . . . thirty or maybe forty years ago." It doesn't take much inquisitiveness from the visitor for Mrs. Todd to tell the intricate story, including an otherworldly moment that she has divulged to few people. It betokens the summer visitor's further admission into Mrs. Todd's charmed circle of intimates.

Through Almiry Todd, Jewett relates Mis' Tolland's tragedy more movingly, perhaps, than the story of poor Joanna. Four Dunnett Landing captains, including Mrs. Todd's father, were celebrating the successful completion of a trading venture to Jamaica. (The location is significant.) As Maine shipping contracted by midcentury, older patterns of trade acquired a new importance. Exchanges grew along the coast and to slave and former slave colonies in the West Indies where wood products and fish were bartered for molasses and sugar. On his Jamaican trip, for instance, Captain Tolland traded a cargo of Maine pine lumber for bags of sugar. A bachelor, he is also one of Dunnett Landing's rare captains who still make distant trips, even as far as the East Indies.

In the course of events, the Maine captains rescue a woman with a guitar who flees from a house where there is a party. She is French, but Captain Bowden knows scraps of the language from travels to Havre and Bordeau. He learns that her husband, a "Portagee," and children died of yellow fever. A "negro" had stolen her husband's money while he was sick. They had intended to use it to take a steamer to France. She tries to support herself by playing her guitar and singing wherever she can earn money, which audiences throw to her.

The captains decide to bring the foreigner back to Dunnett Landing in John Tolland's brig. In retrospect, Mrs. Todd tells her guest, "I always thought they'd have done better, and more reasonable, to give her some money to pay her passage home to France." But this comment tends to absolve the community, and even Mrs. Todd, of any responsibility for what happens. Captain Tolland delivers his sugar to Portland. A Portland justice of the peace, not the Dunnett Landing minister, marries him and the foreigner, who remains nameless throughout the story. Mrs. Todd's mother and father pay visits to the Tollands, but soon they are off to sea. On a second voyage Mis' Tolland stays home. Mrs. Blackett invites her "to a social circle that was down to the meetin' house vestry."

This attempt to incorporate the outsider into Dunnett Landing society ignites the provincial passions that leave the foreigner permanently estranged from the community. When some women in the social circle rise to sing, Mis' Tolland puts her hands to her ears and lets out "a little squeal." The singers are too flat, and in a "pleasant" manner she tries to give them the "right notes." The singers are flat again, and the foreigner "made faces." A hush falls over the circle, the members "settin' around prim as dishes." Mrs. Blackett tries to deliver the foreigner from the tension filling the vestry. She asks Mis' Cap'n Tolland to sing something. Mrs. Todd recalls that she sang a "gay, lovely little song." Then she picks up a pie tin and begins banging it as if it is a tambourine and dancing as she sings "faster an' faster." Some of the men clap loudly as they keep time with the foreigner's singing and banging. Women silently, almost involuntarily tap their feet, the limit of their expressiveness—at least in the church vestry. But a scandal ensues the next day over the foreign Catholic Mis' Tolland's perceived irreverent behavior in the "orthodox" vestry. Mari' Harris, one of the singers and the "Chinee" from *Pointed Firs*, foments the trouble. She confronts Mrs. Blackett and reprimands her for inviting the foreigner. Now we know the source of Mrs. Todd's decades-long hatred of Harris that she inexplicably expresses bluntly at the Bowden family reunion.

We know something else as well. The clash of cultures means that the exotic, expressive outsider from a tropical world will never be fully accepted in Dunnett Landing. The night in the vestry and its aftermath occurred, Mrs. Todd observes, "about the time shipping begun to decay." Creeping insularity, as Captain Littlepage laments in *Pointed Firs*, alters the texture of life in Dunnett Landing.

The Sunday following the controversy over the vestry, Mis' Tolland walks out of the meeting before it's over, providing more fodder for Mari' Harris and her allies. Then the foreigner's isolation from the community is nearly complete when Captain Tolland's ship is lost at sea. With the news, the twice-widowed foreigner suffers a stroke. She dies a few months later.

Mrs. Todd's story of Mis' Tolland is far from over, however. Above all, Jewett complicates the behavior and emotions of the storyteller. In the process, we gain insight into Mrs. Todd beyond the character in *Pointed Firs*. She recounts the story to a mostly passive guest who is enthralled by its dense details and emotions.

Her mother had refused to treat Mis' Tolland as a foreigner, as a castaway after the church vestry tempest. Yet she lives out on Green Island. She enjoins her daughter, "I want you to neighbor with that poor lonesome creatur'. . . . I want you to make her have a sense that somebody feels kind to her." On one of her trips to Dunnett Landing, Mrs. Blackett spends a long time visiting with Mis' Tolland. When she arrives at Mrs. Todd's, her meal is spoiled. With sarcasm, and then embarrassment, the daughter says, "I hope you'll like your supper." Mrs. Blackett erupts, rebuking her daughter for her callousness toward Mis' Tolland: "What consequence is my supper? . . . Or your comfort or mine, beside letting a foreign person an' a stranger feel so desolate; she's done the best a woman could do in her lonesome place and she asks nothing of anybody except a little common kindness." Mrs. Blackett espouses the practical religion of the Old and New Testaments: love the "stranger" as well as thy neighbor.

Mrs. Todd, in contrast, is spurred to strike up a relationship with Mis' Tolland from guilt and a sense of obligation to her mother. Still, the relationship matures. On a visit, Mrs. Todd mentions her mother. The foreigner takes "holt" of her "with both hands an' said my mother was an angel. When I see the tears in her eyes 't was all right between us, and we were always friendly after that." It turns out that Mis' Tolland was a herbalist. That is how Mrs. Todd learns much of what she now knows about the value of herbs.

Yet there are emotional limits to Mrs. Todd's friendship with the foreigner, which she attempts to impute to her youthfulness. There was "no affectionateness with her," she tells her summer guest, with whom she has become emotionally invested. It was Mrs. Todd who had been deficient in affection. After all, the foreigner's relationship with Mrs. Blackett didn't lack tenderness. Despite her friendliness with the stranger, Mrs. Todd confesses, "I never give her a kiss till the day she laid in her coffin and it come to my heart there wa'nt no one else to do it."

Mrs. Todd is not quite finished with her Dunnett Landing tale, nor is the violent storm done arousing memories of the night the foreigner died. "I saw the sails of her narrative were filled with a fresh breeze," the summer visitor recalls. To her surprise, Mrs. Todd inherits the foreigner's estate. She was overcome with remorse, she tells her listener. "There I begun to cry. . . . I couldn't help it. I wished I had her back again to do somethin' for, an' to make her know I felt sisterly to her more'n I ever showed, an' it come over me 'twas all too late, an' I cried the more."

Uncle Captain Lorenzo Bowden became the executor of the estate. He believes that Captain Tolland hid money in the house, possibly in a "chist." He searches exhaustively from cellar to attic. Bowden surmises that Captain Tolland took the chest with him on his final voyage. But he doesn't give up searching through the house. One night he accidentally sets fire to the house from his lamp. It burns down to its foundation. All that remains of the foreigner's life are flowers that she had planted. Mrs. Todd transplants some to her garden to keep the memory of the foreigner alive.

There is still one final twist to the story, which takes the visitor to Mis' Tolland's deathbed. Mrs. Todd is alone "watchin'" over her. Mis' Tolland suddenly sits up in bed and extends her arms toward an apparition in the doorway. "The lamplight struck across the room between us. I couldn't tell the shape but 't was a woman's dark face lookin' right at us, 'twan't but an instant I could see." "'Tis my mother," Mis' Tolland tells her. She seeks assurance that Mrs. Todd also saw the figure. "Yes, dear, I did; you ain't never goin' to feel strange an' lonesome no more." They hold hands, and the foreigner dies peacefully.

"The Foreigner" would have added much to *Pointed Firs*. It shows Dunnett Landing people in conflict, on both the communal and the individual level. It gives depth and complexity to Mrs. Todd. And it ends on a note of imaginative realism.

However one assesses Sarah Orne Jewett's relationship to the American literary canon, she created a body of work that endures. Still, she left much more to say, not only about the shifting sands of Maine coastal life but also about the many other landscapes within the state's coordinates. Mary Ellen Chase stood on Jewett's shoulders. But she explored Maine worlds outside the scope of *Deephaven* and *The Country of the Pointed Firs*. And she did so with a darker view of the coast's decline and of summer people's presence in that history.

2

A GOODLY HERITAGE AND DOWN EAST'S UPHEAVAL

Mary Ellen Chase

In the decades after her death, volumes of Jewett's stories were regularly re-printed, and *Pointed Firs*, with its additions, presided over Maine literature as the finest fictional work the state had produced. In 1925, Willa Cather famously lavished extravagant praise on Jewett's achievement. "If I were asked to name three American books which have the possibility of a long, long life," she observed, "I would say *The Scarlet Letter*, *Huckleberry Finn*, and *The Country of the Pointed Firs*." One might ask, what about *Moby-Dick* or *Uncle Tom's Cabin* or *The Red Badge of Courage*, to name three? (*The Great Gatsby*, certainly an American classic, was only published in 1925.)[1] Few critics would have agreed with Cather's lofty tribute to Jewett. Still, such appreciation and the continued republication of her works suggest the popularity of Jewett as a regional writer at least. Thus, it should not be surprising that a revival of Maine fiction did not occur until the 1930s.[2]

The decade opened with the first acclaimed historical novel of Kenneth Roberts. *Arundel* (1930) focuses primarily on Benedict Arnold's disastrous 1775 march through the Maine wilderness to attack Quebec. Roberts, a Kennebunk native, wrote primarily about wars, often focusing on an individual. His Kennebunkport summer neighbor and friend, the Indiana writer Booth Tarkington, also published two Maine novels in the early 1930s. *Mirthful Heaven* (1930) and *Mary's Neck* (1932) were often humorous portrayals of the doings of summer folk. For my purposes, Gladys Hasty Carroll marks the first significant indigenous imagining of Maine since Jewett.

Born in South Berwick in 1904, Carroll graduated from Berwick Academy and Bates College. She married and was living in Minneapolis when, at the age of twenty-nine, she published *As the Earth Turns*.[3] The novel drew on her experiences growing up in rural South Berwick and her family's relentless work to keep their farm afloat as they produced partly for the market and mostly for their own subsistence. Interestingly, the novel begins with eleven chapters devoted to winter; it opens with a three-day blizzard! We follow the Shaw family through the cycle of seasons to "Winter Again." Unlike Jewett, Carroll privileges winter. It is the season when cold, ice, howling winds, and boredom all tax, and thereby help form, the Maine character. After days and evenings huddled around the kitchen stove, the Shaw family emerges from another winter, their hardihood bolstered and prepared for the toil that lies ahead.

As the Earth Turns became an immediate bestseller, a Book of the Month Club selection, and a Warner Brothers movie in 1934. Carroll's novel offered Depression-era encouragement to its readers. Set in the late 1920s, *As the Earth Turns* depicted a family equipped with the fortitude and skill to weather hard times.

Carroll went on to publish thirteen more novels, a book of short stories, and four works of nonfiction. Yet, despite all of Carroll's success, I think Mary Ellen Chase was a more substantive Maine writer of the 1930s and beyond. She published eight novels, four of which were bestsellers; three bestselling memoirs, two focused on growing up in Maine; a modest number of short stories; scores of popular essays; multiple books for children; a monograph on Thomas Hardy; three biographies; college texts on writing; books on the Bible for general readers; and still more, mostly historical volumes on maritime New England and English novels. In fiction as well as memoir, Chase achieved distinction writing about the Maine coast.

Chase's first and last literary romance was with her birthplace: Blue Hill, Maine. Situated between Penobscot and Frenchman's Bays with the red cliffs of Mount Desert Island in sight, Chase opens her first memoir, *A Goodly Heritage* (1932), with an ode to Blue Hill's beauty. She delineates a landscape with "fields sloping seaward, and rolling hills stretching backward and upward until they are lost in an uneven black skyline of pines and firs." From a distance the evergreens appeared blue, which explains the origins of the town's name. Blue Hill Bay is smaller than its neighbors but by no means a mere "cove." It is almost ten miles wide, with islands large and small stretching twice that far toward open ocean. At the head of the bay "rises the great hill, a landmark to mariners past and present" and, Chase rather imprudently boasts, "a suggestion to more traveled eyes of Vesuvius beyond the bay of Naples."[4]

Chase was born into this Maine coastal world in 1887. During the 1880s, Blue Hill lost more than 10 percent of its population, which stood at 1,908 in

1890, when Chase was three years old. As she grew up, the coastal community continued to shed its year-round population decade by decade, including more than 20 percent between 1910 and 1920, when Chase herself left for good.[5]

Chase was the second born in a family that grew to eight children. Her father, who attended Bowdoin College but did not graduate, was content to be a small-town lawyer, representative to the Maine General Assembly, and municipal judge. He came from a seafaring family whose roots in Blue Hill reached back to the middle of the eighteenth century. Mary Ellen's paternal seafaring grandmother regaled her on Sunday afternoons with stories of adventures on the high seas and visits to exotic places.[6] These firsthand tales of Maine's boundless age of sail took hold in the young granddaughter's imagination. Chase's best fiction grapples with the seafaring heritage of a fictional Blue Hill coastal community as it cozied up to summer people and increasingly lost touch with its own grand maritime history.

Chase's mother taught grade school for two terms and also instructed in Latin at Blue Hill Academy. Edith had married Edward Everett Chase when she was eighteen years old. Mary Ellen attended local schools for twelve years and graduated from the academy. The Chase children also received instruction at home. In her first memoir, Mary Ellen gave a gloss to her home education. She credited her father with sharpening her memory and imparting a love of books. Yet he was a taskmaster, one not unknown for severity. He assigned his children lists of items from the Bible, history, and geography, later testing them and accepting nothing less than total recall. Each night, once supper was completed, he retreated to the house's library to read. The children knew he was not to be disturbed for the rest of the evening. He would die at the age of fifty-one from kidney failure. Interestingly, the first sentence in her second memoir, *A Goodly Fellowship* (1939), reads, "My mother was my first and always my best teacher."[7]

Mary Ellen clung to the fugitive hope of continuing her education at Brown University, the alma mater of her beloved Latin teacher. Her father nixed the idea. He chose the University of Maine. She entered the state school in Orono in 1904, along with twenty other women in an institution of approximately five hundred students. Her father continued to manage her education. He insisted that Mary Ellen experience work before she graduated. For a year and a half, she taught in West Brooksville and Buck's Harbor—small, poor towns near Blue Hill.[8] Chase returned to the university, earning what was in effect a joint degree in English and history in 1909.

Against the wishes of her parents, Mary Ellen set her sights on Chicago and the prospect of teaching. Distance from Blue Hill brought relief from living under her father's thumb. For five years she taught in Wisconsin and Chicago. She spent the summer of 1913 in Berlin and the Harz Mountains studying the German language. A year later, she contracted tuberculosis and lived in Montana for three years as she recovered. During this period Chase began publishing books for children. With a goal of pursuing a career in teaching and writing, she enrolled in graduate school at the University of Minnesota in 1917. Five years later, she received a doctorate and became an assistant professor of English at the university.[9] In 1926, Chase joined the faculty at Smith College in Northampton, Massachusetts, where over three decades she taught such notables as poet Sylvia Plath and Betty Friedan, author of *The Feminine Mystique.* Smith belonged to the so-called Seven Sisters, the elite women's colleges, a kind of female Ivy League.

Chase published her dissertation on Thomas Hardy a year after her arrival at Smith. Most significantly, at Smith she became an enormously popular teacher, a faculty luminary. Especially after she published her bestselling novels, women's clubs in particular sought Chase out as a speaker.[10] Through giving talks across the country she burnished her classroom skills and continued to adapt them for general audiences.

At Smith, Chase met a lifelong mate. Born in England, Eleanor Shipley Duckett was professor of classical languages and literature; she was seven years older than Chase. For most of their years at Smith, they lived in a house owned by the college, close to campus. Unlike the Jewett-Fields Boston marriage, the Chase-Duckett relationship may have embraced physical intimacy. We know from earlier entries in her diary that Chase was open to sexual relations with women.[11]

Chase, like Jewett, developed an outsider-insider connection to Maine. She and Eleanor typically spent leaves from Smith, and sometimes summers, in England. Chase became an Anglophile. One consequence of daily living with an English partner was that she began to speak with a hybrid Down East–Anglicized accent. Moreover, frequently (though not consistently) she adopted English spelling: color became "colour," for example, and labor became "labour." Like Jewett, she converted to the Episcopalian Church from her family's Congregationalism.

Yet, despite her Anglophilia and years living outside of Maine, Chase's native state and hometown served as an axis of her literary imagination. Unlike Jewett, in two fine-grained memoirs and part of a third, the homegrown daughter kept poring over her Maine upbringing. In her first memoir, she made known her gratitude "to the gods who set me in such pleasant places and gave me such a goodly heritage!"[12]

Chase was unwaveringly proud of her family's and of Blue Hill's seafaring past; that history furnished the raw material for some of her best fiction. Moreover, Chase revealed her attachment to Maine in another way: She purchased a summer home on Petit Manan Point, a rock-strewn peninsula far Down East. She spent sixteen summers there with Eleanor before illness forced Chase to sell.[13]

Mary Ellen Chase died in a Northampton nursing home in 1973 at the age of eighty-six. She was buried in the family plot in Blue Hill. When Eleanor Duckett died three years later, she was interred next to Mary Ellen.

The *Colby Library Quarterly* invited Chase to write an article in 1962 for an issue devoted to her work. Her short essay is titled "My Novels about Maine." As she had many times, Chase lengthened the shadow of "the master of us all, the Dean of Maine Letters": Sarah Orne Jewett.[14] More than any other Maine writer, perhaps, Chase labored under the legacy and literary standing of Jewett. She chose to write about themes similar to Jewett's: coastal Mainers, their communities, the decline of ocean-borne seafaring, and, for her, Down East in near thralldom to the summer trade and canneries.

There are crucial differences between Jewett and Chase, however. The latter's best work is historical fiction and doesn't focus on the coast at one moment in time. It sweeps across generations. Also, in contrast to Jewett, Chase transported the reader to sea. She provided a view of seafaring from foc'sle to the captain's cabin to the quarterdeck. Chase didn't attempt to re-create Maine coastal speech. Nor did she include Jewett's eccentric characters in her gallery of Maine coastal people.[15] Still another difference from Jewett is that Chase is scathing in her critique of summer visitors and their disinterest in the history of the communities that they colonize. By the time Chase was writing, the incursion of summer people had significantly altered life along the coast. Chase didn't write primarily for the vacationers, though a writer can never control her audience. As she put it in *A Goodly Heritage*, Maine's proud maritime heritage "still lingers." "Such a possession will remain invincible armor against the new [summer] prosperity of the coast as long as such an inheritance is nurtured and cherished."[16] Thus, if Chase's literary imagination has didactic and interventionist dimensions, it is to preserve and celebrate Maine's seafaring heritage as a way of shoring up coastal people's pride in their own heroic history.

In her essay in the *Colby Library Quarterly*, Chase designated what she considered her most important Maine novels: "The three novels which are based securely upon Maine history and Maine life, both past and present, are *Mary Peters* (1934), *Silas Crockett* (1935), and *The Edge of Darkness* (1957)."[17] The first two novels abide as her best work. *Mary Peters* opens in the early 1880s and concludes more than four decades later. *Silas Crockett*, her most ambitious novel, spans an entire century.

MARY PETERS AND DOWN EAST "RESILIENCY"

Chase wrote from the Depression's depth. Not surprisingly, her literary realism possesses the kind of pointed social criticism that one doesn't find in Jewett. In addition, as someone who focused her scholarly work on Thomas Hardy, fate shadows Chase's characters. But destiny doesn't lead with necessity to doom. Rather, in coastal Maine "resiliency"[18] represents a cultural legacy born of its inhabitants' history, including Chase's family. Mary Peters becomes an embodiment of Down East resiliency. She accomplishes this seemingly against the odds: tragic family fatalities, the passage of time that silts over townspeople's connections to their heroic past, and the coast's material heritage up for sale to outsiders.

Mary was born in Singapore Harbor in 1875. Except for fourteen months as an infant and an occasional term at school, she has grown up on a ship. Her father, John, is one of the last captains who shoves off from Petersport for multiyear voyages to far-flung destinations. When we first meet Mary, she is nine years old and the *Elizabeth* is docked in Cadiz, the major port in southern Spain. Mary awakens and realizes that the ship is "quiet, not plunging and rolling, not pitching or swooping, not whining or groaning in her bolts and beams or rattling her gear." This wonderful evocation of the sensations and sounds of a wooden sailing vessel benefited from more than Grandmother Chase's dramatic accounts of her sea adventures. Mary Ellen had met Lincoln, Joanna, and Maude Colcord at the University of Maine. They were from Searsport, had spent most of their lives at sea, and shared their experiences with Chase. Then, too, by the time Chase published *Mary Peters*, she had crisscrossed the Atlantic four times. Granted, she sailed in steam-powered steel ships. But she did record her observations of the sea, the sky, and the winds.[19] It was a short leap from this knowledge to imagining a wooden ship under one's feet, especially if she had read works such as *Moby-Dick*. Chase is most lyrical when Mary Peters is at sea.

From the quarterdeck, Mary beholds Cadiz for the first time. The "dazzling whiteness of this strange city" fascinates her. Beyond an encircling wall that protects Cadiz from the sea, Mary scans "domes and spires, turrets and pinnacles and minarets . . . with a confusion of homes." The port holds sway "all white beneath a sky of Spanish blue." Cadiz initiates a flood of indelible impressions, including intimations of "some ancient long established seafaring truth." As a symbol, Cadiz is bound up with the journey that deposited Mary in this kind of striking place and, as Chase says in *A Goodly Heritage*, that broadened venturing Mainers' "mental horizons."[20] Once back in Petersport permanently, Mary will dream of Cadiz and recall the white city for the rest of her life.

Yet, as she stares from the quarterdeck, Cadiz also summons for Mary a catalog of counter white images from her mundane Maine world. She recalls, "The white of Monday sheets on Maine summer fields; there were blossoming syringas and lilacs against white Maine doorways and the freshly painted spire of the church at home, on the hill above the sea; and there was the crisp whiteness of a rare party-frock with flounces and ruffles." Formative maritime venturing and Maine as home—Mary will not reconcile these worlds and their symbols until the novel's close. She will create a Maine hooked rug inscribed with the exotic image of Cadiz. She refuses to sell it to summer folk or agents, who are ransacking coastal homes for indigenous Maine artifacts and antiques. But Mary resists corrupting commodification of the rug that preserves the novel's striking first setting.

In *Mary Peters*, Chase portrays vivid scenes of life at sea. Mary's mother, Sarah, transforms the cabin into a school six days a week from nine to twelve. On calm tropical days Mary reads in a corner of the quarterdeck. When there is a warm rain, she and older brother John (named for his father) strip off all but their undergarments and frolic and wash on the deck. Crew members emerge from the foc'sle with items badly in need of washing. From the West Indies to Rio de Janeiro, the *Elizabeth* sails through "undulating meadows of Sargasso," "drifting, nomadic vegetation." The Pacific Ocean is more magical, with whales commonly cresting, dolphins swimming around the ship, and acres of jellyfish, "like globes of fire" at night.

But the sea is not an outdoor aquarium. Chase puts a mature thought in young Mary's head that is perhaps more fitting for Melville's Ishmael: "Even at ten she somehow understood that it [the sea] was too vast to be loved and too indifferent to be hated." Her brother is victimized by the sea's cruelty, as his kitten is washed overboard by a rogue wave. "John saw her terrified face for an instant on the receding back of a giant swell." The kitten disappears in a "burst of spray." John loathes the sea.

John returns home when he is fifteen to attend Petersport Academy. Mary is alone with her parents for two years. Then, when she is thirteen, a new first officer comes aboard while the ship is docked in New York. He is a tall, lean man, handsome and tanned, but not with the leathery face of heavily tattooed crewmembers. William Gardiner is a thirty-year-old Harvard graduate who tried his hand at teaching, which he found dispiriting. The sea is his first love. He takes a special interest in Mary's education. He helps her with Latin, and they read Shakespeare together on the weather deck. Gardiner alters the chemistry of the officers' dinner table. He asks her about books. He is filled with stories and reflections on things, which he drew "out of his mind as a juggler draws one surprising thing after another from a bag of tricks." From the deck he makes observations that broaden Mary's knowledge of the sea. She develops more than an adolescent infatuation with Gardiner. Mary will remember him for the rest of her life, as the end of the novel will powerfully disclose.

One day in Liverpool, Mary's father meets a fellow captain from Petersport. He seeks Sarah's approval before he invites Jim Pendleton to dinner, as Sarah and Jim had once intended to marry. But he met a woman in Brittany, she became pregnant, and he married her, not from love but a sense of duty. They lived in France when Jim wasn't at sea. "He looks bad—and old," Captain Peters reports. "His wife is dead." His first boy has died. A second son, named for his father, is two years older than Mary. She hears the conversation with her parents. Sarah then relates to Mary what happened between Jim and her and his now deceased wife.

Jim Pendleton is dying. He still harbors affection for Sarah and wants to see her for a last time. The dinner is uneventful. The son is tall, shy, and handsome, and he walks with an unexplained limp. The father wants to send his son back to Petersport to be educated in the academy. Mary can't imagine how crucial young Jim will become in her life. She will also realize that his halting step is not the only thing that hobbles him.

After Mary turns fifteen, in 1886, the time arrives for her to return home to attend Petersport Academy. The *Elizabeth* drops anchor in San Francisco, and Sarah and Mary disembark. They stay in a hotel before taking a transcontinental train back east. Then fate intrudes. Overnight the *Elizabeth* is blown down the coast to its destruction on a reef. Mary's father and Mr. Gardiner perish. The latter's body is not found. Mary feels more anguish for Mr. Gardiner even than for her father as the train speeds toward home. During her first night in Petersport, Mary dreams of Cadiz. She is promenading with her father, who "turned all at once into Mr. Gardiner." The catastrophe suggests something of broader significance: a late chapter in the heroic era of Maine seafaring has met its tragic end.

Chase frames the Petersport's distinctive setting as Mary awakens in tears: "She watched the dark hills of Mt. Desert, which on the south enclosed the harbour from the open sea, soften and grow blue before the sunrise. . . . Near at hand tumbled small, uneven fields bounded by stone walls aflame with goldenrod.

An old untended orchard sprawled over a neighboring hillside. Gardens in the rangy disorder of early autumn interspersed the meadows here and there. Rock-strewn fir clad pastures mounted the harbour hills." Yet for all that abides in nature's seasons, Petersport is astir with the uprooting of the old social order.

Most townspeople welcomed, even "rejoiced" at the rise of the tourist economy that increasingly replaced seafaring and shipbuilding as the mainstay of many coastal Maine towns. "There was something immeasurably sad," Sarah Peters reflects, "in the sight of a grandson of a shipmaster in the foreign trade shingling the roof of a summer cottage for his livelihood." Even "sadder" was how summer "strangers . . . knew little and cared less for the boy's history." Over the course of the novel, Chase is a caustic critic of the summer transformation of places such as Blue Hill. In Petersport, the stand-in for her hometown, even the success of the annual August church fair comes to depend on the patronage of summer folk. The novel dissects what we might call the consumption of Maine—outsiders' appetite for prime waterfront property, elegant former captains' houses, and the valuable artifacts and antiques of Maine farmhouses. Still, it is important to keep in mind that artists, not summer people, were the first to discover the sublime beauty of Down East when the region remained largely inaccessible. They represented Down East's first publicists to urban audiences.[21]

When Mary returns to Petersport, the year-round population claimed no foreigners, "not so much as an Irishman or Scotchman." Thus young Jim Pendleton, who lives with his uncle and aunt, receives less than a warm reception. The town's ship captains were expected to become familiar with foreign lands but to marry local women. The best they could say was "at least [Captain Pendleton] escaped alliance with a woman of Latin race."

From his arrival through his scandalous departure from Petersport, Sarah Peters accepts Jim warmly, even treating him as her own son. He is not as well prepared for the academy as Mary. Jim has foreign ways and still is afflicted with a lame leg—and an unsteady character to match.

In Mary's last year at the academy, beautiful Hester Wood arrives in Petersport from a small, poor town ten miles away. She seeks a year of Petersport Academy's superior education to prepare for entrance into the nearby teacher's college. When the woman she boards with becomes ill, the Peterses welcome her into their home. John is smitten with their "lithe and slender" boarder. He dropped out of Bowdoin after two years and turned to farming. John purchased "old Uncle Joel's" rundown farm and has spent several years of unremitting exertion reclaiming the land. It's time to start a family. Jim Pendleton also eyes Hester Wood—but not for marriage.

The school year concludes without controversy. Mary and Hester will begin teacher's college in the fall. Another summer begets more "rusticators" like a biblical pestilence. Alterations in the fabric of Petersport proceed apace: "Boys who planned on college began to see a more immediate and profitable livelihood in carpentry and masonry." Storekeepers raise their seasonal prices and seek out "delicacies" from Boston and New York. The summer economy continues to distance the citizens of Petersport from their noble maritime traditions. The adventurous Maine Yankee mutates into the hireling of summer folk while the merchant transfigures into the "sharpy" of lore, like the Connecticut peddler who sold wooden nutmegs. It is a pessimistic historical assessment. No wonder Mary's memory constantly remains heavily invested in Cadiz and Mr. Gardiner. In the end, to survive, Mary will yield to the undertow of the tourist economy. But she doesn't forsake memorializing her seafaring tradition in the designs of her hooked rugs.

Jim left Petersport before graduation—for good reason, we soon learn. Hester promises to return to Petersport for the August church sale. At that time John sets out to retrieve her. On the way back her hat blows off; she jumps from the surrey, catches her foot, and falls in the road. Hester turns pale and cries uncontrollably. John takes her to the Peterses' home, and Sarah knows immediately what is wrong. The doctor is summoned, and Hester dies bringing forth a stillborn baby.

The narrative moves ahead to 1895. Mary is twenty-five, John twenty-eight. She has been teaching in village schools for five years. Mary muses humorously over the smells of her students in one of the most distinctive and captivating passages in Maine literature. It is worth quoting at length:

> When she bent over the boys at their desks on spring mornings, she smelled barn smells, fresh milk, hayseed, manure, mingled with the scent of pine pitch, which lingered on their fingers from the pricking of pine blisters and with that of the wood which they had carried into their mothers' wood-boxes on their morning chores. . . . There were the smells of soda biscuits, flapjacks, and donuts. . . . There were smells of lamp wicks and soft soap, homemade sausage and apple butter, smells of wood smoke, horse liniments, spruce gum, ham and baked potatoes, apples, baked beans and Johnny-cake and buttered popcorn. Colds brought more smells and made one keenly aware of the rigors of rural pharmacopoeia. Flannel chest protectors gave infallible proof of the plasters of mustard and salt pork, hen's oil, and duck's grease, boiled onions, and flaxseed.

Clearly, Chase drew on her own experience teaching in village schools for this catalog of classroom smells that change by the season. After five years enveloped in these scents, Mary moves to Petersport Academy to teach English.

Mary's life becomes filled with loss that tests her resiliency like the women whose men sailed on perilous and often ill-fated voyages. The casualties and years rush by. Sarah suffers a devastating stroke and is confined to her bed for years. John, who disavowed the indifferent sea, dies ironically on land in a freak accident when a tree he is moving slips from a derrick and crushes him. Sarah finally succumbs in 1905. Mary then telegraphs Jim Pendleton in New York. Sarah would have wanted it that way—yet so does Mary.

Jim stays for two weeks with his uncle and aunt. He is a smooth-talking phonograph salesman. He charms country farming families into purchasing what they can't afford. He also spends much of his time at Mary's brick house, tidying up her flowerbeds and preparing them for winter while she is at school. Jim sheds his salesman's persona for a more subtle charm in her presence. He does not beguile Mary: "She knew him for what he was." And yet he shared with her "all that still gave meaning to her life"—most important, "the swift understanding of Cadiz and Ponta Delgata in the early morning, of fruit-laden boats moving across clear water, of wind-filled sales, and long hours of idle waiting on a still sea." He had experienced "all those things which had quickened her, made her present and future but one with her past." As if to underscore this bond, Jim presents her with a seventeenth-century pocket fiddle: "It was shaped like a tiny boat, with a rounded keel and pointed stern and all the four olive-wood stops which formed its prow were surmounted by a carved serpents head." The artifact is fragile, suggestive of her brittle looming marriage to Jim. He warns her, "I'm always off on some tangent or another. You know that. I'll hurt you." She realizes the truth of what he predicts. "I've never paid much attention to the future," she responds. He returns to New York, and they correspond. Mary will take a risk on Jim, like the chances her family embraced with the sea.

When the curtain falls on another short summer, Petersport reverts to its unhurried off-season state of affairs. Looking downward from the water, fishermen see summer homes "closed, locked, banked and boarded." The brown grass turns "shaggy" on the golf links. Merchants have carted their summer profits to banks for safekeeping. Even the church services are relaxed. In particular, the ministers no longer feel self-conscious about "inadequate sermons." The winter becomes a time to talk about the "queer" summer folk. The sleepy village can also keep close track of how often Mary writes to Jim.

They are married in July standing below the portrait of Mary's great-grandparents, "painted, somebody said, in some foreign port a hundred years ago." Mary resigns from the academy, while Jim continues to sell phonographs to farmers. He carefully chooses the demonstration records he plays to suit his assessment of the customer's taste.

Within six years of marriage, the local market for phonographs shrivels. Jim has to take longer automobile trips in search of customers. Mary hears rumors; villagers greet her with suggestive "glances and pregnant silences." It is 1912. Mary is forty years old. The year also marks the height of "rage for antiques," with tragic consequences for the Maine coast. Old homes such as Mary's and pinched families are stripped of "their rightful possessions" by dishonest "collectors of all sorts," which immeasurably widens the gulf between native and sojourner. Mary has to sell some of her antiques to support Jim and herself.

We might reflect on the transformation of handcrafted artifacts into "antiques," since coastal Maine people and rural New Englanders as a whole sold off chunks of their material heritage. Handmade objects became valuable because they represented the pre-industrial "Age of Homespun." This past seemed a more authentic era than modern times of industrial labor and the mass production of cheap goods. Antiques gave material shape to values that appeared understocked in modern America: character, craftsmanship, simplicity, and good taste.[22] The rugs that Mary Peters hooks are not antiques, but they are "Made in Maine" by hand and reflect the same old-fashioned authenticity that gives cultural currency to antiques.

Did Down East people of the period shelve their history while their towns turned into summer colonies, as *Mary Peters* sets forth? One may be surprised to learn that Blue Hill established a historical society in 1902 and published a modest town history in two installments between 1903 and 1905.[23] More than a few coastal towns and islands Down East generated histories of varying quality during the years covered by *Mary Peters*: Deer Isle (1886); Mount Desert (1887 and 1905); Eastport and Passamaquoddy (1888); Islesboro (1893); and Gouldsboro (1904). Chase's fictional representation of Down East history is not utterly wrong. Rather, it is sometimes overdrawn for dramatic effect or for the purpose of social criticism. Yet Chase also offers the reader a low-to the-ground view of how the texture of Down East communities changed over the course of two generations.

Jim announces in August 1914 that he is going to France to assist in World War I. He can put his knowledge of French to good use working in a noncombat role. However, he never leaves Petersport. He crashes at a high speed into a bridge abutment and is killed. Ellen Peters, John's widow, with whom Jim has been having an affair, is a passenger in the car. She is left a paraplegic.

Partly out of loyalty to her dead brother, Mary consolidates households with his wheelchair-bound widow. She and Ellen sell their spacious houses in the village center and move to John's farm. In Mary's case, a family from Cleveland purchases the Peters homestead. She keeps her father's logs and pictures of the long line of ships that generations of Peters had sailed. In the end, Mary and Ellen work together braiding rugs for summer visitors.

Mary begins to hook rugs that narrate the story of her life at sea—a ship under "full sail in deep blue water," "the palms of the Java coast beneath a tropical moon," lighthouses, ports such as San Francisco, and much more. The summer buyers marvel at her work. One acknowledges her ignorance. "I didn't know there were actually people left nowadays even in Maine who had been to sea," she says. "Then that old town is an actual place," which is precisely Chase's point. History, memory, stories, material objects—all map and preserve the intrepid maritime history of coastal Maine.

But perhaps Chase lacks some balance in her assessment of "newcomers." Mary observes, "To most summer people the coast of Maine has no existence apart from themselves." Yet at least some who took up summer residence in unmodernized communities such as Petersport that retained their historical character came to know and value their town's past. In other words, as a work of historical fiction created by an invested author, we should not expect *Mary Peters* to display the objectivity of a historian. Thus we might ask: Do Petersport tradesmen represent one-dimensional opportunists—betrayers of their history—or are they resilient in their own right? Granted, Mary and Ellen don't use their skill to exploit customers. If anything, the opposite prevails: outsiders underpay for their hooked rugs, and city agents acquire antiques well below market value.

There is one final revealing summer encounter in the novel: A customer mentions that her son's future father-in-law, whose last name is Gardiner, is waiting in her car. Mary learns that his uncle was a first officer who was lost off the coast of San Francisco. Mary races to the car and discovers that the waiting visitor is the nephew of the *Elizabeth*'s William Gardiner, who taught her so much. "I loved him," Mary declares to the nephew, "as I've never loved anyone all my life."

Mary resists selling the beautiful rugs that her grandmother wove at sea. The same is true of a rug she hooks that captures her image of Cadiz. "In my opinion that's the best one yet," Ellen compliments Mary. It lies on her bedroom floor, safe from any summer visitor who would put a price on it. Such a transaction would profane Mary's memory of Cadiz and all it represents by reducing her rug to a summer commercial commodity.

Chase stressed in her essay "My Novels about Maine" that *Mary Peters* (which was the name of her great-great-grandmother) "was created solely for the purpose of showing how a childhood spent largely at sea might help to form a mind and an imagination invulnerable against time, chance and tragedy."[24]

Whether this literary vision represents realism unalloyed with romantic elements in *Mary Peters* is open to debate. It is clear that, among other things, *Mary Peters* advances the most scathing critique of summer people and their adverse effect on the character of coastal residents in Maine fiction up to 1934 and beyond.

In any case, the novel shot onto bestseller lists in America and England. Thirty thousand copies sold in the first year at home, with thousands more sold in England. Chase wrote to her mother that at one London book-signing event she autographed "450 books in all."[25]

Mary Peters was reviewed widely, like most important Maine fiction of the period. On the whole, reviewers gave the novel a highly favorable reception. "This is not a novel but a symphony," the *New York Herald Tribune* Sunday Books enthused. In the *Saturday Review of Literature*, Gladys Hasty Carroll lavished praise on the book. "There is nothing of the hush of a cemetery on a summer afternoon," she wrote. "Rather there is something of the resilience of a springboard, as in *A Goodly Heritage*." The *Boston Globe* called it "a fine and well-written story." The *San Francisco Chronicle* thought it would win the Pulitzer Prize "for the best novel of 1934." The *London Daily Mail* named *Mary Peters* its book of the month for February. "It is impossible to read it without exhilaration," the reviewer wrote.[26]

Of course, there were some less than enthusiastic and even negative reviews. The one that gnawed at Chase the most appeared in the *Atlantic Monthly*, a periodical where she had published. She knew the reviewer. He praised the descriptive and lyrical aspects of the book but thought that, Mary aside, the characters were flat. "John, Ellen and Jim . . . are one-note people." The reviewer also had a problem with Chase's "narrative," saying that she "is uncertain in her development of events."[27] This criticism touched a nerve. Chase wrote to the reviewer and challenged his assessment. Despite this major negative review, Chase could bask in the satisfaction that *Mary Peters* was an overwhelming popular and critical success.

SILAS CROCKETT: FROM CLIPPERS TO CANNERIES

Published only a year after *Mary Peters*, *Silas Crockett* is Chase's most ambitious and acclaimed work. It rests on extensive research and displays deep knowledge of Maine's maritime and coastal history. The novel is a four-generation saga of the Crockett family's changing fortunes. Chase offered her epic as a contribution to Maine social history. In the foreword to the book, she acknowledged that, given her subject, she had "placed more emphasis upon setting and character than upon plot and incident." In fact, the novel is sometimes heavily descriptive and expository—that is, she narrates or writes like a historian. Chase tells rather than shows or dramatizes. It is almost as if she can't make up her mind whether she wants to write fiction or history. Perhaps we need to make some allowance for the historical breadth of *Silas Crockett*. Nevertheless, as in *Mary Peters* her language is vivid and engaging; her characters are also believable.

Silas Crockett chronicles the transformation of the Down East maritime world between 1830 and 1933. Chase has to navigate this journey with fidelity to historical facts winnowed through her literary imagination. She frames her epic as another narrative of declension. Change displaces too much heroic history from the minds of Down East people and radically rearranges their seascape and their economy as well. But something "lingers," as Chase says in *A Goodly Heritage. Silas Crockett*, like *Mary Peters*, represents a kind of intervention in history: In the face of inexorable change, Chase wants to document a noble past and to reanimate Mainers' pride in their own maritime exploits on land and at sea.

We first meet Captain Silas Crockett in 1830, when he is returning to Saturday Cove by steamship from Boston after a highly successful one-and-a-half-year voyage to India and China on the aptly named *Seven Seas*. Silas is the offspring of Saturday Cove's grandee. Captain James Crockett is a retired, accomplished shipmaster, like two generations of his family before him. He owns the town's shipyards and lives in Saturday Cove's most stately house, situated on a hill. Silas is tall, lean, and energetic—restively, even nervously, so. He is meticulously dressed and groomed. He sports "spotless cravats, well-fitting clothes . . . light kid gloves and a Mallacca-jointed cane." Silas's "sleek black hair and perfectly trimmed side whiskers" augment his commanding figure. He is a week shy of his twenty-third birthday and already a veteran captain of the seas.

Silas despises steam power. On the last leg of his return, from Bath to Saturday Cove, he impatiently squanders four days on a small steamer that "coughed and spluttered" its way Down East. Unlike the *Seven Seas*, the steamer is uninspiringly christened the *Island Maid*. Its captain serves as an accompanying foil to Silas. Captain Gilley (who is given no first name) is "a short squat man of fifty." His clothes are grease stained, and "the remnants of his breakfast eggs" cling to his mustache. The talkative Gilley tries to make a case for the challenges of navigating a coastal "tub." There are unmarked "reefs and ledges." Seasonal fogs "thicker than wool off a sheep's back" pose another hazard. Yes, Gilley concludes, inshore waters present more perilous challenges than open ocean.

Silas, of course, is having none of Gilley's blather. He lets the *Island Maid*'s captain carry on without wasting a word on him. Then the tobacco-chewing Gilley makes a prophecy: The age of steam is almost upon them. "There's days coming, young man, when the Atlantic Ocean to a steamer won't look no bigger than Penobscot Bay to a ship with a wind dead against her or no wind at all."

Silas stirs. Standing on his family's maritime exploits and his own command of the seas, basking in New England's glorious age of sail, he delivers a forceful response to Gilley. Silas mocks steam. It may evolve along shore, "not on the broad Atlantic and Pacific where clouds are the only cooling-stations you can fall back on." Crockett then finds fault with himself for replying to such a coarse representative of what poses no threat to the flourishing high tide of sail. Besides, he has more important things on his mind. In a matter of days after his return to Saturday Cove, Crockett will marry Solace Winship. In three weeks he will haul anchor and carry his bride across the seas, a practice that was not widespread on the coast of Maine. But women and children on board give more human interest to both *Mary Peters* and *Silas Crockett*.

Saturday Cove lies well Down East, beyond Mount Desert, "where French-man Bay sweeps on toward Passamaquoddy." As the *Island Maid* crawls from Bath to Saturday Cove, Chase summons the sights and sounds of the bays and inlets that have become hives of shipbuilding. Sawmills buzz, producing miles of board that leave "great mounds of saw dust." Ships stand at varied stages of construction, from simple skeletons to nearly completed vessels undergoing copper cladding below the waterline to prevent rotting and the effect of hitch-hitching sea worms and other marine life. The smell of "tar and pitch" fills the air. Silas sees sheets of canvas as they are shaped into sails. From the *Island Maid* he hears the pervasive sounds of optimism, of progress, of the future: "the mallet and hammer upon wood and iron, and the calls and cries of shipwrights, riveters and framers, tackers and seamers, and the excited shouts of boys lingering to watch." Chase's introductory pages are engaging, even elegant. She suggestively delineates character and setting—the bustling Maine coast in 1830—and draws the reader into her grand narrative.

Silas has expansive dreams. Already highly respected by Boston merchants, he will sail for them again. Eventually he will purchase his own ship. After he makes his fortune, Silas and Solace will retire to a fashionable street in Salem or Boston. As he reflects, "The coast of Maine was a good place to come from but not to end one's days on when the whole world beckoned." Yet a career captain like Silas will have seen the world in his travels. Moreover, the Crocketts for generations have seen fit to return to Saturday Cove—if they survived the seas' whims.

In fact, Silas's two older brothers have already perished. Nicholas died from fever in the West Indies, and Reuben was lost at sea—no one knows where. Perpetuation of the family's maritime tradition now rests solely on Silas, who is far from immunized against hubris.

Silas's arrival at Saturday Cove occasions our introduction to his mother, Abigail. She is another of those stout women like Sarah Peters, and Mary Peters herself, who are common in Chase's work. The Reverend Ethan Fisher, Saturday Cove's throwback Congregational minister, greets Silas at the dock. The good reverend is a thinly veiled Jonathan Fisher, Blue Hill's longtime orthodox pastor. He completed an iconic oil painting of the newly established state of Maine: *A Morning View of Blue Hill Village* (1824). A corner of the painting captured shipbuilding in the village. Chase wrote a biography of Fisher.[28] The "fictional" Fisher offers a Calvinist-laced prayer. Abigail takes exception. She thinks the rigid reverend is more suited for the backcountry. On the coast people "were always more flexible in conception and application . . . and were more inclined to take a chance on the vengeance of God against an idle work now and then." Of Silas's future mother-in-law, Dorcas Winship, Abigail pungently observes that she "knows more about the will of God than God himself knows." Abigail is an independent-minded, resilient woman who has already experienced the crucible of loss. She is not about to interpret it as God's personal chastisement. More loss lies ahead. At one point, Chase describes Abigail in Jewett-like language as "oracular" and resembling "some ancient prophetess."

Abigail Crockett embodies Chase's appreciative but qualified interpretation of Puritanism's role in providing a moral foundation in the settlement of the Maine coast. The Puritan work ethic, communalism, and commitment to education set in place an enduring legacy for Down East. But Calvinism represented another matter, especially given the coast's exposure to cultures around the world. Abigail accompanied her husband to sea; it is not surprising that she is less religiously hidebound than Dorcas Winship. Revealingly, when the betrothed couple consults with Reverend Fisher before they marry, he presents them with a volume written by Jonathan Edwards, the high priest of eighteenth-century Calvinism. Silas tosses the book in the cove. One might add that in Silas's moral universe there is no room for the Puritan sea captivity narrative. Whether threatened by pirates, caught in a gale, or marooned on an island after a shipwreck, mariners' deliverance from such alleged divine punishment doesn't involve prayer and repentance of collective sins. The seamen rely on their own, not divine, agency. Little does Silas know, however, that historical forces beyond his control will determine his fate.

Like Abigail Crockett, Thomas Winship, Solace's father, is a finely drawn character. He is Saturday Cove's quiet hero; his greatness complements, even as it is obscured by, James Crockett's stature. Both men built vessels, and Winship voyaged as a ship carpenter. Retiring from the sea, Thomas refined his architect's imagination and his carpentry skills. Unassuming, industrious, reticent, and bent over like an ancient bookworm, he designs a built landscape for the ages: fourteen churches, academies, and more than a dozen houses with red brick or white clapboards. He incorporates into his work architectural details that he admired in his travels throughout the watery world. He assimilates the outside world into Down East tradition. He resembles Mary Peters, who weaves the memory of her voyaging experiences into her hooked rugs.

After a wedding commensurate with the Crockett family's standing, Silas and his twenty-year-old bride set off on their world voyage. Solace "never liked the sea but she adored her husband." Her name serves as prophecy of her life. And tragedy strikes early in her marriage. The *Seven Seas* makes a call on Marseilles. A doctor assures the pregnant Solace that she has seven weeks until birth is likely. Thus there is time for Silas to continue sailing before dropping anchor so that Solace can deliver in a hospital. The doctor proves to be wrong. Solace gives birth to a stillborn aboard the *Seven Seas* as Silas, with direction from the first officer, presides over the delivery. It will be twenty years before Solace presents Silas with an heir.

The course of Silas's progress is interspersed with the larger context of maritime New England sailing at the summit of its commercial prowess. Here Chase writes as a historian, a more than competent one. During the 1830s, fifteen hundred ships sail every year into Boston; the growth of factories contributes shoes and textiles, among other items, to New England's intricate web of trade and reexchange; and Bostonian Frederick Tudor perfects his ice trade to tropical countries and then to India. In Saturday Cove and along the Maine coast, ship owners and investors, captains and officers, "ate, drank, and wore the products of foreign soil and talked more familiarly of the *Seven Seas* than of Machias Bay."

Before the end of the decade, Silas acquires ownership of the *Seven Seas*. He then sells the vessel to finance a new one, which he christens the *Solace Winship*. He invests his energy and ambition in that long ship with tall sails and more freight capacity. In other words, the *Solace Winship* takes on characteristics of a "clipper ship," those fleet Yankee vessels that were refined in the early 1850s to transport goods to the Far East and gold-fever adventurers to California. Silas spends ten hours a day in the Saturday Cove shipyard overseeing the vessel's construction.

Patriarch James Crockett is no longer alive when the *Solace Winship* is launched. He suffers a major financial setback when a Machias brig in which he had heavily invested was lost at sea. The misfortune stuns James. On a hot August day, a fatal stroke in one of his shipyards ends his life. Silas, for the time being, is the only surviving descendant of the illustrious clan.

Throughout the 1840s, he and Solace sail the ship that bears her maiden name as Captain Gilley's prophecy looms. As early as 1840, while Silas crosses the Atlantic, "clouds of smoke" are caught "up upon his sails." It is the *Unicorn*, Samuel Cunnard's pioneering transatlantic steamship. The *Unicorn* overtakes the *Solace Winship* and leaves a subdued Silas in the distance. Worries about steam power stalk Silas and other captains of sail over the course of the decade. New design only enables Maine's age of sail to persist on borrowed time.

Finally pregnant for a second time, at the age of forty, Solace helps bolster Silas's sagging faith in the future. She remains in Saturday Cove while Silas sails for Australia. In the old Crockett homestead, Solace and Abigail form a gendered attachment shaped by their shared experience and isolation from men: "It was a women's world, patient, unhurried, self-contained, a world of letting well enough alone until the time should come for action." When that moment arrives, Solace gives birth to a healthy boy. Named for Silas's deceased oldest brother, Nicholas Danforth Crockett is five months old when his father sets eyes on him for the first time.

Silas had once told Solace that he "would rather have no son at all than to see him unable to prove himself as a man in the high vocation of sail." He saddles his son with both continuing the Crockett family tradition and a coercive maritime notion of manhood. Chase dissects how a boy is socialized into the world of sail. As Nicholas grows up, Silas presents him with his brother's sea chest; it still bears the name "Nicholas D. Crockett." Silas rows his son out to a ship preparing to sail and explains the significance of everything that is taking place before departure. When he's ten years old, Nicholas and Solace go to sea with Silas. The son has the run of the ship. He is particularly fond of the fo'c'sle and the world of the men sailing before the mast, which Chase describes in realistic details. Nicholas loved this "man's world . . . with its smell of drying clothes and stale tobacco." As the wind howled outside, the men "seem more snug and comfortable within." He enjoyed watching them "sitting about the mess-tub with their spoons and tin basins, ladling out thick pea soup with dumplings and bits of pork, swilling down their cups of steaming coffee, gnawing great fistfuls of hardtack." At the age of ten, it is as certain as the tides in Saturday Cove that Nicholas will pursue a life of sail.

Yet throughout Nicholas's first decade, his father's fortunes fluctuate. The world of sail is constantly in flux. Saturday Cove's piers are rotting and its shipbuilders have left. Then the Civil War writes the last chapter in New England's great age of sail. Already Down East is undergoing what we might call the industrialization of the coast. Canning factories for lobster, pickled herring, and oil from pogies displace shipyards. Recent research documents that by 1880 twenty-three factories were canning food in Maine, many of them along the coast.[29] Jewett never dealt with this part of maritime Maine, but it becomes central to Chase's coastal realism.

Silas does not live to see the worst of the coast's transformation. While removing porcupine quills from a dog that Nicholas acquired, Silas is bitten. He develops an infection and fever and then slips toward death, inveighing against the war and steam with his failing breath. After a life at sea, it's an unheroic end for fifty-seven-year-old Silas. The son will not live half of his father's allotted days, and he will endure a wretched death.

Solace and Grandmother Crockett raise Nicholas. He grows up as his father's son, tall and lanky. A restless, indifferent student at the academy, the only abiding residue of his years there is his love for Deborah Parsons. It is unrequited. She goes off to Mount Holyoke Seminary and the prospect of a world beyond graying Saturday Cove, where there "was little left of the old far-seeing life." Foreign ships no longer call at the Cove. The crumbling shipyards will soon leave behind nothing more than the equivalent of a cellar hole from a once successful farm. Few captains persist in the old sailing ways. Those who stay behind turn to fishing. Herring weirs and lobster traps along with canneries announce the new economy. Saturday Cove acquires its own canning factory, a token of its descent into provincialism and pinched opportunity for those who stay behind. Chase's jeremiad now gathers momentum.

She furnishes a sympathetic depiction of the plight of many young men in Saturday Cove after the war. They stood "knee deep in the holds [of ships] shoveling herring" for the new canning factory. "The men and boys . . . were bronzed and tired. Fish scales clung to their hair and to the stubble of their beards." Such labor forms calluses on more than their hands. They worked "only to get home for a late supper and sleep before the earliest dawn summoned them again to the outgoing boats."

As for Nicholas, he spurns any kind of fishing for a decade. At the age of twenty in 1870, he accepts a "lesser" officer position on the blandly named ship the *Mildred May*, sailing from Boston to San Francisco. Along with everything else in Maine's maritime world, crews have changed. They are less composed of ambitious New England youth, many of whom had aspired to rise through a ship's ranks. Now a more intractable mix of humanity, a kind of floating lumpenproletariat, confronts the officers. In *Mary Peters*, a first officer is murdered with an axe and Captain Peters responds by brutally crushing the mutiny of the non–New Englanders. Nicholas Crockett is elevated to second officer on the *Mildred May*'s return voyage for his skillful management of the volatile crew.

Deborah Parsons has now returned to backwater Saturday Cove. With her father's death, she is unable to continue at Mount Holyoke after one year. Seemingly confined, or condemned, to a place she longs to escape, Deborah views Nicholas in a new light. Given his knowledge of the sea and his skill on a craft, Deborah believes in Nicholas's swift rise to steamship captain as sailing's profitability and prestige plummet. They are married in the spring of 1873, when Nicholas is twenty-three and now first officer on the *Mildred May*.

It is not enough for Deborah. She launches her campaign of quiet argument and acrimony to cow Nicholas into switching from sail to steam. He holds out, viewing steam as a betrayal of everything his father dinned into him. Deborah broods when Nicholas doesn't buckle under her combativeness. The sea emerges as an escape from a domestic drama in which Nicholas's nerves become as taut as the rigging of a ship at full sail.

In the fall of 1875, events accelerate Nicholas's journey from a heroic to a heartbreaking figure. He sets out on the *Mildred May* for Bermuda. The ship capsizes from a gale off Cape Hatteras; a fire soon engulfs the *Mildred May*, and most of the officers and crew perish. But Nicholas manages to escape and commands the only boat that makes it to shore with survivors, who suffer through three days at sea deprived of food and water.

Newspapers pick up the story and identify Nicholas. Letters and telegrams pour in from steamship lines recruiting experienced officers from sailing ships. Deborah, who is pregnant, ratchets up her pressure on Nicholas to accept a steamship position. And now Solace, with new pride in her son and concern for his future, urges him to become a steamship officer, even a captain. Nicholas is unyielding. He refuses a captaincy because "there's not much respect in commanding a thing you have no respect for." Nicholas fends off Deborah's tears and threats: "I'll be proud to have a son of mine know I helped command such a [sailing] ship and he'll be proud too."

Nicholas refuses to draw lessons from the *Mildred May*'s devastation. Sail is more perilous than steam, as the widows of coastal Maine silently signify. But that's what makes it heroic and manly. Nicholas is unable to give the slip to Silas's long shadow. The father implanted in the young son the superiority of commanding a sailing ship over a steamship, dogma that, ironically, supplants the Calvinism that his ancestors rejected. Nicholas can't accept that he lives in a different era, defined by the death spiral of sail. With Deborah's pregnancy, the rational choice for Nicholas is a better-paying position on a safer steamship. Instead, the hope that he will soon have a son only revives throwback romantic notions of sailing's manly challenge.

Fate intervenes, as it so often does in Chase's fictional universe. Unbeknownst to him, Nicholas has already taken his last voyage—at least in this world. A schooner captain happens to see Nicholas in the post office collecting his ample mail with numerous job offers on steamships. Early the next morning, the captain shows up at the Crockett house with an offer. Captain Simpson is a "high-liner," the coastal term for the most successful fisherman and lobsterman. He has a new schooner, and the halibut fishery on the Grand Banks is his destination that very afternoon. But his "best man" has taken sick. He needs six teams of two to man his dories, which will sail off from the schooner. He believes Nicholas is the person to replace his best man. Captain Simpson warns Nicholas that "it's no summer picnic." He promises enticing money for twenty days of fishing, which will enable the schooner to deliver ninety thousand pounds of halibut to Boston.

The Maine halibut fishery has a manly heroism of its own, suggestively immortalized in Winslow Homer's *The Fog Warning* (1885). The oil painting shows a fisherman in his dory, his catch at his feet, as he rows furiously back to his ship while a fog bank rises up over the horizon. Chase gives the reader a graphic picture of the halibut fishery's multiple perils. Sometimes the "fog horn" signaling the ship's location for the dories consists of a conch shell or gunshots. A thick fog increases the danger of being run over by another ship or destroyed by "jagged cakes" of ice. Then there is the numbing cold "in the blank whiteness of winter," when the temperature seems stuck well below zero at noon. The halibut themselves, weighing two to four hundred pounds, pose still another hazard. They have to be clubbed before being dragged aboard. After an exhausting day of fishing, the dory men must sail out again for one more dangerous task: baiting the trawl lines, which, we now know, could number as many as four hundred hooks.[30]

Yet the vulnerabilities of the halibut fishery are still not over. The crew has to maintain watch through the night for ships crisscrossing the banks and for the threat from icebergs. As the *Lydia* heads home with its catch, Nicholas drags himself from his bunk and climbs to the schooner's lookout for his turn at the watch. There, leaning against the mast for some protection from the wind, he apparently falls asleep and freezes to death. His lifeless body has to be pried from the mast. In other words, only death frees Nicholas from his dogmatic manly attachment to the age of sail.

Nicholas's son arrives in the spring; he represents the family's new hope. His mother, expecting a girl, leaves to Solace the choice of a name. "Reuben" was Silas's second brother's name. When the child is four years old, Deborah finally escapes from Saturday Cove. She meets a summering artist from Boston, marries him a year later, and moves to the city. Reuben is left in the care of Solace, who is seventy years old, and her servant Susan Gray, who is fifty. He only sees his mother for brief periods, with years in between visits.

Reuben grows up in the 1880s as a short, squat, and meek boy, which suggests the diminution of Saturday Cove's once adventurous character and the downsizing of the Crocketts, once the town's most distinguished family. He possesses none of the "suppleness of the Crockett men." Nor does their spirit "burn so restlessly" within Reuben. He labors at his studies and remains easily overlooked in school. The boy begets the adult. Reuben will mature into a decent young man whose life continues on a head-down, low-to-the-ground course.

During those years, the world of his ancestors fades away. It is a past that, like an archeologist, Chase excavates as a stay against the corrosive consequences of maritime decline and the emergence of a summer economy. When visitors sail their yachts into Saturday Cove's harbor, they possess no knowledge "that below the soil nearest there were remnants of wharves and docks and building platforms." Only the old-timers cling to remembrance of the communal celebration on the launching of a ship, "the church bells ringing and everybody in holiday dress." Such a collective maritime memory will soon be interred with the passing of Solace's generation.

The 1890s witness summer people's plundering of Saturday Cove. They purchase "land at unheard of prices," they build "cottages, with native labour," and they demand "fresh fish for their tables as well as lobsters and clams." Some summer folk seek out houses that, with their frayed antimodern grandeur, articulate a sense of history. They fall into the hands of "men from Philadelphia and Boston and New York." Solace will not sell the Crockett homestead. Instead, she accepts an offer for her father's house. A Minnesota buyer tenders more money than two Boston maiden ladies; however, she accepts less money to sell the Winship place to New Englanders, who will (presumably) show more appreciation for the house's architectural significance. With the money, she fixes up the Crockett homestead in preparation for Reuben gaining sole possession of it.

Solace dies in 1890, when Reuben is fourteen. His mother comes to the funeral looking "more like a summer visitor than a native." She has no intention of taking custody of Reuben and carrying him back to Boston. To Deborah's relief, Reuben has no desire to go. He remains in Saturday Cove and completes his growth into young manhood under servant Susan's maternal watch.

From the world Chase re-creates, the reader surmises the narrow range of options that Reuben, like other young men attached to the Down East coast, faces when he finishes the academy. Labor for summer people, take up fishing and lobstering, or enter the cannery—these are the principal occupations of the members of Reuben's generation who stay behind. Instead, with his family's maritime heritage at his back, Reuben finds low-paying employment as a clerk with the coastal steamer that shuttles between Rockland and towns east of Mount Desert. He is the first Crockett to compromise with steam and for whom it is not a fraught decision.

The daily repetition of the steamship's circuit is relieved for Reuben by the coast's beauty across the changing seasons: "He never tired of the great curve of shore line sweeping up to Owl's Head, or of the perfect symmetry of Mark Island . . . the purple hills of Camden with Negro Light in their dark shadows, the blue sweep of Eggemoggin, the high promontory of Eagle and the squat coziness of Pumpkin, the spruces that back the great granite cliffs of Heron Neck, and the white lighthouse towers of Frenchman's Bay." Against this captivating background, Reuben begins a quiet grind toward the modest pinnacle of his success. By 1901, when he is twenty-five and a new steamship company is formed, Reuben assumes command of his own ship. He is the youngest captain in the entire steamship line. But it is a modest vessel that plies a limited course. His steamer runs between Rockland and Saturday Cove, the latter well advanced in its progress toward a summer colony.

To be sure, well before twenty-five Reuben's grandfather commanded a ship that braved many seas and oceans. At Reuben's age, his father had the choice of the numerous oceangoing steamships that were recruiting him. Interestingly, after he makes it safely through a powerful gale, Reuben declares to Susan that piloting a coastal steamer poses more challenges than commanding an ocean-traveling vessel. "It's knowing every reef and shoal and sounding of the most tricky coast in all the world," he insists. "It must have been a fine thing to sail in open water hundreds of miles on every side of you. . . . But maybe it's not such a poor job to know how to get through the islands of Eggemoggin Reach and Frenchman's Bay in a fog that's sitting thick on your very pilot house." Ironically, of course, these words echo what the garrulous, slovenly Captain Gilley uttered to Silas at the start of the novel. Now they come from a Crockett descendant! At least death spared Silas and Nicholas from witnessing the family's eclipse, which will scrape bottom in the next generation.

Susan and the townspeople, who barely remember the heroic Crocketts, are proud of Reuben because of his skill in the thickest fog. As she ages, Susan finds her voice as Saturday Cove's scold. "I don't know what this village is coming to," she grumbles to Reuben. "It's getting so that young an' old work only in the summer an' hang round air-tights all winter." They distort their Maine ingenuity, one might say. Winter months find too many Saturday Cove people trying to figure out "how they can cheat them that come here for three months so's to get enough out of 'em to live on the remain' nine." Through Susan, Chase reiterates a theme that she drives home in *Mary Peters*: the summer economy not only distances the locals from their maritime heritage but also corrupts the "traditional" Maine character.

For four years after Reuben becomes a captain, Susan watches his tentative courtship of schoolteacher Huldah Barrett. In one of her colorful localisms, Susan describes it as "the beatingest thing." Huldah is five years older than Reuben. Still, he moves toward a marriage proposal at a glacial pace. They finally wed in 1905, when Huldah is thirty-five and Reuben thirty. She moves into the Crockett house and Susan comes to love her. Then, in 1910, the longtime Crockett servant dies, only the first of Reuben's personal and then professional misfortunes as Saturday Cove and the Maine coast contend with a new incursion of summer people in automobiles.

Huldah is pregnant when Susan dies. On Christmas Eve, she delivers a boy who will be named Silas Crockett II. But the birth has gone terribly wrong. The doctors have no explanation. Huldah becomes a paraplegic. She courageously accepts her fate, and Reuben has to secure care for her and Silas. Expenses leave his modest salary barely enough to support the family.

Young Silas grows up tall and gangly like his grandfather—and great-grandfather. Unlike them, however, he enjoys school and excels at his studies. He provides some compensation for his father's growing dispiritedness in the 1910s and early 1920s. Reuben stands flat-footed as the earth shifts beneath him. Automobiles "thronged the coast roads in summer." His steamer has now been repurposed to transport freight instead of passengers. The former locations of the docks, fish houses, and shipyards are now occupied by the "golf links of the new country club." Reuben mortgages the house to stay afloat. Then he agonizes over selling the family portraits that have dignified the parlor for generations and memorialized the Crocketts' accomplishments. With Silas's permission, he lets them go to a New York dealer. By the age of fifty, Reuben has white hair.

Surprisingly for a work of historical fiction, Chase makes no note of the centennial of Maine statehood in 1920. It was celebrated in many communities.

Chase might have introduced it if only to show that the centennial had meager relevance to townspeople who, like Reuben, were scuffing by or milking summer people while cunningly calculating how better to exploit them.

Silas graduates from the academy at the head of his class. He sets his sights on becoming a doctor, a kind of reclaiming of the Crockett family name and achievement. To finance his first year at Bowdoin, Reuben and Huldah sell off the furnishings of a "great front bedroom" now ordained "antiques." Finally, Reuben acknowledges, the house must pass out of Crockett hands for the first time in four generations. The structure is crumbling around him—as is the very "house" of Crockett—and Reuben is unable to find the money for badly needed repairs. A man from Philadelphia purchases the property in 1930. Perhaps Reuben is prescient for once. Within months of the sale, his steamer, which has been losing money for some time, goes silent.

Reuben and Huldah abandon Saturday Cove for the farthest reaches of Down East, where Maine's version of "Cannery Row," to borrow Steinbeck's term, is concentrated, though Jonesport, Lubec, and Eastport are never identified. Reuben finds a job piloting a ferryboat. Yet his slide in standing is far from the Crocketts' most disheartening, as Silas leaves Bowdoin after two years. Given the family's financial straits, he believes that the money Reuben has saved for college should be put to more immediate needs. Moreover, he is able to work and assist the family.

Silas finds a job at the herring factory and agonizes over taking such lowly, squalid employment. The manager of the factory tells him that in the hard times of 1931, Silas should seize the job "like a gull diving for herring refuse." The manager says more about Down East and the Depression: "This business is about all that keeps the coast alive just now except for the rusticators that are losin' all their money and are bound to lose more." However, Silas is not persuaded by the possibility of promotion or the fact that there are no workers who are "Canucks or Eyetalians or even Irish. They're fine coast-of-Maine stock."

Chase has Silas explore the entire canning operation, which enables her to document the division of labor and assembly-line operations of the factory. He is to start at the lowest rung, except for the men wearing hip boots in the holds of ships "shoveling herring into baskets." For twenty to twenty-five cents an hour, he is to work at the next stage: the cutting tables alongside boys and girls who wield sharp knives to sever the "heads and entrails" of herring. After a week of hesitation, Silas enters the factory.

One final incident sums up the utter dissolution of the Crockett family's standing: Silas falls in love with the traveling nurse who tends to Huldah. At the request of a dying Reuben, Silas and Ann return to the former Crockett homestead to report back on how its new owners are caring for the historic property.

Silas sounds the brass knocker on the door, and an "elderly," "stately" man outfitted in black answers. Silas doffs his hat, not realizing it's the servant. But the irony of Silas II's predicament is devastating. For generations the Crocketts hired servants; they never removed their hats when they greeted them.

Yet many of the Crockett men and women display resiliency, pitching and rolling with family tragedies and the shifting currents of their beloved Maine coast. Solace, Reuben, and Silas II, for example, all embody resiliency, which connects them especially to Mary Peters. Nevertheless, from the great age of sail to the Great Depression, Chase has written an unflinching saga of Down East's transformation as a process of declension.

Silas Crockett was a commercial success in the United States and Great Britain. Chase's work appealed to an audience that *A Goodly Heritage* and *Mary Peters* had created. *Silas Crockett* appeared on bestseller lists in the United States and Britain.[31]

The novel was mostly a critical success as well. The *London Evening Standard* named *Silas Crockett* its book of the month for January 1936. The *Star of London* praised the book for the "sturdy portraits of the Crockett men . . . [and] the charming vignettes of their wives." *The Scotsman* declared, "This is a fine, long, rich book."[32]

Silas Crockett was widely reviewed in the United States. The *San Diego Union* described the saga as "beautifully written." The *Boston Evening Transcript* enthused "that nothing will ever be written which will reveal so clearly the glory and the tragedy which befell the State." The *New York Times* reviewer was also enthusiastic: "By an astonishing selection of quiet incident and descriptive detail she recreates a vanished way of life that is tender and refreshing."[33]

Still, there were tepid and critical reviews. The *New York American* diminished the book with faint praise: "She has written a dignified, provincial story in a quiet vein which guarantees success these days." The *New York World Telegram* reviewer complained that *Silas Crockett* "covers too much ground without making the story vital to the reader." It also lacked the "unity of *Mary Peters*."[34]

Chase was sensitive to criticism. In a long essay in the *Sunday Portland, Maine, Press Herald* in 1936, she responded to some of her New York critics. Chase singled out those who said she was "idealizing a past which was long dead" and "regretting the death of that past." First, Chase turned to her extensive research, which included a visit to a Jonesport herring factory. She wanted to establish that *Silas Crockett* was a work of historical realism, not idealism or romanticism. Despite her lament for Down East's tidal wave of change, she argued that the maritime past remained alive in Maine: "Any state with a noble history such as ours cherishes her past, transmutes it with all its gifts into the present, reminds her children of their heritages." As an example, she suggested that the "great old houses of Wiscasset . . . call that past to mind daily and will hold it tenaciously."[35] Thus Chase's nonliterary mission in *Silas Crockett*, and in *Mary Peters* as well, is to construct a narrative of Maine's coastal past every bit as real and evocative as a Wiscasset captain's dwelling.

Of course, the proletarian novelists of the Depression years might have disagreed with Chase's whole project. Mills had become the state's growth industry during decades before the 1930s. Maine now encompassed industrial workers—French Canadians, Irish, even "Eyetalians," and other groups. They had scant, if any, connection to Down East's history and its white mansions of yesteryear. Such is fair criticism, but it doesn't reduce the *Silas Crockett* saga to pocket-sized historical fiction. Moreover, Chase didn't live to see the establishment and growth of institutions along the coast to preserve and interpret Maine's maritime past. The heroic seafaring era remains very much a part of Maine's collective consciousness.

Six years after *Silas Crockett*, Chase published her most commercially successful novel, which was widely and favorably reviewed. *Windswept* was also the name of her Petit Manan cottage. The book left Chase comfortable for the rest of her life. *Windswept* was reprinted fifteen times by 1952.[36]

Despite its Down East setting, Chase did not consider *Windswept* the third volume in her Maine trilogy. Though it stretches over sixty years, the novel doesn't grapple with the coast's transformation. It is a long story about Philip Marston and his descendants. He is a Maine native and a successful marine engineer in New York City. Far Down East he discovers a seemingly barren part of the coast, a wafer-thin cover for Petit Manan that takes possession of him for its stark beauty. In 1880, he decides to build a summer cottage there. But he is killed in a hunting accident on his land before the house is completed. His teenage son, John, the new owner of the property, decides to complete the cottage in memory of his father. The novel traces the progress of the family and the history of the house down to World War II.

Chase considered not *Windswept* but *The Edge of Darkness* (1957) the final volume in her Maine trilogy. It is very different from *Mary Peters* and *Silas Crockett*. Chase claimed that *The Edge of Darkness*, a "phrase used by Eastern Maine to describe the twilight," was her "favorite of all" she had authored.[37]

The story takes place in less than a twenty-four-hour period and involves the death of ninety-year-old Sarah Holt. The "novel" is short and loosely structured. Holt served as the last connection to the long-gone prosperous shipbuilding and sailing days of the cove. The remote hardscrabble lobstering and herring weir town is vividly portrayed in chapters devoted to particular characters. Holt's death temporarily unifies these individuals because she has had direct or indirect influence on them. However, for all that Chase invested in the moving description of the funeral and the realistic depiction of the townspeople, *The Edge of Darkness* doesn't dislodge *Silas Crockett* as her best Maine book.

For my purposes, Chase was the most important Maine novelist of the 1930s. Though she appealed to audiences across the Atlantic, primarily in England, Maine was the subject matter of her strongest works. Chase never developed a literary approach, such as Jewett's imaginative realism, that might have enabled her to extend her most enduring work beyond the particular. Still, no one has yet matched her combination of historical knowledge and literary imagination to tell an overarching story of Down East Maine's momentous shift from the age of sail to the era of canneries and summer folk.

3

ISLAND VILLAGES AND THE STRUGGLE FOR SURVIVAL

Ruth Moore

Maine year-round island life has been compared to a "lifeboat." Survival depends on "all who cling there."[1] Neighbors and strangers (those not island born) often must "turn to," as the nautical saying goes. Perhaps Melville's metaphor of Nantucket as "an anthill in the sea" is also suggestive.[2] It describes the relentless activity and the cooperation that enable island life to endure. We might take a cue from Jewett's portrayal of Green Island. In Maine, fictional island inhabitants represent the attributes of the so-called traditional Maine character to the nth degree. Mrs. Blockett and William are industrious, practical, unvarnished, and straightforward, for example, and they speak in a distinctive Maine vernacular.

In the mid-1940s, two highly successful authors emerged who wrote extensively about Maine island life: Elisabeth Ogilvie and Ruth Moore. Prominent New York publishers issued their books. Both also reached a wide audience of readers and reviewers.

Ogilvie was not a Maine native, but from an early age she summered on Criehaven, an island next to Matinicus, twenty miles out to sea. She grew up in the Boston area, graduating from North Quincy High School in 1934. Ogilvie didn't attend college, though she did take a writing course at Harvard. She settled permanently in Maine in the early 1940s. By the middle of the decade, as her writing career blossomed, she and her lifelong partner, Dorothy Simpson (who was also a writer), purchased Gay's Island. It lay almost attached to the midcoast mainland at the mouth of the St. George River. In an often-humorous memoir, *My World Is an Island* (1950), Ogilvie related how she and Dorothy made habitable a dirty rundown farmhouse on Gay's, where they were the only residents.[3]

Over the course of a long career, Ogilvie published more than forty books, which included adult and young adult novels, romances, and historical fiction. She is best known for her Tide Trilogy (1944–1947). Set on fictional Bennett's Island, where the lobstering community experiences depopulation and then repopulation, the trilogy draws from Ogilvie's experience on Criehaven.

The first novel in the Tide Trilogy suggests Ogilvie's skill and limitations as a writer. *Hide Tide at Noon* focuses on the Bennett family, descendants of the island's original owners.[4] Ogilvie draws credible and sometimes complex characters. Joanna Bennett, the only daughter among a family of boys, is the central character. She is a strong, mature young woman of nineteen, fully capable of lobstering like her brothers. She is hindered only by her gender. Ogilvie's plot in *High Tide* also revolves around Joanna's levelheaded, forthright, hardworking lobster fisherman father, Stephen. A highly respected lobsterman he struggles to keep his family from fragmenting and the community from splintering as well.

Through the Bennetts, Ogilvie takes the pulse of a lobstering life in decline. She offers a fine-grained depiction of lobstering's vagaries: the challenges of the weather; the unpredictability of the lobster crop; the fluctuation of the market price; the territorialism of the lobstermen and its maintenance that ensures peace and order; and the mutuality that counterbalances the lobsterman's lonesome cowboy of the sea way of work.

Ogilvie represents an ongoing shift away from Jewett, especially from the *Pointed Firs*. Bennett Island is afflicted with serious human failings. Joanna is nearly raped by the island's ogre, she marries a handsome newcomer to the island who is addicted to gambling and secretly weighs down the house with mortgages, heavy drinking is rampant, and the island puts up with a popular harlot.

Yet for all the strengths of *High Tide at Noon* and the trilogy as a whole, Ogilvie's writing has major limitations. There are too many amateurish descriptions of nature. "The bird was the color of a jewel, the sea was full of diamonds, the day itself had a gemlike radiance." Joanna walks along the shore with "the wind from the harbor running boisterous fingers through her hair." There are sentences that fall flat: "the silence in the room was heavy."

Nevertheless, Ogilvie was a popular storyteller. As her obituary in the *New York Times* observed, she spun out "tales of romance and mystery set on the craggy islands off the coast of Maine."[5] Still, I think Ruth Moore, Ogilvie's contemporary, is a far more polished and distinctive novelist. When Ogilvie first heard of Moore, she worried about competition. Ogilvie believed she "had the whole coast to herself." After she read *The Weir* (1943), Moore's first novel, Ogilvie's unease dissipated "because our styles were so different."[6]

Ruth Moore marks a complete break with Sarah Orne Jewett. There is a striking minimalism in her writing. Unlike most writers about the Maine coast, she typically shuns evocative descriptions of nature during the summer. Rather, she foregrounds a fictional setting where men and women scratch out a living; where overexposure to sun, and sea, and dangerous outcroppings partially numb consciousness; where nature is often an adversary. Of the uncommon descriptions of nature in *The Weir*, the most detailed is of dead winter. It is stark and foreboding.

> Comey's Island in the bleak morning light had seldom looked so lonely or so forbidding. . . . Even the spruce trees looked like thin and shrunken ghosts of themselves, their branches, normally green and lustrous in winter, whipped wildly and were covered with white salt rime. . . . Trees, houses, boats, even lilac bushes were covered with white rime. Overhead, the sky was early-morning whitish blue, and against it the swirling masses of vapor were dark, like smoke.

This description, condensed above, comes very late in *The Weir*.[7]

Moore's writing is fresh and inventive in other ways. *The Weir* is dialogue driven. She deploys a distinctive pattern of island speech. It is clipped, not thick like pea-soup island fog. Contractions in particular are creative: "t'warn't," "wouldn't a," "soon's," "mor'n," "good's," and "would'fore" (before). Moore also introduces island neologism: "culch," "oary," "skyvertin'," "high feather," "mealin'," and "hummocky," for instance. The reader has to decode words and phrases in context. Characters often bear colorful names: Jarv, Perley, Jap, Cack, Weeza, among others. Moore is distinctive in another way: she explores genuine evil and untrammeled greed that blights island life or infects the mainland communities to which islanders are connected.

The Weir mentions "rusticators" only to dismiss them: "The summer people who came to Comey's were a cheap crowd." They couldn't afford to acquire property along the coast, "so they bought a little piece of land on the shore of one of the islands and made believe to the natives that they were rich." Despite their absence in *The Weir*, summer people were very present in Moore's early life and helped her go to college. One important vacationer helped her after she graduated.

The lineaments of Moore's life and of her novels reside in hardscrabble Maine. It is not too much to say that swaths of the state barely noticed the Great Depression because they had endured hard times for decades. Such straits set Moore's home island on the path toward depopulation of year-round residents.

The oldest of three sisters in a family of four children, Ruth Moore was born on Gott's Island in 1903. The modest island lies approximately one mile off the southern coast of Mount Desert. The family's house stood on a hill with a view of Blue Hill Bay. Moore traced her family back five generations on Gott's. Like Hardy Turner, the protagonist in *The Weir*, Ruth's father ran a small store in his house, served as the island postmaster, and operated a weir. Consisting of poles, brush, and tarred netting, the weir trapped herring for lobster traps. The Moores, like the Turners, cultivated a garden, milked a cow, raised chickens and pigs, and took in boarders. The family also provided meals to summer people who boarded elsewhere on the island. Ruth worked with her mother tending to summer visitors. She formed friendships with some of the summer people and played with their children as a young girl.[8]

After completing grammar school on the island, Ruth boarded with relatives in Ellsworth to attend high school. She hated her experience there, just as the island boys do in *The Weir*. A classmate recalled, "The snooty Ellsworth kids made fun of her, because she was an 'island girl,' because of the way she talked, [because of] her homemade and unfashionable bright-colored clothes, and also because she was very smart and outspoken."[9]

After high school, two island families encouraged her to go to college. Ruth chose the State Teacher's College in Albany, New York. Decades later, her sister Esther explained to an interviewer why Ruth settled on this school. A summer resident who taught at Albany offered to "sponsor" her, and she was able to qualify for in-state tuition. Another summer resident later claimed that her aunt lent Moore money for college.[10]

She graduated in 1925 with a degree in English; she taught on Long Island, New York, for a year and then left the classroom for good. She moved to Greenwich Village in 1926. A year later Moore became the live-in secretary to Mary White Ovington, one of the three founders of the NAACP. Ovington, who was white, summered on Gott's. A graduate of Radcliffe, she lived in Brooklyn. Through Ovington Moore was drawn into the work of the NAACP. She traveled to Atlanta to document Southern lynchings and she played a critical role in a successful fundraising campaign for the association. Her work with the NAACP proved crucial to her awareness of prejudice and injustice. It represents a source of an important theme that characterizes some of her best work: an emphasis on the malevolence of ethnic prejudice and empathy for the outsider.

Moore returned to Maine in 1931 and enrolled in a master's degree program in English at the University of Maine. She left after one semester and returned to New York in 1932. During the years that followed, however, she wrote to family describing how she was homesick for Maine. "I get homesick when I don't get home in the summer," she told her father in 1936. Later when her writing career began to take flight, she wrote to her mother, "I wish I could make my fortune so I could come home and live for good." Sometimes she expressed her longing for Maine more obliquely. "I wish it would be winter, doggone it," she complained to her mother of the New York City climate, "and we'd get some weather with some guts to it."[11] More than Jewett and perhaps Chase, Moore possessed a fierce attachment to Maine and cultivated a steadfast sense of place. Indeed, on the title page of *The Weir* she placed an unattributed quotation that she applied to Maine: "That was the place that you were homesick for, even when you were there."

In 1940, when she was visiting home, she met Eleanor Mayo from Southwest Harbor, who would go on to become a novelist in her own right. Eighteen years younger than Moore, Mayo formed what became a lifetime partnership with her. We know the relationship was deeply emotional. There is no evidence that it was erotic.[12]

Moore and Mayo lived together in New York. By 1941 Moore was working for the *Reader's Digest* and writing at night. In 1943, after a narrow rejection by Macmillan, William Morrow and Company published *The Weir*. It quickly went through three printings. She confessed to her mother, "I've waited a long while for it."[13] She was forty years old. The novel was also published in England.

With the success of *The Weir*, Morrow was eager for another novel. *Spoonhandle* appeared in 1946. For $50,000, 20th Century Fox bought the movie rights as part of a seven-year contract. Hollywood expected more novels from Moore that could be adapted for the screen. When Moore saw the working movie script for *Spoonhandle*, she claimed that she tried to break the contract.[14] Retitled *Deep Waters*, the movie was filmed on Vinalhaven, with a few days spent in Rockland. Moore hated the film for its compromises with her realism, but it enabled her, finally, to come home. Moore left *Reader's Digest* in 1947. She and Eleanor built a small house in Trenton (now Bass Harbor) at the southern tip of Mount Desert, within sight of Gott's Island.

Over the course of three and a half decades, Moore wrote fourteen Maine novels, three books of poetry, and several short stories. She described her intention "to write as truthfully and accurately as I could about small communities and the life in them which I have known well. My object is to interpret the region realistically."[15] Thus in later years she bestowed her approval on Maine neorealists Carolyn Chute and Sanford Phippen. They tell the truth, she said, "about a segment of Maine life that isn't in accord with the fairyland view of

Maine put out by the Maine publicity bureau."[16] Still, realism is a literary art. A writer engages the world through her sensibility, her ideas, and her deployment of literary conventions. In a word, Moore is a fictional realist, not a reporter. She imaginatively captured the darker elements of the Maine she knew, a place that also produced noble characters.

THE WEIR AND THE MORAL ECONOMY OF ISLAND LIFE

The novel is set during the Depression, though there is only one passing mention to the era, and it's to "Hoover." The islanders have been swimming against the tide for decades as their population has steadily receded. *The Weir* has a strong plot with explosive endings. It follows events in the lives of two families, the Turners and the Comeys, who have intersecting friendships. As the story unfolds, the reader becomes engaged in the daily affairs of all eight of the remaining families on Comey's Island, which lies three miles offshore from "The Harbor."

Hardy Turner is *The Weir*'s principal protagonist. If the island resembles a lifeboat, or if it's a diminished anthill in the sea, then its survival depends on commonly accepted customs, traditions, and practices to regulate economic behavior, to restrain naked self-interest and unbridled competition. "Moral economy" describes such a framework. Though Moore doesn't employ this term, moral economy represents an essential theme of *The Weir*, and Hardy Turner is its exemplar. Yet on Comey's Island and in the Harbor, customary values are frayed. City ways infiltrate, even corrode, life along the Maine coast.

Moore's father informs the portrait of Hardy, just as her mother gives shape to Josie, his strong wife. The fictional characters, however, are far from mere transcriptions of real-life parents. Hardy attended commercial school and studied bookkeeping. His goal in life is to own a small business on the mainland. This modest version of the American dream will upend his life when he transports the values of the island's moral economy to the mainland only to be gulled. Hardy's sole assets as a young man are his native intelligence and his work ethic. He quickly rises to first mate on a successful freighter plying trade routes with South America. He is poised to take command of his own ship.

Josie Scott first meets twenty-six-year-old Hardy in Bellport, fifty miles down the coast from the Harbor. Trimmed in his first-mate uniform Hardy cuts a handsome figure. Josie is nineteen and descends from a long line of seafarers. Her father, Captain Hosea Scott of Bellport and Boston, owns his own ship. He dominates trade between the coast and Nova Scotia.

After a five-day courtship, Hardy and Josie decide to marry. The captain erupts. "No, by God, you ain't goin' to marry any damn Comey's Islander." When they persist, the captain vows not to attend his daughter's wedding. Hardy confronts his prospective father-in-law, looks him straight in the eye, and tells the captain he's welcome at the wedding. If he still objects, "I'd advise you to go som'ers else." Hardy's forthrightness earns the captain's respect—and his participation in the wedding.

Then another crisis surfaces. Hardy wants to return to Comey's Island, where twenty families still live. Josie resists, especially when Hardy is a step away from rising to captain of his own ship. "It seems an awful come down," she cries. "I don't want to go over with them people." She slurs the islanders. Such an attitude will recur in *The Weir*, including in abusive form. In the end, Josie swallows the common mainland contempt toward the islanders. And, as we shall see, in one of the most finely wrought scenes in the novel, Josie will face down this disdain for the islanders when her son is suspended from the mainland high school on suspect grounds.

Hardy envisions his return to Comey's as temporary. He still hears the siren call of the mainland and the fulfillment of his bourgeois American dream. When we first meet Hardy, he has been on the island for more than two decades. He and Josie have three children: twenty-two-year-old Leonard, fifteen-year-old Haral, and eleven-year-old Mildred. Hardy's mother, a salty eighty-six-year-old, lives with the family. She comments on daily domestic affairs and tests Josie's forbearance. When the soap in the house is changed, "Grammy" lashes out at Josie: "You'd use a cow turd if the feller on the radio said to." One of Grammy's roles in the novel is to provide the reader with some comic respite in a drama that often turns bitter, even deadly.

Hardy is in the seventeenth year of working his weir, after giving up lobster-ing. The sea is unpredictable, and, over the years, the Turners, like the real-life Moores, have sought other sources of support. They have a garden, a cow, and chickens and once took in boarders; Hardy operates a small store in his ell and serves as postmaster. Still, Hardy has little to show for years of labor. He finds himself at a midlife crossroad. He has lost confidence in his weather eye. Though partially protected by ledge, the weir has been totally destroyed by storms twice and partially damaged once. Each time money and labor are required to rebuild the weir. The nets have to be dropped in a storm to prevent damage. Hardy has become overcautious. He imagines what is being said about him: "Somebody broke wind and Hardy has dropped his nets down." At other times he dithers; then he's forced to row out to the weir in the middle of a stormy night to save his nets.

Hardy's loss of confidence in his ability to divine the weather is symptomatic of a larger self-doubt. He lives from season to season with little to show for his labor. Soon he will be too old to venture out to a business. With each passing year, his American dream fades into youthful fancy. Hardy's life is a weir; he's caught in a web of responsibilities and routines. Before long there will be no escape.

Several incidents involving the weir reveal Hardy's commitment to the island's moral economy. Mackerel have been scarce for the season. Some become trapped in his weir. Usually Hardy gives them to islanders rather than taking advantage of his good luck. This time he hands the mackerel over to son Haral, who plans to sell them. He wants twenty-five cents for each fish, so he asks for thirty and then drops the price. In other words, Haral peddles the fish and manipulates neighbors instead of simply offering them for sale. He has been spending time at the Harbor and imports its way of economic exchange in place of his father's. He doesn't even save one mackerel for the family.

When Hardy learns what has happened, he explodes: "A quarter apiece! After dinner, young man, you take fifteen cents of that money to every person you got it from." Haral resists; he spends the money at the Harbor.

Each time Hardy raises the flag on his weir, signaling that he has herring, he treats everyone equally. He also offers the herring at a fair price to the first comers. Thus, if Hardy hasn't accumulated riches over the years, he has accrued social capital—his fellow islanders trust and respect him for his evenhanded adherence to customary practices. When he fails to lower his nets and a storm blows up, Hardy rushes out to save his investment. The lobstermen and fishermen put their lives at risk rowing out to help him, thereby reaffirming the communal safety net. "It ain't property they're doing it for," one lobsterman's wife says. Her comment reminds Josie that "they're doing it for Hardy." The island as a lifeboat spurs the community into action.

At the end of the season, Hardy benefits from a strong run of herring. One day two cannery ships arrive and their skippers engage in a bidding war. One familiar master, Eddy, is from the Harbor, where a cannery employs scores of townspeople. The other is a stranger. They bid up Hardy's haul from ninety cents for a bushel of herring to a $1.35 when Eddy drops out. In the middle of the bidding, the stranger's name is revealed, and there is a raw display of Down East racism against "Marceau." "Frog, eh," Eddy says. "What you doin' round here with white men?" Unknown to Hardy, Mildred has rowed out to the weir and she is hanging on the freshly tarred netting as she watches the bidding. After Hardy sees her with tar on her face, he, too, makes a racial remark: "You look like spots coming out on a nigger." Just as Moore strove to capture island speech realistically, she refused to avoid its racist elements.

What is interesting about the bidding war for Hardy's herring bounty is his passiveness. In fact, he never says a word. He doesn't auction off his herring; that's not customary practice. Before Hardy even sets a per bushel price, he is made an opening offer. Hardy earns more than $800 on that sale alone. For the season, his exceptional profit is more than $3,000. He sees that money as a grubstake for finally fulfilling his American dream.

In contrast to the Turners, the Comeys are a family riven by conflict. Sarah Comey has been widowed for three years. Her husband and oldest son perished in a gale within sight of the island. If the son hadn't been drunk, Sarah believes, the tragedy might have been averted. She is a strong, caring, and prescient mother. Sarah nurses the island sick, who welcome her large, calloused, yet comforting hands. Sarah, for all her similarity to strong women in Jewett or Chase, represents a significant alteration; she possesses physical strength, for one thing. Like Sarah and her deceased husband and son, the Comeys are among the island's most physically imposing residents. Twenty-three-year-old Joe is six feet, two inches and nearly two hundred pounds. Sixteen-year-old Sayl (Saylor) is already six feet. The Comeys have black hair and ruddy complexions stretching back to their grandfather.

And then there is Morris Comey, who embodies the kind of evil that one doesn't find in Jewett or Chase. Morris seems to carry some recessive Comey genes. He is not even five feet tall. He has light hair, blue eyes, and "delicate" features. His malevolence is a product of his biography. Morris ran away from home at age fifteen to escape his father's autocratic ways. He vowed not to return until Clyde Comey was dead. For twelve years he worked as a crewman, mostly on freighters, never having the physical stature to serve as an officer. He knocked around the globe; ironically, he took orders from men just like his father, apparently endured ridicule for his size, and served as a soft target for bullies. No one knows how he learned of his father's death. But Morris returns to Comey's at the age of twenty-seven and arrogates to himself the role of man of the family. His mother is ever vigilant of this son who disavows Comey's Island values, including everything associated with what we have been calling moral economy.

Morris claims that only he knows how the "real" world works. The islanders inhabit a sinking fantasy, as illusory as Atlantis. Yet his ruthlessness evolves from his brutish experience at sea. He is a social Darwinian. It's a fish-eat-fish world, we might say. Morris instills fear in Comey's inhabitants and provokes his mother's constant vigilance over the family and her protectiveness toward Joe.

Joe and Leonard Turner are best friends (so are Sayl and Haral). Leonard has his own small fishing boat. He also shares ownership of deep-sea fishing nets with the two older Comey brothers. Morris wants to build the biggest, fastest fishing ship on the island. Unfortunately, he can't do it on his own. He borrows money from his brother. One day Joe and Leonard decide to go fishing without Morris. He hears the boat engine start while he is reading the newspaper. Sarah watches him. Morris doesn't move; not even a muscle in his face twitches. His mind races as he plots the cruelest revenge.

The island poolroom is an opportune setting for his public humiliation of Joe. Morris is a pool sharp. No one will play with him for money. Lord of the poolroom, Morris swaggers in and before the gathered men flings $1,200 on the table where Joe is shooting a game. He is buying out his brother's share of the new boat, preferring to owe the bank money. Morris pulls out a quitclaim and tells Joe to sign it. "Or get someone to write your name for you and you put a cross next to it." Joe is stunned and pleads with his brother to go to the boat with him because this is private business. Morris only pours mockery on "lamebrain." He's wise to the point where Joe is defenseless; Joe's a bit weak in his upper story, so to speak, and he's docile, never taking advantage of his superior size—especially over his diminutive brother. Joe signs the quitclaim. He's smart enough to know that the details of how Morris brought him to heel will ricochet around the island and across the three miles of water to the Harbor.

Joe and Leonard continue to fish with Morris, but they plan to partner on their own. Joe has $1,200, and Leonard can sell his small boat for $800. They will have enough money to build a good vessel. Still, they need more money to have a design drawn and molds created for the boatbuilder. Joe and Leonard fall back on customary island practice of sharing knowledge about boat design. They ask Morris for his drawings and molds, which are gathering dust in the loft over the woodshed. Once again Morris repudiates the island's moral economy and the community of people who cling to it. He wants to be paid. "Chrise, the way you people around here feel," he tells Leonard, "if a man's got a good thing he ought to share it with everybody. Well, it's you that's out of line with the rest of the world. It ain't me." "You people," like Josie's old "those people," marks Morris as the outsider that he is and the outlaw that he will become. Sarah Comey hatches a plan to help Joe and Leonard. It will have deadly consequences.

One of the most compelling incidents in *The Weir* derives from Moore's experience as an island girl attending Ellsworth High School. But she complicates this past personal treatment when she transmutes into fiction. Moore reimagines mainland high school prejudice against islanders in scenes layered with irony on top of irony.

The Comeys have never valued education. But Joe insists that a reluctant Sayl attend the Harbor high school and offers to pay for his room and board. Josie and Hardy Turner possess some education. She in particular accepts it as a given that Haral will go to high school. It isn't long into the semester before the school's contempt for the island boys incites controversy.

A series of circumstances conspire to expose disdain for Sayl and Haral lurking just beneath the surface. Due to a shortage of books, the first-year students have to read *Macbeth*, an advanced assignment. The teacher, Miss Rayne, is brand new; she has no experience and is unfamiliar with Shakespeare, who writes in a foreign language as far as she is concerned. On this particular day, Miss Rayne is unprepared, as she went out on a date the night before.

Rayne resorts to having the students simply read and explain passages from *Macbeth*. Then she singles out Sayl to interpret one. "Dun know," he mutters. She orders him to stand and to direct his comments to her, "not to your stomach." She cuts into him, and the class sniggers. "That's a perfectly simple passage . . . if you know how to read." Sayl is embarrassed and blurts out, "Them three ole wimmen was cookin' rotten guts in a kittle." Laughter ripples through the class, inflaming Miss Rayne. "This is no place to show how ill-bred you are." She demands an apology. Sayl stands mute; the sting of his humiliation deadens any impulse to apologize. The teacher orders him to the principal's office with a note. As he leaves the room, he rolls his eyes at Haral, who cackles. Then he roars, no longer able to contain his "suppressed laughter." He is ordered to the principal's office as well.

Mr. Benson is off teaching a class. Sayl then urinates in a potted geranium on the windowsill. His counterattack on the school escalates. He urinates in Benson's hat. He is in effect voiding himself on the authority of the school, his way of announcing that he will never return. At the same time, his behavior only seems to confirm the school's view of islanders. It could be invoked, ironically, to disarm any of Comey's critics of the alleged injustice done to Sayl and Haral.

Mr. Benson arrives and reads Rayne's note. He lashes out at Sayl and Haral. "You boys who come in here from the islands," he fumes, "you think you can act the way you're allowed to at home. Now, here in this school we're civilized." Then comes the smear that most enrages the islanders: "The next slip out of you and you'll go back to Comey's Island, or whatever other foreign country you happen to come from." He orders the boys back to their classroom. Instead of returning, Sayl and Haral escape from a basement window and go home.

They relate the details of what happened to them. One of the words in the passage that Sayl was asked to explain is "entrails." He and Haral had consulted the dictionary, and it said "guts." The island is in an uproar, especially about the principal's insults. Someone has to confront him. Sarah Comey declines. Joe is not suitable. The task devolves to Josie Turner. In other words, the woman who is not a native islander and who once shared the mainland's low opinion of "those people" on the island sets out to defend Comey's.

Still, when Josie dresses up for her mission, she is not, ironically, an islander but the daughter of Captain Hosea Scott of Bellport and Boston. In her exchange with Mr. Benson, Josie adopts a calm bearing and an economy of direct words that deprive him of a defense. Since his hat dried out by the time he went home, Benson doesn't know that Sayl has urinated on his head. Moreover, given his biased perception of the islanders, he would have expected a rough-edged emotional visitor instead of a lady of proper dress and demeanor.

Haral said "that you called people over on Comey's island foreigners, and said that we let our young ones talk nasty in our homes." Then Josie gives Benson a kind of benefit of doubt: "It didn't seem to me likely that you said just that." He turns as scarlet as Sayl did when Miss Rayne chastised him. Benson stammers; Josie has mined the truth. "Well I-I don't believe I remember quite what I did say," Benson offers. "I was . . . angry. The other boy has been hard to manage." Josie's response is measured but dogged: "I ain't got any doubt Haral has, too. But no worse'n other boys . . . He's had a decent bringin' up." "I'm sure he has," Benson lies. "Then you didn't say what they say you did?" Josie counters. Benson, in fear for his job since the islanders are so irate, then claims, "I think the boys repeated to you what they thought I meant."

Josie thanks him and leaves knowing that he has been spouting weasel-worded responses to her. Haral is sent to high school in Bellport, where he can board with relatives. Sayl's schooling is over.

Sarah Comey initiates a hazardous scheme to help Joe and Leonard build their boat. She has Joe feign illness one morning so that only Morris and Leonard head out for a three-day fishing trip. She and Joe spend hours copying Morris's prints and molds. They are handed over to the boatbuilder to start work on the vessel. It takes shape over the winter, and visitors to the shop remark on its resemblance to Morris's boat. However, Joe and Leonard have purchased a much larger engine than what powers Morris's craft. He visits the boat shop and becomes suspicious. He checks his drawings and models and sees that they have been disturbed.

As the boat nears completion, the island men realize it's an improved reproduction of Morris's. Sometimes seriously, other times jokingly, they speculate that the boatbuilder has an excellent memory. The men take satisfaction in how Joe and Leonard have outfoxed Morris. One day in Jake's bar at the Harbor, Orin Hammond, a fisherman, is buying drinks to celebrate what Joe and Leonard have put over on Morris. Hammond was in the poolroom when Morris humiliated Joe.

Morris walks into Jake's and realizes that the men are making sport of him. Orin seizes an opportunity to avenge Joe's humbling in the poolroom. He buys Morris a drink and then grabs "him by the back of the pants and his coat collar" and lifts him so that they are both at the same height. Morris is now drinking at a "man-size" bar, Orin says. One can assume that Morris endured similar barroom incidents during his twelve years of knocking around global ports. He doesn't resist Orin. When he is lowered, Morris straightens out his clothes and calmly walks out of Jake's.

Shortly after, Morris exacts his revenge. Orin drowns under puzzling circumstances. His halibut trawl drags him under water. He is found with a hook through the palm of his hand, a common occurrence in the fishery. It is mysterious, however, that, unlike all fishermen, Orin didn't have his knife readily available to cut his hand free of the net. He always carried a knife with his initials on it in a leather sleeve attached to his belt. The knife is nowhere to be found. The sheriff dampens suspicions that gravitate toward Morris because there is no evidence. Soon, however, the truth will emerge.

When Joe and Leonard finally take their boat home, Morris suffers another humiliation. Halfway from the Harbor, the boats confront each other. As if in a rage, Morris runs circles around them. Then, in a contest of superiority, Joe and Leonard easily power past Morris. He hatches his revenge, setting off a cascade of actions and reactions too numerous to detail. Sarah has to physically intervene in the dead of night to save the new boat from Morris's attempt to destroy it. He tries to cut the boat from its mooring so that it will crash into ledges overnight. She loses her life in a struggle with Morris. He perishes as well. Orin Hammond's knife is found on Morris's boat. The latter's death restores the island's moral economy.

The Turners' final predicament is far less dramatic than the Comeys' but more related to Moore's Maine themes. As the time approaches to repair the weir for another season, Hardy loses heart. He has long admired Willard Hemple, a successful grocer at the Harbor. He has known Hemple from boyhood. They were also classmates in commercial school. While Hardy went to sea, Willard wisely started a grocery store in what became a growing cannery town. Sitting on a crate, Hardy watches "the customers come and go and the stream of business that went over Willard's counter." Hardy's American dream has been focused on Hemple's store for years. The two old classmates have carried on a running conversation about Hardy's purchase of the business. Now Hemple is eager to sell. He knows the balance sheet of Hardy's life, the modest windfall from last year's weir fishing. Hemple profits from Hardy's longing to make a change and his view of the store owner as an embodiment of the American dream.

Hemple is also a slick-speaking merchant, a Yankee sharpy who knows how to move a bill of goods. In turn, Hardy can't even squeeze a profit from his house store. He extends credit and enables people to work it off—helping him repair the weir, for example. Hemple and Hardy operate their stores within different moral economies. For the former, people are merely customers; to the latter, neighbors are confederates of the anthill in the sea.

Hemple gives Hardy the hard sell. He invites him into his large, new $1,200 refrigerator with its impressive array of hanging animal flesh. Hemple claims he wants to rebuild his garage. He makes Hardy an irresistible offer, so much so that the islander repeats its details for reassurance. He accepts Hemple's word. Hardy traffics not simply in money but also in friendship and trust. The spoken agreement is as binding as the printed document. Hemple offers to sell the store, the stock on its shelves, the freezer, his furnished house, and sixteen acres of woodlot for $6,500. Hardy will pay $2,500 down and $500 a year plus interest. He reaches for the brass ring. In the end, Hemple will treat his friend little better than the carcasses suspended in his freezer.

Josie learns of Hardy's agreement with Hemple after the fact; she doesn't want to leave Comey's Island. The Harbor, after all, is a gritty place dominated by the cannery. In a memorable description, Moore extends Chase's representation of the cannery town. The changing of the tides "never quite cleaned away the refuse and grease spilled out from the vents of the sardine factory." Nor did the coastal winds blow "away the heavy stench of frying oil hanging in the air over the town." Along the shore "all the homes showed signs of wear and weather—paint scaled off, a gutter dropped here, there a rotten doorstep replaced with a rickety box." The town's appearance divulged how the people were "too tired and discouraged to mind that their houses weren't anything more than a place to eat and sleep and shelter." The merchants and factory bosses lived "on the hill above the shore road"; here there "were strong old-timers, like the Comey's Island houses, with solid gables, white paint, and wide comfortable barns."

When the islanders find out Hardy is moving to the Harbor, other families decide to follow him, a testament to his standing on Comey's. This respect shifts to empathy at the Harbor. Hardy has the equivalent of a near-death experience when he visits his newly purchased store, while the family takes stock of Hemple's former house. As he unlocks the store, Hardy walks into a nightmare. The interior has been stripped down to its light fixtures and bulbs. Rows of shelves are empty. The freezer is gone; only wires protrude from where it stood. The floor is strewn with packing material and empty boxes. Hemple has fleeced Hardy. The house is also neglected and grimy.

He heads toward the hill of tidy homes where the grocer has moved. Hardy confronts Hemple in his yard. He angrily reminds him that the sale included the stock and freezer. Hemple falls back on the deed, which doesn't specify those details. "You mean your word ain't worth nothin'?" Hardy presses Hemple. "Nothin' in a court of law," Hemple responds. He is starting a new store with Hardy's money.

Perhaps Morris was right after all. The islanders are out of step with the rest of the world. Hardy transacts business with Hemple guided by the moral economy that sustains Comey's, which keeps the island as lifeboat from capsizing. Hemple inhabits a world where words mean nothing unless they are printed on official documents, where legalisms, lawyers, and judges regulate the smooth operation of business. Hemple snares Hardy like the herring trapped in the weir. Leonard deplores his father's blind trust. "Why didn't he stay over on the island where he belonged!" Leonard angrily criticizes his father to his fiancée, Alice Lacy. "He was a man on his own ground. Look at the way people always come to him when there was a tough job to do."

Moore might have ended the novel at this point, with Hardy's American dream shattered and his future uncertain. Instead, Alice Lacy proposes another sale, which will at least enable Hardy to restock the store. She has rebuffed Leonard throughout the novel. Alice comes from the Harbor and doesn't welcome the life of a fisherman's wife on Comey's. To help support her father, she has worked in a Boston factory from November to April for several years. She has a change of heart. Alice has always loved Leonard, even though she became engaged to the dead Orin Hammond. She has saved $600. She and Leonard plan to offer it to Hardy for the Comey's Island house. The ending may seem rather confected, but it does suggest that Hardy's future will entail an ongoing struggle for survival, with Josie compelled, perhaps, to join the cannery workforce.

The Weir was an impressive commercial success, especially for a first novel by an unknown author. The book was published at the end of February 1943, while war raged in Europe and the Far East. *Publishers Weekly* reported three weeks later that *The Weir* had already gone through its third printing. Four thousand copies were sold within a week of publication. "The firm says it is one of the most successful first novels it has ever published." The director of publicity for Morrow wrote to Moore telling her that three thousand copies had been sent to Portland bookstores alone. *The Retail Bookseller* named *The Weir* its "Editor's Choice" for February, praising its "always compellingly real and vital" characters.[17]

Moore's novel was reviewed from New England to Florida and throughout the Midwest, the Southwest, and California. Such a response suggested the broad midcentury interest in Maine literature, especially work set along the coast. The critical reception was overwhelmingly positive and mostly enthusiastic. "It is a first novel that is rare," the *Boston Globe* reviewer wrote, "because there is nothing amateurish about it." *The Weir* possessed "the power to swoop you into its turbulent atmosphere." The *New York Herald Tribune* roundly praised *The Weir*, observing that it's "surprisingly enough her first novel." The *New York Times* sounded a similar note: "She writes in language that captures the sound and heart of her characters and tells her tale with restraint and salty humor that is their own. A notable first novel."[18]

Other reviewers described *The Weir* as "sinewy" or as "one of the finest novels to be written about the Maine coast" or compared it to the classic *Ethan Frome*. The *San Francisco Chronicle* noted, "Miss Moore writes seriously, permitting herself no flourishes, keeping steadily to her pattern which involves the struggle for a way of life by two generations as well as the ancient struggle of good and evil." In a capsule review, the *New Yorker* mentioned a criticism that struck a minor note in *The Weir*'s reception: there is "a spot of melodrama at the end."[19]

Morrow sent a copy of the novel to Mary Ellen Chase. After she read it, Chase sent a letter to Polly Street, publicity director for Morrow. Chase wrote that she loved *The Weir* and that she would recommend it to friends and especially to "audiences with even greater enthusiasm." She gave the publisher permission to quote anything in her letter for promotion purchases. Obviously,

Moore made an unanticipated major breakthrough with *The Weir*.[20] No wonder Morrow was eager for a quick follow-up novel.

SPOONHANDLE: GREED, ETHNICITY, AND INCORRUPTIBLE ISLANDERS

Moore's second novel, published in 1946, advances similar themes and characters as *The Weir*. Spoon Island is a flagging, inbred community preserved in brine for more than five generations. Its hardworking men make a meager living as sea harvesters, and their women folk stretch dollars that ebb and flow with the lobster catch. The islanders' speech overflows with colorful localisms and neologisms: "aigs" (eggs), "aidges" (hedges), "jealsy," "kit along," "knuckly," "goveled," "joppy," "queered the sale," and many others.

Once again, a corrupt storekeeper is central to *Spoonhandle*'s plot. Pete Stilwell is no Willard Hemple, however. Stilwell gratifies his appetite for wealth and power by a sinister plan to gain control of the island and most of its inhabitants. Moore also persists as a minimalist when it comes to representing Maine nature. Her longest description is of the Maine that summer people never see:

> Day after day in the changing weather high clouds soaring, storms driving low, the land huddles into itself. Saltwater curdles into slush against the shore, then, slowly, into grainy pale-green ice, fissured by tides and flung in crumpled blocks up and down the beaches. The spruces crack and snap on a windless evening and let go their load of snow, so that a wood lot in the cold seems to be talking to itself in a language of small stirrings, whispers and sighs. There is nothing people can do with land like that, bitten four feet deep with frost, secret and uncommunicative under the snow.

"Off-season" is *Spoonhandle*'s literary peak time.

But for all the continuities with her first novel, Moore has more balls in the air in *Spoonhandle* than in *The Weir*, and she manipulates them with dexterity. First of all, summer people help propel the novel's plot and, with the complicity of Pete Stilwell, rearrange the island's seascape and the lives of *Spoonhandle*'s inhabitants. In addition, the novel offers the most sustained sympathetic subplot involving an immigrant family since the Janowskis in *As the Earth Turns*. Joe Sangor is a native of the Portuguese Azores—that is, he is a born islander who is shunned by his new fellow islanders. His outsider status culminates in a gruesome, yet heroic, death. Two very different love stories form additional subplots. Thus, along with tart humor, they afford the reader some relief from the treacherous and tragic elements in *Spoonhandle*. The love stories also suggest why Hollywood found so much potential in the novel. All of what Moore juggles in *Spoonhandle* makes it a richer, more complex novel than *The Weir*.

Spoon Islanders live astride a physical setting ideal for summer development in 1936–1937, the time frame of the novel, when the Depression has partially and temporarily relaxed its grip on the nation. The island consists of two parts. Big Spoon resembles a horseshoe. Its prized western side, "the Spoonhandle," faces open ocean. The eastern shore is rocky and near the mainland, to which it's connected by a pre-automobile wobbly wooden bridge. At the center of the horseshoe lies a natural protected harbor, ideal for yachts and cruisers. Big Spoon is four miles long and three miles wide. Little Spoon falls within the harbor and is two miles long. Only a muddy mussel bar, which fills at high tide, separates the island from Big Spoon. The brothers William and Hod (Horace) Stilwell are the sole inhabitants of Little Spoon.

The Stilwell family dominates island life. Forty-five-year-old Pete, the would-be family patriarch, is the single most powerful islander. He graduated from commercial school but hides his diploma. He runs his store under the guise of a simple country merchant who makes an effort to speak in dialect. In fact, throughout *Spoonhandle* guises recur, cutting across genders as well as locals and summer people. Like his father and grandfather before him, Pete Stilwell controls the levers of power on Big Spoon as storekeeper, first selectman, harbormaster, and real estate agent, once outsiders discover the island. He is a major purveyor of petty or calculated gossip. He's also a cheat—both of the piddling kind and of the type who would dispossess his neighbors of their valuable land. A deftly drawn Yankee sharpy, Pete engages in a game of wits with the most powerful prospective summer resident. His neighbors are no match for the scheming Pete.

At forty-seven, widowed sister Agnes (Aggie) is the oldest member of the family. She has graduated from normal school, but *Spoonhandle* offers no hint that she has ever taught. She married a shoe salesman and boasted that he was actually an executive. Pretension is her calling card. As one Spoon Islander observes of Aggie, "she'd dress up to go to the backhouse." She is aligned with Pete and like him lives in a big white house purchased with her father's money.

Aggie asserts her influence over Big Spoon through the Ladies Aid Society. Her crusade of the moment focuses on the sale of beer at the Do-Drop-Inn.

Aggie seeks to prolong Prohibition, which ended in 1933. When a majority of the Ladies Aid Society fails to do her bidding, Aggie is undeterred. With all the self-importance of a Stilwell, she confronts the earthy Mag Snow, proprietor of the inn. Mag gives Aggie a tongue-lashing and dismisses her as a "filthy-minded old flounder!" If Aggie is losing her grip on the Ladies Aid Society as well as on Big Spoon's omens of change, she has never possessed influence with her two younger brothers since they became adults.

Thirty-seven-year-old Willie and twenty-six-year-old Hod adopt a semi-reclusive life on Little Spoon. Their father lorded over them, dispensing verbal and physical abuse. Willie and Hod also made good targets for their domineering older siblings. Thus, the two Little Spoon Islanders have long been alienated from Pete and Aggie. Willie showed no interest in education as a young man, no raw ambition to improve his lot. In frustration, his father gave Willie Little Spoon and vowed to disinherit him. He never got around to changing his will, however. Hod completed three years studying engineering at the state university. When his father died, Hod quit school and accepted Willie's invitation to live with him in the fixed-up shack of an old Norwegian sailor. The two brothers trap lobsters and fish. They earn reputations for industry as well as eccentricity. They are tall, lean, and muscular with "mops" of dark hair. Hod is especially handsome. One would never know Pete is their brother, for he is "stout" and stooped with a "pink round face."

Willie and Hod befriend Joe Sangor. Hod in particular forms a close relationship with the outcast Azorean and his family. On a freezing winter day even Hod's engineering skill is unable to get Willie's aged boat to run smoothly so that the brothers can motor out to fish. It needs to be towed to Josh Hovey's boat shop, two miles away on the mainland in Bellport. Hod walks down the wooded Spoonhandle to Joe's house at the point. The Azorean can't tolerate Spoon Island's winter cold and dampness, so the family all but hibernates until spring. The joke in the village is that they "holed up like squirrels from November to April."

Hod's approach to Joe's front yard provides Moore with an opportunity to depict realistically a Depression-era setting not uncommon on Maine islands or along the Down East coast. In the midst of scenic beauty, some residents curated collections of "useful" oddments. In fact, in *The Weir* Hardy and Josie Turner live next to the colorfully named Jap and Cack Comey, who preserve a front yard not unlike Joe Sangor's. Hod sees "an old sofa [with] dripped springs and stuffing over the woodpile. On it Joe has piled his year's salvage from around the shore." He has collected everything from "old lobster traps, odds and ends of rope, logs and buoys" to "rusty pans and bits of china." The yard also contains "a broken kerosene lamp, some oil drums," and a "rusty kitchen stove complete with a pipe." For Joe the yard is a repository of potentially useful castoffs—castoffs like the Sangors themselves.

Joe had fished with Willie on the Grand Banks. Willie invited him to settle on Spoon Island. He bought twenty acres from the Pray brothers on magnificent Spoon Island Point. It has not yet been aestheticized and commodified. That will soon change. Joe has been in America for twenty years but still has trouble understanding and speaking English. Virtual exile from the community helps explain Joe's lack of facility with the language. But his wife speaks English and Joe's deficiencies strike one as cultural resistance. He longs to return to the Azorean archipelago and claims, or imagines in his mind's eye, that on a clear day he can see the islands from his ocean-facing windows. Joe and Hod share food before the latter explains the reason for his visit. Despite his dread of the cold and his own sputtering old boat, Joe leaves his cocooned life to tow Hod to Bellport.

Josh Hovey is a tobacco-chewing-and-expectorating old salt who has grown wise and well connected from years of interactions with natives and summer folk at the boatyard. As to the people from away, Josh tells Hod, "some's all right, I guess, but some of 'ems barstids." Of course, Pete Stilwell, not a summer resident, will prove to be the biggest "barstid" between Bellport and Spoon Island. Willie's time-worn boat is not worth repairing, Josh concludes. But he has one that he bought for $1,000 from a summer resident who needed money quickly. The cruiser is worth much more. He offers to sell it to Hod for $1,200 with a down payment of what it would have cost to repair Willie's boat and no time limit on paying the balance. Hod bristles at what seems to be an act of "charity." Josh is known as a wily owner of the boatyard and shop. But that is a bit of a pose, like Pete's more malevolent public persona as a simple country shopkeeper. Hod presses Josh for an explanation. "I hear a lot of talk," he says. "I ain't one of them that thinks Willie's a screw ball. . . . I know the deal he gut from Pete and the old man." Josh realizes the "spot" Willie will find himself in "if he don't have no boat't work with." The boatyard owner will emerge repeatedly not as the crusty, even cussed trader but as an unlikely hero, the quiet conscience of his corner of coastal Maine. From his strategic perch, he comes to know the "right" people and the latest hearsay.

In fact, Josh's boatyard functions as a node in the exchange of information and gossip that links Bellport and Spoon Island, where Pete claims to get "all the news hot off the griddle." Sometimes he has just cooked it up. Mag Snow's

Do-Drop-Inn represents another site where gossip is swapped. Back in Bell-port, Connie's Diner serves up recycled hearsay and warmed-over, lousy food.

Hod visits the diner after leaving Josh. Connie is the sullen, acid-tongued owner, cook, and waitress. She, Josh, and Mag of Do-Drop-Inn are sources of Moore's rich, varied humor in *Spoonhandle*. Connie caters to the locals and thus doesn't double prices in the summer, which earns her social capital in the form of respect and appreciation that carries her through the long off-season.

A woman at the next table speaks to Hod as he's mulling over the new cruiser. Through the scrim of time and change, Hod has a flash of recognition that thrusts him back to his youth. He realizes it's Ann Freeman, daughter of lobsterman Paris. Hod and Ann had passed the milestones of school as class-mates. Ann had graduated from Bates College, studied at Columbia University School of Journalism, worked for a newspaper in New York, and published a novel. The island girl is now a sophisticated, creative urbanite, so much so that Connie thinks she's a "fruit" (the local lingo for summer people). Connie is al-lergic to Ann, smartly dressed in a pantsuit. When Ann asks her to reheat Hod's meal, Connie returns feeling that she has been abused: "My feet do hurt. I've got very coarse veins you could anchor a punt with." As to the food, Connie tells Ann, "You don't own me a cent. I feed the fruits for nothin'." In the end, she charges a dollar with the stipulation, "And don't leave no tip. If I ever found a tip, I'd drop dead." Ann leaves five dollars.

The native arrives two miles from home only to receive an uncourtly greet-ing. Ann asks Hod for a ride to Spoon Island. She then makes him blush with her city forwardness: "You're still the handsomest man I ever saw. Are you still one of the nicest?" Hod's tongue-tied. They cruise home with Joe Sangor huddled below, all but embracing the engine for warmth. Joe's passion for his family represents one love story in *Spoonhandle*. It ends in tragedy. Another between Hod and Ann takes place in fits and starts over the novel's course.

The desk drawer in Pete's store office shelters the outline of his far-reaching ambition. It contains a map of all the valuable shore lots on Spoon Island and inscribes his scheme to transform a community on the skids into an affluent summer colony. Nelson Witherspoon is pivotal to the realization of Pete's de-signs—and so is brother Willie.

If we reflect for a moment on the treatment of summer people in Mary Ellen Chase and Sarah Orne Jewett, it might clarify how Moore's Nelson Wither-spoon marks a new literary turn. Chase piled disdain on summer people, but she did so mostly from a comfortable literary distance. She assails them as group and laments their effects on coastal life. We do come to learn much about Jewett's summer travelers/narrators. Still, they are not permanent summer folk. They do not own, nor do they wish to buy, coastal property or Maine antiques. In Nelson Witherspoon, Moore creates a close-to-the-bone portrait of an entitled summer sojourner.

Witherspoon wants to purchase Little Spoon Island entirely and rename it for himself. After all, the island already contains half of his last name, as if God designated it for him. With the wealthy Witherspoon in place, Pete Stilwell can trade on his status to market the other waterfront lots, once he has swindled them from families who have possessed the properties since the middle of the eighteenth century.

Witherspoon is a sixty-year-old businessman from a long-established family in Baltimore. While still in his thirties, he purchased a hundred acres of waterfront property in Bellport and built a spacious summerhouse. He continued to augment his wealth through a once stagnant family business, the Chesapeake Hemp and Manila Corporation. Witherspoon's business acumen and drive revitalized the company into a prosperous operation with foreign branches. The Depression appears not to have seriously affected his bottom line. Witherspoon has thoughts about the country's economic condition and believes, as he tells his aide-de-camp, Bundy, that he has an explanation for what is wrong: "If the common people of this country had the brains to save their money for a rainy day, instead of blowing it on luxuries they didn't need, there never would have been a depression."

Witherspoon's top-down view of the world extends to all males beneath his station. As with Bundy, he diminishes them to their last names. The most serious personal campaign the privileged businessman wages is with midriff bulge. He incessantly exercises his stomach muscles, eats the finest cuts of meat, and enjoys the best seasonal vegetables. Dessert is out of the question. With his trim figure and flock of red hair, Witherspoon doesn't look his age. Yet his subordinates call him "Old Pinky." It is, perhaps, an act of retaliation with multiple meanings. "Old Pinky" reduces the boss to the smallest digit of his hand. Witherspoon also has a reddish complexion.

Witherspoon tries to enlist Aggie, Hod, and Pete to persuade Willie to sell Little Spoon. He sends Aggie a fur coat, claiming that it is only a year old and his wife has outgrown it. Suspiciously, it shows no sign of wear at all. It seems as if Old Pinky deemed it too unrespectable to send such an expansive gift to a woman other than his wife. Thus he developed what appears to be a frail cover story. Anyone other than Aggie would have seen the "used" coat for what it is: a necessary fiction, a guise for a condescending bribe so that she will plead Witherspoon's case to Willie. Aggie has no hold on her brother, but she has gained a coat that she wears around the village, in a parade of pomposity. It serves as a fake emblem of her dead husband's "wealth."

There is no sleight of hand in Old Pinky's attempts to induce Hod. If Witherspoon purchases Little Spoon, then Hod would have a job. "I shall want a good man to run my cabin cruiser," he writes to Hod. "The job pays $200 a month, uniforms, and found [free room and board]." Witherspoon's haughtiness knows no bounds. A uniform for an independent, self-sufficient Mainer such as Hod, a college-educated engineer, would reduce him to Old Pinky's summer water jockey.

Witherspoon and Pete need each other. Unbeknownst to Witherspoon, however, Pete possesses no leverage over Willie. The outsider relies on the local merchant for advice. In turn, Pete realizes how crucial Witherspoon is to his dream of an exclusive summer colony on Big Spoon. They toy with each other. Pete adopts the guise of a Maine hayseed. When he writes to Old Pinky, he litters his letters with spelling and grammar errors. He even rereads the correspondence and adds more mistakes. Witherspoon is not fooled; he sees Pete as a competitor. Thus he investigates and discovers that he graduated from commercial school. Pete knows how to overcharge and shortchange his neighbors. Witherspoon doesn't let on that he sees through Pete's Maine-country-bumpkin masquerade.

He sweetens his initial miserly $500 offer to Willie. "Three thousand dollars is a lot of money, Stilwell," he tells Willie, though it's loose change to Witherspoon. "You could buy any place around here for that." Willie replies respectfully in the local argot: "Don't know's I'd feel to home in any place, Mr. Witherspoon." In contrast, Old Pinky counters with bombast in his own monied mother tongue: "Nonsense. With money, a man can feel at home anywhere." Later in the novel, Moore puts a striking thought in Witherspoon's head, a kind of joke he once heard: "What a wonderful world God could have made if He only had money." It persuades Witherspoon that he is trying to do God's work on Little Spoon—making a small corner of Maine into a personal heaven. In the end, he raises the ante to $8,000, then to $15,000. The raggedly dressed Willie stands tall as one island man who can't be bought, even for "God's work." He has not been posing as a pigheaded country Yankee to skin Witherspoon, as the businessman once thought.

The hard-charging Old Pinky is not to be frustrated by a village crank in his quest for a scenic piece of paradise, where he could command a manor "through the mellow summers of his declining years," he reflects. Witherspoon lets Pete know that he will visit Big Spoon for Christmas. It is 1936, and the Depression already long in the tooth. From his office Pete sees Witherspoon's Chrysler sweep to a stop. Pete slips into his public persona; he leans back in his chair, puts his hat over his face, and snores. However, Witherspoon is not taken in by his acting the part of a homey country merchant in a sleepy Maine village.

Witherspoon has Doyle, his chauffeur, and Bundy, his on-call assistant, with him. He has a plan. On Christmas Day they will scour the island in quest of a scenic, private location. They will dress as duck hunters so they don't arouse suspicion. At this point, dissembling has emerged as a running motif of *Spoonhandle*: Pete's guise; Aggie's coat and the larger façade of her husband's life; Josh Hovey's shifting Yankeeness; and the hunting outfits. Moreover, Pete is already engaged in a cynical, veiled process of dispossessing his neighbors of their most valuable land.

It is winter on Big Spoon, when the wind smells of "cold and salt and spruces." Witherspoon and his trusty assistant set out to initiate a bit of God's work, equipped with hunting jackets, "high-laced" boots, and shotguns. They tramp along the coast of Big Spoon, evaluating "every cove, every headland." The two men make their way to the Spoonhandle's overgrown road and discover the magnificent point of the peninsula and Joe Sangor's home.

They knock on his door and Joe half opens it. The sight of the gun alarms him. Once before a man had appeared at his door armed, that time with a pistol. It was the sheriff who came to repossess Joe's piano. A salesman in Bellport had duped the "Portygee." Joe had paid $50 down and then $50 on installment. He understood that he owned the piano. But the sheriff showed up to reclaim the piano for Joe's failure to make additional payments. Now he exercises caution, until Witherspoon offers the fisherman $3,000 for the house and his twenty acres on Spoonhandle Point.

Joe and Mary react as if they have been presented with a huge Christmas gift. It's far more money than they have ever seen. With the windfall in hand, they will be able to return to "their own people" in New Bedford and purchase a house. Joe will be a step closer to the Azores. They will never make it home to New Bedford, however. The sale of Spoonhandle Point sets in motion a rush of events culminating in tragedy for the Sangors. In the meantime, Witherspoon allows the family to stay in the house until the spring, when construction will start on his mansion.

Even before Witherspoon purchases Spoonhandle Point, Pete has executed an ingenious conspiracy to monopolize ownership of his neighbors' soon-to-be valuable shore property. The map in his drawer then slowly springs to life with fresh names and a new future for Big Spoon. The island will go the way of Bellport, "from a village of independent fishermen and farmers, their own men who took nothing from anybody . . . to a town full of domestic servants." Or, as Josh Hovey caustically and colorfully puts it to Hod, in Bellport "good upstandin' men . . . make reg'lar goddamn prayer-rugs out of themselves, all summer long." Again, Mary Ellen Chase mined this thematic vein. But she didn't exhaust its literary lode. Besides Witherspoon, Spoonhandle represents other crucial differences with Chase's treatment of summer people buying up the Maine coast. Moore portrays a sinister insider, an embodiment of greed and small-pond power, who furtively and all but single-handedly rearranges Big Spoon's seascape and transforms its summer economy. At the same time, Moore depicts heroic islanders who stand up to Witherspoon and Pete Stilwell.

Before Christmas Pete plants the news that someone who is interested in buying "spruce woodland for pulpwood" came to the island the previous month. Pete just happened to write the man's name down: Joe King, Box 48, Bellport. Word spreads quickly through the island's gossip circuit. Joe King is actually a young clerk in the office of Pete's Bellport lawyer. As the letters of inquiry arrive from the island, Pete travels to Bellport to set prices. He stints his neighbors, most of whom live from lobster catch to lobster catch. Paris Freeman, Ann's father, a proud, independent, hardworking lobsterman, receives $3,000 for forty-five acres. Curiously, Joe King is only interested in woodlots that abut the shore. Days before Christmas, nearly 150 acres of Spoon Island's waterfront are transferred from the straw purchaser to Pete Stilwell for $1. Joe King receives $25.

Pete employs Bellport real estate agents to sell Spoon Island's pristine shore land; they freely invoke Witherspoon's name and the fact that he has already bought twenty acres. Soon Pete begins to fill in his map, his words in black ink standing out from long-faded lines. Farrell from New York, Washburn from Beacon Hill, Jennings from Baltimore—the list goes on. At Molino, he pauses, thinking he may have admitted the wrong type. Molino turns out to be a respectable businessman in Philadelphia, not some Al Capone spin-off. Pete has to draw the line somewhere, however. Bergstein represents that boundary.

In April, as Witherspoon is building his estate house and Joe Sangor prepares to leave, Hod visits Josh Hovey. He pays the boatbuilder the last $500 he and Willie owe on their cruiser. They talk about what is happening on Spoon Island. Josh, a gatherer of gossip, tells Hod what Bill Pray related to him. When Pray read in the Bellport newspaper about Joe King's sale of his land to Pete, he confronted the merchant. Pete seizes the moral high ground. He allegedly accuses his neighbors of selling their property to pulpwood cutters who would lay waste to the land, leaving stumps and piles of brush. "Anyone who'd spoil land as sightly as spruce lots on the east side of Spoon Island, ought to be hung." The Ladies Aid Society, pressured by Aggie, praises Pete as a "public-spirited citizen."

Even as the summer colony begins to take shape, Hod tells Josh that Spoon Islanders don't blame Pete. They blame themselves. It's their fault that they sold too soon; "they didn't have Pete's vision." This strikes one like the perspective that Maine writer Robert P. Tristram Coffin offered in the mid-1930s about Robert Frost's poems. Coffin described Frost's Depression-era, rural Yankees who don't put the onus for "their troubles on the capitalists or the environment, but on the way life is built and the way they're built."[21] Yet Josh reveals details suggesting how Pete duped his neighbors.

Josh first became suspicious when he knew, as a boatbuilder, that there was no demand for pulpwood. In fact, there was a glut. The only Joe King in town was a local kid in Pete's lawyer's office. He served as the front for Pete's devious scheme. Hod leaves Josh infuriated, yet frustrated by not knowing what to do.

Bellport on April Fool's Day hasn't quite fully emerged from mud season. Hod follows the "mud-ridden streets" as he heads for Connie's Diner. "In the April sunlight, watery and thin, Bellport drooped like a hen that had been rained on." Main Street had yet to acquire its summer shimmer: "Half the plate glass windows . . . were boarded up, the planks splintery and weathered." Joe Sangor yells out a greeting to Hod. Rough-talking Connie says something that will turn out to be prophetic: "Ain't two people in this town ever treats a guinea anything but stinkin'?" Moore revives the issue of ethnic prejudice with a vengeance. "Otherness" becomes a prescription for tragedy.

Joe has bought an old truck, piled it high with the family's possessions, and will leave the next morning. It's in O'Brien's garage being inspected. Hod repeatedly asks Joe to look at the truck. But since he has money, Joe doesn't want to impose on his friend. He invites Hod to a farewell party that night at the Do-Drop-Inn. The gathering will never take place.

For the first time, Hod pilots a boat that he and Willie completely own. The sun sets on Spoon Island, and Joe hasn't arrived. Hod learns from the drunken foreman on the Witherspoon place who has come from Bellport that police were all over the road. He calls O'Brien's Garage and finds out Joe left two hours earlier. Hod presses the mechanic about what had been repaired on the truck. He claims they cleaned a "sludgy carburetor" and "fixed the steerin' rod." Hod fears the worse. He suspects the garage exploited an outsider who is not considered fully white by the locals.

Hod borrows a car, drives toward Bellport, and comes on the accident scene. Furniture is strewn across the road. Joe and two of his young sons are dead.

Hod learns that Joe lost control of the truck on a curve, the truck turned over, and soon the gas tank exploded. The coroner's report is terse: a drunk Portygee who was unfamiliar with the truck lost control at a curve at the bottom of a hill. The coroner does tell Hod that the state police found the "truck's steering rod broken."

Joe's death redeems something, but not before the story of the drunken Portygee overruns Bellport and Spoon Island. After Joe's funeral, Hod stops in Pete's store to buy cigarettes. There is a large crowd, men and women who surprisingly turned out for the Portygee's funeral. Not Pete. He is maligning Joe and his ethnic brethren: "Most of us leaves the drunken driver to the Portygees, y'know." Hod enters, and Pete continues to defame Joe. "Drunker'n a hoot-owl, the way them fellers git, the minute they lay their hands on a quarter," Pete pronounces.

It is too much for Hod. All of the animosity toward Pete that has taken up residence in Hod's psyche across the years boils over. He grabs Pete, drags him over the counter, and repeatedly and forcefully slaps his bug-eyed brother, who lets out "squeals of pain." Hod gives his audience something to gossip about, a requiem for his friend: "Joe Sangor wasn't drunk . . . his wife said at the inquest he couldn't drink without getting sick." Hod goes on to relate Joe's sacrificial heroism: "He burned to death trying to get his two kids out from under a truck load of furniture." Hod inspected the truck: the steering rod had not been repaired. He reprimands his audience of men and women for their failure to accept those who aren't island born and who possess "funny names." The Sangors are as "decent human people" as the native islanders claim to be.

Hod then turns back to Pete and his land swindle. He discloses Joe King's identity and his relationship to Pete's lawyer. "I'll probably go to jail for slapping the puss of your damned public-spirited tree savior, there." Hod walks out; the stunned, slack-jawed crowd watches him leave. The ground has shifted after the most dramatic scene in *Spoonhandle*. The islanders will no longer look at Hod as an odd fellow. He carries Spoon Island's conscience on his broad shoulders. As Bill Pray says the next morning, "This whole town'd go along with him to jail if Pete arrests him."

The badly bruised Pete knows better. He is no longer viewed as an untarnished man of vision. Yet he will continue to accumulate power over islanders' lives and derail any boycott of his store. Shortly after the confrontation with Hod, however, Pete and his wife leave the island in his Chrysler on a trip to California. He's building a new supermarket modeled on Griswold's in Bellport. Its shelves will be stocked with special items, at high prices, for the summer trade. Spoon Island represents the lodestone of Pete's life. Or, to put it another way, he's a man of no account without a cash register close at hand. He cuts his trip short to return before the opening of his store in July. If he has lost whatever civic power he wielded over the community, he exchanges it for tighter economic control.

During his absence, the islanders have patronized Myron Osgood's small store at another corner of Spoonhandle. Like Witherspoon's arrival on Christmas Eve, Pete pulls in front of Osgood's store in his Chrysler. He makes Myron an irresistible offer. Pete needs someone experienced to help him with his new store. He will assume Myron's bills, pay him for his stock and "goodwill," and give a "stiddy" salary. Myron accepts. What he doesn't know is that Pete is already planning to reduce his hours in winter and "lay him off when trade was slow." The islanders will be completely dependent on Pete, for few will go to the trouble of shopping in Bellport.

Pete consolidates power over his Lilliputian realm in other ways. He is an intermediary between summer people and the islanders. When the former need cooks, maids, caretakers, and boat pilots, they seek Pete's recommendations. He urges Henny Pray, the highly vocal and independent Bill's wife, to accept a maid's job at Molino's house. "Oh the job pays sixty a month, maid's uniforms, and three meals a day." He gives her a note to take to the family. The fiercely independent but struggling lobsterman Paris Freeman accepts a year-round job as a caretaker. The steady pay is too much to resist: "Sixty dollars a month all winter, a hundred for four months in the summertime."

Pete's treachery aside, Moore presents the transition to summer economy with some moral ambiguity. Islanders divest themselves of their independent sea life and spirit, at least for the summer interlude. But as the ironically named Paris Freeman reflects, "The grinding, uncertain, business of making his own decisions was over forever." He is relieved and "felt himself relax all over." Perhaps Witherspoon and other summer people are doing "divine" work. They and Pete, Old Pinky muses, are "the source of the sleepy village's awakening, the people dusting themselves off, expectant now of better things to come . . . work, wages, an upstanding town instead of an ingrown community headed toward decay."

Moore skillfully threads a love story through *Spoonhandle*'s overarching plot of greed and villainy. Moore' s realism doesn't lapse into melodrama, though Hollywood took the novel in that direction. Rather, she underscores how love emerges from the integrity of two very different characters' lives. Ann Freeman's fondness for Hod bursts into love after she witnesses his confrontation with Pete.

When she temporarily returns to Spoon Island, Ann is not simply seeking peace and quiet to complete her new novel. She is also recoiling from a personal relationship with another journalist that has dissolved. She takes an immediate shine to Hod, but it's not amorous. Ann is an outsider/insider. She has no intention of engaging in a new romantic relationship, especially with an islander.

After her initial encounter with Hod upon her arrival in Bellport, Ann observes him and Willie mostly from a distance. She ruminates on the brothers' reserve, suggesting a broader pattern of Mainers' behavior, beyond Hod and Willie. Ann believes that the islanders' silence (with the exception of Pete), "their shyness and modesty—their reticence with outsiders was more than half made up of the fear that they might not say or do the proper thing; that they might, in some way, let themselves be vulnerable." Moore's experience on Gott's Island surely informed such a shrewd observation on the relationship between Maine folk and summer people.

Over the course of more than a year Ann and Hod go through a fitful relationship as they slow walk toward mutual love. Ann is restless under her father's overbearing parenting. He complains about the cost of wood she burns up heating a room where she writes, an activity that mystifies him as work. All in all, Paris treats his adult daughter as a fourteen-year-old. Hod has cords of wood delivered in a gesture of generosity toward Ann. But Paris will never accept anything with a hint of charity and orders the wood returned.

Ann seeks freedom. She buys a fish house from a kind widow; it belonged to her husband. Ann sets up a writing studio. Hod, along with Willie, makes repairs and improvements. She grows fond of Hod, but he misinterprets her intentions and is rebuffed. He has clumsily made himself vulnerable to a big-city woman. Humiliated, Hod stays away from Ann's retreat for weeks. But as the novel progresses, her relationship with Hod not only is repaired but also crosses over to affection. Hod's kindnesses and gentleness awaken her emotional attraction to him. Still, she is guarded. Then a turning point arrives—Hod's confrontation with Pete and the disclosure of Joe Sangor's avoidable tragedy. Ann happens to be in the store when the incident occurs. "Hod," she says, holding his bruised hand, "that was the most wonderful thing I ever saw." From that point the mutual love turns passionate. It leads to physical intimacy and then marriage, with her father kicking and complaining along the way. The love story is well told because the characters are both smart and strong. They are also strikingly different individuals. Urbane Ann is a writer; she knows how to express herself. Insular Hod is an engineer—a doer rather than a talker.

Spoonhandle was a commercial and, on the whole, a critical success. William Morrow published an initial run of thirty-five thousand copies on June 12, 1946. The company aggressively promoted the book with full-page advertisements and personal communications between the company's director of publicity and more than twenty-two hundred book stores across the country.[22] By July the book shot onto the bestseller lists. It rose to number two in Boston. The *New York Herald*'s survey of major bookstores across the country ranked *Spoonhandle* at number nine, on a list with Taylor Caldwell, Somerset Maugham, and Upton Sinclair. In mid-September, among twenty city bestsellers *Spoonhandle* stood at number seven, behind Robert Penn Warren's classic *All the King's Men*.[23]

In the "Book of the Month Club News" for July 1946, noted Vermont writer Dorothy Canfield asked, "What! Another book about Maine?" She went on to praise Moore for serving up "the real stuff"—that is, "the kind of folk who live in the real North Country of New England." Canfield singled out *Spoonhandle*'s "authentic picturesque turn of phrase, [and] the crisp locution." But she considered the love story between Ann and Hod "not especially original or true" and "below the high standard of the rest of the book."[24]

One reviewer posed a probing and suggestive observation about Maine's literary tradition: "One speaks about a Maine novel and it connotes something; the same isn't equally true about New York or Connecticut and Missouri." Of the many novels about the place "flung into the Atlantic," the reviewer argued, "few [are] as deeply evocative of its spirit as Ruth Moore's *Spoonhandle*." She has managed to tell "a story that penetrates the bedrock of the people."[25]

Newspapers from Philadelphia to Chicago to San Diego lavished praise on *Spoonhandle*. The *Philadelphia Inquirer*, for example, wrote extravagantly that the "novel will rank as one of the best written of contemporary authors and perhaps gain a place in the lists of all-time masterpieces." What troubled some other reviewers, *Spoonhandle*'s "kaleidoscopic shifts of action," did not bother the *Inquirer*. Its reviewer claimed that Moore handled "her material so cleverly that no continuity is lost."[26]

In contrast, the *New York Times* and *New York Sun* found much to criticize in Moore. For the *Times*' reviewer, Moore's characters were mere types. As a result, "nowhere does the author search very deeply into human souls." Given the author's aims, and apparent skill, "*Spoonhandle* is an adequate and even successful book. But beneath its situations and its people there remain meanings and implications unrealized." The *Sun* reviewer leaned on sarcasm. *Spoonhandle* was little more than "a prosy, prosaic narrative about folksy homey people on a tiny island off Maine." Moore showed "snatches of skill," but she needed to "remember to get the maximum out of one thing rather than the minimum out of many."[27]

Moore could find reassurance in praise from many other reviewers: the *Hartford, Connecticut, Times*, the *Times Literary Supplement*, and the *Chicago Tribune*, for example.[28] Perhaps the most colorful Maine image came from a Chicago reviewer who saw *Spoonhandle* as confirming that coastal people "are as amphibious as seals."[29]

Moore, of course, didn't focus only on island communities. One needs to say a few words about non-island novels before summing up Moore's achievement. Enlarging the depictions of the Harbor in *The Weir* and Bellport in *Spoonhandle*, she presented a full-blown portrait of a coastal fishing community in *Candlemas Bay* (1950). The gripping plot follows the fortunes of the Ellises, the fishing town's founding family. Once among the town's wealthiest families, the Ellises find themselves in a struggle for survival. Moore again weaves an unusual love story through the now grim, then heartening depiction of postwar coastal life. *Candlemas Bay* was one of her most successful novels, a bestseller, a Literary Guild and Book of the Month Club selection, and a *Publishers Weekly* Editor's Choice.[30]

Still, I think *The Walk Down Main Street* (1960), her eighth novel, remains a more resonant book. Set in the late 1950s after the Soviet Union had launched the Sputnik spy satellite, Moore dedicated the novel "To School Teachers with Admiration." The original book cover captures the idyllic ensemble of some Maine coastal towns. Main Street is constructed of white clapboard and red brick. The compact business district occupies the foreground. A white-steepled church reaches for heaven in the background. A civic building with neoclassical white columns stands across the street from the church. Late in February, fresh snow perks up the landscape and signals the persistence of winter. Main Street is narrow, like the townspeople we will discover. In fact, *The Walk Down Main Street* may be read as Moore's *Peyton Place* (1956), minus its erotic scandals. Moore's novel examines the corrosive currents of anti-Semitism and an impoverished civic life. Most reprehensible, perhaps, the nameless coastal town is in thrall to high school sports, especially basketball, and scrimps on academics. Crude ethnic prejudice pervades town life, having endured through the mists of the past, as references to the "Klew Klux" suggest.

The novel begins with old Martin Hoodless, a cranky Yankee and mossback patriarch, who sets out to do his morning chores. His last name suggests an unreconstructed former member of Maine's KKK. Hoodless is the only character who speaks in a thick accent. Throughout *The Walk Down Main Street* there are allusions to television and its full-course menu of Westerns and situation comedies. Moore may be suggesting that television is reshaping local speech. More clearly, television has eroded civic life. No one wants to serve on the school committee, except a troika with vested interests in public education, and particularly in the basketball team. They are the gatekeepers who, with the complicity of the townspeople, favor sports over learning. They also maintain the ethnic "purity" of the town's teaching ranks.

An extraordinary chorus of sounds disrupts Martin Hoodless's quiet morning. The church bells ring simultaneously, the tannery whistle blows, the fire whistle blasts, the fog warning at the point sounds on a perfectly clear day, and even the coastguard cutter from the nearby base joins the cacophony. There is a parade with fire trucks coming along the highway from downtown. Cheering high school kids hang on the vehicles' sides and rears. Cars blowing their horns follow, with the high school principal part of the procession. Martin sees a neighbor, the mother of the basketball team's star, writing on a white sheet. He immediately thinks of the KKK. "Oh, hell, no," his neighbor responds. "We give all them [sheets] away to the kids" for Halloween. The novel resurrects memory of a time in the not too distant past when the KKK weaponized bigotry in Maine towns and cities. Martin learns that the morning's ruckus is for the basketball team, winners of the state championship by two points the previous night.

The Walk Down Main Street then goes on to dramatize the importance of basketball, especially to small northern Maine towns, which, one might add, persists today. High school basketball seems the only community activity that disengages people from their television sets. The sport helps townspeople cope with long Maine winters. The success of a team boosts town pride.

The champs march down Main Street and are celebrated like war heroes, most notably in their "hangouts—the drug store, the restaurants, the poolroom." Moore deploys the basketball team to illuminate the post-WWII emergence of a teenage subculture. Carlisle "Shirttail" McIntosh, a senior, and his fifteen-year-old brother, Ralph, are members of the team. They are also grandsons of Martin Hoodless. The brothers live with their widowed mother and their sister on Martin's farm. The grandfather's anger toward his grandsons accumulates because he can't get them to complete their chores. They have too many teenage distractions; Martin tries unsuccessfully to impose on them youthful responsibilities that hark back to a bygone era.

Coach Chet Alison drills the team at the expense of classes. He has played college and professional ball. For him, winning is a springboard to a larger school and better pay.

The only one who challenges Alison's appropriation of valuable class time is science teacher Al Berg, known to the students as "Buggsy." He is a dedicated, demanding teacher of chemistry but no match for Alison, who has the principal, the school committee, and the town on his side. Berg is a "Jew-boy," or "kike," who was only hired because the position paid so little and there were no takers. In other words, Moore examines how, even after Sputnik's launch in October 1957, with its attendant alarm over American scientific know-how, chemistry is an afterthought to basketball.

The school committee has already decided that Buggsy will be fired. Before any formal meeting, the members come together in the backroom of Win Parker's gas station. He serves as chairman of the school committee. Parker is a repository of crude ethnic jokes, which he draws on to regale listeners. In an earlier era, one suspects, he would have served as the local Kleagle of the KKK. Parker sells heating oil to the high school and gasoline for school busses. Harry Troy, a second member of the committee, owns the supermarket and supplies food to the high school for lunches. Doc Wickham, the school physician, rounds outs the educational powerbrokers. They settle things, such as Al Berg's fate, in the back of the garage before public meetings. They all have sons on the basketball team. The hometown heroes ultimately lose in Boston Garden to a racially mixed team.

Moore went on to publish six more novels after *The Walk Down Main Street.* If we consider Sarah Orne Jewett as primarily an author of novellas and short stories, then Ruth Moore's achievement is notable. She abides as one of the most accomplished novelists of Maine life in an important watery subregion of the state. Among other things, Moore wrote about more than Maine Yankees. Immigrants and ethnics find a place in her novels, even if it is as outsiders. From her work with the NAACP to characters such as Joe Sangor and Al Berg, Moore inveighs against intolerance and its consequences. To be sure, Jewett also wrote about immigrants, but not, as we have seen, in her most significant work, except for "The Foreigner." Perhaps Moore's activities with the NAACP also help explain the limits of her realism. Moral ambiguity has all but taken its leave from Moore's literary universe. Major characters, for example, are typically assigned to good and evil camps.

II

THE NORTH COUNTRY
AND BACKCOUNTRY

4

FROM BANGOR
TO THE BORDER

Three Writers of the North Country

People in the state believe that everything to the south of where they live is not the "real" Maine: one occasionally hears variations on this idea about the state. A partially tongue-in-cheek observation, it nevertheless possesses an element of truth when it comes to Maine's cultural geography—that is, how the state has been imagined over time. The image of the pine tree represents one way of charting the emergence of the north country as a real and symbolic landscape that became increasingly important over the course of the nineteenth century and beyond. When Maine secured independence from Massachusetts in 1820, its state seal prominently displayed a pine tree in the foreground with a moose reclining in the background. A farmer and a sailor flanked the pine, representations of the "real," indigenous folk of Maine, to the exclusion of the north country's native people. The lumberjack is implicit in the pine's privileged positioning. Until 1909, the state flag displayed a single pine against a white background. Then the state seal's ensemble was transferred to the Maine flag. By the middle of the nineteenth century, the "Pine Tree State" condensed and secured Maine's identity as New England's outback.

Other developments signaled the economic and political rise of the north country in the nineteenth century. Bangor incorporated in 1834. The thriving "Queen City" on the Penobscot, the lumber capital of Maine, New England, and beyond, adopted a seal with a pine tree front and center. A year earlier the state capital shifted from Portland to Augusta. Portland's aggressive efforts to reclaim its "rightful" political standing were to no avail. The state's largest city didn't represent Maine's growing heartland. A generation later, Maine's land grant university was established more than a hundred miles north of Portland, in a small lumber-processing town. In other words, Maine's nineteenth-century, geographically informed actions and symbolic choices remain with us in more crucial ways than the presence of Bangor's Paul Bunyan "statue," a token of its glory days.

To reiterate a point from the prologue, the expansive north country is part of the largest congressional district east of the Mississippi. From Bangor it stretches east and north to New Brunswick and west to Quebec Province. Despite the presence of vast forested land, the north country consists of diverse landscapes.

Three highly successful writers published major novels set in different locations and depicting distinctive aspects of Maine's north country. Ben Ames Williams (1889–1953) offers a colorful portrait of Bangor's rise to America's lumber capital between the War of 1812 and the Civil War. Elizabeth Coatsworth (1893–1986) crafts an engaging story set in one of those far north unincorporated plantations on the edge of lumbering country. Cathie Pelletier (b. 1953) transports the reader further north to "Mattagash," where place matters like family and history and the very air the "Mattagashers" breathe. Taken together, these three writers capture something of the north country's varied places and people.

BEN AMES WILLIAMS, BANGOR, AND THE EMPIRE OF PINE

Ben Ames Williams was born in Macon, Mississippi, and grew up in the southern Ohio town of Jackson, where his father was the editor and publisher of the local newspaper. Over the course of his youth, Williams visited Maine frequently. After graduating from Dartmouth College in 1910, Williams became a reporter for the *Boston American*. He met Kenneth Roberts, the future historical novelist who was a reporter for another Boston newspaper. They formed a friendship that would lead to mutual critical readings of their writing.

Williams worked during the day as a reporter and wrote stories at night. After repeated rejections, he finally published his first story in 1915. He resigned from the newspaper, and his mother promised to provide the difference between his journalist's salary and what he could earn through his writing. Soon he began publishing in some of the best periodicals of the day, including *Collier's*, *Maclean's*, and the *Saturday Evening Post*. He also experienced much success with the less prestigious *Country Gentleman*. His early novels were first serialized as short stories.

Between 1919 and 1949, Williams endured among the most prolific, popular fiction writers in the country. He published more than thirty-five novels as well as collections of short stories. He lived outside of Boston and also wrote, from the spring through early fall, at "Hardscrabble," his farm in Searsmont, Maine, a town south of Waterville. One of his books was a collection of short stories, *Fraternity Village* (1949), based on life in Searsmont. Maine and "Hardscrabble" were so central to Williams's life and writing that when he died, his ashes were scattered on his beloved farm.[1]

Some of Williams's novels were bestsellers. Hollywood made several of his works into feature films. Thus, after a short apprenticeship, Williams thrived as an impressively productive writer, an almost unchallenged commercial success, and an often critically well-received author as well.

Williams wrote historical novels, adventure tales, and mysteries set in different parts of the country. For his historical works he conducted extensive research, which only makes his literary output even more remarkable. For *Splendor* (1927), a historical novel about Boston, he said that he read all of the city's newspapers between 1877 and 1922. Williams set a lofty literary goal. He longed to "build [him]self into a writer not only with a popular appeal but with a claim to real rank among those who were worth while [*sic*]."[2] The latter goal proved elusive. Though he was a good storyteller and an often-deft portrayer of character, his novels were sometimes verbose. Given the speed at which he produced his major fiction, one wonders whether he had time for serious revision. For example, a long chapter in *The Strange Woman* (1941) plunges important characters into the maelstrom of the Civil War. William's literary credo called for books with "gusto." "They each deal with vice," he explained, "with vicious men and women, with vicious society."[3] *The Strange Woman* keeps faith with this realistic literary creed.

The novel is one of his two important works of Maine historical fiction. A year earlier, he published *Come Spring*, a nearly eight-hundred-page, meticulously researched fictional history of the founding of Union, Maine, a midcoast town.[4] Remarkably, a year later Williams published his almost seven-hundred-page novel on Bangor, which also showed impressive research. If Williams never actually attained "real rank" as an American writer, at least he deserves recognition for his strongest literary achievements. *The Strange Woman*, for instance, not only traces the life of a character conflicted between virtue and viciousness but also offers a portrait of Bangor in its lumbering heyday that is more vivid and persuasive than anything (and there is not much) produced by historians to date.[5]

In a preliminary acknowledgment to *The Strange Woman*, Williams discloses that his original intention was "to present a picture of life in Bangor and the Penobscot Valley through the years immediately preceding and during the Civil War." He referred to 1855–1865. "But before the actual writing began," Williams continues, "the central character [Jenny Hager Evered] assumed command of the book," and its time line changed. Williams explained that the book "became much more a study of character than an historical novel."[6] Yet place remains far more than mere setting in *The Strange Woman*. As the lumbering capital of America, even for a short period, Bangor developed as an exceptional Maine city. Jenny and the other major characters in the novel lead lives that intersect with the world that the white pine creates. A white pine is imprinted on the book's spine as well as on its title page.

Since all aspects of Bangor's boomtown crisscross with Jenny's life, we need to rough out the plot, without allowing her to take over this analysis the way she came to dominate *The Strange Woman*. The novel begins in 1814. The British have ransacked Bangor homes, even using furniture for campfires while ignoring the residents' split wood. Jenny Hager is four years old. Her mother, Moll, decides to run off with a handsome British lieutenant. She offers the lieutenant a colorful description of Dan Hager, her husband, as some primitive backwoodsman: "He is a hairy man, with more whiskers in his nose and his ears than a boy like you will ever have on his chin and all are stiff as bristles on a pig." Here is the image of the shaggy woodsman who surfaces in Bangor after months in the forest snorting like a barnyard animal in mating season. Dan is no lumberer, however, except when he needs money and treks into the woods poaching pine that he doesn't own.

Moll begs Jenny to come with her. She refuses. She wants to stay with her father, the first man whom she will come to dominate and destroy. In a word, Jenny will be empowered, not traumatized, by her mother's departure. She grows up into a beautiful, beguiling young woman. Men and boys take notice. She uses her charms to manipulate and control her six-foot-seven-inch father, until the besotted hulk, who will drink himself to death, physically abuses her.

Jenny then flees to the house of merchant Isaiah Poster. He is widowed and sixty-five, more than three times Jenny's age. He sends his son Ephraim off to Harvard because the young man has eyes for Jenny. After consulting the town "fathers," Isaiah marries Jenny, offering her comfort and security. She, in turn, provides Isaiah with companionship in his old age.

With his lust for Jenny thwarted, Ephraim Poster frequents Boston's barrooms and bordellos rather than Harvard's classrooms. Fellow student John

Evered, an exemplar of virtue who will eventually marry Jenny, helps "Eph" turn his life around. He comes back to Bangor and begins to work with his father. Isaiah is one of Bangor's kingpins. He is a merchant and an investor in ships and forestland. Jenny seduces Eph. Then she tells him that she will reveal that he slept with his father's wife unless Eph kills Isaiah. On a canoe trip to inspect forestland, Eph is responsible for a series of events that lead to his father's death. He is disgraced and then abandoned by Jenny. Eph reverts to the dissolute ways of his youth and perishes in New York. Jenny is now responsible for three deaths: Eph, his father, and her father. She then devotes her wiles to causing the moral destruction of two men who will be compelled to live with the consequences of her duplicity.

Jenny is suddenly a rich woman. She is also a devoted member of the Congregational Church and a fervent supporter of abolition and temperance. Jenny straddles the pious and profane worlds that define Bangor, though not in equal proportions.

By happenstance, John Evered rescues Jenny when they have to abandon an old Rockland steamship in a storm. They fall in love, and Jenny thus marries Eph's old Harvard friend. John helps manage the expansive Bingham estate, an early, famous, private Maine land purchase from Massachusetts. He also takes control of Jenny's business interests. John is incorruptible, which only rankles Jenny. She pays a black washerwoman to charge John with sexual assault. An impressive cast of leading citizens testify to John's character, and he is acquitted.

Jenny has already been involved with the seduction of an elder of the church, Lincoln Pittredge. She convinced him to testify against John. After the acquittal, the elder is discredited. He doesn't know that Jenny is pregnant with his child. While John is off for an extended inspection of forestland with two of their four boys, Jenny delivers a girl, named Moll for her mother. She is born in the old homestead, which is now a waterfront brothel.

John remains loyal to Jenny in an increasingly loveless marriage. He is adored by his sons and treated contemptuously by his wife. As the Civil War marches toward its end, Jenny begins to show symptoms of a grave illness. She gradually wastes away, seemingly from cancer. Just before Jenny's life is extinguished, she summons to her bedside both the lawyer who argued in court for John's conviction on sexual assault and the disreputable publisher who first printed the story. She revises her will. It disinherits John, the two sons who have gone South and become Confederates, and the two older sons, for not killing their brothers in the Civil War. Her now seventeen-year-old daughter, who still lives in the Bangor brothel where she was born, inherits Jenny's estate. She reveals that Elder Pittredge is Molly's father. Jenny had paid to have the entire will published in the newspaper. Her revelation serves as a humiliation of John, punishment of her sons, and a shock to Bangor's pious community, of which she has been such a devoted lifelong member.

Some readers found *The Strange Woman* an immoral book. Williams claimed that, as with his other books, evil doesn't triumph in the end, arguing that "the reader abhors the woman [Jenny] herself and feels pity rather than esteem."[7]

Perhaps. Yet Jenny continues to destroy men—her own family—from beyond the grave. More certainly Jenny's evil is archetypal; she is an Eve, a Jezebel, a character of biblical proportions. Or, to put it another way, Jenny is an outsized male construction of woman as temptress, the serpent in the garden.

Over the decades when Williams's novel follows the course of Jenny's devious destruction of men, Bangor comes to life as the so-called Queen City. It prospers from lumbering, shipbuilding, and the exchange of goods, especially sawn boards. The brothels and grog shops that make up the "Devil's Acre" along the waterfront propagate Bangor's reputation as a libertine place. *The Strange Woman* is a heavily secular book, but there is another side to the colorful town and to Jenny. She is a leading member of her church. There is a respectable religious dimension to Bangor. An important Congregational institution, Bangor Seminary, was founded in 1814. Williams alludes to the "seminary" a few times. In a sense, *The Strange Woman* rehearses Maine's secular founding by fishermen, farmers, and lumberers, with religion arriving later, after a seedbed has been sowed. Maine was no Massachusetts Bay Colony, and Bangor is no "city upon a hill."

Williams presents a historically sound view of Bangor when the British occupied the town in 1814: "The village of seven or eight hundred people sprawled pleasantly, across low hills on either side of Kenduskeag Stream, with scattered farms bordered by the black masses of the forest. . . . Some of the houses in town were no more than cabins, but most of them were more substantial." Bangor, though small, has moved beyond its frontier stage. The town boasts some progress toward stability such as the presence of a courthouse and a hotel.

Williams is often unclear about dates, or the chronology of the events in Jenny's and Bangor's life, which is to say that he is not a historian or even a full-fledged fictional historian in *The Strange Woman*. He is heavily invested in the protagonist's personality or, we might say, in her personality disorder.

Bangor's explosive growth took place between 1820 and 1850, when the city's population grew to well over fourteen thousand. In 1846, Henry David

Thoreau first visited Bangor and left a memorable commentary on the city, which was included in his classic *The Maine Woods* (1864). "There stands the city of Bangor," he wrote, "fifty miles up the Penobscot, the principal lumber depot on this continent, like a star on the edge of night, still hewing at the forests of which it is built." He saw the city "overflowing with luxuries and refinements of Europe, and sending its vessels to Spain, to England, to the West Indies for its groceries."[8]

Devil's Acre certainly didn't escape Thoreau's notice, though it eluded his written record. *The Strange Woman* takes the full measure of Devil's Acre, including an anti-Irish riot. Spring reanimates life in the seasonal watering hole and the line of bawdy houses that extends up from the Kenduskeag Stream. Lumbermen drive white pine because it is lighter than hardwood and thus floats more easily to sawmills in Bangor and towns to its north on the Penobscot. Woodsmen receive their season's pay in the city. It serves as the financial capital of northern Maine.

As Williams presents it, the "sober" people of Bangor "dreaded" the spring, for "the dives began to be reopened, and every stage brought from Augusta and Portland and even from Boston rough men and women coming to re-populate the district along the stream." Rum flows freely and "the bawds are waiting." Williams is realistic, yet restrained, in his representation of Devil's Acre; the word "prostitution" is never mentioned, and only once are readers given entrée to a brothel (and it doesn't involve a liaison). Devil's Acre helps define Bangor's distinctiveness within Maine. Pious people—like hardheaded Yankees—mostly turn a blind eye to Devil's Acre: it's a cost of Bangor's prosperity. Men who perform grueling work during the coldest months of the year need some release. They are joined by sailors from hundreds of ships that carry wood products to distant ports. Williams even suggests, probably accurately, that bawdy "establishments" are "sometimes secretly or openly financed by Bangor men."

The ill-fated Elder Pittredge rails publicly against the city's "leprous scab of Iniquity." He calls for one hundred men to reduce the Devil's Acre to ashes. But the only destruction in the elder's moral wasteland is a targeted one. It reveals the anti-Irish, anti-Catholic sentiment that agitated midcentury Maine and New England.

Ma Hogan's is a popular house of ill repute. It apparently has Irish harlots who service their countrymen as well as others. Many of the Irish migrated to booming Bangor from Nova Scotia. The riot at Ma Hogan's electrifies Bangor and thrills Jenny, who is a bystander. One of Ma Hogan's girls allegedly steals money from a sailor-customer. The rumor spreads, and soon the waterfront is crowded with men carrying torches. They shed shadowy light on drunken figures taking apart Ma Hogan's house with axes and crowbars, presumably looking for the sailor's money but actually with the real goal of destroying this Irish establishment. Soon a bonfire rages as doors, shingles, and beds are tossed from the house into the flames. The bawds have been dragged out and dunked in the stream.

But Ma Hogan, an ironfisted madam, refuses to leave. She appears on the second floor after the front of her house is torn away. Ma fights off the men; she is slugged and gets up bleeding. "You God damned rats and cowards," she yells. "Ain't there one single solitary Irishman in the lot of you? No by God, or he wouldn't stand there and let men treat women so that never did any harm to them." A brawl ensues, but the Irish are outnumbered. Not only does the whole episode showcase prejudice, but the tumult and Devil's Acre in general also suggest how Bangor has not yet shed its coarse frontier origins.

The riot takes place more than a decade before Thoreau's visit. Williams memorably describes the busyness of Bangor and its effect on the still-primitive lanes in the center of town: "The streets had turned to a quagmire as the frost went out of the ground." The town improvises. "Pot-holes were filled with branches cut off and thrown loosely in. . . . The mud turns to dust and back to mud again." Horse teams and oxen carrying heavy building materials "churned up holes which were never filled." There are no sidewalks—only footpaths with walkers "forever dodging teams or carriages." Williams probably based these details on newspapers of the era. We presume he read the *Penobscot Journal* because he quoted from it in the novel.

Bangor in the mid-1830s, the decade of its fastest growth, is a boomtown with an epidemic of land speculation and fraud. The forest is too vast for people's imaginations to grasp or for surveyors to plot. Boundaries blur in the woods or are simply transgressed. Surveyors are subject to bribery. Property is bought and sold blindly. Owners sometimes show one section of forest when they are actually selling another. Bonds trade in place of land. Paper proves more tangible than the dominion of white pine whose scope traders are unable to fully comprehend. All of this is to say that Williams's deciphering of Bangor's speculative lumber economy and the corruption that accompanied it represents one of the high points of *The Strange Woman*'s historical context.

Isaiah Poster exercises caution when it comes to land speculation. On Eph's return from Harvard his father initiates the son's tutelage of Bangor's "pyramid" of paper. Speculators aren't interested in land; the Maine woods represents terra incognita to them. "The Coffee House is packed all day" with speculators from Bangor to Boston "dickering for bonds," Isaiah tells Ephraim. "What's a bond?" he asks innocently. The subject has escaped his classical Harvard education. Isaiah begins his son's introduction, and the reader's as well, to Bangor's parallel economy.

Someone draws up a bond with a promise to deed land to a buyer "at a certain price a year from now, or five years or ten." A man acquires the bond, waits for the underlying land to appreciate or, more commonly, sells it to someone else. The new purchaser continues the process. In this way, bonds circulate; they are traded and also function as an alternative currency. But what happens when the original maker of the bond doesn't own the land? Someone makes quick money and leaves town. Moreover, even when land is owned, the forest is subject to risks such as sudden fire. In addition, the pine may be "concussive" (soft on the inside). Isaiah will only buy a bond if he has seen the land—hence the nearly seventy-five-year-old father's excursion into the woods that ends with his death.

Much later in the novel (the date is not clear), John Evered fills in some detail of the speculation that remains rife. He serves as the legitimate assistant agent for the Bingham estate. John explains to a visitor how debt supplies the oxygen for Bangor's speculative bubble. The visitor remarks that in Bangor "no one seems to lose money! Every seller makes a profit, or says he does." John describes how purchases are typically made with a "note"—that is, an IOU. Deeds are then sold and resold. They flood the marketplace as a form of money. Such a system is not underwritten by specie or hard money. Wildcat—or wild west—banks conspire in this devil-may-care economic system. They issue debt far in excess of the specie on hand to support it.

Shortly before the "Panic" of 1837, the nineteenth-century term for a depression, Bangor's Congregational minister delivers a jeremiad against what is happening to the city. He catalogs all the types of corruption in trade and issues the formulaic sermon's prophetic warning for "the loss and ruin and destruction sure to ensue." Bangor's bubble bursts in 1837 with the ripple effect of the federal government's withdrawal of funds from state banks. For all the detail he provides about Bangor's boom, Williams only gives a nod to its bust. The decisive Panic is only a short narrative bridge that he must cross. The Panic purged the economic excesses of the 1830s, paving the way for less explosive, sound growth. Population figures bear out Williams's thumbnail discussion. Instead of swelling by 200 percent, as the city had in the 1830s, Bangor population grew by 67 percent in the 1840s. It remained a flourishing city.

In 1846, the spring movement of lumber was disrupted and the harvest partially destroyed, when ice clogged the Penobscot two miles above Bangor. Ice jams represented another risk that speculators and investors faced. Williams clearly researched in depth what happened in 1846, for he reconstructs events in exacting, colorful detail.

The jam built up with ice that was two to three feet thick. Exhausted men using ice pokers failed to dislodge cakes that were pointing in all directions. "The air was full of a grinding, groaning noise; there was a rumbling and a squealing everywhere in the ice mass." Torches, lanterns, and bonfires illuminated the night sky as people stood on banks and on the bridge watching as nature took possession of their lives and of the lumber drive. The Penobscot and its tributaries swelled from heavy rain and melting snow "draining . . . off seven thousand square miles of wilderness." The river's water rose to historic heights and began to overflow the Penobscot's and then Kenduskeag Stream's banks. The force carried sawmills toward the sea and swept away cut lumber piled on the river's banks; new boards floated through Bangor's streets.

Part of the jam dislodges, propelling chunks of ice and more water toward Bangor. It is the middle of the night "when there came in the constant grumbling and complaining of the ice a new note; a shrill and ominous sound." Church bells ring, warning citizens to seek the safety of higher ground. "There it draws?" Elder Pittredge cries out. A "grinding roar" erupts as the "ice tumbling and cracking" wedges "solidly in the narrows below the town."

Among the places Pittredge visits to warn inhabitants is one of the more carefully managed brothels. It's the old Hager house, which Jenny rents to the madam. The moral muddle of Jenny's life spans Devil's Acre and Bangor's leading house of worship. In one of the brothel's rooms, she lies in bed. Jenny shows the elder their daughter, who is only three hours old. Pittridge is horrified. Jenny has broken the elder's final thread of self-respect. He flees, staggering and swimming through the icy waist-high water that engulfs the city. He will never surface again.

The destruction around Pittridge as he gropes his way through water and fog parallels his moral collapse. He hears the "crash" of buildings as they strike the ground. "Ice masses pound against frail, wooden walls still standing." Panicked voices fill the night.

All in all, Williams's compact description of the ice jam and its aftermath is handled skillfully. There is no question that Bangor incurred extensive damage. Yet the city appears to have recovered quickly. When Thoreau visited Bangor several months after the late March ice jam, he made no mention of its effects.

Slavery intrudes on midcentury Bangor in ways that reveal the views of Jenny, John Evered, the community, and Williams as well. A slave named Atticus escapes from Georgia on a Bangor schooner. The "darky," as the ship's captain refers to him, finds refuge on the Evereds' property. But John, ever the one to follow the law, says that he's private property and must be returned to his owner. John's position provokes an early rift with Jenny. She is an abolitionist; in fact, she's portrayed as an uncompromising radical, even fanatic abolitionist. In other words, Jenny is represented as unhinged when it comes to slavery. "I'd like to see every slave owner whipped till his back is as raw and bleeding as the lacerated backs of his miserable slaves," she tells John and her oldest son Dan. And recall her order to sons Dan and Will when they join the Union Army—to kill their two "Southern" brothers if they confront them during the Civil War.

In one sense, such tortured moralism represents the dominant side of Jenny's "strange" character. But in another sense her kind of extreme emotional makeup, with some adjustments, was commonly imputed to nineteenth-century northern abolitionism during the period when Williams wrote. Indeed, it was not until the civil rights movement that we would come to see abolitionists as more than the offspring of firebrand John Brown. Jenny, as a kind of stand-in for Brown, provokes a civil war within her family.

"Nigger lover" is inscribed on the Evereds' barn. When Atticus's slave owner tracks him down, the prevailing sentiment in Bangor seems to be for the slave's return. Attempting to resolve his moral dilemma, John offers a high price for Atticus's freedom. The owner refuses to sell. Since his arrival in Bangor, Atticus has been complaining about the cold. Williams makes much of this, which is absurd; after all, Canada was the last stop on the Underground Railroad. As to the coming winter, Atticus says, "Time it gits tuh be cold lak dat, I'm gwine wish't I'd stayed in Savannah, Gawguh." Williams presents a view of slavery as a benign institution. Dan tells his mother that Atticus claims "being a slave was just having a good master and plenty to eat and a warm cabin and having it warm weather all the time." Atticus is ready to return with his master. He praises his liege lord as a "'good man' who provides plenty to eat and a warm cabin." The two Southern brothers also write letters to Dan defending the humane slave system.

Such views were commonly held, even among academic historians, in 1941. Two years earlier, *Gone with the Wind* was a blockbuster movie; it won the Academy Award for Best Picture in 1939, over stronger competition.[9] Once again, not until the civil rights movement was the "moonlight and magnolias" view of Southern history administered the last rites. However, it was too late for Ben Ames Williams.

In the main, *The Strange Woman* was well received. The *New York Times* heaped praise on the book: "Mr. Williams has written the most original and controversial novel of his career." The reviewer suggested that Williams would reach his broadest audience to date. The *Saturday Review of Literature* agreed with the *Times*. "Mr. Williams' latest book is one of his best, and that rates it as very good, a very good story indeed." The *New Yorker* praised *The Strange Woman* "as a lively, readable piece." *Booklist* was less enthusiastic: "The style matches the heroine's emotions in flamboyant abandon."[10] The novel was reprinted in 1943 and adapted for a Hollywood movie in 1946.

When it came to Bangor's lusty age of excess, the movie was no match for Williams's often rousing and dependably realistic portrayal of Maine's pine tree capital. Bangor's tumultuous days of extravagant wealth and speculation reside in the distant past. Yet the city endures on the edge of a thinly populated frontier where pine trees far outnumber people. Moreover, Bangor's municipal seal and Paul Bunyan statue suggest how the city's frontier past remains part of its collective consciousness. Perhaps, too, as the site of Maine's first (and highly successful) gambling casino, Bangor has taken a step back toward its secular origins. Interestingly, Bangor Seminary, founded in the year *The Strange Woman* opens, has abandoned its historic campus because of dwindling enrollment. The seminary's goal of educating ministers for frontier Maine's moral uplift no longer has takers. Maine is one of the most unchurched states in the country.

ELIZABETH COATSWORTH AND THE UNINCORPORATED PLANTATION

Elizabeth Coatsworth was one of Maine's most prolific writers. Primarily the author of children's books, her *The Cat Who Went to Heaven* (1930) won the prestigious Newbery Medal. Coatsworth also published volumes of poetry as well as novels. In addition, she authored reflections on life in her adopted state such as *Country Neighborhood* (1945) and *Maine Ways* (1947). *Personal Geography: Almost an Autobiography* (1976) stands as her most intimate book. Though choppy, both in style and in the subject matter of narrating a life, *Personal Geography* nevertheless furnishes the best information on Coatsworth's solidly upper-middle-class background, elite education, and extensive travel from childhood to young womanhood.

Coatsworth was born to a highly successful grain merchant in Buffalo, New York, in 1893. Her family lived with her paternal grandmother in a house designed by the famous architect Henry Hobson Richardson. The family summered on the Canadian side of Lake Erie, in four cottages they owned. At the age of five Coatsworth traveled across Europe, England, Switzerland, Germany, and Italy. She also sailed for Egypt and explored the desert riding donkeys. "The most vivid memories are Mt. Vesuvius and Egypt," she reflected seven decades later, "so strange and so different that when I went there again twenty-five years later it was as if I had been away only a few weeks."[11] The family moved to Pasadena, California, for two years, and Elizabeth attended private school. The Coatsworths spent a month exploring Mexico, enjoyed another month on California's Catalina Island, camped in Yosemite National Park, and visited Seattle.

When the family returned home, Coatsworth attended the private Buffalo Seminary. She went on to Vassar College, graduating as salutatorian in 1915. The following year she received a master's degree from Columbia University. Then it was off to the Far East for thirteen months. Her travels included the Philippines, Indonesia, and China—the latter her most seductive destination.

Already a sophisticated cosmopolitan young woman, Coatsworth was a fledgling writer of poetry. Her first book of poems was published in 1923. In *Personal Geography*, she explained how 1929 marked a significant change in her life. (It was not because of the stock market crash.) "Travel had been my greatest joy. It continued to have a place."[12] But she met and, a year later, married Henry Beston, a Harvard graduate and the author of *The Outer House* (1926), a well-received account of his year spent in a small cottage at the edge of the ocean on Cape Cod. When they married, Elizabeth was thirty-six years old, Henry forty-one.

In 1930, Macmillan released Coatsworth's most successful children's book, *The Cat Who Went to Heaven*. A year later, Elizabeth and Henry moved to Maine. They called "Chimney Farm," on Damariscotta Lake, home for the rest of their lives. There they raised their two daughters and pursued writing careers. Henry published his much-admired observations of rural life, *Northern Farm: A Chronicle of Maine*, in 1948. By then Elizabeth had published multiple books across three genres: children's stories, adult fiction, and personal essays. Henry died in 1968 and is buried at Chimney Farm. Elizabeth continued to live at the farm with a housekeeper.[13] When she died in 1986, her body was interred next to Henry's.

Coatsworth's most important Maine works are her four "incredible tales." They were published between 1951 and 1958. The first three are set in northern Maine; the last takes place on the midcoast. Given their character as fables, the significance of Coatsworth's incredible tales extends beyond Maine. Not for nothing is *The Enchanted*, the first volume, still in print.[14]

The four tales are novellas, or "novelettes," as some critics referred to them. They contain approximately 120 pages of printed text. For lack of a better term, they represent a distinctive form of Maine "magical realism." That is, the incredible tales are firmly grounded in the subsoil of realistic detail. They also incorporate elements of the fantastical, the mythical, and the supernatural. The magical side of the incredible tales evolved from Coatsworth's writing for children and from her study of Wabanaki mythology. After the publication of the second novella, the *New York Times* claimed that Coatsworth "had created a rich, fresh medium that is at once original and yet a revival of a tradition neglected in this material age."[15]

The Enchanted is the most appealing of the incredible tales for at least two reasons. First, it is something of a mystery story involving the strange Perdry family, who periodically disappear. The novella skillfully discloses the plot at a measured pace, like the slow trot of the Perdrys' boney old horse. Second, *The Enchanted* is the most lyrical of the incredible tales. Its poetic language captures the beauty and majesty of the Enchanted forest.

We might add that the novella also suggests how *space* is transformed into *place*. "Funny how there wasn't a dog in the settlement," the protagonist reflects, "if you call three houses in a hole in the wilderness a settlement." Over time he is initiated into the local knowledge of Enchanted forest. He comes to appreciate how its majestic yet forbidding nature is also layered with human activity, artifacts, stories, and myths—all of which transmute the Enchanted into a distinctive place.

The vast majority of Mainers, not to mention vacationers, have probably never heard of Enchanted Township and don't know where it's located. The north country is simply too vast for even the native born to master its geography. One can't find Enchanted Township on most maps of Maine. Such an absence brings to mind Melville's famous observation about the pagan harpooner in *Moby-Dick*: "Queequeg was a native of Kokovo, an island far away to the West and South. It is not down on any map; true places never are."[16] We can make a less lofty argument about northern Maine's townships or plantations, as they are also called. These remote unincorporated places represent a distinctive geopolitical aspect of northern Maine. Taxes aren't collected to support local civic institutions, which don't exist. Plantations are appealing havens for libertarians.

To locate Enchanted Township, one has to rely on the granular geography of the *Maine Atlas and Gazetteer*. There one finds Upper and Lower Enchanted Townships, well west of Moosehead Lake and east of Jackman. The original hardcover of *The Enchanted* has imprinted on its front a close-up map of the township, as if to assure the reader that a place with such an unusual name actually exists. All of the geographical names Coatsworth uses in her novellas refer to places that one can locate on the atlas.

The tale takes place from spring to fall. One of the three dwellings in the plantation is a tar-paper shack; another was forsaken and has only been occupied since April. The third has been empty for two years. The owner made a good living raising and caring for lumber horses, but his wife suffered a nervous breakdown, apparently from the oppressive seclusion of the Enchanted. The township "lies in the heart of forest country and is seldom entered except by lumbermen bound for some winter logging camp from which they return with curious tales." That is to say, one who experiences Enchanted forest fails to leave unchanged—for good or for ill.

Coatsworth observes epigrammatically, "A man may step from his house intending no more than to buy shaving soap at the corner drug store and return with his life changed, or perhaps never return at all." For young Dave Ross, the protagonist, Enchanted Township represents his trip to the drugstore.

Dave and a real estate agent arrive in the Enchanted settlement to look over the once-thriving farm, the forest looming over it. "Pretty lonely here," the real estate agent tells him. But Dave seeks solitude after "living pretty close to a lot of people" for too long. He grew up an only child, with apparently emotionally distant parents, who now live in Florida. This solitary son ironically withdraws to Enchanted Plantation; yet he secretly wonders what his life would be like as a member of a large family. The Perdrys, all nine of them, have taken over the other vacant Enchanted farmhouse. When they pass by in their surrey, Dave automatically and repeatedly assumes the family is French Canadian. Such a hasty judgment may be taken as more than a stereotype. It's a reminder of his conflicted self. Presumably a large French-Canadian-like family is what he secretly yearns for. The identity of the strange family that dwells with Dave in the hole in the wilderness serves as *The Enchanted*'s sustaining mystery.

After he purchases the farm for a paltry sum, Dave devotes his time to the wearisome work of restoring the property from the ravages of neglect. He makes preliminary arrangements with a lumbering company to raise and board horses. He is too busy and then too exhausted to visit his nearest neighbor, who lives in the Enchanted's tar-paper shack. His name is John "Chip" Chandler. He was born in the woods and spent his working life there as a blacksmith. Now retired, he is a repository of fantastic tales about Enchanted forest. In other words, he's an insider, a bearer of local knowledge. Chip will introduce Dave to the Enchanted forest's magical elements. The blacksmith will chip away at Dave's city-born skepticism.

Dave's gathering curiosity about the Perdrys leads him to Chip's doorstep. The solitary old man turns out to be talkative. He warns Dave to "watch your step" when it comes to the Perdrys. Chip disabuses Dave of the notion that they are French Canadian. "I don't think they call themselves French Canadians." Again he cautions Dave, "Just go slow" in dealing with the Perdrys. Rather than diminish Dave's interest in the family, Chip's words only fuel his growing fixation on the Perdrys.

The aged blacksmith then warms to the subject he knows most keenly—Enchanted forest. "Boy, the first growth spruce I've seen back in the Enchanted! And pines. They rise up like they'd never stop." The sheer abundance of the Enchanted has apparently spared majestic original growth timberland. Dave will eventually venture into this sort of fairyland forest. If he doesn't emerge transformed like, say, Hawthorne's young Goodman Brown, he will walk out of the wilderness with a new knowledge of the plausible and fantastical events that have come to define the Enchanted as a distinctive place.

"There's plenty of reasons for the name," Chip tells Dave. "Queer things happen in all the woods, things no one would believe who hadn't been there." The Dead River disappears before it surfaces again. Yet it can be heard "like water singing" before the river reappears. "The men generally work together," spooked by the loud voices they hear.

Dave receives such talk as so much dross. In turn, Chip has an audience after living through the winter with his dog and chickens, with no one else in the settlement. The blacksmith sounds out Dave: "I suppose you wouldn't call it queer if you chased a buck into a thicket and it came out the other side a black bear?" Coatsworth draws on traditional Native belief to enrich the lore that lumbermen acquire over a lifetime in the woods and that endows the Enchanted as a storied place. All creatures embody spirit; some change form.

In *Mountain Bride* (1958), the third incredible tale, Pamola, a bird-spirit of Wabanaki mythology, appears. He is an eagle who is part man, part moose. Pamola can also take other animal forms. He serves as a guardian of Mount Katahdin's summit, where a treacherous peak along the "knife edge" bears his name. As Thoreau observes in *The Maine Woods*, invoking Native belief, "Pomola [*sic*] is always angry with those who climb to the summit of Katahdin."[17]

Both *The Enchanted* and *Mountain Bride* are steeped in Native mythology. Lumbermen and the Native trappers they know in the woods "don't explain things your way," Chip informs Dave. He goes on to relate a long story of a skilled Native hunter who for family reasons tracks moose for three days to a clearing in a woods. He strikes his tomahawk in a tree, hangs up his snowshoes, and begs the moose to become one of them. His wish is granted. "Nice legend,"

Dave tells Chip, who doesn't know what the word means. From the Enchanted, Chip has formed a kinship with Native people. He's unwilling to divide the world between the mythical and the real. Of the story, Dave asserts, legend means it's a fairy tale. "You'll find yourself in the middle of one of them legends if you don't look out." Chip's final words will prove prophetic.

Dave gathers his lantern and leaves for home. The light against the Enchanted's immense darkness unnerves Dave, suggesting how Chip has sparked his imagination, given a glimmer to his sense of place. During the spring weeks he has labored unremittingly, followed with evenings consumed by fatigue. Now, as he walks home, he muses on Enchanted forest's name and feels its presence: "The Enchanted. The name cast its own spell. Mile after mile, the woods lay about him, closing him in, impenetrable and as far as he knew pathless. Not a lighted window, not another lantern broke its darkness; not a human sound broke its silences. . . . But were the woods sleeping?" Even as he labors during the day Dave feels, though he can't see, the Enchanted's mountain. The wilderness shields the mountain from view. Nor can the flatlander visualize it through his forested imagination.

Dave finally meets the mysterious Perdry family in early summer. They raise no farm animals to feed their large family. In fact, they only own old "Blackie," the horse left behind to starve to death, which miraculously survived the long winter. One morning, while Dave shingles his barn roof, the Perdrys arrive in their surrey. The three boys and their father jump out, mount the roof, and start to assist Dave. The four girls and their mother go directly into the house. Dave has seen the girls picking berries, which they are especially fond of consuming—the first hint of the Perdrys' identity.

On the roof the father introduces the brothers. But Dave has difficulty telling them apart—they look so similar with their roundish bodies. The Perdrys work facilely, without the need for conversation. "A sixth sense told" them if "one needed more shingles or nails," Dave observes. Small wild animals take notice of the Perdrys when they are outside, typically freezing in place. Hints of their identity emerge over the course of the Perdrys' visit. The astute reader is a step or two ahead of Dave. He remains chained to his clichés. "They must be French Canadians." Then he surmises, "they might be part Indian."

When it's time for a midday meal, Dave and the Perdrys enter the house, and he is surprised with how Mama Perdry and her daughters have domesticated and feminized the interior. They have scoured the rooms and added flowers and fragrances to them. The baked beans and biscuits give a homey aroma to the farmhouse. Tellingly, in the midst of a jovial meal, a chair crashes to the floor upstairs. The startled Perdrys jump and shove away from the table. Apparently they take the noise for a gunshot—yet another intimation of who they are.

The four daughters look like their brothers. They're egg shaped and difficult to distinguish from each other. Dave singles out Molly, his future wife, by the leaves and flower she wears in her hair. He is overwhelmed by the fellowship that envelops him. The Perdrys' family harmony and neighborliness clash with his libertarian-leaning view of life that led him to the Enchanted in the first place: "He had seen human beings as isolated creatures facing the surrounding universe . . . alone, now carried along on the sunlit current of individual life, now struggling and drowning in its back flood." Increasingly drawn into the Perdrys' orbit, Dave thinks he has found the large, convivial family for whom he has secretly yearned. He overlooks the Perdrys' quirks and discards Chip's advice to exercise caution with them. Instead, the Perdrys "elect Dave an honorary member" of their flock.

Midsummer arrives. With no farm animals, the Perdrys have no need of haying. Instead, they burn their fields to foster the growth of blueberries. Then the family disappears.

Dave begins harvesting his hay. At the end of a long day, he spies Chip sitting on the stone step in front of his shack. Dave decides to pay him a visit, hoping to extract information about the Perdrys. The Enchanted's splendor towers over the two figures as dusk begins its slow descent, lending singular splendor to the setting. "Above the forest the evening sky was almost white, but not white enough to quite dim the brilliance of the planet quivering low over the tree tops like a single drop of dew." Such recurring poetic language engages the reader perhaps as much as the mystery of the Perdrys.

Dave prods Chip, hoping the old blacksmith will reveal what he knows about the family. But Dave has already set aside Chip's advice to exercise vigilance when it comes to the strange neighbors. He has visited them a few times, and he and Molly are in love. Chip muddles the enigma surrounding the Perdrys: "They live mostly on tea and bread and what berries the girls pick. Ever since they come here in April." Dave believes that the Enchanted has made Chip "cracked" about the head. He has yet to venture into the Enchanted forest with "its almost unknown ponds and mountains, vast groves and its streams which disappeared and were lost to sight." Someday, Dave thought, he will find the time to explore the Enchanted, yet "not for long enough to go crazy" like Chip. Still, the blacksmith's stories serve as prologue to Dave's eventual encounter with the Enchanted, under Molly's tutelage.

On his way home, he sees a light in the Perdrys's house and discovers they have returned as undetected as when they left. He and Molly kiss and vow to be married. The Perdrys welcome the addition of a "son" to their family, giving them the symmetry of four boys and girls. Dave feels as if "he were marrying all the Perdrys, Molly in particular, but still all of them."

They are wed in late summer, and for their honeymoon the couple sets out on a camping trip for a few days in the Enchanted forest. In many respects, this excursion represents Dave's initiation into the Enchanted as a place and not simply as formidable space. The Enchanted has overshadowed all of his industry in fashioning a well-groomed pastoral outpost with the forest "walling in his sunlit fields." The sunrise "became caught in the darkness of its high pines." Night arrived "earlier because of the forest." Once Molly and Dave enter the forest, Coatsworth's writing becomes the most lyrical in *The Enchanted*.

The four-day camping outing has the aura of an archetypical fairy tale. It's sort of a rite of passage to a new level of knowledge. Molly knows the terrain as reliably as a creature of the forest; in actuality, she is one. No wonder her senses are on constant alert as her "sleek head turns from side to side." She all but leads Dave by the hand. He is apprehensive. For Dave, a city boy, the Enchanted rekindles Chip's strange stories. Unbeknownst to him, long before they arrive at the falls, "like hot silver pouring between black rocks," Molly has heard its "music." On the way they come upon a clearing, the site of an old lumber camp. All that remains of the human hand are crumbling foundation stones, an apple tree, and lilacs. Nevertheless, these markers inscribe human activity on the landscape; they reveal stories about place.

Molly and Dave establish their camp at the head of the falls, under a pine with "its roots getting their hardy living from cracks and crannies of the stone." Though they are only on the outer edge of the forest, they feel its weight, its immensity, and how it's "profoundly non-human." The early darkness redoubles the Enchanted's gravity. Molly doesn't want to be left alone; she knows the wilderness too well.

The next day Dave stumbles on new lumbering artifacts that tell stories, which give material shape to the Enchanted's history and help create a sense of place. Dave discovers rubber boots nailed to a tree. Molly, his interpreter, demystifies what they have chanced upon. The boots mark a lumberman's grave. It is not uncommon for them to perish by drowning when the logs are driven down rivers in the spring. Molly has seen boots throughout the Enchanted. But Judson Platt, the name on a simple marker, didn't fall victim to the river; rather, the Enchanted forest itself ensnared him, according to history or legend or some hybrid of the two. Like a giant pine, the story's taproot is difficult to determine. Judson Platt "heard a voice calling him which none of the others heard," Molly tells Dave. He became separated from the lumbermen. Once a snowstorm started, Platt couldn't be traced. "Some people say he went crazy. But it was the voice of the Enchanted."

Dave and Molly remain at camp on the last day of their outing. They sit resting against "their" pine tree's trunk, almost spellbound by the Enchanted. They stare into the water, "always new water flowing by," with "ripples of light, yet always essentially the same stream catching the sunlight in the same net of motion." After hours of tranquility, they both turn restless. Molly misses her family. Dave's thoughts drift to his farm. His masculine mind conjures up a set of pastoral images, a counterpoise to the forest's untamed nature. Dave thought "of the fields he had cleared and the shine of the new shingles in the morning sunlight, and the broad backs of horses, and the plowing he meant to begin."

The Enchanted jumps to autumn. Molly is pregnant, with the baby's arrival set for the spring. One day Dave and Chip set out for the Forks, a real Maine place and "accidental sort of town," where the Kennebec and Dead rivers intersect in West Forks Plantation. It is adjacent to Enchanted Plantation. Molly has no interest in towns of any size. Dave is on a mission to purchase a mare for his growing stable of lumbering horses. He returns with a tomcat that unnerves Molly, who protects herself with a broom. It is the first of two incidents that drive Molly back to her family.

Ed Jordan, the manager of the lumbering company, arrives unannounced. He wants to inspect Dave's farm and the progress he has made acquiring reliable horses. Jordan is invited to stay for supper. Dave beheads three young chickens, tosses them in the sink, and tells Molly to broil them. She is horrified. The Perdrys don't consume animal flesh. Molly even objected to eating trout that Dave caught on their camping trip. He is not unwilling but unable to make sense of the cumulative evidence of Molly's alternative incarnation. She flees to her family rather than prepare the chickens. When the men return from rambling over the farm, it's Chip who has broiled the chickens.

In October, the Perdrys, including Molly, melt away once again. Even Chip never tires of the Enchanted's beauty at that time of year. He stares "at the woods, whose outer wall shone in lemon and bronze and scarlet and rich pine green in the sunlight across the fields." Yet in the midst of all this brightness, "shadows lay forever unpierced not twenty feet from open land." Such beauty of light and darkness seems lost on Dave. He is now obsessed with the Perdrys, but Chip will not answer his questions and pare back the family's mystery.

A stranger appears with a dog to hunt for partridge. As Dave works in his fields, he hears three quick shots. When the hunter drives out, Dave asks him about his luck. It was "rotten," the man replies. "I started one covey and I'm sure I winged a bird, but it got away." Now Dave will learn what has been increasingly under his nose over the course of the plot.

He returns to the house, and all the Perdrys are there. Molly rushes into his arms; there will be no more tacking between forms of life. Jasper's arm is bandaged and in a sling. In a flash, the Perdry peculiarities since the spring cohere. "What did you do to yourself, Jasper?" Dave asks, anticipating the answer. "I stopped some birdshot," Jasper replies. "A fool was shooting down in the alders and didn't see me coming up the path." The Perdrys form a partridge covey! Perhaps translating Coatsworth's example of magical realism into a more recent idiom, we might ask: What do partridge really want? Or, alternatively, what is the hidden life of partridge? Or, most important, it would seem, what can we humans learn from partridge? We might also ask: Can indigenous mythology still inspire interesting Maine and American literature?

The Enchanted was generally well received. The *New York Times* reviewer expressed enthusiasm for the book: "In less skilled hands this might have been a half-baked fairy story, sloshed with overwriting." But Coatsworth "drags the reader into her own acceptance of the strangeness of all nature. . . . *The Enchanted* is not only a beautiful [story], but one which is essentially believable." The *Library Journal* praised the book's evocative descriptions "of farm and woods life, of gentle people." The *Christian Science Monitor* welcomed *The Enchanted* as "a happy fantasy for the discerning reader, reminiscent of certain tales of childhood." *Kirkus Reviews* was more tepid: *The Enchanted* was "a pleasant reading experience if you are addicted to Maine ways and fairy tale surprises."[18] A year after its release, the novella was published in London.

For all of their appeal, the incredible tales did not suit everyone's taste in an age of Cold War, McCarthyism, existentialism, Freudianism, and the struggle for civil rights. None of the four novellas achieved the status of, say, *Catcher in the Rye* (1951) or *On the Road* (1957). Yet the follow-up volumes to *The Enchanted* were again commercially successful and noted for their distinctiveness by reviewers. They widened Coatsworth's depiction of Maine's remote north country.

Silky (1953), the second novella, is distinguished by its stark portrayal of northern Maine poverty.[19] It also incorporates supernatural interventions. Cephas Hewes lives in the backcountry of the Mills, a speck of an apparently unincorporated town where lumber was once transported to sawmills. Lumber companies have heavily denuded the landscape. Cephas's farm is on the verge of financial collapse. All around him are abandoned farmhouses that are sinking into their cellars. Cephas's own house, built well over a hundred years earlier, is rotting around him. Ceilings are collapsing from a leaking roof, rats infest part of the house, and the exterior badly needs painting and extensive repairs. Cephas has few skills. Moreover, he suffers from depression.

Adding to his gloom, Cephas's wife of thirteen years, Verda, is expecting their fourth child. She was once beautiful, as he was tall and handsome. But Verda has grown "fleshy" and turned into a slatternly housewife who has capitulated to the hopelessness of their lives. "Somebody help me!" Cephas cries out. Soon he has trouble keeping the gate to the family burial ground closed. He is on the fast track to his own emotional graveyard.

Shortly after Cephas utters his pleas for help, a mysterious young girl appears; she has long straight hair like silk. The reader later learns that a distant relative of Cephas, who had constructed the house, lost his only child, a young daughter, to illness. She is buried in the family plot.

"Silky" has temporarily come back to life. She rescues Cephas and Verda. In a crisis, without a doctor or Cephas present, she delivers Verda's baby girl, who will be named Silky. The mysterious young girl never appears again, and the gate to the burial ground remains shut. Silky leaves behind a way for Cephas to relieve his poverty. Her father had built a library of first editions of famous works that he ordered directly from London. They are now highly valuable. Cephas only learns this when one of his children, at Silky's suggestion, looks at the books and takes one to her distant school. The sale of a few books will more than solve Cephas's financial problems. He and Verda even rekindle their love. The novella has too much of a storybook (or a children's book) ending: They lived happily ever after.

Silky's strength resides in its grim portrait of northern rural poverty rather than in a lyrical representation of nature, as in *The Enchanted. Mountain Bride* (1954) resembles more the latter than the former.[20] The novella is set at the foot of Mount Katahdin. There are wonderful descriptions of the mountains shifting moods: "like a specter Katahdin appeared against the sky, rising above the countless trees that before had hidden it. The rains had washed the granite slopes bare, but still the crevices were white with the winter's snow, and on this the light of the unseen moon shone and glittered coldly." Katahdin towers over the lives of the main characters.

Pete Fournier serves as a park ranger and lives year-round in a log house at the foot of the mountain. He is part Native American. He possesses superior hearing and the power of presentiment. Coatsworth imputes these abilities to his Native blood. She does the same with Pete's daughter and granddaughter, who have wild streaks and naturalness, like Katahdin's feral state. Coatsworth's essentializing of Native people represents a problem with *Mountain Bride*. It is as if anyone with "Indian" blood will never get lost in the woods.

Ethel Fournier, Pete's wife, is no woodsy person. She stays inside and copes with her isolation through obsessive crocheting and constantly reading her Bible. Sylvie, their seventeen-year-old daughter, has been missing for nearly two weeks at the beginning of the story. Her parents fear that she has run off to be married. When she returns, Pete and Ethel press her to reveal whether she is married and to whom. She is cryptic, coughing up the name "Ola," which is part of Pamola. Drawing on a story her father used to tell her, and partly out of curiosity, she repeated an appeal to Pamola to come to her in her loneliness. The Native spirit appeared and took Sylvie to his cave on Katahdin's summit. However, she doesn't reveal any of this to her parents.

Shortly after Sylvie's return, she tells her parents that she's pregnant. Sylvie and her daughter Claire live in the Fournier household as time races forward and the daughter of Pamola is ten years old. Claire embraces life in the shadow of Katahdin. Over those years, Pamola appears in different guises, including a traveling French-Canadian salesman and a dog, at first friendly and then vicious.

Finally, Sylvie and Pamola meet at a site where deer go to die. He pleads with her to return with him to his cave. She resists, and Pamola leaves her with a long red mark shaped like lightning that covers the side of her head and face.

More than the first two incredible tales, *Mountain Bride* is a dated work. Nevertheless, beyond its literary merit as a four-season depiction of Katahdin, the novella serves as an exploration of Wabanaki spiritual beliefs that make Katahdin a Native sacred place. What other major Maine writer, we might ask to Coatsworth's credit, has set a work of fiction at Katahdin, cloaked in awesome nature and legend? From a Wabanaki perspective, however, *Mountain Bride* and *The Enchanted*, to a lesser extent, represent acts of cultural appropriation.

CATHIE PELLETIER AND "MATTAGASH": THE NORTH'S NORTH

Say *Allagash* to most southern Mainers, at least, and the name will most likely call to mind a popular, locally brewed craft beer. Allagash is also the name of a microscopic town—a cartographic pinprick—engulfed by forest on the Canadian border. Between 1986 and 1991 Cathie Pelletier burst onto the national literary scene as the epic novelist who poured twelve hundred words into a teacup, a far-off town of several hundred residents with a rapidly dwindling population.

Though she has cultivated a following, Pelletier remains perhaps insufficiently appreciated within her home state and inadequately recognized in contemporary American literature despite widespread and favorable reviews of her novels. They are far more than humorous postcards from the edge of Maine. The Mattagash trilogy, where she established her literary bona fides, brings together dark humor and tragedy as well as compassion for many of her characters' predicaments. She adds a distinctive literary voice to Maine letters and to recent American literature in general.

Yet Carolyn Chute, Pelletier's contemporary, became a national sensation with *The Beans of Egypt, Maine* one year before the first Mattagash novel. Moreover, Chute herself attracted extensive press interest in the way she lived and the persona she presented to curious big-city interviewers: a member in good standing of the overlooked rural down and out in the age of Ronald Reagan. (See the next chapter.) With two more novels over the next ten years after *The Beans*, Chute seemingly overshadowed Pelletier as an original indigenous voice from Maine's social and geographical margins. Still, Pelletier deserves recognition for her own achievements, which include an adept portrayal of an impoverished rural family that is sharply different from Chute's Beans. One might also argue that, on the whole, Pelletier has had a more productive literary career than Chute.

Pelletier was born in Allagash in 1953, the youngest of six children. Her father, a lumberjack who ran his own business, was a French-Canadian Catholic. Her mother was Scots-Irish and Protestant. Pelletier grew up in the Protestant Church. She showed her keen intelligence in school, skipping both the sixth grade and her senior year of high school. At sixteen she enrolled at the University of Maine at Fort Kent, approximately twenty-five miles from Allagash. The following year, she was expelled for what she now describes as "childish insubordination and campus pranks."[21] Violating curfew and pulling a fire alarm reflected her early rebelliousness.

With a friend, she then hitchhiked around the country, traveling through Tennessee. She felt some bond with the state. "I knew I'd come back to live there," she has written. "The South spoke to me. It's that simple."[22] Of course, it's not that simple, for she has never authored a book about the South, though her songwriting may have provided an outlet for her regional sentiments. All of her twelve novels are set in Maine. She wrote two of these under the pseudonym K. C. McKinnon. The McKinnons were one of the founding families and longtime community leaders of Allagash. Many townspeople are related to this local royalty, including Pelletier. The McKinnons are a pivotal family in the Mattagash novels.

After three months of hitchhiking, Pelletier returned to Allagash. The university readmitted her, and she graduated in 1976. Pelletier then set out for Nashville. She hoped to carve out a career in songwriting. She also briefly studied creative writing at Vanderbilt. Pelletier had already authored a book of poetry, *Widows Walk* (1976), published by the University of New Brunswick. At Vanderbilt she was encouraged to write fiction. Several years would pass before she took up this advice.

Pelletier remained in Nashville for thirty years; during much of that time she lived with a country music star. The transplanted Mainer experienced modest success as a songwriter. But beginning in the mid-1980s Pelletier's turn to fiction yielded fruit. Within five years she published three novels with arresting titles: *The Funeral Makers* (1986); *Once upon a Time on the Banks* (1989); and *The Weight of Winter* (1991).[23] The first Mattagash novel was a "notable *New York Times* book of the year." The third won the New England Booksellers Award. Then Pelletier shifted to another Maine town before she returned to Mattagash in 2005 with the publication of *Running with the Bulls*, which won the Paterson Prize for Fiction. Of all the Mattagash novels, Pelletier considers *One-Way Bridge* (2013) her best.[24]

According to Pelletier, *The Funeral Makers* was written five years before it was released. She had no knowledge of Chute, who had been publishing short stories. She disavows any influence from Chute, and her novels bear out this contention.[25]

Pelletier is Maine's northernmost successful literary novelist with a national audience. Her two McKinnon novels were mass audience romances written under a pen name, apparently to safeguard her literary reputation. The first, *During the Harvest Moon* (1997), sold well, and Pelletier received a million-dollar advance for *Candles on Bay Street* (1998), which was translated into ten languages and adapted for a movie.[26]

In 2013, Pelletier moved back to Allagash with her husband. She returned to care for her ninety-three-year-old father. She now resides in the house he built along the St. John River. Allagash's population of approximately two hundred stands at a historic low, a steady fall over the decades from its high of 680 in 1950. There were 480 Allagashers in 1970, when Pelletier was booted from the university. By any measure, then, the real town, like the fictional Mattagash, has always been a backwoods village.[27]

Pelletier has said that she "keep[s] a map of town as I work so I can remember which characters live where."[28] A childhood friend, who has also moved back to Allagash, says of Pelletier's characters, "I know all these people."[29] To such comments, Pelletier has a writerly response: "Even if I started with a real person, the character often takes over and creates his or her own life."[30] Further-more, Pelletier doesn't see herself as strictly a Maine writer, a latter-day local colorist. She has said that all of her novels have "the same message, that we're all just human beings doing our best while affected by our environments."[31] Yet that environment is often so particularized, even miniaturized, in the Mattagash novels that perhaps it gnaws at Pelletier's quest for a kind of universal human-ism. One finds unpersuasive her claim that in the novels "the only thing I relied upon is the Allagash wit, the old Irish wit."[32]

Since Pelletier maps a real geography, unchanged except for most names, onto the fictional town, it's helpful to fix Allagash's coordinates before examin-ing her novels. The town lies well north of Quebec City. Allagash is a woodsy hamlet at the top of Maine, 340 miles from Portland, or more than six hours driving time. Two hundred and thirteen miles separate Allagash from Bangor; most of that stretch consists of forested terrain. One reaches the border town of Fort Kent, the largest community near Allagash, with a population of ap-proximately twenty-five hundred. A narrow, winding twenty-five-mile road, filled with frost heaves and potholes in Pelletier's fictional world, connects to the lumbering town. Allagash-Mattagash geography represents a sequestered, bracing "environment" of the hardy, the entrapped, or those such as Pelletier who flee or long to leave a remote town on the skids.

The Funeral Makers raises the curtain on Mattagash in 1959. *Once upon a Time on the Banks* is set ten years later. *The Weight of Winter* assesses the state of af-fairs in Mattagash in 1989. I'm going to focus on *The Funeral Makers*, arguably the best of the trilogy. But I'm going to draw on all three of the initial Mattagash novels. They compose a saga of an isolated lumbering crossroads in sharp de-cline that survives, against the odds. Pelletier views her characters through the prism of a literary imagination that fuses gallows humor, hijinks, tragedy, and social history, not quite in equal parts.

Thus the novels have continuity well beyond the ongoing inability of women to scrub pine and spruce tar from their lumberjack husbands' clothes. It is as if they can't eradicate some original sin. Pelletier provides a dollop of Allagash-Mattagash history that suggests what happened in the beginning to set the town a bit off-center.

During the 1830s, settlers made their way to what would become Mattagash. They were Scots-Irish Protestants from New Brunswick. Pelletier makes con-tinual references in the three novels to the Irish brogue or "country twang" that one can still hear in Mattagash, but she fails to bring the reader within earshot of this local inflection. She is less hesitant when it comes to re-creating Canuck speech in *Once upon a Time on the Banks*, with its characters from "Frog Town" (Fort Kent).

The first migrants were loyalists; they supported the king of England. They settled on land they believed belonged to Canada. The state of Maine contested this claim. Both jurisdictions coveted the miles of valuable virgin forest that enclosed the future Mattagash. Maine constructed Fort Kent and Fort Fairfield to secure its interest. The federal government settled the so-called Aroostook War, by treaty, in 1842. Maine received most of what it claimed. With a scratch of the pen, the loyalist pioneers found themselves wedged into Maine.[33] In short, Mattagash originated in a geographical miscalculation.

The town grew from the founders' offspring and their progeny, though some French Canadians and Irish Catholics also later settled in Mattagash. The McKinnons, a founding family, became local civic leaders. Given the town's size, over generations the founders' seed became mixed with that of people who couldn't trace their genealogy back to Mattagash's origins. As a consequence of intermarriage, many townspeople became "genetically linked like paper dolls."

Mattagash's birth and development serve as more than historical background to the novels. The past often bursts into the foreground. Other elements help unify the trilogy. The subject of how Mattagashers imagine their town spatially recurs. First of all, they think of themselves as living at "Maine's North Pole" or "next door to the North Pole," as a character observes in *The Weight of Winter*. Throughout the trilogy the seasons are frustrating, even painful for their brevity or intensity—that is, for the lopsidedness of nature. Winter has moxie in Mattagash.

When they live so far in the real and imagined magnetic north, how do Mattagashers conceive of Maine's south? A character in *The Weight of Winter* refers to "down in faraway Bangor," where the nearest English television station broadcasts. In *The Funeral Makers*, Old Man Gardner notes, "When the birds go south I'm satisfied they winter somewhere down around Bangor." The comment is humorous. Still, it suggests how north and south are imagined relationally, especially in a provincial village where the trees "saw a lot more of the world than the people did."

Or consider Portland, "where there is a rare book store on every block," as it's described in *The Funeral Makers*. The city registers differently from Bangor on Mattagashers' mental map. They view remote Portland through a glass, darkly, as "a city in that part of the state." Maine's "metropolis" could be Boston, or even New York, for all they think.

From the opposite angle, Portlanders in the novel have their own perspective on the north. When the visiting funeral maker from Portland discovers a stolen car in Mattagash that belongs to his son, he's appalled to learn that the nearest police are thirty miles away. "He was relieved to be a southerner," the father reflects. Resentment and even revulsion between the visiting Portlanders and Mattagashers gives starch to the plot and subplots in *The Funeral Makers* and *Once upon a Time on the Banks*. In *The Funeral Makers*, the McKinnons and the Ivys (the latter from Portland) gather in Mattagash as Marge McKinnon lies on her deathbed. She is only fifty-nine and has led a tragic life. Marge is far from the only poor soul in the family who suffers from depression. Her father was a fanatic minister-missionary. Traveling missionaries occasionally stayed with the McKinnons. Marge fell for a handsome, eloquent preacher who seduced her and led her to believe they would marry. When her father exposed the visitor as no minister, as nothing but a married con man with children in Portland, it crushed Marge. She donned the veil of celibacy for the rest of her life, living on a diet of Chinese tea and polished rice.

Circumstances forced Marge, as the oldest daughter, to assume responsibility for her two younger sisters, Pearl and Sicily. Their mother died within days of giving birth to her last child. Then her father strode off to China to save souls and contracted a deadly disease. After her sisters married, Marge lived a solitary life in the McKinnon homestead.

The youngest McKinnon daughter, forty-six-year-old Sicily, is married in misery to Ed Lawler, principal of the grammar school. The marriage originated in a deception, just like the founding of Mattagash. Sicily led Ed to believe that she was pregnant. He had to marry her and resented it for the rest of his life. Ed also thinks of himself as an utter failure. Who would want to preside over a school in the far North Woods where one committeeman thinks a bachelor's degree means someone who is not married? Ed suffers from acute depression, which manifests itself in his beer-guzzling, chain-smoking habits. He possesses a sharp and sometimes morbid sense of humor. His in-laws, the Ivys of Portland, are undertakers—"funeral directors," they keep correcting the other family members. Ed has nothing but contempt for them. He tells Sicily, "You don't need me there to listen to the death freaks from Portland lick their lips and plan a funeral as though it was their dinner."

The funeral makers from Portland establish the novel's unresolved tension between the big lights from the city and the backwoods people of Mattagash, who don't even have running hot water yet. In fact, many Mattagashers still use outhouses. One local resident offers a backwater philosophic rationale for his outhouse: "People got no business shittin' in their house." He leaves his outhouse without frills. Some Mattagashers, however, take pride in their structures as if they were bathrooms: "Women painted them bright colors and planted flowers about the door, laid bricks in the earth path for a cobblestone effect, or painted two discarded tires white and sank them into the ground where they became a gateway for an outside path." In other words, the appearances of outhouses in Mattagash inscribe differences in rank and the strength of a family's aspiration to eventually defecate in their house.

In a kind of repudiation of Mattagash, Pearl McKinnon, the second oldest of the sisters, had set off for Portland at the age of eighteen in the quest for better prospects (economic and marital) than her Mattagash hometown had to offer. She met Marvin Ivy, who was studying to become a lawyer. But he found the work too challenging and turned to the funeral business instead. Pearl promptly suffered a nervous breakdown.

By the time the family returns to Mattagash, Pearl, now fifty, and Marvin have a grown son, Marvin Ivy Jr. He joins his father in the business of caring for their "house guests," as Marvin Sr. refers to embalmed corpses. Junior is a slovenly womanizer; his wife, Thelma, is brought low from what appears to be neurasthenia, and she devours Valium in place of liquor.

Marvin Sr. transports his trade to Mattagash in more ways than one. Sicily Lawler fears shaking his hand, knowing what he does to the departed. People imagine that poor Marvin's clothes have absorbed the chemicals of his trade; he transmits the rancid odor of death. His profession is engraved on his frozen stone face.

But the most important tension between Mattagashers and the Portland mourners resides with Pearl Ivy, one of their own who has become urbanized. "What must Pearl think each time she comes home," Sicily reflects defensively. "She must feel like that Margaret Mead when she stepped off that boat into that litter of natives." Mattagash has no funeral home. The nearest is in Watertown. Pearl tells Sicily how Portlanders "would think it a really barbaric and strange custom to wake a loved one at home." From Junior's spacious new Packard to their up-to-date city mortuary practices, the Ivys represent the social distance between Portland and Mattagash.

Interestingly, daughter-in-law Thelma Ivy, trapped in a mutually loathsome relationship with Junior's mother, vows to tell "all of Portland," now that she had seen Mattagash, how her mother-in-law had treated her so wretchedly. What could one expect given "how shabbily Pearl had been raised in a town of rusting chainsaws, pulp hooks, and a family of nitwits"? The return of the native does not mean her Mattagash ways are safely sealed in a mason jar back in Portland, however. Pearl sometimes drops her guard and reverts to Mattagash type. In *Once upon a Time*, for example, she "sipped her milk loudly. She was no longer in Portland, Maine. She could guzzle as she pleased."

The Giffords enrich *The Funeral Makers*'s gallery of characters who are simultaneously realistic and comically or tragically off-kilter. The Giffords consist of three generations of family living under patriarch Bert's roof. They include a thirty-one-year-old grandmother. Bert and his thirty-two-year-old son, Chester Lee, embody what Karl Marx referred to as the "lumpenproletariat," the lowest level of workers, often engaged in petty crime, who lack class consciousness. Bert does some part-time guiding of canoers and hikers during the summer. Chester Lee, whose five brothers are in the penitentiary, fails to hold a job in the woods for any length of time. Bert fakes a back injury to collect a monthly government check, and the husband-less Gifford women receive welfare. The Giffords are strikingly different survivors from Carolyn Chute's Beans.

Bert and Chester Lee supplement the family income through thievery. Albert Pinkham, the oddball owner of a four-room motel, says he attached it to his house so that the Giffords wouldn't carry it away. Bert bequeaths his "back problems" and thievery to the next generation of Giffords. By *The Weight of Winter*, Pike, Bert's son, embodies his father's moral defects; he also adds alcoholism and domestic abuse to the Giffords' rap sheet.

In *The Funeral Makers*, Chester Lee has cultivated a relationship with fourteen-year-old Amy Joy Lawler. She is the daughter of Ed and Sicily McKinnon Lawler. Pudgy and pimply Amy Joy mistakes her infatuation with Chester Lee for true love. He has an unflinching justification for pursuing a fourteen-year-old: "Hell, it ain't like I got a bushel to pick from." But his predatory relationship also stems from another motive. He possesses "the means to bring the House of McKinnons crashing to the ground," especially if he forces Amy Joy to live in the Giffords' "menagerie." One might argue that Chester Lee nurtures a kind of class consciousness. Primitive resentment and revenge drive him, however; he possesses no feelings of solidarity with Mattagash's working class. Whatever latent class consciousness he may harbor, it is not the type that advances the interest of workers. In the end, Chester Lee will conquer not one but two McKinnons. That represents his personal class triumph.

Mattagash's American Legion Hall, once the scene of lively Saturday night dances, stands abandoned with peeling paint and an unsecured door. It serves as a stark signifier of the town's decline. Chester Lee has set up his dank den in the basement among spiders and mice feces and the reek of mildew. A thin mattress forms a twin bed, with a folded woolen coat as a pillow. An overturned potato barrel makes a bedside table. In the sordid bowels of the patriotic hall, Chester Lee steals Amy Joy's virginity.

Yet a more momentous triumph is to come. Chester Lee retreats to the hall for more than sex; it's also a place of escape from Mattagash's scrutiny. Sicily knows that Amy Joy has been spending time there. She climbs down the stairs to rescue her daughter. Chester Lee is alone. He begins to sweet-talk Sicily among the "boxes of newspapers and pamphlets that had melded together [and] gave off the aroma of basement living." Growing up, Sicily's older sisters dispossessed her of a sense of self-worth, even as a McKinnon. She has been love starved with Ed for decades. Now the forty-six-year-old stands emotionally naked and needy before a lowlife Gifford, who tells her how beautiful she looks. A few more words of flattery, and Sicily finds herself on a filthy mattress with outer garments and undergarments removed. Pride soon filled the "Gifford household that one of their own had scaled the McKinnon walls."

Still, Chester Lee pursues another conquest that leads to his demise. While Marge is dying, Amy Joy has been sleeping at her house; she makes a lame attempt to help care for her aunt. Now emboldened by his sexual conquests, Chester Lee finds "something about crawling between the whiteness of McKinnon sheets in a McKinnon house as a challenge any true Gifford would take up." He climbs into Amy's room and begins setting upon a surprisingly spindly body. It's Junior's wife Thelma, who awakens and yells, "Rape!" Gifford flees, steals Junior's Packard, and heads toward Watertown, where he can turn and make his escape south on the highway. He plows into two deer; the Packard crashes into trees. Chester Lee meets his end.

This death is one of three that take place in rapid succession. They suggest how, for all its humor, *The Funeral Makers* is also a novel about tragedy, about the end of things: the "fleeting" summer (when the events occur), the Lawlers' marriage, Amy Joy's innocence, the decade, and Violet La Forge's last hope.

She is a stripper performing in Watertown and a prostitute in Mattagash. Violet's real name is Beth Thatcher, and she comes from a small Maine town, down on the New Hampshire border. She seizes on balding, beer-bellied Ed Lawler, seemingly her only educated customer, as someone who "might be the end of a long, bumpy ride." Well endowed but forty-six years old, Violet finds herself caught in a performance circuit located in the land of "pulp and guns." She wrests a scant income from stripping and drumming up a few customers who will pay for her body. Exploited by owners of dives like "Vic's Playpen," Violet sometimes has to give away sex. Other times she is cheated of her wages. Given Violet's age and the lineaments of her life, Ed Lawler looms as a way out of her misery.

Yet he views his life as made of "crepe paper." Ed's father was a teacher, and Ed spent part of his boyhood in Massachusetts. However, his father established an unspecified relationship with a student. His letters of recommendation only hinted at what happened. The Lawlers hastened off to Mattagash when Ed's father was offered the principalship of a two-room wooden grammar school. Ed followed his father into the school and then to the principal's office. He had become tethered to Mattagash by Sicily's deceit.

Fly-fishing while guzzling beer during the summer constitutes Ed's only enjoyment in life. Mattagash's communal highpoint only underscores its benighted backwoods ways. Work becomes sport for a day. Lumberjacks compete in all manner of contests, from felling trees to debarking them.

Fall arrives early in Mattagash; Ed hates the season, and not just because it presages winter bearing down on the town with six feet of snow and "temperatures that fell to 20 and 40 degrees below zero," which helps drive him, and other Mattagashers, to the bottle. He's also irritated with the way townspeople gild fall foliage as if less than three weeks of a colorful landscape provides compensation for what Mattagashers have to endure for the rest of the year. Black flies and mosquitoes even blight the evanescent summer. (The season "comes and goes on mosquito wings," motel owner Pinkham laments in *Once upon a Time*.) Principal Lawler is weary of hearing how the leaves look prettier each year. "Can't the goddamned leaves just get so pretty and then they can't get any goddamned prettier?" Then the start of the school year is disrupted after three weeks for northern Maine's potato harvest. Whole families leave for the farms where they labor for hard-earned paydays. Even lumber trucks shift to hauling potatoes. Fall reminds Lawler that he is a failure. He's principal in a dog patch, where no self-respecting educator would choose to come, let alone stay for good.

Thus, autumn arrives "like a knife, slicing leaves off trees, embedding itself in Ed's fat gut with a thrust that left more fear than pain." He retrieves a gun hidden behind books in a drawer and drives to the empty school. In the principal's office, Ed puts the gun to his temple. His past races headlong by him. He pulls the trigger. His suicide is simultaneously an escape from oppressive Mattagash and, ironically, the permanent lodgment of Ed's memory in the town's history and mythology.

Ed leaves suicide notes for Sicily and Amy Joy. He tells his daughter that he loves her. Yet she brought no joy into his life, provided no reason for him to keep on living. In the subsequent Mattagash novels, as people die or leave and Amy Joy matures, her character assumes an increasingly critical role in the plots.

Marge dies after Ed. Marvin Sr. had been growing impatient to get his hands on the body. At one point, he lets loose his frustration: "That's one long last breath. She's been drawing it since the phone call yesterday." After the funeral the Ivys drive home to Portland, not to return for ten years.

In *Once upon a Time on the Banks*, a decade has passed and Mattagash has continued its tailspin. The population has fallen by nearly 20 percent. It stands at 456 inhabitants. But as Mattagash's slide persists, the Giffords are thriving, as they breed, collect disability and welfare checks, and keep a sharp eye out for larcenous openings. Their glowing Christmas lights in April betoken the boundaries of what Mattagashers call "Gifford town." One resident observes of the family's neighborliness, "If you're in trouble they'd take the shirt right off your back."

Familiar sights and sounds denote that spring (or, rather, what Mattagashers call spring) has arrived. Melting snow reveals the debris that clutters "Big Vinal" Gifford's front yard. "The pile of used tires that had sprouted there last fall . . . was still blooming. Hubcaps glistened in the soft April sun." Trucks and "gutted" cars "rested on hardwood blocks at various angles." It is a familiar setting that recurs in Maine literature from Ruth Moore to Philip Booth's poem "Maine" to Carolyn Chute to Cathie Pelletier.[34]

A second sign of spring in Mattagash derives from nature: the opening up of the river and the return of its familiar current coursing over rocks, a hymnlike reminder of nature's continuity. Yet, for all of spring's progress, winter in the far north makes an about-face before it departs for good. Snow falls continuously on May Day.

The McKinnons and the Ivys from Portland come together again, not for a funeral but for a wedding. At twenty-three years old, Amy Joy is engaged. With a declining population, marriages across ethnic and religious lines become more common, further thinning out the McKinnon blood. Amy Joy has fallen in love with a French Canadian from "Frog Town." Jean Claude Cloutier works as an auto mechanic, which means that black grease has taken up permanent residence beneath his fingernails.

Cloutier speaks in Canuck rather than in Franglais, a mixture of French and English. While Pelletier again refers to the persistence of a "distinguishable country brogue" in Mattagash, the reader has to imagine the particularity of local speech. At the same time, she skillfully re-creates the tortured diction of the Canuck idiom. Jean Claude calls Amy Joy about breaking off their engagement: "I jus have some bad thoughts go in my head, me . . . I tink, may-bee, you and me, we break hup, hus . . . hits jus, well, she [his mother] doan want us to tie da knot, her." Nevertheless, the engagement proceeds up to the wedding day, when Jean Claude jilts Amy Joy. His brothers have spirited him off to Connecticut, where French-Canadian and other northern Maine expatriates have found factory jobs.

Once upon a Time on the Banks continues to dissect the social tensions between Mattagashers and Portlanders and their imagined geographies of Maine. Sicily's self-image shrinks to a "country mouse" in the presence of Pearl, her "citified sister." Albert Pinkham provides motel rooms for the Ivys, but he reserves nothing but contempt for Pearl, "with all her city airs and bloated sense of self-importance." She seems convinced "that her shit didn't stink." Junior Ivy's wife, Thelma, reencounters the North Woods, and it fosters anew her mental mapping of Maine beyond Bangor. As the pines rush past her, she seems to be journeying "into the heart of the forest . . . just to surface nowhere." At one time she held a southern Maine perspective on the north. Beyond Bangor, one found "no houses. No hospitals. No schools. No people." Through marriage she had acquired another view of the north. Her dismissal of the region now takes a different form: "She wished greatly that the world had indeed dead-ended at Bangor, and that if you ventured any farther you would fall off the edge."

The Mattagash saga continues with *The Weight of Winter*. At just short of five hundred pages, the third volume swells to twice the length of *The Funeral Makers*. Pelletier continues her characteristic humor but offers a somewhat darker view of Mattagash, whose population has shrunk to approximately 360.

Winter has arrived days before Thanksgiving. It snows constantly. Townspeople have to get accustomed to the sky "dull gray with snow, the mountains dark whales beached on the horizon." The "meteorologists down in faraway Bangor" too often botch Mattagash's forecasts, which are taken as a personal slight. Who cares about the small-town people that far north? Their viewer ratings don't matter, it seems. The meteorologists are like "the shits in Augusta [who] thought the road ended a foot north of Bangor."

Now forty-five, Amy Joy remains single, with few marriageable men her age available in Mattagash. She lives with her mother in the McKinnon homestead. Sicily's friends have died or else live at Pine Valley nursing home, known unofficially as "Death Valley." Albert Pinkham resides at Pine Valley, his motel in ruins. He sits in a wheelchair with his head on his chest, all but drooling on himself.

Pine Valley cares for Mattagash's oldest citizen. At 107, Mathilda Finnelson has one foot in the graveyard; yet she retains her memory and imagination, silent partners that fill her days. Pelletier devotes chapters to the centenarian. Pelletier's refreshing, adroit re-creation of Mathilda's ruminations fills in her story of remarkable endurance; she also illuminates Mattagash's history over Mathilda's long life. In *The Funeral Makers*, Pelletier similarly explores the churn of Marge's deathbed self-loathing. She deploys Marge's turbulent recall to tell, among other things crucial to the plot, how she fell in love with the missionary imposter.

Pelletier's third novel examines new ways that Mattagashers cope with five to six months of winter. Snowmobiles blast "through the quiet of the woods . . . despoiling the white blankets of snow in all the fields with their tracks." Other "new gods" of winter fill Mattagashers' lives: satellite dishes, VCR movies, and "the burgeoning state lottery." As the town's metabolism alters, the appetite for gossip grows. Two Mattagashers drive around at night, their eyes peeled for signs of suspicious activity. One monitors her police scanner, waiting for something to happen and then taking pride in being the first to know and tell.

The excessive flow of alcohol ineluctably leads to domestic violence. Pike Gifford grabs his wife, Lynn, twice, pins her to the wall, and threatens to kill her. The first time, his oldest boy—"that yellow trickle of piss," Pike calls him—swings a baseball bat and knocks his father unconscious. The second time, the boy retrieves his hunting rifle. But he accidentally kills Pike's best friend and drinking partner.

The Crossroads, a newly opened bar, serves as the hub of Mattagash drinking. A campaign, led by women, crops up to shut the place down, which will only move drinking back to a domestic setting. However, some Mattagash wives are opposed to closing the Crossroads, as it will mean that their men will spend too much time at home. A voting booth is set up in the gym, with a shower curtain, of all things, to ensure privacy. The Crossroads is forced to close.

Over three Mattagash novels, Pelletier doesn't significantly alter her engaging storytelling style: its sassiness, quirky characters, farcical and dark humor, bouts of violence, and examination of generational change. She immerses the reader in her dissection of a town in decline and largely isolated in the northern wilderness from the rest of Maine. Fleeting or formidable seasons shape the rhythm of life in Mattagash. In *The Weight of Winter*, a character looks at a sweatshirt emblazoned with the ironical "Aroostook County the Crown of Maine." Mattagash is part of the crown of Aroostook, but there is nothing regal about it.

With her Mattagash trilogy and subsequent novels Pelletier surpassed Ben Ames Williams and Elizabeth Coatsworth in her literary achievement as a writer about northern Maine. She established herself as a sharp-witted chronicler of life in a pint-sized backwoods village. Pelletier represents the most prolific literary voice of the state's north country. Her varied humor enhanced the Mattagash novels' appeal to a wide audience. Some readers doubtless found the humor entertaining and failed to give sufficient due to Pelletier's representation of the human predicament. Her publisher printed twenty-five thousand hardcover copies of *The Funeral Makers*, an impressive run for a first-time novelist. A producer purchased movie rights.

Each book in the Mattagash trilogy received mostly favorable and sometimes enthusiastic reviews, though some critics inevitably dissented. Susan Kenney, a novelist from Colby College, heaped praise on *The Funeral Makers* in the *New York Times Book Review*: "The book is at once hilariously funny, irreverent, comic tragic, and lyrical." Kenney also found the novel "large, wide and deep."[35] At the opposite end of the critical spectrum, *Kirkus Reviews* saw *The Funeral Makers* as wanting. The reviewer noted that Pelletier "has a sharp feel for broad comic dialogue and farcical doings, but the undercurrent of the worst small-town mores, unrelieved by fleshed-out characters, muffles the laffs."[36]

The *New York Times* again gave Pelletier an enthusiastic endorsement for *Once upon a Time on the Banks*. Fannie Flagg, the noted novelist, believed that Pelletier's second book fully lived up to the promise of the first. In the *Washington Post Book World*, Vermont writer Howard Frank Mosher agreed with Flagg: "Funny doesn't begin to describe these shenanigans, and yet, as in most comic fiction, there's a current of human wisdom running straight through the novel from beginning to end." The *Los Angeles Times* reviewer seems to have taken himself too seriously and the book not at all. "Forget Winslow Homer, Kennebunkport, LL Bean, blueberries and lobster rolls," he suggested of tourists' totems of the "real" Maine. Mattagash, he wrote dismissively, represented "a grand place for a writer to be from and terrific people to remember from a distance of 2000 miles and 20 years."[37]

The Weight of Winter received wide praise. The *Boston Herald* devoted the cover story of *Sunday People*, its weekly magazine, to Pelletier. It noted that *The Weight of Winter* was already in its second printing. *Booklist* stressed how Pelletier "has sympathy to let her characters behave in outrageous or brutal ways without turning them into caricatures who can elicit only one response."[38]

Clearly the Mattagash trilogy proved to be a critical and commercial success. Moreover, this accomplishment occurred almost contemporaneously with Carolyn Chute's emergence as a national literary sensation. Though people made superficial comparisons of the two new Maine authors, Chute inhabited a strikingly different social and literary world from Pelletier.

5

THE BACKCOUNTRY AS MAINE'S APPALACHIA

Carolyn Chute

For more than a generation, Carolyn Chute (b. 1947) has given voice to the backcountry underclass, at first to unstinting critical praise and phenomenal commercial success, followed by more muted reviews and modest commercial reward. At the time she published her breakthrough novel, *The Beans of Egypt, Maine* (1985), Chute was living with her husband, Michael, on welfare and food stamps in North Gorham, Maine. The good fortune of *The Beans* enabled the Chutes to move to Parsonsfield, Michael's hometown, nearly fifty miles from Portland, where they built a simple house in the woods.[1] Parsonsfield informs the novel's setting.

North Gorham and Parsonsfield enable us to map the backcountry as the thinly populated subregion approximately fifteen to fifty miles from the heavily settled coast. It is important to keep in mind that the kind of southern Maine backwoods world that Chute explores actually characterizes large swaths of the state, including the north country. A generation ago, farming and lumbering were more common between Gorham and Parsonsfield than they are today. Of course, even in 1985 exurban sprawl intruded on the backcountry. In *The Beans*, two well-to-do outsiders driving fancy cars build large colonial houses across the road from the Beans' trailer. According to the Federal Census, Parsonsfield's population grew by more than 35 percent in the 1980s, to nearly fifteen hundred inhabitants.

With her first novel Chute made a national splash that was at least equivalent to Stephen King's reception a decade earlier. Within two months of its publication, *The Beans* went through four printings and sold more than seventy thousand copies. In Maine, booksellers scrambled to keep their shelves stocked.[2]

Moreover, not only did readers embrace the book, but it also provoked intense interest in the author. Newspapers and television networks requested interviews. Since Chute had no telephone, she gave interviews from a neighbor's house and even in a Gorham general store.[3] Such backcountry celebrity stemmed in part from a quotation on the dust jacket of *The Beans*: "This book was involuntarily researched. I have lived poverty. I didn't CHOOSE it. No one would choose humiliation, pain, and rage." Unfortunately, the quotation seemed to leave little imaginative daylight between Chute's life and the literary characters she created.

She repeated the quotation in interviews, cultivating the persona of a country author who, like the Beans, knew dire poverty from birth, with its attendant moral upheaval.[4] Chute often pontificated as spokesperson for the fictional Beans. "The poorer you are the more you love your children" represented, at least in part, her explanation of the Beans' hypersexuality, which embraces incest. As to the Beans' physical violence, including against women, "Their masculinity is at stake and they become very fragile, vulnerable."[5]

Chute grew up in Cape Elizabeth, an attractive seaside suburb of Portland, which was already affluent during her childhood. She has described her up-bringing as comfortable but "very boring" and "very protected."[6] Her father, a native of North Carolina, worked for an electric supply company. A Maine native, Chute's mother was apparently a stay-at-home mom.

Carolyn's fall from comfort began when she dropped out of high school at sixteen and married a man who worked for a bread company. They lived in South Portland, and she gave birth to a daughter, Johanna. After seven years of marriage, during which she had already begun to write stories, Carolyn asked for a divorce. She now became self-supporting. A succession of menial jobs followed: she worked in chicken and shoe factories, labored on a potato farm, and drove a school bus, among other low-paying employment.[7]

She married Michael, a seasonal handyman, in 1978. Then she completed her high school degree and took psychology and creative writing classes at the University of Southern Maine's campus in Gorham. She also served briefly as a part-time suburban reporter for the *Portland Evening Express*. Chute continued to write fiction, and she placed stories in prominent magazines including *Grand Street* and *Ploughshares*.

Chute dedicated *The Beans* as follows: "In memory of real Reuben. Who spared him this occasion? Who spared him rage?" "Reuben" was the stillborn son she bore in 1982. Chute blamed her loss on the lack of prenatal care. In the early 1980s, the Chutes typically lived on several thousand dollars a year. During those years she continually discussed what became *The Beans* with Michael. His knowledge of Parsonsfield and its inhabitants sparked her imagination.

With the advance for *The Beans*, the Chutes bought a headstone for Reuben and built their small house on a dirt road in the woods of Parsonsfield. They managed with an outhouse and without a television, telephone, or computer.[8]

THE BEANS OF EGYPT, MAINE AND LIBERTARIAN RAGE

Chute's novel was born into a world with "Reaganism" at high tide. It was a period filled with references to the urban underclass, "welfare queens," tax cuts, and "trickle-down" economics. *The Beans* disrupted this discourse and called America's attention to the rural underclass. As we shall see, the opening of *The Beans* captures the difference between the skilled laboring class and the unsteady underclass. The latter category consists primarily of people who labor, when employment is available, for minimum wage (or lower) at often-hazardous jobs that provide no benefits. In other words, the underclass refers to people who try to support themselves through the kind of work that Carolyn and Michael Chute undertook. *The Beans* evokes the native Maine world of "minimum wage with a view."[9] Consider Beal Bean, the protagonist of Chute's disquieting novel. He is a stutterer with a severe learning disability. He can neither read nor write, like Michael Chute. The stress of chronic poverty destabilizes his family life and generates Beal's self-destructive rage.

Rather than the underclass, the *New York Times Book Review* referred to the Beans as "infernally white-trash."[10] They were often portrayed as the literary cousins of Faulkner's Snopes or Caldwell's Jesters of *Tobacco Road*. Moreover, college courses on "White-Trash Literature" typically included *The Beans*.[11] Thus some reflections on the multiple sources and regional primacy of so-called white trash are illuminating. Of course, mid-nineteenth-century Northern abolitionists argued that slavery eroded the work ethic of ordinary Southern whites and created a class of poorly educated and minimally motivated marginal people whose existence was redeemed only by their racist belief in white superiority to blacks. Southern slaves in turn apparently clung to their own view of the region's "po' white trash."[12] And so did the Southern slaveholding elites, revolted by the real and perceived coarseness of the region's "red necks" that they nevertheless racially exploited to maintain the system of black bondage.

Chute repositioned the *Times'* poor white trash to New England or, more precisely, to Maine. She did so as the coast grew more affluent and L.L. Bean increasingly emerged as Maine's signature company, whose values and customer-centered business practices seemed to represent the state's essence. In short, *The Beans* disrupted the images in the L.L. Bean catalog, the work of the state publicity bureau, and the primacy, even exclusivity, of the coast in defining the state. The Beans wouldn't touch a lobster with a barge pole despite the crustacean's widespread symbolism along the coast and its ubiquity on the Maine license plate beginning in 1988. Not surprisingly, some residents of the hinterland painted over the license plate lobster, and Chute offered "macaroni and cheese" as a more representative Maine dish.[13]

The Beans alternates between chapters narrated by Earlene Pomerleau, from an early age, and those penned from a third-person point of view. Each has a different artistry. Earlene's observations and thoughts appear to be artless, though they are skillfully crafted. The other chapters possess more straightforward literariness. Chute's ability to evoke the sights and sounds of the Beans' world constitutes a significant literary achievement. Sometimes these details are minor, but they provoke a sudden recognition, like the car with the "Bondo color fender."

Chute adroitly introduces the class division between the Pomerleaus and the Beans in the novel's opening scene. Moreover, she does so in Earlene's distinctive voice: "We've got a RANCH 'cause it's like houses out west which cowboys sleep in." A picture window represents a defining architectural accent of a ranch house. But instead of "cattle eatin' grass on the plains and cowboys ridin' around with lassos and tall hats," the picture window frames the Beans' cluttered front yard: "tires, radiators, parts to old bicycles . . . around a skidder motor covered with a rug." The Beans' lives are decidedly messier, given the cast of her father's words: "Daddy says the Beans are uncivilized animals. PREDATORS, he calls them. If it runs a Bean will shoot it. If it falls a Bean will eat it, Daddy says, and his lip curls."

Daddy is Lee Pomerleau, a slight man with delicate hands. He is a skilled carpenter, building objects for his church's sales, such as birdhouses and breadboxes. He also whittles small artistic figures. His skills enable him to secure employment throughout most of the approximately seventeen years during which *The Beans*' small-scale drama takes place. The Pomerleaus are devoutly religious; they belong to the Fundamentalist Baptist Church and accept the literal truth of the Bible. Gram Pomerleau throws the fear of God into Lee and Earlene; she spouts scripture the way the Beans spit out profanities. Early in the novel she discovers Earlene and her father in bed together taking a nap, partially unclothed. Earlene rubs his sore back. Gram also finds out that they sleep together at night. In tears, Lee repeatedly tries to assure fire-breathing Gram that nothing untoward has happened. Earlene and her father live alone; her mother is institutionalized in a psychiatric hospital. Lee's tearful self-abasement before

Gram raises suspicion. Perhaps his sleeping habits are innocent, or possibly his guilt represents desire similar to that of the incestuous Beans.

A gravel driveway separates the ranch house that Lee built from the Beans' mobile home, "one of them old ones, looks like a submarine." The Beans have all-season Christmas lights, that beacon of poor rural Maine, around their trailer. Lee erects a sign that affords no protection for Earlene's quarantine from the Beans: "No Turning in Driveway!!!! Keep Out!!!!" The driveway sets apart the "respectable" working-class Pomerleaus from the underclass Beans. "Earlene," Lee commands, "don't go over on the Beans' side of the right of way. Not ever!"

When he's not looking, Earlene ventures across the driveway. She is both repulsed by and curious about the Beans. The plot's thrust follows Earlene's descent into what becomes the Beans' domestic abyss. Interestingly, as the novel progresses, Lee's driveway signs fade badly and are nearly blown away every day when Rubie Bean turns his lumber rig around within inches of the Pomerleau car. Lee never protests. The Beans apparently intimidate their slight, defenseless neighbor.

We might pause to reflect on the representation of religion in *The Beans*. Of course, the only time the trailer dwellers invoke God is as part of curses. Yet both the Beans and the Pomerleaus delineate two sides of religion in Maine. The state, along with Vermont, is among the most unchurched places in the country. Thus the absence of organized religion, or any faith, in the Beans' lives typifies much of the state, including rural areas. This is not to suggest that the Beans simply represent the consequences of a life devoid of religious fellowship and belief. Conversely, as mainline churches have declined in rural Maine, small Fundamentalist Baptist and Pentecostal churches, such as the Assembly of God, have filled some of the void. The Pomerleaus stand for this other side of religion in rural Maine. Lee's car has bumper stickers: "Jesus Saves" and "Honk If You Love Jesus." One might argue that for all of its fanaticism, Lee's religion still serves as a moral and cultural resource that helps him consolidate his respectable lower-middle-class sense of himself. (Of course, such men don't sleep with their eleven-year-old daughters.)

Reuben Bean and Beal Bean are the two major male characters in the novel. When Rubie pulls his lumber rig into the yard it feels as if the earth shakes. The truck has dents where Rubie has pounded his fists when he's not punching holes in walls, or striking his wife or live-in girlfriend, or beating a game warden within inches of his life. He's a tinderbox who goes through life with unpredictable outbursts of rage on objects and people.

Rubie is a hulk of a man; all the Beans are tall, and some of them are bulky. Rubie's rawness, a kind of impulsive primitivism, is fully on display at the dinner table. He makes "snorting noises" as he eats and uses his sleeve in place of a napkin. He "belches" without restraint. His hands are missing fingers. "One nail is shaped like a claw, and with this one he picks something from his back teeth." Food sticks to his "whiskers" as he finishes eating.

While driving his truck, Rubie is easily provoked into road rage. When another logging truck passes him, their mirrors touch. The familiar driver honks his horn and then races his empty rig ahead. Rubie seethes. He floors his truck, "spit springin' from his mouth like a dog. Spit foamin' off his mustache." He manages to pull alongside the truck that passed, and his ex-wife, who is traveling with him, says, "I was embarrassed to have that fella see my husband droolin' like a Christly hound."

Lee tells Earlene that the Beans' jaws have that "Cro-Magnon look." Their "mouths always got slack. And in the slack is their chunky yellow teeth." Granted, this is Lee's class-inflected reading of the Beans. Nevertheless, for much of the novel Chute veers from realism into a harsher, more deterministic naturalism. In this view, environment heavily shapes character, often eliciting instinctual or baser elements of human nature, a kind of reversion to an earlier evolutionary stage. Among other behaviors, the Beans breed like feral cats. Even Beal's dog, "Jet," is pregnant early in the novel and delivers a litter beneath Aunt Roberta's "wee green house," one of the annoying descriptions that Chute repeats excessively along with the Beans' "fox-like eyes."

The naturalistic representation of the Beans endows the novel with some literary shape. It's doubtful, however, that Chute self-consciously crafted a literary naturalism or even knew what the term meant. A reporter from the *Washington Post* described "one bookshelf in the front room of the Chute house." Chute estimated that "she had read about 30 books in her life, mostly things friends recommended."[14] Willa Cather was mentioned. Chute stammered through a vacuous answer. In fact, she was a poorly read author when she produced *The Beans*. She appears to have thought and wrote in a literary vacuum. No wonder noted novelist Anne Tyler observed after Chute's second book that she wrote as if she hadn't read another work of fiction.[15] Yet literary unaffectedness proved liberating. In many respects, *The Beans* reads like a work of literary folk art. Some chapters, for instance, are an unconventional half a page long.

One of Chute's finely wrought confrontations, which brings Rubie's scattershot fury to a boil, involves game warden Cole Deveau. The Beans are not crooks, shirkers who feed off the government like Pelletier's Giffords. The Beans have a libertarian streak that manifests itself in one way through their disregard for game laws. Rubie settles on a new object for his rage. He slaughters young deer in a field. The game warden comes upon the killing field and knows there is only one inhabitant of Egypt capable of such a senseless act.

The showdown between the warden and Rubie is imbued with Western elements—a kind of shootout. Deveau locates Rubie working in the woods with his two sons, their movements making "the sound of sucking mud as they raise their feet." Given the savagery that follows, the mud suggests a kind of primordial ooze—that is, literary naturalism. Survival belongs to the superior brute. Rubie issues a warning. After ordering Deveau to move, he drops a log from his boom that rolls toward the warden, who has to jump quickly out of the way. Then they square off. Deveau has pulled Rubie's rifle from the cab of the rig. "I can understand bein' a glutton for meat, Rubie, but what you left on the power line isn't meat . . . it's a friggin' holocaust. Haven't you got a sprig of conscience?"

Rubie denies the accusation, but Cole has interrupted his woods work because he has trampled on more than game laws. Cole has already disarmed Rubie, but then he ignites his reptilian brain. Cole knows the rifle was a gift from Rubie's father. But he grinds it into the mud until the rifle is half-buried. Rubie walks toward the warden, seizes the gun, and with two hands swings it repeatedly into Deveau, knocking his teeth out and crushing bones before hacking away at the warden's midsection. Rubie points the gun into the fallen warden's neck "and dry-fires over and over and over." His sons have to pull him away. Rubie's wrath seems to know no bounds short of murdering a symbol of authority.

Subsequent events transform Earlene's picture window into live television, when the posse comes for the outlaw, or the police arrive in force to arrest the ruthless criminal. Rubie drives into the trap shirtless and slimy with work sweat. His skin is slippery. The police have to beat him into submission. In the end, Rubie faces a fifteen-year sentence in the state prison.

With Rubie's removal, Beal Bean emerges as the primal male in the novel. He is the son of Merry Merry, the adult Bean daughter with the mental capacity of a child. She is kept under lock and key for her own safety. Beal's father is apparently an outsider with a face as "gray and grained as barn board." At thirteen, Beal Bean is tall and brawny. Since he has repeated grades, he looks outsized in Earlene's fifth-grade classroom. Swollen pimples "as big as plums" bulge across his face. Chute stresses the physical "otherness" of the Beans, though that seems at odds with her professed fellow feeling for the underclass. "In school under them lights all the Beans are purple." Beal's greasy black hair excretes the "smell of a kerosene stove." Earlene imagines that "if you tossed a match at a Bean, they'd burst into flame."

The Beans has a certain haziness when it comes to the passage of time. Chute only uses the present tense. In a whirl, we now encounter Beal when he is nineteen, Earlene still in her midteens. His facial lumps have receded to "pimple scars, [as] concave as cellars holes." Since the age of thirteen, as Rubie rages in the mobile home, Beal has slipped away to Aunt Roberta Bean's house. Beal's world is filled with aunts by birth and by marriage. They pluck out their eyebrows and then paint black lines. The blood Beans are physically bigger than their in-laws. A tall fecund Bean by birth, Aunt Roberta acquiesces to regular incest with Beal, at least by the time he is nineteen. Such incest, along with driving a powerful lumber truck, suggests a rickety scaffolding on which to erect the Bean sense of masculinity. Beal may come to father as many as five of Roberta's nine bedraggled children.

Chute carefully details the odd physical attributes of Beal's favorite aunt. Perhaps Roberta herself is the promiscuous consequence of incest. She is tall but has "the head of a 15¢ turnip." Her smile reveals the teeth of a "Doberman, long, fat, yellow, sharp." She wears clothes soiled with "spilled coffee and year-old blood." The smell of "fruity" babies fills her house. Roberta exemplifies characteristics of some creature of the forest primeval.

Still she possesses a kind of country neighborliness, an undesigning naturalness, as March Goodspeed (an appropriate name for a highway engineer) finds out. He's the recent Massachusetts transplant who lives in the big house across the road and drives a fancy Lincoln. One morning he can't get his car started. Roberta arrives with her brood of children and chickens in train. He repeatedly resists her offer of help, like a trainer "commanding a huge but humble dog." One child spits on the car in what seems like an instinctive act of resistance. Chickens peck away at Goodspeed's hubcaps. Roberta retrieves her fenderless truck and jumper cables. Goodspeed gets out of his car only to be repelled by Roberta's stench, the very stitching of her clothes and pores of her skin permeated by the smell of food. The engineer views her children as a "bizarre litter of moles." To Goodspeed's relief, the car starts and he makes his escape.

Roberta mounts two more guileless overtures toward Goodspeed. In one, she shoots rabbits—a vital part of the Beans' diet, even for breakfast—cleans the best parts, and puts them in a bread bag. Roberta then ties the bag to Goodspeed's doorknob and tapes a note to the door: "WELCOME TO EGYPT HERES A LITTLE PRESENT." It's a gesture that underscores how the middle-class Goodspeed and the underclass Beans eat, live, look, smell, and procreate so differently from each other. When he is stuck again and Roberta reaches out to assist him, Goodspeed has a question: "Do you know anything about . . . someone fastening a bag of . . . chicken meat on my front door?"

Along with the tension between the Pomerleaus and the Beans, the encounters between Roberta and Goodspeed constitute the principal clashes of class in *The Beans*, until Beal's demise near the novel's end.

Over the course of Earlene's growing up, her father periodically forces soap or shampoo into her mouth to punish and purge words he finds offensive. The puritanical regime of Lee and Gram leaves Earlene conflicted. She views the Beans as both off-putting and liberatingly seductive. After Gramp dies, Lee sells the ranch and moves in with Gram. Lee and Earlene have added physical space to their class distance from the Beans. Yet she is about to be raped by the rutting Beal, setting in motion not her conversion to the Pomerleaus' Fundamentalist faith but her rite of passage into the Bean tribe.

Though Earlene is in her late teens, Lee persists in punishing her, this time for smoking, by pouring shampoo in her mouth. "Praise God for His Mercy. . . . Praise!" he shouts. Earlene "vomits . . . a foamy wob of orange." In effect, she ejects his religion. Earlene then attempts to run away, which only results in miring her in Egypt.

Hitchhiking in the rain, Earlene watches vehicles pass until a logging truck driven by Beal Bean stops. He drives her directly to Aunt Roberta's house and leads her up into the attic, where two boys awaken. Beal proceeds to overpower Earlene. "I ain't gonna do nuthin', you know . . . you know . . . with you," she protests. She joins her hands in prayer. "Beal! Please!" Earlene does remove her clothes and thinks of Gram's words: "God only gives you one chance." She also recalls the stories Gram's brother told about how to survive when you confront a black bear: lay still and the animal will lose interest in you. With his long black beard and bulky frame, Beal is a bear of a man. He forcefully positions Earlene's hips. "Ohmagaud," she mutters and struggles with her arms and legs as "his vast hairy front" pushes against her. When he stops, "she feels the hot arc of Bean's seed. She pictures millions of possible Bean babies, fox-eyed, yellow-toothed, meat-gobbling Beans." Earlene struggles to her feet "gasping for breath."

Chute has now added rape to incest, promiscuity, domestic violence, and the brutal beating of a representative of the law to a supposedly sympathetic portrayal of underclass life. In many respects, she appears to pathologize the rural underclass in ways that parallel how politicians and others in the 1980s represented the urban (black) underclass. Such moral confusion represents the fundamental thematic flaw in *The Beans*. As for Earlene, she is soon pregnant and trapped in her father's house. She gives birth to a daughter, Bonny Loo— an outback, Bean-like name. And akin to the learning-impaired, illiterate Beal,

Bonny Loo will become a special needs child in school. Her grandfather later tells Bonny Loo that "if he ever finds out who her father is, he will KILL." This sounds like bluster from the diminutive Lee. Bonny Loo's father should be obvious to all. Among other Bean features, she shares their fox-colored eyes.

Again, chronology is illusive in *The Beans*, as choppy chapters shift back and forth between Earlene's first-person point of view and the author's third-person perspective on the Beans. Several years after Bonny Loo's birth, Earlene falls into a deep depression. She refuses to eat, bathe, or leave her bed. In turn, since the rape, Beal's licentiousness persists. He continues to sleep with Aunt Roberta while adding Madeline Rowe, Rubie's girlfriend when he went off to jail, to his conquests.

Roberta, already established as a character who is a kind of earth mother in extremis, rescues Earlene in an undeveloped subplot. With no apparent provocation, she marches into Earlene's bedroom while Lee is at work. She lifts Earlene from her bed, uses the now deceased Gram's wheelchair, and pushes Earlene into the sunlight and fresh air. Her recuperation has begun.

Then Beal reenters Earlene's life. The Beans have always repelled her, but so has the repressiveness of her Fundamentalist lower-middle-class upbringing. There is a brief mention of a wedding, which Lee Pomerleau fails to attend because his back hurts. Madeline Rowe serves as Earlene's maid of honor, but that doesn't discourage the girlfriend from kissing Beal passionately on the lips.

Beal and Earlene move into Rubie's tar-paper shack, with plastic on the windows. There are no year-round Christmas lights because the structure lacks electricity. Rubie has put his fist through all of the cupboards. He has also knocked out Madeline's front tooth. Chute deploys teeth as a signifier of class throughout *The Beans*. Beal's teeth become "penny-colored along the gums." Bonny Loo's school reports that she has gum disease, betokening the family's slide into the underclass. Of all the major characters in *The Beans*, only Earlene's teeth are not described.

Soon after the marriage, Beal's economic prospects go into a tailspin. The only work he can find is "limbin' pulp" six days a week; it pays less than the minimum wage. His boots are rotting. "He smells of pine," Earlene complains in bed. "Sometimes I see him suck on his knuckles in his sleep, the hands black with pitch." More than once Earlene falls to her knees and kisses Beal's feet, in a kind of ritualistic total submission to the Beans. After Dale Bean, the ten-pound future bruiser, arrives, Earlene pleads with Beal to apply for food stamps. But backcountry libertarianism paralyzes him: "Once you get in the old welfare game, they got a trail on you . . . 'cause, lady . . . when you're poor you stink!" Government help also subverts Beal's manhood, his sense of himself as a rugged self-reliant individual. "What good am I?" he asks self-pityingly. "I musta' come outta my mother's asshole." In the discourse of the 1980s, welfare queens reside in the inner city, not in rural, white small towns like those of Maine, where everybody will know who's on the dole.

Not surprisingly, except to Earlene, on the heels of his humiliation Beal demands sex. And he wants it "dog-style." This need suggests the multiple functions of sex in *The Beans*. In Beal's desperation, it represents the last shred of manhood that he controls.

Just before Thanksgiving Day, an appropriately named Mayflower truck backs into the driveway of the new house across the road, with its lamppost and fancy Chrysler. Shortly thereafter, Beal carries his rifle outside and begins shooting at the house's windows. It's his last outburst of primitive rage; the act seems only remotely related to a class consciousness that Beal would be unable to articulate. He never blames anyone or anything for the disintegration of his life. The newcomers summon the police, who riddle Beal's body with bullets.

Earlene orders the undertaker to "burn" Beal; cremation is not a part of her vocabulary. In a brave, original, and jolting passage, Chute has Earlene imagine what happens to Beal's imposing body. Lying on the sofa she visualizes "the broad architecture of my husband's back curl up, drizzle off the bone, gurgle into a pool the color and texture of hot chicken fat which will be cold chicken fat . . . in time." Distributing the deceased's ashes appears to be a ritual of another class.

In the aftermath of Beal's death, Earlene's church reaches out to help her. She also benefits from food stamps. Then Rubie returns, or what remains of the former behemoth of backwoods Egypt, Maine. A heart attack in prison, where he claims to have died and come back to life on the shower room floor, has defanged the man who once stormed through life. His eating etiquette hasn't changed, however. He finds that Madeline has left to marry the owner of Egypt's hardware store.

Rubie's afraid of dying, so he sleeps in a chair, constantly awakening when his heart races or he imagines it pounding in his chest. Rubie's sons give him a low-level job "runnin' a chipper." The Bean who used to back his truck into the Pomerleaus' gravel driveway and the little girl in the picture window settle in to domestic life together.

The reviews that gushed over *The Beans* represent too many to cite. "The national media . . . are like pet geese," Chute observed. "One honks and they all start honking."[16] *Boston Magazine* was impressed with the sounds in *The Beans*. "The book is so aural it rings in your ears." It celebrated Chute for contributing "to American literature a voice so fresh, so fully realized that it should floor you, overwhelm you." The *Christian Science Monitor* praised Chute's "brisk imagery, shrewd character development, plotting (episodic but brisk) and affectionate common sense." But the reviewer expressed a reservation: "For despite her writerly brilliance, it's a book of appalling images, not easy to get through." The *Hartford Courant* reviewer was one of the most enthusiastic boosters of Chute. *The Beans* showed that she possessed "uncontaminated talent and awesome power."[17]

The Beans made the short list of the *New York Times* Editors' Favorites. But the *Times* published a review that upset Chute. The female reviewer focused on the novel's incest. She seemed to suggest that *The Beans* had much to do with the "metaphysics of incest." Chute appeared to offer an "ancient apologia for incest (if you ain't good enough for your own family, who are you good enough for?)."[18]

Ten years after the release of *The Beans*, a new publisher issued what Chute characterized as the "finished version."[19] She described the original novel as "a clumsy youthful attempt at the art of writing." She changed words and sentences that she thought conveyed her immaturity as a writer. In a remarkable postscript, she sought to establish *correct* interpretations of *The Beans*. Chute disputed that Lee Pomerleau and Earlene ever engaged in any kind of incest or that Beal raped Earlene. With respect to the latter, she claimed that "Earlene never says no." She went on to offer the "correct" interpretations of Roberta's action toward March Goodspeed and to wish she had made her an aunt by marriage to circumvent incest.[20]

Chute's new version of *The Beans* and its remarkable postscript display naiveté and misunderstanding of imaginative literature. First of all, it assumes that a novelist knowingly exhausts the meaning of the words she puts down on a page. The reader's only task, Chute seems to suggest, is to decipher, to decode, the author's intention. But readers bring different experiences to their interaction with a novel. A published work of fiction doesn't belong solely to its author. Sent out into the world, it becomes part of a community of general readers, reviewers, teachers, and students.

LETOURNEAU'S USED AUTO PARTS: CAST-OFF PEOPLE AND JUNKED CARS

With the surprising critical stir and brisk sales of *The Beans*, Chute's publisher urged her to dispatch a new novel building on her first. *Letourneau's* appeared three years later (1988). It solidified Chute's reputation as an authentic voice of the backcountry's desperately poor working-class folks.

In addition to their bracing portraits of the rural underclass, the two novels share other elements. Both adhere to a choppy style, for instance, and the use of the present tense, which once again befogs the passage of time. Yet there are crucial differences between the novels. For one thing, *Letourneau's* possesses no distinctive first-person voice comparable to Earlene's. Chute tempers the naturalism of *The Beans*. There are no characters in *Letourneau's* like *The Beans'* raging bulls, Rubie and Beal, or the default sexual object, Roberta.

All this is not to suggest *Letourneau's* inferiority to *The Beans*. Both books transport the reader through the thickets of the working poor's lives. *Letourneau's* offers a more nuanced, sympathetic representation of this underclass. Furthermore, in some respects it's a more complex novel than *The Beans*. For one thing, it has a larger cast of characters, so much so that Chute diagrams their relationships as a prelude to the novel. Still, these family trees by no means encompass all of *Letourneau's* characters. Moreover, Chute employs an effective conceit that helps unify much of the novel. The figure of Big Lucien Letourneau hovers over Egypt, and therefore over most of the narrative. He owns the sprawling salvage yard. Outside of the woods and a local mill, it's the town's principal employer. He's also the proprietor of the incongruously christened "Miracle City," a last-stop residential haven for those evicted by landlords or simply dispossessed by life. In other words, Big Lucien is a weighty figure in Egypt. Yet we only come face-to-face with him on the novel's last page. Despite his physical absence, Big Lucien takes shape through his presence in the lives of his former wives and girlfriends, as well as through his salvage yard workers and Miracle City residents. He saves much more than used auto parts in Egypt.

The novel begins portentously with an oddball salvage yard worker, Crowe Bovey. He is married with five children. But he has spent the last three days with a twenty-year-old college student, indulging in sex on her waterbed. His hands are "tattooed by auto grease" and "wrecked with sores," the badges of his salvage yard labor. In fact, he is Big Lucien's best worker. His labor and lust are summed up by the fact that he "smells like the inside of a motor running hot."

Over the years Bovey has purchased and traded for antique and up-to-date rifles. He loves to kill crows and small animals. In this sense, he bears a mild resemblance to Rubie Bean. Bovey displays some of his rifles on his truck's gun rack. The vehicle lacks a rebel flag sticker commonly placed on a rear window to announce proudly that the owner is a "Maine redneck." It takes no leap of the imagination to envision Bovey as a forerunner of some Trump enthusiasts or that people like him, with grimy hands and a passion for guns, resent how elites on the coast condescend to hardworking backcountry folk and their mores.

Interestingly, Chute appears to anticipate such a political prospect. Maxine, an ex-wife of Big Lucien and mother of five of his children, smokes Tiparillos, wears "cowboy" boots, listens to country and western music, and works in the mill. She seems like a figure from another region, part of Chute's ongoing project to disrupt the imaging of Yankee Maine. Maxine (even her name is resonant, like Crowe's) paints in gold letters on her truck's tailgate "God Bless America . . . God Bless President Reagan." She displays a bumper sticker, "Reagan-Bush '84," and later adds a new one: "More Nukes, Less Kooks." Maxine's former brother-in-law, Armand Letourneau, tells Bovey that public radio represents nothing less than "Commie radio." These characters suggest Chute's political perceptiveness more than her prescience. Nevertheless, it's not too much to contend that Maxine, Armand, and Bovey embody the rural working-class antecedents—the resentments—of a political world to come. Rural Maine, after all, voted heavily for Donald Trump a generation after the publication of *Letourneau's*.

His lust spent, Bovey drives home after his three-day tryst only to discover a crowd and fire engines in front of his house. His entire family has perished in a blaze. Bovey shows no emotion. Rather, he drives off to the salvage yard. In the aftermath of the family's catastrophe, Bovey picks at his scabbed hands; it strikes one as the only way he can express the raw sore of his complicity in his family's demise.

Big Lucien offers Bovey a few days' shelter in his large unpainted house behind the salvage yard. The stay turns into an indefinite residence. Bovey moves from sleeping with his arms crossed and head down on a table to a makeshift "room" under the second-floor stairs. The house serves as a kind of homeless shelter for people and stray cats, an expression of Lucien's "heart of gold," we are repeatedly told. His current wife, Karen, her two children, and Lucien's mother and oldest sister occupy the house, as well as a senile old woman rescued by Big Lucien. Karen describes the state of affairs in Lucien's house: "You never know who's gonna to turn up here. Every morning's a new surprise! Dogs in the barn, drunks on the floor . . . pregnant cats in the tub . . . half-wits watching my TV." She has not said more than a few words to Lucien in three weeks. Though married, he continues womanizing, even whoring. His boundless generosity in Egypt suggests an effort to right the scales of his serial sexual indulgence.

One thing seems clear: The reader confronts the problem of taking the measure of Big Lucien's deeply flawed morality and arraigning it against that of E. Blackstone Babbidge, the other major male character in the novel. Babbidge, known as "Gene," is a religious fanatic, a native of Maine's most northern Aroostook County. He speaks in a county dialect, we are informed, though it is not captured in dialogue. He weighs his words by the thimbleful. Babbidge is a Vietnam vet in his midforties. Of less than average height, he possesses a thick neck; a bushy, mostly black mustache; and "icy" blue eyes. He worships twice a week at Egypt's Fundamentalist Baptist Church. Babbidge also presides over his family of ten children as a severe patriarch. He takes his belt to their bare flesh whenever one steps out of line. He has not always been so austere, however, as we will learn when his drug-addled singer-musician half brother visits and turns over the rocks in Gene's background.

Babbidge works in the salvage yard, and he marries one of Big Lucien's many former girlfriends. Lillian Greenlaw gave birth to one daughter, June, or "Junie," by Big Lucien. Junie will emerge as a major character in the novel. Her physical appearance shows convincingly that she springs from Big Lucien's loins. Where Lillian is blond and fair, Junie bears the results of the "dark, dark blood" of her father. She also has "the Letourneau lip." The young teenager shares some of Lucien's untamed side as well; her sexual license develops as she grows toward young womanhood.

Babbidge forbids his children to play in the salvage yard; they carefully defy him. Junie has unfettered freedom to explore this graveyard of American consumption, this potter's field of the nation's romance with the automobile. She enjoys leaping from car to car and dodging workers. She loves rifling through cars for anything valuable. Junie finds money and oddities, such as a baby dog preserved in a jar. It's the kind of thing that she might show people for a fee. Junie dreams of getting rich, and she skips school as she invents schemes to shake down tourists.

Junie also sells condoms at school. She leads her mother to believe that she is having sex with Babbidge's oldest son, Luke, the tough-minded manager of a potato farm, who makes nightly rides to berate workers to be more productive. Junie accompanies him. However, Luke will not be the Babbidge that she seduces.

Like Junie, the salvage yard workers also retrieve things left behind in cars, which have passed their road life for one reason or another. Someone discovers a bug zapper, for instance, a "yuppie" invention that perhaps has no place in Egypt, where people have learned to live with black flies and mosquitoes.

Another worker retrieves a short sleeve BOWDOIN shirt, which would be ludicrous for someone in Egypt to wear in public.

Gene Babbidge doesn't confine his cruelty to his children. He possesses a pack of dogs that are chained for life outside his son Luke's house, where he and Lillian live temporarily. The animals have no shelter and suffer through the seasons, poorly fed. Babbidge's justification to his family for the dogs' treatment is as terse as it is morally threadbare: "Life ain't no Walt Disney pi'ture." In one of the many colorful images in *Letourneau*'s, Junie's half sister seethes that what Babbidge "really needs is an egg beater up the ass."

One night, while Babbidge and most of the kids are at midweek prayer, a truck from the salvage yard appears some distance from the house. The dogs bark fiercely. An outburst of rifle fire continues until all the animals are silenced. From the house it's difficult to identify the shooters. One assumes that animal-loving Lucien could no longer tolerate Babbidge's treatment of his dogs and that for Crowe Bovey blasting animals was as pleasurable as sex with a woman other than his wife.

Babbidge shows no reaction to the slaughter. He is as tightly spooled as thread on a bobbin. Later, his second oldest son, Mark, challenges his father in a suggestive way. First he accuses Big Lucien of the killings. He taunts his father that he won't confront the boss because the "man of gold . . . has him by the balls." Then Mark pursues another tack: "But thirteen dogs dead ain't much of a massacre, is it, Dad? You've probably seen PILES of human people in Nam. Death probably don't bother you one little bit." Though he fathered ten children and beats them regularly, Babbidge remains dispassionate in the face of Mark's onslaught. His past is posted territory. "Simmer down, Mark," his father tersely responds.

The family moves to Miracle City after a year of living with Luke. Big Lucien secures a small trailer for them on acreage he owns and devotes to the formation of Miracle City. A hippie commune formerly occupied the land. Perhaps they coined its name. Now Miracle City represents no utopian aspirations. It's the gathering place of Egypt's underclass. Lucien locates trailers of various sizes and vintages for them. Shacks spring up like toadstools. Salvage yard workers use cheap particleboard to toss together "camps" with no plumbing, for people in immediate need of shelter.

A former hippie and ex-wife of Big Lucien returns to Egypt after ten years in California. Chute delivers a sharp rebuke to the hippie movement, even though she lives a kind of back-to-the-land counterculture way of life. Scars are etched into the hippie's body, the result of a knife attack by her boyfriend, who presumably was high on LSD. She uses an aluminum cane. Her body has become markedly bottom heavy. Her outlay for a decade as a California hippie amounts to a lifetime of bodily wear. With her youth squandered, people don't recognize her. Big Lucien has a particleboard shack built for the refugee.

Miracle City keeps overrunning Big Lucien's land—Egypt's perverse model of a suburban subdivision or, alternatively, a kind of Wild West ramshackle squatter settlement erected according to necessity, not design. It reaches a tipping point. The town selectmen mobilize to rein in Miracle City's threat to Egypt's landscape aesthetics, and thus to the town's appeal for prospective new residents "from away." The selectmen grandfather existing trailers and camps but prohibit any further development. The code officer constantly polices Miracle City in his Caravan, what the locals dub a "yuppie bus." Big Lucien tries clandestinely to shoehorn hidden trailers and camps onto his land. He doesn't fool the code officer, who orders people to vacate their only shelter. There is loose talk of shooting the oppressive town official. The dispossessed settle for hanging him in effigy.

One of the more poignant scenes involves Severin Letourneau, Big Lucien's nephew. A landlord evicts him and his family from their apartment because they owe back rent. As if eviction weren't enough, he lectures them, offering a patronizing, yet prominent, 1980s view of poverty: "It's not my fault you people can't manage your money right . . . or don't have the initiative to get better jobs or training or however that goes." That is, "you people" suffer from personal and cultural deficiencies that exonerate him and society. Chute's novels offer a rejoinder. Invariably her major characters possess no impaired work ethic. Among other things, they lack opportunity.

Big Lucien places Severin and his family in a trailer, but it's not grandfathered. They try to fool the code officer by taking periodic refuge in a tool shed. They use candles for light and a Coleman stove for cooking. The family sleeps on mattresses. Severin's aunt, Big Lucien's sister, insists that any home, no matter how humble, needs a crucifix. She gives Severin a "pink plastic Jesus," a resonant symbol in its brittleness and the only thing that hangs on the shed's walls. A salvage yard worker visits and his words suggest the tension between the law and morality, or compassion: "You mean this lean-to–chicken shed, or whatever it is . . . is grandfathered . . . the nice trailer, it wasn't?"

In an essay published six years after *Letourneau's*, titled "The Other Maine," Chute went off on a rant about town code enforcement and what she saw as the campaign to situate the backcountry landscape under the canopy of "The Way Life Should Be." "Lots of us have assorted useful stuff around our yard: tractor parts, truck tires, wooden skids, plastic industrial pails, rolled up chicken wire," she lists along with other items. Such front yards, town officials say, put off tourists and disrupt Maine's cultural and economic investment in Vacationland. The selectmen create the "nightmare" code officer because "tourists like to think we are all sitting up here in front of the fireplace," she grumbled, "with fashionable sweaters, pedigreed dogs, perfect teeth, softly waved hair . . . inside our manicured white New England houses with short grass and . . . [a] hot-top driveway."[21] That Mainers themselves increasingly buy into the state's manufactured tintype particularly set off Chute.

No one in *Letourneau's*, except perhaps the selectman and the code enforcer, sees themselves as inhabiting Vacationland. As the authorities thwart the expansion of Miracle City, life goes on in its grandfathered trailers and camps. In Babbidge's, undersized trailer mattresses fill the floor night and day. Lillian scrambles to feed the family as Chute depicts privations of the underclass's diet. The family drinks Kool Aid. Potatoes are a staple of their supper. They consume deer meat and something called "fast meat," which even liberal amounts of ketchup don't make palatable to Mark. He spits out his first bite. "What was that! The gums of somebody's false teeth?" Nevertheless, Babbidge never fails to say a prayerful thanks over whatever meager provisions Lillian places on the table. His religious fundamentalism seems to have anesthetized him to the family's allotted life. Soon Babbidge finds himself dismounted from his high horse.

Junie has quit school to work in the mill. Her pay helps the family plod along. Lillian's hatred for Babbidge swells as he sits every night in a large chair amid a snarl of mattresses. He wears his work shirt and battery-acid-stained pants, watching television. One night Babbidge picks up Junie from her late shift at the mill and takes her to tow away an apparently repossessed car. She teases him, dancing suggestively when he finishes hauling the car onto the back of the truck. "Don't mess around with me . . . unless you mean real business." After some playfulness, she starts to unbutton his shirt. She is naked. "I'll do anything you want," Junie entices Babbidge. "ANYTHING." He turns her around and, doggy-style, gives her a few thrusts; his carnal appetite is satisfied in seconds. It's typical of Chute's male-centered, loveless, farm-animal-like sex. On the way home she thinks of her sexual encounters with boys at the mill. "I hate your ways, you old thing," she derides Babbidge. "You make love like an old wild goat."

Babbidge's half brother, Ernie Train, arrives for a visit. He reveals a crucial part of Babbidge's past that humiliates him. A country singer who has performed nationally, Train is something of a local celebrity. Their grandmother in Aroostook raised him and Babbidge. She favored the latter, according to Train, so much so that she would have had Babbidge's "shits bronzed." Ernie appears to have squandered his money on women and drugs. He seeks a "loan" from his half brother, who is in debt himself.

Ernie turns on Babbidge, telling of his hippie past. He does more. He produces a picture of a naked hippie Babbidge that he has shown women across the country who didn't believe his description of Gene's physical attributes. Junie hogs the picture of a bearded, long-haired hippie with a dangling member so long it could pass for a true-to-life picture altered into a trick "believe or not." Babbidge gets up from the table and collapses on a mattress with a tattooed arm across his eyes. "That's what I call my B.C. picture of Gene," Ernie offers. "BEFORE CHRIST."

When they're alone, Ernie keeps tearing at his brother's emotional scar tissue. "Ain't NOBODY snort more coke, gulp more V. O., and gobble up more acid than you used ta." Ernie ends up professing his atheism and then hanging himself in Miracle City's woods.

Junie is soon pregnant from her fleeting encounter with Babbidge's manhood. Her half sister persuades her to move to their father's house. Crowe Bovey is still camped out under Big Lucien's stairs and rescuing parts from junked cars.

In addition to Miracle City, the salvage yard represents Big Lucien's second contribution to life in Egypt. Chute deploys it to disrupt images of pastoral Maine, to comment on American consumption, and to suggest how compassion can prevail even in a junkyard. Consider the last point. Big Lucien employs more men than he needs, some of them part-timers who just need assistance. When money gets tight, he forgoes salvaging parts for saving lives. He brings in the big crusher, which just pancakes cars that are sold immediately by weight for quick cash.

If the office wants a part, it relies on a walkie-talkie and calls: "Headquarters to Wasteland . . . Headquarters to Wasteland." Yet the salvage yard signifies more than a wasteland. It abides as a kind of memorial to former dreams and to the marketers of American consumption. Cars come in a blur of brands, styles, colors, and sizes. There's a junked car for everyone. The crusher performs its last rites, indifferent to the bygone status of American automobile culture. The massive machine "eats a couple of Mavericks, a Bobcat, a Satellite, a Vega, a Bronco, and a good looking Dodge Ram. . . . The fork loader gores a Pontiac . . . backs up . . . rams it . . . gores it again."

A blue Baptist bus stands in the middle of the salvage yard, spared from the crusher. It seems to offer workers some relief during Maine winters. Armand Letourneau, Big Lucian's brother, asks in Canuck, "A big fat goof God made in making hell a hot place . . . aye? He would get to torture sinners lot worst have he make nine below and a . . . big wind."

It is no exaggeration to suggest that the men have a measure of pride in their employment in the salvage yard. They work for a benevolent employer. Though the pay is low, they avoid labor in the woods and the mill. The men seem to wear their work shirts all the time—at home as well as on the job. Babbidge has a well-stocked wardrobe of three "Letourneau's" shirts. He doesn't wear anything else.

As Junie's pregnancy progresses, she regularly sleeps with Crowe Bovey, who is camped out under Big Lucien's stairs. He assures her that sex will not affect the baby. Surely his kind of low-grade intimacy runs little risk. "His love making is only a few hard jabs and then it's over." Once again, it's Egypt's version of barnyard copulation. With Junie, evenings pass as Bovey drones on about his first passion: his gun collection.

Perhaps improbably, they decide to elope before the baby's birth. Bovey dresses in a button-up sweater for the marriage. A few days later, to solve their impoverishment, "Crowe combs his hair, combs his beard, puts on his plaid shirt and his brown dress up button-up sweater." The change in clothes and grooming signal a moment of transformation. He packs his valuable gun collection in boxes and "wrapped in blankets," carries it out to his truck, and drives away. When he returns, the collection has been sold and he cries. He grieves, finally, for the loss of his family, it seems, not only for the sacrifice of his guns. He doesn't—or, rather, he can't—explain his tears. He and Junie now have money for a house. Chute has devised something of a too tidy resolution of the tensions in the lives of Junie and Bovey.

A few pages later, the last in the book, we finally come face-to-face with Big Lucien. We already suspect he's not physically huge. His oldest son, Norman, who hates his work in the woods, is not large, and he fits into Big Lucien's hand-me-down salvage yard shirt. More important, his younger brother, Little Lucien, who also works in the woods, lifts weights fanatically and comes to resemble a "Mr. Maine." The fifteen-year-old, we are told, represents the Big Lucien, and Big Lucien is the Little Lucien. Still, there remains a certain mystery surrounding the meal ticket for many in Egypt.

The father has been whoring and drinking in Portland, the distant metropolis in the backcountry's cultural geography of Maine. He spent the night in jail. Now ex-wife Maxine has arrived to return Big Lucien to his native domain. She circles the police station several times as Chute builds the reader's curiosity. Big Lucien finally appears: "He has thinning hair. Work clothes. He has narrow cringing shoulders like he's ducking a thrown shoe. . . . A small man.

What someone would call a 'shrimp.'" The reader should not be surprised or disappointed. The diminutive man has a big heart offset by a boundless libido. Chute leaves it ambiguous whether Big Lucien supports his ex-wives and the trail of offspring those and other relationships spawn. But the reader is left to grapple with the moral calculus of Big Lucien's life—his sexual self-gratification versus his large heart.

Reviews of *Letourneau's* were mostly positive, if, on the whole, not quite brimming with the enthusiasm for *The Beans*. Cathie Pelletier reviewed the book enthusiastically for the *Atlanta Journal Constitution*. "Few authors write with such detail, with such memory for despair, with such painful yet remarkable insights into a portion of the country that still sees fit to bless the country and the president who are, at least in part, responsible for their discomfiture." Though the reviewer for the *New York Times* found fault with some of Chute's techniques (how she overused capital letters for emphasis, exclamation points, and ellipses, for instance), he nevertheless found much to praise in *Letourneau's*. She had a fine eye for detail. Chute also "superbly rendered personality." He concluded that *Letourneau's* is an "energetic and unsentimental book." The *Boston Globe* praised Chute once again for "speaking for Maine's voiceless in *Letourneau's*."[22]

Of course, there were dissenters. The reviewer for the *Providence Journal* sharply critiqued *Letourneau's* as he had reacted to *The Beans*. He accused Chute of exploiting the poor, of taking literary advantage of "our fascination with the seamy, amoral aspects of life among the poor and anonymous." Moreover, *Letourneau's* "has barely a semblance of a plot." And she failed to show how society shaped her characters' impoverishment.[23]

The last point possesses merit; Chute has never seemed to develop a coherent politics, even after she formed the peaceful 2nd Maine militia and invaded the State House with kazoos. She became an avid advocate for the Second Amendment and an enthusiastic gun collector. As late as 2008, she told *The Week* magazine that the 2nd Maine militia was not political. "Political means you're taking a stance on how to fix it [society], but I don't think it can be fixed. It's humans. How do you fix humans?"[24]

Following *Letourneau's*, Chute received a prestigious Guggenheim Fellowship. Her first two books seemed to represent something of the high-water mark of her career. Chute's writing hit a soft patch immediately thereafter. Her third book was long winded and disjointed. *Merrymen* (1994) swelled to nearly seven hundred pages. It contained an estimated four hundred characters. Chute's editor facetiously called it *"War and Peace* in a small town."[25] *Snow Man* (1999) returned to the length of *The Beans* and *Letourneau's*, but it was not well received by critics. Then there was a ten-year drought as Chute labored to carve out new works from twenty-five hundred pages she had submitted for a novel.[26] She made a comeback with *The School on Heart's Content Road* (2009), a *New York Times* Notable Book of the Year, and *Treat Us like Dogs and We Will Become Wolves* (2014), whose critical reception resounded with the strongest praise since *The Beans*.[27]

Treat Us like Dogs won the Pen New England Award for Excellence in Fiction. The sprawling nearly seven-hundred-page "novel" contains some of Chute's best writing. It's also a complex work overpopulated with characters and with preachy passages. As with *The School on Heart's Content Road*, Chute provides readers of *Treat Us like Dogs* with a glossary at the end of the novel. But she recommends that readers not consult the reference! Both novels examine the Settlement, a self-sufficient community of mostly marginal people in Egypt. Gordon St. Onge, the polygamous so-called Prophet, presides over the community and fathers upward of twenty of its children. He is thirty-nine years old and six feet, five inches tall, rugged and handsome. He refrains from sex with married women in the Settlement, but not with others. Much of the plot is propelled by his interactions with Ivy Morelli, a petite twenty-four-year-old reporter who investigates rumors about the Settlement. The fallout from her story about the community and his sexual relations with a fifteen-year-old artist create problems for St. Onge. The Prophet and the reporter are vivid characters, as is St. Onge's former wife, a Passamaquoddy from northern Maine. The young artist is also a complex character.

Treat Us like Dogs shifts from omniscient author to multiple first-"person" narrators, including interplanetary "advanced people." The question of what is actually happening at the Settlement amid all the rumors helps sustain the reader through Chute's literary kaleidoscope. And so does her colorful, inventive use of language. A drenching rain falls like a "nail gun." "The hair on Ivy's neck moves spiderishly." Fireflies form trails of "hiccuppy wattage." The Prophet becomes "beered-up." The picnic table at Kool Kone "is a gooey, relishy, choclaty mess." A character's hair is "wetly black." Trying to solve a philosophical problem is "like an upside bug on a hard floor trying to square up."

To be sure, Chute's quest for the striking use of language sometimes misfires: "There was a pissed-off-looking red sunset with purple worms over the top edge and a bottom layer that looked like human organs, veiny and orange." Moreover, her rush of words and characters occasionally obscures the plot. Nevertheless, both *Treat Us like Dogs* and *School on Heart's Content Road* show Chute's growth as a writer over three decades, since her first two Egypt books brought to life the backcountry and its hardscrabble people for a large national audience.

Chute represents a highly distinctive voice in Maine and in American literature. Her originality shines through her best work—*The Beans* and *Letourneau's*—despite her novels' limitations, including a literary vision that bogs down in a moral muddle in her first book. In both form and substance, she is a literary subversive. Chute disrupts the L.L. Bean-coastal-tourist bureau imaging of Maine. The prosperous 1980s, with the pathologizing of the poor, represents her high historical moment. To the backcountry as Maine's Appalachia Chute brings the revelatory point of view of one who grew up on the coast but before midlife found herself mired in rural poverty.

III

MILL CITY AND MILL TOWN

6

ETHNICITY AND THE MILL CITY

Gerard Robichaud and Elizabeth Strout

"The Pine Tree State" and "Down East" don't lend themselves to images of an industrial landscape. Yet Maine is a well-watered state. Given its size, nature has endowed Maine with some of New England's longest rivers: the Penobscot, Kennebec, and Androscoggin, to cite the most important. These rivers, along with more modest ones (the Saco and the Presumpscot, for example), supplied waterpower for early industrialization. Over time, textile, shoe, and papermaking cities and towns came to define significant parts of Maine's landscape.

Lewiston, thirty miles northwest of Portland on the Androscoggin, developed into Maine's premier industrial community. With a population of nearly thirty-nine thousand in 1940, Lewiston stood as Maine's second largest city, according to the US Census. By then what had originated as a Protestant town had evolved into an overwhelmingly Catholic ethnic city.

Two novelists, writing more than a generation apart, have explored the experience of sharply different ethnic groups in Lewiston. Gerard Robichaud (1908–2008) published novels that fictionalized first- and second-generation French-Canadian life in Lewiston, followed by Livermore Falls. Franco descendants still constitute the single largest ethnic group in Maine. Nearly one-quarter of the state's population claims French ancestry.[1] Robichaud examines the constituent elements that sustained French-Canadian and then Franco-American identity over time.

Elizabeth Strout (b. 1956) created the fictional Maine mill community of Shirley Falls in her impressive debut novel *Amy and Isabelle* (1998). After winning the Pulitzer Prize for *Olive Kitteridge*, a collection of stories mostly about a colorful coastal Maine retired teacher, Strout returned to Shirley Falls to examine the progress of Somali immigrants, the largest group of Maine newcomers, after the turn of the twenty-first century.[2] Lewiston served as her real-life case study.

In pairing a Pulitzer Prize winner with a rather obscure writer who published only two novels, I don't mean to suggest that their literary achievements resemble one another. Robichaud's most important work, *Papa Martel: A Novel in Ten Parts* (1961), displays his skill as a storyteller who created believable and sometimes moving dialogue. But its principal significance for my purposes is the insight the novel offers into the distinctive, durable aspects of French ethnicity in Maine.

PAPA MARTEL: FRENCH CANADIANS AND FRANCO-AMERICANS

Tens of thousands of immigrants primarily from Quebec but also from the Maritimes (principally New Brunswick) flocked to New England's industrializing cities after the Civil War, continuing into the early twentieth century. In Maine, Canadians resembled Mexican immigrants in one important respect: Their new country shared a border with the old homeland. In both Maine and the Southwest, immigrants commonly crossed and recrossed borders. Proximity to the homeland and preservation of the native tongue intersected.

Nevertheless, among the French, permanent communities, or "petit Canadas," developed across New England and generated novels written in French from as early as 1878. Two generations passed before publication of the first Franco novel in English (1938), a marker perhaps of the group's protracted progress toward acculturation and, especially, assimilation.[3] *Papa Martel* appears to be the first, and only, novel about the French-Canadian experience in Maine. Moreover, with its sequel, *The Apple of His Eye* (1965), Gerard Robichaud remains the only published Maine novelist to date who devoted his work to examining the world of French-Canadian immigrants and their children. (A retired Maine professor has self-published novels in French.)

Biographical information on Robichaud is meager, even in the well-endowed Franco-American Collection at the University of Southern Maine's Lewiston-Auburn campus. Robichaud's mother returned to her hometown, St. Evariste de Beauce, Quebec, for her son's birth in 1908. She did so at the urging of her doctor, who claimed health benefits if her newborn first breathed "her natal air."[4] Thus Robichaud arrived in the world after a border crossing that cultivated a kind of mystic bond with the homeland.

His father, a skilled carpenter, came to Maine as a young man to work in the woods. After he married and settled in Lewiston, he accepted jobs throughout Maine while the family remained behind. The fictional Papa Louis Martel is also a traveling carpenter-contractor, in partnership with a fellow French Canadian. He is unable to read or write. Given the close parallels between the novel and what we know about Robichaud, it seems safe to posit that his father was illiterate.

Except for the novel, we know little more about Robichaud's mother, other than that she died when he was ten, as occurs in *Papa Martel*. Robichaud and a brother were sent to an asylum for children, overseen by Catholic nuns. At the age of twelve, he returned to Quebec and entered a preparatory school near Montreal that groomed boys for the priesthood. But he left the seminary at the age of nineteen, frustrating the family's pride in giving one of their own to the church.

After a short stint working in a Connecticut bank, Robichaud made his way to Greenwich Village. A young man far from the world of Lewiston, and liberated from his family's expectation of gaining a priest, Robichaud apparently became caught up in the Village's cultural ferment during the years of the Depression. He supported himself by working as a bellhop for at least part of that time. In 1941, he joined the army, served for four years in the Pacific Theater, and was decorated for his service on Iwo Jima.[5]

Robichaud returned to New York City and apparently met his future wife Elizabeth on VJ Day. We know nothing about her, except that after Robichaud studied in a nondegree writing program at Columbia University in 1951, she encouraged him to develop and pull together his family stories. She had heard and read colorful and heartbreaking tales of his family's life in Lewiston. Doubleday, a leading New York publisher, released *Papa Martel* a decade later. Its success led to Robichaud's second novel with Doubleday, *The Apple of His Eye*. *Papa Martel* is far superior to the latter work both for its literary merits and for its particularized portrait of French-Canadian family life in Lewiston. Robichaud lived to one hundred and continued to write into his nineties. But he published little before he died in Auburn in 2008.

Papa Martel takes place in "Groveton" (Lewiston) with flashbacks to Quebec and New Brunswick that fill in the stories of Louis Martel and Cecile Bolduc, his wife. The book is not so much a novel as a plotless, loosely laced series of family stories. Papa Martel, the benevolent patriarch, provides whatever unity the novel possesses. In many respects, Robichaud has penned a fictionalized biography of his father. A vibrant family life pivots around him. Yet Maman, over her shortened life, abides as a forceful family presence in her own right.

Robichaud situates *Papa Martel* between 1919 and 1937. We might reflect on some major developments in Lewiston during those years. In 1920, a resurgent Ku Klux Klan spewed its anti-Catholic, anti-immigrant bile in the city and burned a twelve- foot cross. That same year Francos represented nearly 50 percent of Lewiston's population and established it as a bilingual city. Over the course of the 1920s and 1930s, a French-Canadian self-consciousness began slowly to evolve into a Franco-American identity, a measure of acculturation, though the French language continued to dominate in the community's churches, schools, and homes. In 1920, more than 50 percent of working Franco men and more than 83 percent of their workingwomen labored in mills. Beginning in the mid-1930s, Lewiston's textile industry slid into its long decline. The Lewiston and Auburn shoe workers staged a bitter strike in 1937, and the governor had to call out the Army National Guard.[6]

With the exception of some gestures toward the transition from French Canadians to Franco-Americans, *Papa Martel* acknowledges none of the significant, even tumultuous, events that occurred in Lewiston between 1919 and 1937. There are only a few references to the Depression and the plight of the mills. By noting these silences, I do not intend to suggest that as a literary contribution to social and cultural history, *Papa Martel* lacks sufficiency. Nor do I mean to propose that Robichaud should have written a different book. Rather, if one takes account of what he chose not to write about, one may gain a better sense of Robichaud's achievement in capturing the texture of life in a traditional Maine French-Canadian family of the first and second generations. In other words, Martel offer entrée into a petit Canada world, into the community within the community.

The French, more than other immigrant groups, displayed ethnic persistence. "Survivance" is often the preferred label for this ethnic pattern. In *Papa Martel*, the patriarch muses over cultural adhesives that ensure French persistence: "their hardy attachment to the Catholic faith, their strong traditions of family life, [and] a common French language." As the Martel family demonstrates, such elements underscore endogamy—marriage within the group. In 1920, for example, 93.5 percent of French marriages were endogamous, compared to 75 percent for the Irish.[7] In addition, the family's pride in French history, in the "coureurs de bois" and the era when their ancestors possessed so much of North America, underwrites ethnic identity. After all, the French were in the New World before the Pilgrims.

Thus *Papa Martel* explores the density of French ethnicity and its resulting persistence. The two wives of Papa Martel, and his children, can acculturate—that is, adjust to American culture—but do not fully assimilate. They remain attached to the French language, to marriage with fellow Francos, and to life in their "petit Canadas."[8]

It's a bone-chilling snowy January night in Groveton, Maine, when we first meet the Martels. Louis and Cecile have been married for seventeen years. They have six children (another has died), five boys and one girl, ranging in age from six to sixteen. Cecile is nearing the end of her eighth pregnancy. They live on the second floor of the Pelletier block, a large multifamily apartment building.

Their tenement is well appointed with sacred objects of their faith. Crucifixes hang in all the bedrooms. A print of the "Blessed Family" is fixed over the wood and kerosene stoves, where the family huddles during the winter. A white Madonna rests on a table next to the marriage bed with a votive candle and Rosary beads. The apartment contains holy water.

Before Cecile gives birth to a girl who will be named for her mother, Robichaud skillfully provides the backstories to her marriage with Louis. It illuminates several aspects of the French experience, both in the homeland and in America: family size, dire poverty, the mythologizing of the past, and the historic animus toward the English, who, in the eighteenth century, conquered first Acadia and later Quebec.

Louis was the youngest in a family of seventeen from New Brunswick. The "rhythm method" was the only form of birth control available to all pious Catholics, but the French appear to have had especially large families. "Marry and multiply," Louis will urge repeatedly to his last single daughter. Despite the migration from dire impoverishment in New Brunswick, he cultivates an imagined past: "Acadee! He said and sighed. Sweet Acadee!" At the same time, he transports to Maine and will nurture over the course of his life a "hatred [of] all Henglish hairistocrats!" English is the Protestant language. "To speak to God in Henglish? Sounds wrong to me." Maman will realize the importance of English for her children. In other words, she will see their future as Franco-Americans. Louis, who can neither read nor write, will remain secure in his primordial French-Canadian identity.

He comes to Maine to work as a logger. But during the summer and fall he labors as a carpenter in Quebec. Cecile's father, a successful landowner, hires

Louis to do work at his daughter's convent. He sneaks a glimpse of his future wife clothed in her religious habit and his body quivers; he drops his hammer. The next day they engage in a conversation. The nun discovers he is illiterate and tries to get him to read his name.

Unbeknownst to Louis, Cecile Bolduc leaves the convent, giving up her teaching of girls, because of neurasthenia. Interestingly, she will never display symptoms of the nervous disorder after her marriage. Louis returns to her town the summer after their first encounter in the convent. He happens to see her in church, and from there the courtship begins. It is something of an unlikely marriage given their different educations and social backgrounds. Yet Cecile recognizes Louis's native intelligence and his skill as a carpenter. He goes through an apprenticeship, becomes a union carpenter, and settles in Groveton. With a partner, who can drive to jobs around Maine and out of state, he becomes a contractor. The narrative closely follows the arc of the Martels' marriage and domestic lives.

Though *Papa Martel* is a story authored by a man mostly about a man, Maman emerges as a character with a resolve that will not be broken by her husband or the parish priest. The latter visits the Martels to collect school tuition. Maman seizes the occasion to suggest the Franco-American future for her children. Drawing on her social background and experience as a teacher, she offers a critique of the parish school her children attend. The school, she insists, devotes too much time to religious activities at the expense of academic subjects. Since the French language, like a totalitarian dogma, exercises dominion over the school, Maman reserves her strongest criticism for the status of English. "Why they have an average of half an hour a week," Father Giroux, "the Napoleon of the school system," responds. That is precisely Maman's point: "Not enough in an English-speaking country." Maman will have to withdraw her children from school before Father Giroux revises the curriculum to put more stress on academics and English. The priest capitulates, though Maman's victory seems too easily secured.

Later we see Maman reading both the *Groveton Daily Herald* and the French *Le Messager*. The two papers suggest the essence of her exchange with Father Giroux. Maman surely values the preservation of her French language and heritage. However, she also wants to acculturate to their new home. To her children she reads "biographies of the great men of the Church of France, of Canada and of the United States." When Louis complains about "Henglish" as a Protestant language, she reprimands him: "It is the language of Shakespeare, of Milton, and of those who make money in the business world." From Shakespeare to money, from English to business, such juxtapositions suggest Maman's cultural literacy and pragmatism.

Father Giroux meets a different kind of quick-witted resistance from Louis than what he encountered with Cecile. His position reveals a working-class, churchgoing French Canadian's philosophy of life's precious simple pleasures. Father Giroux wants him to come to a meeting with other men of the parish and swear off alcohol, which is acquired illicitly. It is 1921, the second year of Prohibition. Louis and Pete Young, the only Protestant in the novel, are fermenting applejack in the cellar. Louis finds the priest's exhortation for abstinence oppressive. Before he refuses Father Giroux, Louis reflects on what gives shape and satisfaction to his domestic life: "A man's castle was built of little liberties, little indulgences, little pure sins, rewards for avoiding the big dirty sins." Louis, the illiterate immigrant who makes his living with his hands, defends his ground against the seminary-educated priest. The pope is no teetotaler, Louis points out. "He's an Eyetalian. He likes his Guiney red too." The Martels express their resistance to Father Giroux respectfully. That is how they have been raised. In addition, they plan to send their son Emile to a school in Quebec that will prepare him for the seminary.

The applejack in the cellar constitutes one of Louis's little pleasures. He plans to split it with Pete. Beyond this Protestant, Louis has only one other non-French individual in his acquaintance. A regular poker game adds another small pleasure to Louis's life. It consists of his French cronies, including the family doctor. One Irishman gains admission. Louis exemplifies Franco resistance to assimilation. From church to marriage to residence to work partners, ethnicity yokes Louis to a group solidarity and security. He may temporarily leave the physical bounds of his petit Canada, but he carries its cultural topography on his person.

As the Martel children grow up, complete high school, and marry Franco spouses at very young ages, Robichaud makes note of the Depression, as one would genuflect in church—it's obligatory and fleeting. Louis asks himself of the marriage of Maurice, his second oldest son, to Muriel Jolicoeur, "What could a man do for his children, these years of economic depression?" He welcomes Maurice and his wife for supper on alternate nights, when they don't eat with the Jolicoeurs.

The era's tumult fails to register with any weight in *Papa Martel* for at least two reasons. Robichaud's preoccupation involves the density of French-Canadian family life, and especially the way the Martels transport their Catholicism from church to home and back. In a word, *Papa Martel* offers an exceptionally interiorized perspective on French-Canadian life. Moreover, Robichaud represents Papa Martel as a self-employed, self-made man, albeit of modest social mobility, not a mill hand. He and Cecile overcame hardship after marriage. They spent their first Christmas in a shack that he constructed of salvage lumber, comforted only by a wood-devouring stove. Now, though he continues to live in a flat within the parish bounds, he also owns a two-room cottage, with a large screened porch on a lake beyond Groveton's grit, that he built by himself. In fact, he constructed most of the other lakeside retreats. He worked on "Sundays, when no one was looking." Such actions, like his resistance to Father Giroux, suggest how Louis, though a devout Catholic, is not a stiff-necked one.

Maman falls grievously ill in 1927, at the age of forty-eight. She is hospitalized, apparently with cancer. At nine o'clock each night the entire family gathers. They kneel and face the print of the Holy Family. Louis leads them in recitation of the Rosary—two holy families, sacred image and humble Martels. Some readers undoubtedly found the scene inspirational. (Long after the publication of *Papa Martel*, Robichaud said the book brought out "the priest in me.")[9] Cecile dies and the family begins a traditional mourning ritual: a year without movies, music, or dancing, along with the obligation to dress in dark clothes.

Two years before his mother died, Emile entered a preparatory school near Montreal, at the age of fourteen. He represents the family's offering to the church. For a devout family like the Martels, there is no greater honor than to have one of their own in the priesthood. It ennobles the family's standing in the parish. Yet Louis, even as he swells with pride over Emile, worries about his son's long trajectory toward the priesthood. "Was not Groveton dotted with boys who had started out the same way [as Emile] and were now garage mechanics, or dentists, and married?" One can only wonder about the disappointment of Robichaud's family when he left the seminary. The author obviously, at least in part, relives his experience through Emile, who will eventually detour from his path to the priesthood.

Emile returns to Groveton during vacations and summers. Louis arranges his room in a way that inscribes the father's respect for Emile and his hope for his son's future. "A luminous Sacred Heart," an artifact that seems particularly French-Canadian, sets the seminarian's room apart. Louis also creates "a small altar with real candles." The still-teenage Emile is viewed as a scholar on church law. The seminarian supplants the pastor when the family needs to clarify church teaching. When Papa Martel falls in love with a much younger nurse, for instance, Emile researches canon law to make sure church teaching presents no obstacle.

In 1930, three years after Cecile's death, forty-eight-year-old Louis first spies Monique Beaulieu at a local baseball game. She is thirty-two and unmarried. Such an exceptional status in a French-Canadian community appears to reside in the medical judgment that she is unable to conceive—a drawback in an ethnic group that values large families. She walks back and forth and comes close to where Louis is sitting. He's immediately attracted to her. Louis makes a quick, revealing assessment of her ethnicity: "with a full face, calm dark eyes, [and], white skin—a *Canadienne* for sure." Such a racialized eye erases the history of physical intimacy between the French and native people—something Elizabeth Coatsworth captures in Pete Fournier, the game warden in *Mountain Bride*. Famous Lewiston local son Marsden Hartley also presented a very different physical view from Robichaud's character in his brawny dark-skinned portrait titled *Canuck Lumberjack at Old Orchard Beach, Maine* (1940–1941).

Louis's initial description of Monique represents a crude example of what we now recognize as objectifying women—that is, treating them as a physical thing, especially a sexual object. He compares Monique to a mare: "Left flank. Right flank. Slowly. Gently. But ready to buck! Slowly. Gently, and now the twitching of the mane, ready to buck, ready for the deviltry to begin." Not long after he meets and courts Monique, another (non-French) woman enters the story, and Louis eroticizes her as the racial "other."

Felix, Louis's third oldest son at age twenty, spends long hours in the gym in between his work lugging fifty-pound bags of coal in winter and blocks of ice in summer up flights of tenement stairs. He emerges as a skilled amateur boxer with a string of victories behind him. He is scheduled to fight for the amateur championship of Maine. Felix appears on the threshold of turning professional. As Dr. Lafrance proclaims to his poker companions, "This is a matter of race. We now have, my friends, a chance to put up a French Canadian Jack Dempsey for the big title, one day." Louis learns at the poker game that Felix has not been training hard enough. He has been spending too much time with a Spanish waitress, Lucia Lopez.

Louis decides not to leave Lucia under wraps. With Monique and son Laurent and his wife for cover, he visits Lucia's restaurant for a lobster dinner. They are unaware that Louis's sole end is to take the measure of Lucia, especially her physical attributes. Even though he defends her against Laurent's assertion that she "gives it away," Louis's observations exoticize Lucia as he objectivizes her: "Nice ankle . . . dark-haired . . . lustrous hair . . . sad dark eyes . . . generous frontage." The last is a nice turn of phrase; it avoids more explicit language that might have offended Robichaud's audience in 1961. Louis goes on: "Quick with the hands, efficient, and what a set of restless hips."

Her hips have been too restless. Felix confides in his papa that he's responsible for Lucia's pregnancy—and that she's already married! Such adultery establishes Lucia's moral otherness. Papa explodes, only to calm down and apologize to Felix. He breaks out the whiskey and then urges Felix to get a good night's sleep. The very next morning, his trainer visits Louis to tell him that Lucia went horseback riding and the "great big trouble" has vanished. It all seems too easy and hasty a resolution to Felix's moral dilemma. Did the whole episode really happen in the life of the Robichauds? As a novelist, could the author not figure any other way out of such a profound moral predicament for a devout French-Canadian family except an overnight miscarriage induced by horse riding? In short, the resolution of this potentially rich incident in *Papa Martel* remains unsatisfying.

As the maturing of the Martel siblings continues, other "crises" unfold, though not involving "big" sins such as Felix's. Therese, Louis's oldest daughter, and her husband, Antoine, are in the fifth year of marriage, and childless. She despairs; he turns tight lipped. They have nephews and nieces all around them. Therese's high school classmates already have well-established families that will continue to grow. "From ironing their husband's pants, some women got pregnant," Therese reflects. It's a witty lament, but she feels like a woeful failure. Her efforts to fulfill the era's prescribed role for women, especially French-Canadian mothers—marry young and give birth every two or three years—have come to naught. An increasingly "crotchety" Dr. Lafrance offers no advice; he shoos Therese and Antoine out of his office. The parish priest proves equally ill equipped to address their frustration. He recommends adoption.

At her grandmother's funeral, Therese recalls the stories she once told about St. Anne de Beaupre, a beautiful basilica in a small town on the banks of the St. Lawrence, in Quebec, an official shrine where miracles had occurred. Grandmere told Therese that she had witnessed a man paralyzed below the waist toss his crutches to the ground and climb the church steps to the saint's statue. The site was a sacred place that drew French people from both sides of the border. Therese dedicates novenas and "special prayers" to St. Anne. In addition, she devises a bargain with the saint: she offers to make a pilgrimage to the shrine "if she is blessed with a child." As if to enhance her odds, Therese lights a candle to St. Anthony every night. She also solicits advice from Emile. In a letter from the seminary, he urges prayer to St. Gerard Majella, "the patron saint of pregnant women." Through Therese, Robichaud explores the rich devotional life of French Canadians, especially women, that extends beyond church ritual. Saints and shrines acquire special importance at moments of crisis. They shape the pious life of French Catholicism, offering direct access to the supernatural.

As the grandchildren keep arriving, even Louis, at age fifty-two, fathers a child with the supposedly sterile Monique. Papa Martel's *joie de vivre* increasingly derives from his large family. Therese finally gives birth. Only his second oldest daughter, Marie, remains single. A twenty-year-old student-nurse, she values her independence, even from the family and ethnic community. Marie represents the process of acculturation *and* assimilation. To Papa Martel's accusation that she is "too fussy," Marie responds, "There's a depression." Her seminarian brother fails to intimidate Marie: "There's a depression, Emile. You may not know it from living in your Grand Seminary." She goes on to warn Emile not to forget after his ordination that "a depression is a grave sin . . . a mortal sin." Implicit in Marie's moral outrage lies a criticism of the church that Emile's response confirms: "It's a new theology . . . never heard of it."

The final grand scene of *Papa Martel* takes place in 1937. There is an ebullient family gathering that Louis presides over to celebrate the marriage of Cecile, his youngest daughter, to Tom McLaughlin. In control of the party and in high form, the patriarch pokes fun at the absent groom. "I have nothing against the Irish," Papa Martel all but bellows. "They fought the good fight against the Henglish haristocrats." Yet that doesn't sufficiently redeem the Irish when it comes to his daughter's marriage. For Papa Martel, matrimony should express ethnic pride and loyalty. As he puts it, "What can an Irishman do here that Canadians have not done, and better?" Of course, many of Papa Martel's comments elicit guffaws because they are part of the merriment. But on the whole his words convey the first generation's ethnic solidarity that persists into the next generation and beyond. Group songs such as "Alouette" and "Vive La Canadienne" energize the party and invigorate group ethnic identity.

As it turns out, Tom is only Irish by birth. His parents died while he was still an infant. He spent the first ten years of his life under the care of the French Sisters of Charity. The French Dominican Brothers then educated him. Tom, Cecile explains, "never spoke a word of English, except during English class." He even talks in a "Maine patois." When Tom finally arrives, the family warmly greets him, the women kissing his cheek and tousling his red hair. In a sense, Cecile's marriage falls within the group; she will wed a man who, except for the accident of his infancy, is reborn as French. He's also a talented cornetist and has already left the unassimilated ethnic ghetto. He plays in a New York City jazz band. The newlyweds will live in the city.

For all his humorous bluster at the pre-wedding party, Papa Martel is wistful. Except for Marie and two-year-old Louis Jr., his children have moved out, though they reward him amply with a new generation. Still, now in his midfifties, Papa Martel feels time nipping at his heels. In his final act, Louis steals twenty minutes from God, measuring it against his life's ledger.

The clock is about to strike twelve when the overnight fast begins in preparation for receiving Holy Communion the next morning. Members of the family crave onion sandwiches, however, after eating lobster much earlier. Papa Martel plays God; he stops time by inserting his finger in the clock's mechanism to "muffle" its sound at the strike of twelve. In the perspective of a long life, it's a little sin, which Papa Martel rationalizes with humor: "Lord what's twenty minutes to you, when you possess Eternity? Remember too that in fifty years or so I've never missed Mass and in that time, in your Name I've suffered many a boring sermon. . . . Against that Lord, what's an onion sandwich after twelve?" Papa Martel's spontaneous, and humorous, prayer serves as a kind of benediction to the novel. It also carries another implied criticism of the church, this time for adherence to a myriad of unyielding rules.

For all of its flaws—the absence of a plot, its implausible turns, and its heavy silence on the Depression's hardships and millwork's drudgery—*Papa Martel* has offsetting strengths. Robichaud's realistic portrait of the patriarch is persuasive; he creates crisp and effective dialogue, and flashes of wit and humor light up the narrative. Above all, *Papa Martel* captures for the uninitiated the intimate life of a French-Canadian family over two generations. It's an important contribution to Maine's social and cultural history.

After the publication of *Papa Martel*, Robichaud informed the *Library Journal*, "I wanted to tell the story of a healthy and lively family. . . . I wished to speak of births, deaths and marriages, of love and customs that last, of faith that endures, of superstitions that still cling, and also with humor to treat of ecclesiastical rigidity and institutional pompousness, the slow tempo of adolescent growth, the demands of the flesh, and the wisdom and follies of French-Canadian folk ways."[10] On most of these points, Robichaud succeeded.

Surprisingly, *Papa Martel* was not reviewed anywhere near as widely as the other works in this study. Perhaps editors deemed its ethnic focus of not enough significance. *Book Review Digest* contains no entries for *Papa Martel*, and neither does the *New York Times Index*. The judgment of *Kirkus Reviews* probably comes close to the novel's critical reception: "An unpretentious book whose interest lies in the loving and accurate description of a region hardly touched upon in contemporary fiction."[11]

Still, *Papa Martel* proved successful enough for Doubleday to release Robichaud's second novel. *The Apple of His Eye* appeared in 1965. The novel is set in Groveton Falls, a mill town on the Androscoggin River (Livermore Falls, apparently). The novel, unlike its predecessor, depicts the town's physical setting: the "cotton mills, box shops, and pulp mills" that blocked "the Androscoggin from view"; the "stinks of saltpeter and sulphur" that hung over the town; and the thriving commercial heart of Groveton Falls, with its Doughboy statue and Dreamland Theater, whose Westerns swell the imagination of the town's youth.

Ten-year-old Michel Dumont, orphaned by the death of his parents in an automobile accident, is the novel's protagonist. The plot revolves around his guilt for keeping a substantial amount of money that doesn't belong to him. He finds the money in the coat of a dead and buried man who worked periodically for his father. Michel has kept it for four months instead of giving it to the nuns for the poor. The man left no family. During confession Father Prevost tells him he must give the money away, "restitute" it. The rest of the novel follows Michel and his friends as they go about giving the money away. A subplot centers on Michel's Uncle Victor, a bachelor womanizer from Boston. He returns to Groveton Falls to settle his nephew's affairs. Michel is destined for an orphanage. Surprisingly, Uncle Victor meets a woman he falls in love with. He decides to settle in his native Maine town, which he spurned for the big city. Michel will stay with him, and Uncle Victor will soon marry.

The Apple of His Eye is a light, unsatisfactory novel. Though it takes place in an almost exclusively French-Canadian world, the novel reveals far less about that ethnic group than *Papa Martel*. Robichaud lived out his long life as the author of only one significant novel.

ELIZABETH STROUT: NEWCOMERS AND NATIVES IN THE POSTINDUSTRIAL MILL CITY

Elizabeth Strout (b. 1956) is one of contemporary America's finest novelists. Five of her seven novels are set in Maine, including the Pulitzer Prize–winning *Olive Kitteridge* (2008). Strout's imaginative investment in Maine offers eloquent testimony of her personal attachment to the state and to her astute understanding of its people. Her consistently wide critical acclaim and commercial success signify, however, that she is far more than simply a Maine writer.

Nevertheless, when a recent interviewer asked her about her "relationship with Maine," she offered a compelling response: "That's like asking me what's my relationship with my own body. It's just my DNA."[12] Strout grew up between Durham, New Hampshire, and Harpswell, Maine. Her father was a science professor at the state university in Durham, and her mother taught English at the local high school and writing courses at the university. Her father described the family as "poor," but a more accurate characterization would be frugal.[13]

Strout spent summers in Harpswell, a beautiful town on a slender peninsula that extends from Brunswick into Casco Bay. Her parents built a house next to her grandmother's; it perched on a granite outcropping at the water's edge. Strout passed much of her time during the summer at the country store watching and envying tourists. Sometimes they photographed her, capturing in their imaginations an indigenous country girl as authentically Maine as the lobster traps along the main road. Such photographs "infuriated" her mother. Her reserved father, in turn, might be set on edge if Strout talked too much at family gatherings. They had a prearranged signal—he put his hand to his tie—for Strout to restrain herself.[14]

After graduation from Durham High School, she enrolled at Bates College in the shopworn mill city of Lewiston, whose post-9/11 race-colored events propel *The Burgess Boys'* (2013) plot. Since her parents neither watched television nor subscribed to a newspaper nor went to the movies, Strout underscores her unsophistication when she entered Bates. She says that the only two movies she had seen were *One Hundred and One Dalmatians* and *The Miracle Worker*.[15]

After graduation from Bates, Strout moved to England for a year. Then she came home to attend law school at Syracuse University. There she met her first husband, who was Jewish and from New York City. She graduated in 1982, moved to New York City, and taught at a community college. She had already soured on practicing law. Her marriage produced a daughter, but it did not last. Years later she met her current husband, a native Mainer, at a book signing. Jim Tierney is a former attorney general who teaches at Harvard Law School.

Strout had only published a handful of short stories, some in women's magazines, by the time she was forty. Then her first novel *Amy and Isabelle* became a national bestseller. "It was a long haul," she has reflected. "I kept going, long past the point where it made sense."[16] A kind of New England persistence, or fear of failure, led to impressive affirmation. After two bestsellers, her third novel, *Olive Kitteridge* (2008), won the Pulitzer Prize. It is not really a novel but a collection of stories about an eccentric, forceful former schoolteacher and her mild-mannered, retired pharmacist husband. Olive gives unity to the stories; yet her presence doesn't register in all of them. (And one story is nothing less than a farce.) Most recently, Strout has returned to her cranky character in *Olive, Again* (2019).

The Burgess Boys, which continued Strout's string of bestsellers, is a much more ambitious book than *Olive Kitteridge*. Strout says that she spent seven years researching *The Burgess Boys*.[17] It is a grand American book fruitfully compared to Philip Roth's *American Pastoral*. *The Burgess Boys* is a major Maine book, perhaps a great Maine novel equaling the achievement of Sarah Orne Jewett in *The Country of the Pointed Firs* or any of Ruth Moore's best work.

Such an evaluation might seem extravagant for a novel whose plot and subplots unfold both in Shirley Falls, Maine, and in New York City, where both Burgess boys live and work. But the family's secret original sin, which takes permanent root in the lives of siblings Jim, Bob, and Susan, transpires in Shirley Falls. It informs the boys' decision to turn their backs on the mill city. *The Burgess Boys* dwells on the particular and reaches toward more universal themes. To identify a few: place and leaving home; global migration; racial and religious intolerance, not only in Maine but also across the contemporary world. Strout is also a connoisseur of small things: Maine's short dark, cold days of winter, for example, with chilly houses and sweaters worn constantly, like armor against an invader.

We are introduced to Shirley Falls in *Amy and Isabelle*, Strout's finely crafted debut novel.[18] Isabelle, a single mother, and sixteen-year-old daughter Amy have moved down the coast to the larger town. Isabelle is in pursuit of a better job, and brighter marriage prospects. She harbors a dark secret and is overprotective of Amy, who chafes at her mother's control. A young girl who has vanished adds mystery to the novel.

The coast represents, perhaps, an unlikely location for a Maine shoe mill town. Shirley Falls assumes some of the iconography of a familiar city. The "roiling water" of the "sudsy" river crashes "over granite rocks." A bridge spanning the river defines the two parts of Shirley Falls. Isabelle and Amy rent a carriage house on the "good" side of town where the Congregational church is located. Each weekday morning Isabelle crosses the bridge for her secretarial job in the mill.

She works in a "fishbowl" office, a room with large glass windows. They enable fellow Congregationalist Mr. Avery to oversee the office staff. He delegates responsibility for these women to Isabelle, whose separate desk placement delineates her difference from the gossipy all-Franco-American office staff. The benevolent (or bored) Avery runs the office and the mill with cultivated disinterest. Though we are never afforded a view of the manufacturing process, we are introduced to aspects of working in a mill. When Amy draws close to her mother, she detects the "faint odor of damp brick" that

Isabelle emits. A "dead . . . putrid yellow" river whose "foam" collects at the river's "edge" divides the town's prosperous and working-class precincts. To Isabelle, Shirley Falls "appeared to be city."

Lewiston inhabits Strout's mental map of Maine's industrial landscape. In *The Burgess Boys*, she strains to keep Shirley Falls within the imagined bounds of a Maine mill town. She slips into referring to it as a city; she also represents Shirley Falls' ensemble as a cityscape. Whenever Bob Burgess's college girl-friend—now his ex-wife—visited Shirley Falls, she would climb a hill "at the edge of the small city, and she would look down over the spires of the cathedral, the river that was lined with brick mills, [and] the bridge that spanned its foaming water." Mill towns don't have cathedrals.[19]

Even before she spent months or years with Lewiston's Somali community conducting research for *The Burgess Boys*, Strout claimed a special relationship with the city. She told one interviewer that Lewiston is "a town close to my heart because I went to college there." To another, she described how "on the wall [of her office] is an old photograph of the Libbey Mill, in Lewiston, where her grandfather worked." She informed Minnesota Public Radio that the Burgess boys as "characters came to her years ago." The novel only emerged, however, "when she found a way to connect the characters to the growing Somali community in her home state of Maine." [20] Her intensive engagement with Lewiston's Somalis bolstered her personal and imaginative investment in the city.

The Burgess Boys recalls recent Lewiston history. Strout redeploys some of that history for imaginative purposes and devotes chapters to Somali perspectives.[21] Thus it is helpful to review the crucial, provocative racial developments in the city after 9/11 that garnered national attention.

With a population that was 97 percent white, the 2000 Federal Census established Maine as the least racially diverse state in the Union. In Lewiston, where Franco-Americans still constituted the largest ethnic group, the white population stood at 96 percent. Significant numbers of Somalis began to arrive in 2002. By the fall, upward of twelve hundred refugees had settled in a tattered section of downtown Lewiston, where rents were cheap among empty stores, tattoo parlors, and adult bookstores.[22]

The Somalis were secondary migrants. After spending years in Kenyan refugee camps, the Lewiston Somalis had first settled in Clarkston, Georgia, outside of Atlanta. But drugs, violence, and limited support drove them north, first to Portland and then to Lewiston, where apartments were cheaper and more readily available. The city was also much safer than Clarkston, though Lewiston had its own drug problem.[23] It is also important to note that the Somali refugees received only eight months of welfare support from the federal government.

They forfeited that benefit when they remigrated. To refugees hampered by language and lack of transportation but eager to work, Maine's five-year welfare limit proved attractive.

In the fall of 2002, the Franco-American mayor ignited a community controversy. He released a public letter to Somali elders and leaders instead of consulting with them privately. The letter appealed to these Somalis to stem the influx of their compatriots. The mayor asked the Somalis to "exercise this discipline." Then, in a statement that could only inflame progressive segments of Lewiston's white community, he wrote, "We have been overwhelmed and have responded valiantly. Now we need breathing room. Our city is maxed financially, physically and emotionally."[24]

The *New York Times* announced, "Mixed Welcome as Somalis Settle in a Maine City." The reporter heard rumors of free gifts galore that the federal government allegedly showered on the Somalis: cars, grants of money, air conditioners, and a jump to the head of the line for subsidized apartments.[25] The mayor's letter brought to light white grievances that had been festering for a year. The Somalis were sponging off hardworking taxpayers. In turn, his letter kindled Somalis' suspicion of municipal government and fear of white neighbors.

Still, the mayor's letter and the ensuing distrust on both sides rallied religious leaders, state officials, and ordinary citizens who welcomed the Somali refugees. In January 2003, a local Many and One Coalition staged a march and rally of approximately four thousand supporters of diversity. The governor and attorney general spoke to the crowd. The white supremacist World Church of the Creator held a recruitment rally in another part of Lewiston that attracted only forty people.[26]

In the aftermath of the rallies, life on the surface appeared to return to normal. But cross-cultural fears, resentments, and simple misunderstandings persisted as the Somalis continued to settle in Lewiston. Strout effectively captures this alteration to Lewiston's social fabric through Susan, the only Burgess sibling who has remained behind in Shirley Falls, and Abdikarim Ahmed, the Somali who opens a café-store, the first refugee business, during the years following the dual rallies. Somalis continued to relocate to Lewiston and to open businesses in long-vacant storefronts. Then, in the summer of 2006, Lewiston was again thrust into the national spotlight.

A thirty-three-year-old local man rolled a frozen pig's head, which had begun to bleed, into a mosque. Quickly arrested, he offered the defense that he intended a joke and didn't know that the storefront was a mosque or that pork is forbidden in Islam. At one point, he claimed the pig's head, which he launched down the mosque's center aisle, slipped from his hand. The attorney general charged the perpetrator with a civil rights violation. Maine Superior Court issued an injunction ordering him not to have any contact with the mosque or its members. A violation would lead to jail time and a heavy fine. Many members of the mosque said they forgave the desecrator. The imam told the *New York Times*, "Most people feel welcome, but after these incidents not all." He went on to plead, "Mainers have to understand that this is the new Maine."[27] Strout's mother sent her the story about the mosque's desecration. It took flight in her literary imagination.

Before she could tell the story of a Somali community based in part on actual events in Lewiston, Strout conducted a kind of ethnographic fieldwork. She has described how she drove by a Lewiston school to observe: "I wanted to see, with the little kids, if they were playing with white kids, and so I would just watch and watch and watch." She ventured into what was at the time the lone Somali store and won the confidence of community members. Some Somalis invited her to their homes. "It took a long time," she has reflected, "but it was so *interesting*."[28] Once she came to understand Lewiston's Somalis sufficiently— the women who had experienced years in refugee camps, now with "ravaged" faces, and the men who congregated on the sidewalk because they missed the Somali sky—Strout was ready to write.

She ingeniously tells two divergent, then intersecting, stories of the Burgess family and the Shirley Falls Somali community, especially store owner Abdikarim Ahmed. The troubled narrative of the three Burgess siblings, on its face, constitutes the novel within the novel. Their adult emotional dysfunction, it would seem, derives from the Burgesses' early family fall from innocence. When Jim, the oldest, was eight, and the twins, Bob and Susan, were four, their father, a foreman in a mill, died in his own driveway. One day he parked his car at the top of the steep driveway and walked down to check the mailbox. Bob fooled around with the gears; the car rolled down the hill and killed his father. Such is the foundational narrative that the Burgesses carry into their early fifties when we first meet them. Yet it rests on deceit that is revealed too late, it seems, to reclaim the family's emotional life.

Jim represents the Burgesses' alpha male. After the state university, he attended Harvard Law School on a scholarship. Jim soars to the top of his profession as a result of securing the acquittal of Wally Packer, a national black "crooner" accused of having his white girlfriend killed. As with the O. J. Simpson case, toward which the Packer trial gestures, everyone believed the singer was guilty. Packer went free and Jim joined a top-drawer Manhattan law firm. Helen, Jim's wife, comes from a monied Connecticut family. They live comfortably in the fashionable Park Slope Brooklyn neighborhood. Their three children are away at college.

Jim professes to hate Shirley Falls. Yet he secretly reads the local paper every day. One can infer that he sees how he might have attained great political success in Maine. Tall, handsome, and eloquent, Jim surely would have become Maine attorney general, then governor, and possibly United States senator, if he had stayed home. But he fled Maine after a brief stint in the attorney general's office. His hate for Shirley Falls is perhaps as much self-hate. Beyond his rejection of public service, Jim has other grounds for self-loathing, as he discloses near the novel's end.

Hapless younger brother Bob is also a lawyer. His professional engine has been at low idle for decades, however. He labors in the trenches as an appeals lawyer at Legal Aid. In other words, even in this public service lawyerly realm he's on the second team. Likeable and "big-hearted," Bob's life nevertheless is in disarray, traceable perhaps to the trauma of what happened to his father. Through the mists of a four-year-old's perception, Bob never saw, or later recalled, what actually occurred with the gears. He only knew what Susan yelled: "It's all your fault, you stupid head." He also saw his father's body lying at the foot of the driveway covered with a blanket. Even for a four-year-old—or, rather, especially for a four-year-old—this sight becomes etched into his psyche for life.

For Bob, adulthood seems to lengthen into an extended act of penance. Unable to produce a child, his marriage dissolves, though he and his ex-wife, Pam, remain fond of each other. They regularly have lunch. Pam remarries, but Bob scuttles a second marriage when his prospective bride demands that he break off the relationship with his ex-wife. He refuses. Bob lives alone in a downscale section of Brooklyn. In his isolation, he increasingly embraces the bottle as his companion.

Big brother Jim has never mentioned the accident that engendered so much upheaval in his family. Like his handling of witnesses in court, Jim knows his brother's vulnerabilities. He throws verbal punches and then retreats to his corner. His preferred names for Bob are "slob-dog" and "knucklehead." Bob absorbs these blows with no one to defend him, though his sister-in-law, Helen, likes him. Bob is tall like Jim and sports a mop of grey hair.

The Somalis enter the Burgess boys' lives when Susan calls Jim, not Bob. Her son Zach has thrown a pig's head into a mosque, "during prayer. During Ramadan." To Helen, Jim relays in detail what Susan said actually happened. The melting pig's head bled on the carpet running down the center aisle. The poor mosque couldn't afford to replace it. Thus, following Islamic law, the members scrubbed the carpet seven times. Months earlier, when Bob learned from Susan that Somalis were settling in Shirley Falls, he told Helen. She asked two revealing questions: "Why are there Somali people in Maine anyway? Why would anyone go to Shirley Falls except in shackles?" Helen's dismissive view of Maine is that of a well-heeled Connecticut native whose primary task in life is to hire good domestic help. Bob's retort to her is refreshing: "They are in shackles. Poverty's a shackle."

The police still haven't found out that Zach is the person who carried out the desecration, which he claims was a prank, not a hate crime. Susan wants to turn him in to the police before he's caught. She's hoping Jim will accompany Zach to the station. But Jim and Helen are about to set off on a vacation to St. Kitts, with the managing partner of the firm and his wife. Bob, who happens to be present when Susan calls, offers to go by borrowing Jim's car and driving to Shirley Falls. (He's afraid to fly.) Jim is skeptical, and not only of Bob's ability to carry out the task of handing Zach over to the authorities. He knows that Susan and Bob hate each other. Beyond their father's tragic death, the brother and sister grew up attached at the hip by their mother, who referred to them as "the twins." Moreover, Bob is not licensed to practice in Maine. He can do no more than accompany Zach to the police station and sit passively as Zach is booked and then let out on bail. Even so, Bob will stumble into an unfortunate blunder.

Susan Olson lives with Zach and an elderly woman renter in a three-story house outside of Shirley Falls' center. At fifty, her hair was "mostly grey" like Bob's. Seven years earlier, Susan's husband hastened off to Sweden, leaving his bitter, divorced wife to raise their only child. Zach's father came from the small northern Maine town of New Sweden. He moved to old Sweden to get in touch with his roots, he said. Zach stacks shelves at Walmart, spends his time listening to music in his room, and has no friends. He may not be a skinhead but he appears to fit the profile of a slow-burn resentful loner.

Susan has not seen Bob in five years, but there is no warm greeting. In fact, even when Jim later arrives in Shirley Falls after his vacation, she musters only a partial hug, leaning in so that their shoulders barely touch, while bending her torso away from his. Susan keeps her house thermostat on permanent chill, so much so that Bob constantly wears his coat, even when he sleeps for the night on the couch. The house's microclimate suggests the emotional frostiness of the Burgess siblings' relationships.

Susan's domestic habits remind Bob of the Maine he left behind. She serves dinner, or supper, at 5:30. Macaroni and cheese and microwaved frozen lasagna represent the house cuisine. Or, alternatively, she simply doesn't want to exert herself to cook for a twin brother who is still under censure for childhood culpability in their father's death. "I miss Jim. No offense," she humiliates Bob. More precisely, she misses her oldest brother's legal skill, not his aloof company. Bob needs wine; all that Susan has on hand is Moxie, which seems like overkill in Strout's depiction of the family's Maine tastes. Yet the Catholic Church's billboard reads, "Jesus is our savior, Moxie is our flavor," which seems believable given Lewiston–Shirley Falls' proximity to the beverage's birthplace.

Bob finds Susan in a swivet over Zach's stunt and Somali refugees' inroads into the city. She and many others in Shirley Falls refer to the newcomers as "Somalians," an act of verbal resistance. She seethes with white grievance against the Somalis. If the mayor who wrote the public letter to the Somalis were a character in *The Burgess Boys*, Susan would surely rally to his defense. "Look," she grumbles to Bob, "they keep coming and coming and there was hardly enough money and so the city had to get more from the Feds, and, really, Shirley Falls, when you consider how unprepared it was, has been great to them." The diction suggests how Susan has been waiting to pour forth her pent-up frustration with and anger against the "Somalians." Her self-congratulation echoes the mayor's letter.

Susan is an optometrist at the mall across the river from Shirley Falls. It establishes a setting for cross-cultural misunderstanding. The Somalis wander in, not knowing that an appointment (a cultural convention) is required. They haggle over prices, a custom of Somali bazaars. When Susan attempts to examine a Somali woman's eyes, "she acted like I was putting a spell on her." Then Susan raises the inflammatory issue of clitoridectomies, which Bob tells her have long been outlawed in America. She dismisses offhand the claim of some residents that the Somalis are no different from French Canadians in Shirley Falls' past. Among the distinctions Susan cites, the most important appears to be that "they're Muslim."

Susan represents the swirl of cultural tensions, misconceptions, and urban myths that unsettle the white city as the presence of Somalis grows. Though she is as thin as a scarecrow, Susan doesn't come across as a stick figure whose sole purpose is as a stand-in for what a swath of Shirley Falls believes. She shares with Bob a still-festering backstory from childhood. Her husband has abandoned her in midlife; no one has offered her help, she complains, but they have been solicitous of the Somalis. Moreover, Zach has doubtless heard around the supper table the kind of anti-Somali bill of fare that Susan serves Bob. Zach's assertions that he only meant his act as a joke don't wash.

Bob wades into the current of misunderstanding and tension that has enveloped Susan. He goes to a convenience store at a gas station to buy wine. A Somali woman stands behind the counter. Bob's eyes need to adjust, like emerging from a dark theater on a sunny summer afternoon. "In a Shirley Falls convenience store the clerk was always white," he reflects, "and almost always overweight." Colorful Somali garb brightened up the drab mill city. But it requires constant optical adjustment.

Bob backs away from the store and nearly hits a Somali woman in a "long red robe" with a scarf "covering her head and most of her face." She starts yelling at him in a foreign language. The clerk comes out of the store. Bob is unsure whether he hit her and wants to call the police. The Somali clerk wants no part of the law. "You were trying to run the car over her. Go away crazy man," she shouts. Bob hasn't hit the Somali woman, but he calls the police to report the incident. An old high school classmate is on duty. He tells Bob that the Somalis are "whack jobs. Forget it. They're jumpy as shit."

Bob turns Zach into the police. They book and fingerprint him and then lock him up in a cell until a bail commissioner arrives. The brief incarceration horrifies Zach. He and Bob leave the police station after posting bail. Bob says something amusing to his nephew and Zach smiles. A photographer snaps his camera. The next morning the picture appears on the local newspaper's front page under the headline "NO JOKE."

Bob calls Jim on St. Kitts to forewarn him of what has happened, particularly the smiling photograph of Zach. "You're a fucking mental case, Bob! An incompetent mental case!" At that moment, Jim realizes he will have to go to Shirley Falls to save a nephew he wouldn't recognize.

Before she leaves for work the next day, Susan piles on. "You've always been useless," she unloads in a reenactment of a longstanding family dynamic. For Bob, it's just another minor flesh wound; over the years the onslaught of such cutting remarks spills blood that goes unseen. He retreats to the porch for a cigarette or two. Unitarian minister Margaret Estaver arrives, hoping to see Susan and Zach. She and Rabbi Goldman are spearheading a rally for tolerance. She wants to assure Susan and Zach that the effort is not against him. Estaver looks about Bob's age; she wears glasses and has unruly hair and a warm personality. They have a brief exchange, and he feels a slight stir. But he is so anxious to flee from Shirley Falls that he takes a costly taxi to the airport in Portland. He leaves Jim's car behind but carries away his original fall from innocence and his siblings' corrosive new expressions of contempt for him.

Paralleling our introduction to the Burgess boys and Susan as individuals and as members of a profoundly impaired family, Strout turns to the Somali perspective on the state of affairs in Shirley Falls. She seemingly draws on "field notes" as well as her literary skill to come to terms with the refugees and integrate them into the plot's trajectory. The latter presents a challenge because the secret story of the Burgess boys is so explosive; its disclosure will upend family history. Nevertheless, Strout devotes chapters to the Somalis' lives, and she writes with sensitivity about the complexity of their community. She doesn't paper over differences among elders and clans. Nor does she elide the later arrival of the Bantus—"their skin as black as winter night sky"—in Shirley Falls (as in Lewiston). They are an ethnic group with their own language, and descendants of slaves brought to Somalia from Tanzania and Mozambique. As black Somalis, the Bantus are a racial minority within a society that self-identifies as Arab.[29] For all her cultural knowledge of the newcomers and her sensitivity to their plight, Strout writes as a novelist, not an anthropologist.

The principal Somali character in *The Burgess Boys* is Abdikarim Ahmed, an elder who owns a café-store, which serves as a gathering place for his male compatriots. As a character, Abdikarim may be asked to carry too much water for the Somali community as a whole, but his emotions and perceptions are far ranging. He's angry with the police, but ultimately he will be forgiving of Zach; he will see in court that the trembling defendant is no more than a boy. Abdikarim's aversion to revenge and violence has been forged in the blast furnace of Mogadishu's terror and in the searing criminality near Atlanta.

In the aftermath of the attack on their storefront mosque, Abdikarim and his fellow Somalis exercise caution. They don't walk near doorways at night, they keep lights out in their apartments, and their children remain inside all day. The Somalis fear what racist ruffians might do to them: "those who drank beer in the morning on the front steps, thick arms tattooed, driving loud trucks with bumper stickers that read: 'White Is Might, The Rest Go Home.'" Still, Shirley Falls is not Clarkston, Georgia.

Abdikarim's café-store contains a large window that frames the small daily indignities that the Somalis endure. Bullies screech their trucks as they drive by his business. People stare into the store as if it's a zoo. Teenagers yell names from across the street.

Despite the arrest of the person who victimized them, the Somalis have an uneasy relationship with the police. Abdikarim relates to Rabbi Goldman what happened after the imam reported the mosque's desecration. Two armed policemen arrived, looked at the pig's head, turned toward one another, and grinned before they laughed. They had no interest in how the pig's head and its blood defiled the mosque. In the aftermath of the incident, the carpet's nap apparently absorbed the cleaning fluid. The acrid odor of xenophobia lingered.

The rally for tolerance is well intentioned. It represents a significant expression of acceptance of the newcomers in Shirley Falls.[30] Still, the Somali

community appears to be divided over the rally. The event seems to rein-
scribe the Somalis' outsider relationship to "their [new] village, their town,
their country."

Strout's introduction of the Somalis captures the hostility to their presence
in Shirley Falls, as well as the tensions within their ranks. Her exploration of
the community grows as she takes us deeper into the story of changing mill city
and of the Burgess family's hidden history. In a double achievement, though not
without wooden elements, Strout tells the stories of a native-born family on the
edge of dissolution and of an "exotic" community of newcomers reconstituting
itself in the world the Burgess boys have left behind.

Bob returns to his routine in New York. After work he settles on a stool, the
loner's stump, at his familiar Ninth Street Bar and Grille. He drinks beer and
orders a hamburger. That is, he favors a diet little better than Susan's. Since he
left Shirley Falls, the police chief has held a press conference with the FBI but
no representative of the Somali community. The small-time chief is a publicity
hound. He assures Somalis of their safety. He monitors the wretched racism on
the internet, suggestions like importing ovens to Shirley Falls.

Jim and Helen know Bob's routine. They enter the bar and grille, with Jim
spring-loaded to hold Bob accountable for what he did in Shirley Falls. "Knucklehead," Jim greets Bob. "He had gone up to Maine and done nothing except respond like an idiot, panic, and leave their car up there." Jim remains self-assured
that he can counter Bob's gaffe and help Zach. He knows the attorney general
from their early days working in that office. Jim considers him a "moron." He
can't imagine the attorney general filing a civil rights charge against Jim Burgess's nephew. The famous hometown lawyer has been invited to speak at the
rally. Surely he can deploy his formidable oratory in a way that will help Zach.
Jim's whole strategy will backfire, to Zach's misfortune. The New Yorker has
become disconnected from customary Maine courtesies.

Jim and Bob drive toward Shirley Falls on the Maine Turnpike at twilight.
The younger brother has an altered impression of the prospect around him,
perhaps because he expects to see Reverend Estaver. "He gazed out the window
at the black stretches of evergreens, the granite boulders here and there." Bob
had forgotten the stark beauty of Maine and those short days of late fall when
evening creeps up on you silently, like the years that just slip by as you arrive at
midlife. "The world was an old friend, and the darkness was like arms around
him." Jim has a different response: "This is just unbelievably depressing."

Strout has actually transposed the rally in response to mosque's desecration
from what was actually the reaction to the mayor's letter. Scattered clusters of

Somalis punctuate the assemblage of white Maine faces gathered in the park. Margaret Estaver cheerfully greets Bob and enthuses over the crowd. "Jimmy" Burgess talks with the attorney general. The speeches begin, and then the attorney general is announced. He climbs to the bandstand. Continually "flipping his bangs out of his eyes," he comes across as ill at ease. The attorney general knows the eloquent Jim Burgess will follow immediately.

He introduces the famous lawyer. Bob's perceptions of his brother are telling, as Jim goes on talking about his native community and its resolve to protect newcomers. Jim "showed no fear," Bob reflects. "He never had." He continues in a vein that reminds one of Philip Roth's panegyric to Seymour Irving Levov, known as "the Swede," a Viking-looking flawless three-sport Jewish athlete, in the Pulitzer Prize–winning *American Pastoral* (1997). "Look at him, his big brother," Bob takes stock. "It was like watching a great athlete, someone born with grace, someone who walked two inches above the earth, and who could say why?" As the secret plight of the Burgess boys thrusts forward toward tragedy, Strout's novel increasingly acquires the character of a powerful American saga.

Jim receives sustained applause for his speech, unlike the attorney general. They shake hands; Jim greets the governor, the next speaker. Then he leaves— "always on the exit ramp," Susan has described Jim in the past.

For all of his eloquence, Jimmy has become unmoored from his Maine roots. His rhetoric far outshines and humbles the attorney general. He doesn't stay to hear the governor's address. Later he contacts the assistant attorney general in charge of civil rights. His reputation as a high-flying New York lawyer doesn't help matters; it only stiffens her spine to follow the letter of the law as she sees it. The attorney general will not stand in her way.

After the rally, Somali men gather in Abdikarim's café. He finds the demonstration of support "amazing." Some agree; others want to wait and see what good it actually produces on the ground. Whenever the men gather, talk turns to the homeland. After all, they are refugees, not willing immigrants. While violence, rape, and robbery continue to afflict Somalia, the men are still offended by a congressman's recent pronouncement that their country is a "failed state." Strout shows how, though they have been driven halfway around the globe, the refugees retain strong emotional ties to their homeland. *The Burgess Boys* consistently allows the Somalis to speak for themselves, as they react to local events and to the tumult in their native country.

In silence the brothers drive back to New York the day after the rally. Strout now deploys the landscape to suggest their barren relationship: "They drove beneath a gray November sky. The bare trees stood naked and skinny as they passed them. The pine trees seemed skinny too, apologetic and tired. . . . They drove by fields that were brownish gray." Coming at the end of book two, the passage augurs, perhaps, Jim's fall into a sunless, depleted existence in the last book.

Jim Burgess suffers an unaccustomed legal defeat, and it arrives from Maine at the hands of the attorney general and his civil rights assistant. "Those stupid pukes," he rails. "I hate the stupid state." A civil rights violation has been filed against Zach. Jim's mission to Shirley Falls has poisoned Zach's legal plight: "The whole reason I went up there was to make sure this idiotic liberal fascism wouldn't happen."

Zach's hearing takes place a week after the rally. His famous lawyer-uncle from New York fails to appear. Why would he return to face another setback for an unfamiliar nephew, for a distant sister? Jim eases what's left of his conscience by recommending a solid local lawyer.

Abdikarim Ahmed is the first to testify. He relates what happened when the pig's head came through the door, including that a little boy fainted. But he speaks "with little affect, warily and wearily." Mohammed Hussein follows and more forcefully confirms what Abdikarim said, that he was "very frightened." The judge allows him to describe the refugee camps in Kenya to establish a context for Zach's violation of their right to worship and their ensuing fear: "bandits . . . came in the night to rob, and rape and sometime kill." Now, in their down-at-the-heels Shirley Falls neighborhood, they found themselves "threatened, attacked, robbed and the women frightened by pit bulls."

When the assistant district attorney stares down at Zach in his shiny new off-the-rack suit, he trembles. He can't hold a glass of water and spills it. Abdikarim watches from the audience with compassion. Later he tells his niece, "You didn't see him. He's not what we saw in the newspaper. He's a frightened . . . child." In other words, Zach doesn't resemble the tattooed muscle-bound neighborhood men with a swagger who taunt the Somalis. Yet others of his countrymen don't agree with Abdikarim's conclusion that Zach is a scared boy, not a hateful young man.

The assistant district attorney is unrelenting in disputing that the incident with the pig's head was simply a joke. Zach's big-shot uncle seems to be on trial as well, for sticking his New York nose where it didn't belong. Her interrogation is blunt and passionate, his replies tentative and terse. An underachiever at school, Zach has never been a talker. After recess, the judge declares Zach guilty of violating the Somalis' right to freely practice their religion. The court orders him to stay two miles away from the mosque and to have no contact with Somalis. Any violation of the injunction will result in jail time and a heavy fine.

Bob and Reverend Estaver drive in her untidy car "along the river, the empty old mills to their right." Bob learns that she is twice divorced, fifty years old, and a Maine native. One of her husbands was Jewish; she sometimes says "Oy." Bob has also picked up the expression, to Jim's aggravation, from his Jewish colleagues at Legal Aid. Zach's travails have brought together two middle-aged people who need one another.

Once again Strout briefly interjects a slice of Abdikarim's history in a way that some readers may find contrived. It is about a far more frightening experience in Mogadishu than the pig's head, a prelude to seeking shelter in Kenya. Abdikarim and his son Bashi were in their store. A truck "screeched" to a stop in front of his shop. Young boys with "thin arms" and "heavy guns strapped over their shoulders" jumped from the truck. They then destroyed "the counter, the shelves," creating "horrendous chaos, the surging wave of hell cresting over them." Fifteen years later, in Shirley Falls, the youth, guns, violence, and fear for their lives still haunt him. Nevertheless, unlike other Somalis, Abdikarim doesn't want Zach to be further prosecuted.

But that is the FBI's intention, his lawyer tells Zach. Soon he goes missing, and Susan calls Jim. But her big brother's personal and professional lives are in a free fall toward dissolution.

The first indication of problems occurs when a female friend of the family sees Jim and a young woman having lunch. She tells her husband, the managing partner of the law firm. He assures her that "Ari" is a paralegal. He has often seen her eating lunch at her desk from plastic containers. Jim probably took her out as a reward for work well done on a successful case. Then one morning another signal appears in the narrative's early warning system. Jim uncharacteristically says, "Helen. You are so good. . . . You're a good person. I love you."

Jim, Helen, and Bob travel to Shirley Falls. The brothers' mission is to help distraught Susan sort out what she should do about Zach's disappearance. (He has actually flown to Sweden to be with his father.) They stay at a hotel across the river and encounter a Somali chambermaid dressed in traditional garb that covers part of her face, like the French nuns from his youth in Shirley Falls, Bob recalls. Strout seems to suggest that the traditional attire of Catholic nuns was once as exotic on the Shirley Falls streets as the dress of contemporary Muslim women.

Standing in the dark on the balcony of the hotel with Bob, Jim acknowledges his failure to protect Zach. He made matters worse with his speech and his call to the assistant district attorney. "I was considered the best criminal defense lawyer in the country once. Can you believe that?"

They hear the river flowing swiftly and thundering against granite boulders. It is a fitting sonic setting for the time bomb Jim detonates—his private secret that has shaped the course of the Burgess boys' lives. Jim was the one at the gears when the car rolled, picking up speed, toward the accident that took one life and permanently altered the lives of four others. "I pushed you into the front seat before Mom came out of the house. Way before the police came, I'd climbed in the back." After graduating from Harvard, Jim felt a moral obligation to come back to Shirley Falls, atonement for what he had done. "I was supposed to stay here and take care of everybody." Instead, within six months, once his mother had died, Jim made off from Shirley Falls, putting distance and then time between the past and present.

Bob refuses to believe the story. Perhaps he can't because it would involve an imaginative reconstruction of his life's architecture. Bob has been the family goat for fifty years. He accuses Jim of making up things. When that doesn't work, he simply tells Jim that he's drunk. Bob asks, why now? Jim's reply is short and seemingly believable to his brother: "Because I couldn't stand it." Bob's New York therapist once drilled into him, "Stay in the present," a bit of cognitive behavioral therapy or Buddhism, or both. He will have to stay in the present to salvage Jim's life.

The Burgesses leave Shirley Falls when Zach calls. Since he's in Sweden, he hasn't violated the judge's injunction to stay away from the mosque and the Somalis. Later, his local lawyer learns that the US attorney has decided not to pursue a hate crime charge against him, dividing the Somali community in the process.

Many in the Somali community are angered that Zach has appeared to jump bail for his trial in June. Abdikarim would like to see the misdemeanor charge dropped. His shop is now surrounded by businesses, as the Somalis help rejuvenate downtown Shirley Falls: "A translation service, two more cafes, a store that sold phone cards, a place for English classes." Over at Margaret Estaver's church, Bantu women, in the main, line up twice a week for the food pantry. This short report on the Somali community is all but tacked onto the end of a chapter.

The collapse of Jim Burgess's comfortable life gains momentum. One day the paralegal who was spotted having lunch with Jim hand delivers a complaint against him to the managing partner of the law firm. He closes the door to his office, but then he realizes that she might be sitting before him holding the equivalent of "an automatic machine gun." They go for a public walk to discuss her sexual complaint against Jim. Her name is Adriana, and she lived below Bob, quarreled constantly with her husband, and called the police when he became physically abusive. As she was moving out, Bob suggested that she apply to his brother's law firm for work. Ironically, Bob becomes indirectly and unintentionally linked to the collapse of Jim's world.

Adriana is no legal rube. She has drafted a four-page complaint of sexual harassment against Jim. She claims not to have consulted a lawyer. Adriana has preserved everything from text messages to hotel receipts.

In the midst of this crisis, while they are sitting on a shaded bench, Jim's partner and family friend can't resist stealing an assessment of Adriana's body: "Her legs were perfect, without veins or splotches, just smooth shins neither tanned nor too white." The legs suggest the young flesh that enticed, or ensnared, middle-aged Jim. In this case, the male gaze "nauseated" Jim's partner. He knows he will lose a good colleague and friend. He also thinks of Helen. Adriana asks for a million dollars. The final settlement amounts to half of that, but it will come from Jim's equity in the firm.

Jim stumbles through a series of lies to Helen and another affair, this time with a married "life coach." When Helen exposes this relationship, the sordid truth of what happened at the law firm marks the end of their marriage. Jim leaves with the clothes on his back and the burden of adult children who are furious with him. Helen purges her home of everything that belonged to him, from clothes to the flat-screen television.

As the narrative of Jim's demise and its aftermath gathers momentum, Strout shifts back to Shirley Falls. Joyless Susan, with her heavily pilled sweaters, still refers to the refugees as Somalians. She draws a selective historical comparison to Shirley Falls' French Catholics: their large families, like the Somalis', had the purposeful effect of overtaking the native born. Susan remains an unreconstructed nativist.

Strout seems to shoehorn—or crowbar—the Somalis back into the novel. Of Abdikarim, she told an interviewer, "Once I made this decision to have a marbleized Somali point of view running through the text, it didn't seem like a struggle to take him on."[31] "Marbleize" is a provocative image that distills her narrative design. It also offers a way of thinking about American ethnic and racial assimilation, which, of course, the Somalis are far from achieving in Shirley Falls.

Abdikarim worries that the sudden notoriety of Somali pirates will lead people to believe that all Somalis are pirates at heart. He's also alarmed by, and fails to understand, how newcomers become hyphenated—how the children of his community are referred to as Somali-Americans. He wants to preserve an unalloyed Somali identity. His niece Haweeya complains to Margaret Estaver about American kids: "I want my children not to feel—what is the word?—entitled."

The plot quickly returns to New York after this seeming snapshot of Somali life in Shirley Falls. Bob has been kept in the dark about his brother's fate until he visits Helen and she tells him of Jim's squalid affairs. Jim now teaches at an elite upstate college. Bob drives to see him. Jim hates the place, and they drive off to Shirley Falls. Zach is coming home from Sweden the next day. Bob has a future with Reverend Estaver. At the bus station, waiting for Zach, Bob and Susan all but push Jim on the bus back to New York, presumably to see whether he can reconcile with Helen. Jim's departure and Zach's arrival—the uncle and nephew with uncertain futures—closes the novel.

Since it immediately followed a Pulitzer Prize–winning work, and because Strout took risks with such an ambitious book, *The Burgess Boys* received a range of responses from reviewers, most positive, but some sharply critical. Consider the *New York Times*. The *Sunday Book Review* lavished praise on the novel: "Strout handles her storytelling with grace, intelligence, and low-key humor, demonstrating a great ear for the many registers in which people speak."[32] A reviewer for the daily *Times*, in contrast, found much to criticize. For starters the reviewer apparently had no awareness of the national coverage of the pig's head incident. Thus she observed, "The awful act in *The Burgess Boys* is so strange that the book can hardly accommodate it." She concluded, "For all its potential and Mrs. Strout's proven skill, *The Burgess Boys* asks too many questions and offers too few interesting answers."[33]

The *Washington Post* reviewer enthused over the novel: "The broad social and political range of *The Burgess Boys* shows just how impressively this extraordinary writer continues to develop." He thought that she effectively told the story of "moldy" family "tensions" and examined the "prejudices that continue to reverberate through American culture since September 11."[34]

The *Los Angeles Times* offered a more mixed review. Strout's "prose sings," the reviewer observed, and she displays a "knack for dropping in on characters and illuminating their lives in a few sentences that is compelling." Yet the novel presented problems: "glimpses into foreign lives are quickly overshadowed by the travails of the Burgess family."[35]

If too many of Strout's loyal readers became wrapped up in the Burgesses saga, Somalis appear to have had the opposite response. Minnesota Public Radio, for example, announced, "Local Somalis cheer Elizabeth Strout's focus on hate crimes." The book attracted enough interest within the Minneapolis Somali community—the largest in the country—that Strout's book tour for the paperback edition brought her to the city, where she did a special reading.[36]

Strout's cross-cultural appeal represents a significant achievement. Her ambition to execute two stories of markedly different people that crosscut and then diverge remains impressive, if awkward in places. And the graceful, incisive prose that she deploys to examine changing Maine and America makes *The Burgess Boys* a major work.

7

THE MILL TOWN
IN TURMOIL

Richard Russo and Monica Wood

Beyond modest-sized mill cities, manufacturing towns have helped define Maine's far-flung industrial landscape. Indeed, mill towns have historically outnumbered their urban counterparts. From Jewett's Salmon Falls to Brunswick, Rumford, Jay, Millinocket, Dexter, Winslow, and Bucksport, for example, town-centered industrialism has crisscrossed the state. Maine's manufacturing geography maps an important, though often dimly perceived, reality on the ground. Small-scale industrialization has far surpassed dense urban mill development.

The recent history of these Maine mill towns mostly constitutes a late stage in New England's deindustrialization. First textiles, then shoes, followed by papermaking have fallen prey to globalization. Some town manufacturing economies endure, with fewer jobs and depopulation. Others have lurched toward a new postindustrial landscape. Still others remain mired in terminal stagnation.

Pulitzer Prize–winning Richard Russo (b. 1949) and Monica Wood (b. 1954) depict different company mill towns at distinct stages of their development. Russo's Empire Falls is on the cusp of reinventing itself as it tilts toward a postindustrial service economy. Wood's Abbott Falls, a unionized paper mill town, engages in a divisive fight to preserve jobs and save a working-class way of life.

Russo and Wood employ markedly different literary styles. The former prefers long novels with intricate plots, subplots, and a large cast of characters. Russo's "blue collar novels" brim with varied forms of humor, from incandescent wit to more earthy hilarity. Wood is a far more linear storyteller. Also, her literary vision invests less in humor than Russo's. These and other stylistic differences mean that Russo and Wood construe their fictional Maine mill towns in different ways.

Yet, for all their differences, Russo and Wood have things in common. Both grew up in small manufacturing communities dominated by one industry. Their fictional representations of Empire Falls and Abbott Falls are informed by research into their communities' history. Both identify with the working class, and they handle most of their central blue-collar characters compassionately.

RICHARD RUSSO: THE REINVENTION OF THE COMPANY TOWN

After Russo won the Pulitzer Prize for *Empire Falls* in 2002, he gave many interviews, which continued with subsequent novels. He also published *Elsewhere* (2012), an unusual memoir. It was as much about his mother as him. Or, more precisely, the memoir is the story of their lifelong, extraordinary relationship. The interviews and the memoir enable one to sketch Russo's background, including important aspects of his intellectual biography.[1]

Born in Johnstown, New York, in 1949, Russo grew up in nearby Gloversville. The city of 23,634 in 1950 was known for its tanneries and fine leather glove manufacturing. Over the eighteen years that Russo lived in Gloversville, the city slid into an economic tailspin from which it has never recovered. Global competition and shifting fashion undermined the glove industry. Poor job prospects set in motion a steady decline in population, which has continued to this day. Perhaps with some exaggeration, Russo has recalled, "By the 1970s [Gloversville] had become a Dresden-like ruin." In *Empire Falls* (2001), an old photograph of a bustling town center prompts the major character to reflect that now "you could strafe it with automatic weapons and not harm a soul."[2]

As Gloversville's economy spiraled into decline, Russo's parents' marriage dissolved. They separated when he was very young and later "Jimmy" and Jean Russo divorced, when "Rick" was in high school. His father apparently had no consistent presence in Russo's life and provided no child support. A participant in D-Day and awarded the Bronze Star, Jimmy Russo worked briefly as a glove cutter and then found more stable employment as a union road construction laborer. He liked to drink and talk within the camaraderie of bars. Jimmy Russo was especially fond of gambling.[3]

Despite his father's absence in his life, Russo has said that he experienced a happy childhood. He lived with his mother on the second floor of her father's two-family house surrounded by relatives. Jean Russo worked as a telephone operator. Later she found employment at General Electric in Schenectady, an hour drive from Gloversville. Russo played sports, served as an altar boy, attended public schools, and graduated from the Catholic Bishop Burke High School. His mother had always encouraged him to aspire toward college as a means to escape Gloversville's straitened economic opportunities, not to mention the toxic waters and carcinogenic landscape left behind by the leather industry.[4] The city suffered from an elevated cancer rate and his grandfather died from emphysema, linked to his work in the tannery. In other words, Russo did not have to fully invent a world for his first two Mohawk novels. He saw first-hand Mohawk-Gloversville's economic plight, and, through family members who were employed in the leather industry, he knew both its inner workings and its perils to a long, healthy life.

Russo decided to attend the University of Arizona because its tuition was inexpensive. What he didn't expect was that his mother would decide to go with him. Jean Russo had developed an emotional dependence on her son as he grew up. She would follow him around the country as he pursued an academic career. His father told him not to let his mother go with him to Arizona. "You *do* know your mother's nuts, right?" he later asked his son. She suffered, Russo recalls in *Elsewhere*, from what at the time was referred to vaguely as "nerves."[5] Jean's actual illness, he much later realized, was most likely undiagnosed obsessive-compulsive disorder. He would deal with its consequences for the rest of his mother's life.

After their drive across the country, Russo helped her find an apartment in Phoenix. She couldn't drive, nor did she have a job. He headed south to Tucson. Constant telephone calls kept Russo informed of his mother's slow progress in Phoenix. He returned to Gloversville in the summer to work on road construction with his father. As a result of these periods of interaction, Russo says, he came to better understand and accept his father. In *Elsewhere*, Russo reconstructs a kind of fatherly apologia. "I should've thought about you more," Jimmy Russo admitted, "but you were easy to forget. There was always something going on, a horse at the track that couldn't lose or some poker game. You seemed to be doing fine without me."[6]

Russo also discovered something important about his father: he was a great barroom storyteller whose creativity shifted as he moved from one drinking hole to the next.[7] Russo appears to suggest that he inherited some genetic storytelling ability from his father, enabling him to become a fiction writer. He dedicated his second novel, *The Risk Pool* (1988), to "Jim Russo." His father had died of cancer at age sixty-four.

Russo stayed in Tucson for twelve years. After earning his bachelor's degree he married his wife, Barbara, in 1972, while pursuing his doctorate. He received the degree in 1979. Russo remained at the University of Arizona for an MFA in creative writing, an unusual turn for someone who had just been awarded a PhD. He had struggled to complete his dissertation on the now obscure early American writer Charles Brockden Brown.[8] Russo discovered that he was not cut out for academic writing and publishing. "Creative writing," he has explained to interviewers, "gave me another avenue, and it saved my life."[9]

With scholarly and writing degrees, Russo possessed a bit of an edge in a glutted academic market for English PhDs. Nevertheless, for a decade he lived an "academic nomadship,"[10] as he sought a job that would provide him with time to write. Russo taught in Pennsylvania and Connecticut, where he published *Mohawk* (1981). He then accepted a creative writing position at Southern Illinois University. He moved his mother to Carbondale. Russo was teaching at Southern Illinois when he published his second Mohawk novel, *The Risk Pool* (1988). But life in Carbondale proved unsatisfactory. "We were anxious to put southern Illinois's buggy, humid, tornado ripe summers behind us, not to mention its passive-aggressive religious fundamentalists," he relates in his memoir.[11] A part-time position at Colby College appealed to Russo because it would free up time to write. "Besides," he told an interviewer, "I think living in the Northeast is just better for me personally. I just like it better."[12] With Barbara and their two young daughters, he moved to Waterville in 1991. After much difficulty because of her obsessive fussiness, Russo also settled his mother nearby.

Two years after he arrived at Colby, Russo published the book before *Empire Falls* that changed his life. *Nobody's Fool* (1993) introduced the engaging, hapless "Sully" of North Bath, New York. Russo cowrote the screenplay for the movie, which boasted an all-star cast headed by Paul Newman. The great actor also appeared on the cover of the paperback edition of *Nobody's Fool*. The novel's commercial success and, more important, Russo's introduction to lucrative screenwriting soon enabled him to leave his position at Colby. He told an interviewer that he worked on three screenplays for about six weeks each while writing *Empire Falls*.[13] He grew familiar with Hollywood's ways. At the same time, the Russos moved from Waterville, which resembled Gloversville and Empire Falls, to the upscale coastal town of Camden.

Interestingly, the first novel that he published after leaving Colby, *Straight Man* (1997), is a hilarious satire of academic shenanigans and infighting at a poorly funded state college in Pennsylvania. He had taught at Penn State in Altoona, yet another blighted city. *Straight Man* draws on more than one of Russo's academic pauses during his nomadship.

Academic types emerge in *Nobody's Fool* and *Empire Falls*. Russo's rejection of literary scholarship appears also to have involved a kind of allergy to most academics, who are satirized in *Empire Falls*. For example, the local beat cop observes the faculty from nearby Fairhaven College, who begin to patronize the Empire Grill when its dinners evolve into creative "grille"-like cuisine. To the cop, the professors are like a flock of exotic birds. They prefer Volvos, "plain-Jane" wives, "chinos and a tweed sport coat over a light-blue shirt with a button down collar." The cop is befuddled: "Why did they all have to wear a uniform, these college professors?" In any case, Russo's good fortune enabled him to flee the vein of pretension and conformity he apparently sees lodged in academic life.

Though he has published consistently since *Empire Falls*, nothing of Russo's has surpassed the critical standing of that novel. He wrote the script for the HBO miniseries, starring Paul Newman again. It was filmed in Skowhegan. The miniseries and the Pulitzer Prize brought further attention to Russo's work. He has continued to live in Maine, now in Portland. In fact, he has resided in the state far longer than he has lived anywhere else. But since *Empire Falls* he has only set a sixty-seven-page novella and a few short stories in Maine.[14] He has also published an occasional nonfiction piece dealing with some aspect of Maine life.

Empire Falls, like much of Russo's work, is a throwback novel. He possesses a literary preference for nineteenth-century writers rather than more proximate modernist and postmodernist fictional innovators. In interviews he has identified Charles Dickens as his favorite author and *Great Expectations* as the most influential novel giving shape to his own work. Like Dickens, Russo prefers drawn-out storytelling with a large cast of characters, numerous subplots, and an overarching plot than emerges at a slow pace and in a nonlinear way.[15]

Sherwood Anderson represents one twentieth-century writer who Russo acknowledges was enormously important. *Winesburg, Ohio* (1919), a classic portrait of small-town America, evokes the place through chapter-portrait-stories of individual inhabitants. For Russo, Anderson wrote "about [small town] people's lives that were every bit as rich, multi-dimensional, full of the same dreams, fears and anxieties as big city people."[16]

Over three novels (excluding *Straight Man*), Russo sharpened his Dickens-style storytelling focused on small communities reeling from economic dislocation. Then he published *Empire Falls*, a culmination of a literary style he had honed over two decades. *Mohawk* lays down a marker of the literary distance Russo traveled from his first book to the Pulitzer Prize. *Mohawk* originated with a long prospective novel he completed before leaving Arizona. Mostly set in Tucson, the draft also contained a lengthy flashback to Gloversville, a place that he knew far better than the university city. One of his creative writing teachers, who had befriended the aspiring novelist, read what Russo had produced. He concluded that the work was "inert" except for the flashback, which possessed spark. Russo salvaged forty pages from the original work, switched his focus back east, and produced a more-than-four-hundred-page novel based on the Gloversville that he vividly recalled. After multiple rejections, *Mohawk* was published as a Vintage Contemporary.[17]

Set between the tumultuous years of 1967 and 1972, the novel evinces little of the era's conflicts, except for a local draft dodger who is chased by the Secret Service. The citizens of Mohawk are inward looking, preoccupied with weathering their town's economic collapse. They seemingly push politics to the periphery. The novel's structure tests readers' patience, and endurance. Major and minor characters proliferate, subplots multiply, and unity recedes in the onslaught of particulars. Russo has described *Mohawk* as an "ensemble novel with a dozen or so important characters and employing numerous points of view."[18]

The novel also foregrounds brutal violence, fratricide, suicide, and incest. It does contain noble characters: A young hero saves a brain-damaged man from a hospital under demolition. A longtime tannery worker with a moral spine resigns quickly from his newly assigned foreman's position because he cannot avert his eyes from an entrenched ring of robbers who pilfer skins as compensation for seasonal layoffs and occupational hazards.

Then, too, the goodhearted, awkward naïf, Dallas Younger, emerges as a humane character, a man with virtuous instincts and vulnerable human weaknesses. A tall, handsome man, marred by two false front teeth (which are suggestive of other imperfections), he serves as *Mohawk*'s main character, for lack of a better choice in Russo's bulging gallery of dramatis personae. He represents the first of Russo's blue-collar "everymen." Younger is a highly skilled automobile mechanic and an inveterate small-time gambler, like most of the working-class men around him. He is divorced from Anne Grouse, another major character; they have a son of draft age. Younger has been absent from his son's life; yet he's always ready to help in a crisis. He's especially attentive to the welfare of his brother's widow, for example.

In *Mohawk*, Russo fails to choreograph satisfactorily the multiple components of his roundabout storytelling style. As one critic has put it, "The novel's sixty-seven short chapters depict nonlinearly and often obliquely the complicated relationships among the primary dozen or so characters."[19] Still, Russo's representation of the dying mill town itself constitutes a significant achievement of *Mohawk*.

The Mohawk Grill anchors a forlorn downtown where the large Montgomery Ward building stands empty. Other businesses are boarded up. Harry Saunders, the diner's proprietor and a forerunner of *Empire Falls*' more fully developed Miles Roby, watches his patrons pore over their horse racing forms. The Off Track Betting Parlor, like the diner, caters to the working class in particular. Gambling represents Mohawkers' principal diversions: horses, the numbers, and regular poker games.

Economic headwinds have hastened the tannery industry's dissolution. Toxins have flowed freely into Mohawk's bloodstream. Those who stay behind suffer from elevated cancer rates and shortened life spans. For decades the unregulated tanneries have poured poison into Cayuga Creek, where the fish are so deformed that the waters are no longer restocked. Life goes on in Mohawk with a seeming acceptance, or fatalism, about the way things stand. Revealingly, one worker espouses the view, apparently widely held, that for all of a tannery's hazards to workers' health, "where would a man like me have been without that mill?" In summary, the voice of protest is muted in *Mohawk*.

Yet humor informs Russo's depiction of the townspeople in ways that give the reader a partial reprieve from the gloom that hangs over Mohawk. A character blows cigarette smoke from "weedy nostrils." Dallas Younger's son grows up tall and as "lanky as undertakers in the movies." Two elderly sisters, one a widow, compete over who bears aging's greater emotional and physical afflictions. The widow deploys her "upper hand" over the still-married younger sister. But then the latter's daughter divorces Dallas Younger, and her husband dies. She now holds the power to thwart her sister's manipulation and to assert preeminent hardship. Nevertheless, the younger sister proves "too kind to press unfair advantage, and the two agreed that each had leaden crosses to bear."

Russo sharpened his wit and comedic dialogue over his next New York novels. Then *Straight Man* turned into a satirical farce of academic life and took aim at an old chestnut: the disagreements in academia, especially in English departments like West Central Pennsylvania's, often turn rancorous, paradoxically, because relatively little is at stake.[20]

By the time Russo had made a literary detour with *Straight Man*, he had already established a reputation as a novelist of blue-collar America. But in his focus on class, Russo bears little resemblance to the proletarian writers of the Depression. He does express admiration for John Steinbeck, whose works bear the imprint of militant novelists of the 1930s and 1940s.[21] Still, one finds no class conflict in Russo's blue-collar world, no neo-Marxism, no union activism, or, indeed, no ideology at all. Moreover, despite possessing a name ending in a vowel, Russo displays no interest in ethnicity, though in novels such as *Empire Falls* he describes a town that immigrants built.

Russo serves as the fictional tribune of small-town blue-collar life in post-industrial America. Those left behind survive without an ideology. (Globalism has not quite been fully singled out as the cause of their problems.) Unions have vanished, if they ever existed. Families rupture from the pressure of patching together a livelihood and a life. In short, Russo's historical moment and fictional world are by necessity markedly different from earlier proletarian authors.

At nearly five hundred pages, *Empire Falls* is substantially longer than *Mohawk*. Both novels possess similar structural elements: intricate plot twists, sundry subplots, and numerous major and minor characters. But Russo controls and deploys these literary components with far more skill in his fifth novel than in his first. For example, with two exceptions, the subplots are closely related to the novel's through line. The humor in *Empire Falls* is sharper and richer than in *Mohawk*. Italicized flashbacks that bookend the novel and appear at other points provide context and coherence to the knotty plot. They also refuel and propel the drama.

Russo told an interviewer after *Empire Falls* was published that his novel focuses more on class than place. And yet he has advanced a strikingly different view of the critical importance of place in his fiction. In an essay about writing fiction, he has stressed "that place and people are intertwined, that place is character, and that to know the rhythms, the textures, the feel of a place is to know more deeply and truly its people."[22] In other words, class is inscribed in real places, on the ground, in material ways. But Russo resists foregrounding class conflict in any proletarian kind of way.

Empire Falls is a fictional composite of real Maine places, "such inland towns as Lewiston, Madison, and Skowhegan," Russo says.[23] Waterville, where he lived and taught, also seems to have contributed significantly to Russo's imaginative construction of Empire Falls. The novel surrounds that fictional place with the names of real Maine communities: Orono, Augusta, Farmington, Blue Hill, Castine, and Portland, for example. Russo is unconcerned with being labeled a regionalist or a Maine writer. Though they transcend the local, class and postindustrialism still manifest their workings in place-specific ways.

In an important respect, then, shifting his blue-collar townscape from New York to Maine required Russo to grapple with the Pine Tree State's industrial history, which differed from Gloversville's. "It forced me to think about history and myth and to do more research,"[24] he acknowledged. Russo discovered Maine's historic status as a "colony" of Massachusetts. Hence the black-and-white limousines, real and alleged, that periodically appear parked outside Empire Falls' shuttered mills bear Massachusetts license plates. Russo has also noted Maine's distinctive appeal to him as a place. "Maine's culture of hard work and unpretentiousness suited me." He has said other things about the state's distinctiveness as a place. "One of the things I love about Maine is that it seems far outside the culture," an increasingly arguable point. In Maine, he has observed, "people are courteous to each other."[25] All of this is to suggest that though a shared blue-collar plight crosses state lines, Empire Falls emerges as a rather different postindustrial place from Mohawk.

The contemporary town of Empire Falls takes shape in the novel through physical descriptions, characters' actions, and flashbacks. The opening flashback describes how the Knox River endowed Empire Falls with abundant water power. Elijah Whiting first engaged in logging in the nineteenth century, but the family then expanded to textiles, shirt manufacturing, and papermaking. The enterprises drew "Irish, Polish, and Italian immigrants who came north from Boston and . . . French Canadians, who came south, all of them in search of work." Smokestacks up river at the paper mill remain monuments of the Whiting empire. For generations they exhaled "sometimes white, sometimes black smoke," until the stacks no longer emitted their soot and clear sky meant rough sailing. We get this history and more from the opening flashback that doubles as a well-told stand-alone short story.

Elijah Whiting built a large Georgian "mansion" in Empire Falls that fell into disrepair like so much of the town's housing—sagging porches, sinking foundations, and peeling paint. The mansion was ultimately donated to the town, which bore the financial burden of restoring the structure for civic purposes. It became the sleepy office of Town Planning and Development. The past has left other imprints on the townscape. On Front Street, which parallels the river, the poorest French-Canadian immigrants had taken up residence. The mills disgorged changing, dyed water. Years later "patches of fading chartreuse and magenta" still sully the banks.

The Whitings own the Empire Diner and most of the town. They have made no improvements to the shabby eatery in decades. Since the Rexall Drugstore has been demolished next door, the diner affords a clear view down the now ridiculously named Empire Avenue to the textile mill and its abutting shirt factory. "Both had been abandoned now for the better part of two decades, though their dark, looming shapes at the foot of the avenue's gentle incline continued to draw the eye."

Miles Roby, the novel's protagonist, runs the Empire Diner; he doesn't own it. His ex-mother-in-law, the widowed Bea Macieski, is the proprietor of Callahan's Bar, another blue-collar gathering place. Perhaps Callahan and Macieski suggest the process of ethnic succession—of one group taking the place of another in the process of social mobility. More likely, given Russo's seeming disinterest in ethnicity as a category of identity, a few names only represent remnants of Empire Falls' historical non-Anglo majority. Shabby Callahan's barroom has an even more wretched bathroom. When its frozen pipes leaked behind the wall, workers cut multiple huge holes as they tried to find the source of the problem. The holes were never repaired. For Miles, "This crapper . . . was his hometown in a nutshell." The holes, for instance, parallel the empty lots in the heart of Empire Avenue, where buildings have been demolished, as if the wrecking ball could solve the town's problems.

The initial flashback introduces us to Charles Beaumont Whiting, the grandson of Elijah, known as C. B. in Empire Falls. He has been dead for twenty-three years. But the consequences of his marriage and affair still reverberate in Empire Falls. Thus his life provides crucial context for the sinuous plot.

C. B. graduated from Bowdoin, like all the Whiting men, and then spent the better part of a decade traveling in Europe and Mexico. Below the border he exhausted his days "living a life of poetry and fornication." His father called him back to Empire Falls and "a life of enforced duty and chastity." But in an act of rebellion, he crossed the iron bridge over the Knox River, separated himself from the town's working-class people, and built a hacienda with a studio. Weak-tea verse constituted his only artistic aptitude.

As he laid out plans for his lawn with a gazebo, C. B. confronted a natural obstacle to his ambition. Refuse, including a dead moose (a resonant Maine symbol), accumulated along his riverbank property. At the so-called Robideaux Blight, a protrusion on the opposite bank, the river narrowed and its current slowed. The Blight belonged to the Robideaux family, French Canadians who farmed the opposite side of the river. The entitled Whiting was not to be thwarted by nature. He purchased the Robideaux property, bribed state officials, and dynamited the Blight. The Knox now flowed swiftly by his gazebo and carried its flotsam downstream to Fairhaven, where there was a dam—and a college. C. B. had been warned about the danger of altering the course of the river. It will have deadly consequences; Whiting will reach beyond the grave to avenge his cursed marriage.

The real Robideaux blight in C. B.'s life, it seems, was his wife. He couldn't blast her away, though he would try. Francine Robideaux, the farmer's daughter, matured into an attractive young woman and a graduate of Bowdoin. From her modest background, the college gave birth to a lissome, wily young woman. She graduated "no longer recognized as a Robideaux in deportment, speech or mannerism." Carefully observing her fellow students, she "adopted their table manners, fashion sense, vocal idiosyncrasies and personal hygiene." In a word, Bowdoin anglicized her, provoking the ire of her French-Canadian family. Bowdoin sharpened her intellect, steeled her upstart ambition, and burnished her social skills. Francine, not C. B., would become the ruthless power broker in Empire Falls. Townspeople could no more defy her than resist the force of gravity.

In theory, Francine, ten years younger than C. B., represents an infusion of new ethnic blood into an old Yankee family. C. B.'s life, and his hacienda, suggests the Whitings are in terminal decline by the third generation. No wonder C. B. is a physically diminutive man. Francine further reduces him to a boy. She calls him "Charlie"; no one had ever referred to him that way. His typical response to Francine is "Yes, dear."

From this backstory we are thrust forward more than two decades to present-day life in Empire Falls. All the Whiting men are dead, and Francine, who is in middle age, controls the town from the hacienda when she is not in Boston or Florida. In particular, she owns the Empire Grill and, for personal reasons, which become increasingly clear over the course of the novel, she manipulates the long-suffering Miles Roby. Francine's motto in life is "Power and Control." Forty-two-year-old Miles represents her principal pawn. His early manhood has raced by in the neglected grill in the midst of a scruffy mill town. Only the promise of owning the diner has kept Miles shackled to its griddle. He didn't intend for his life to unwind this way.

Miles's late mother urged him to go to college as far away as possible from Empire Falls. She didn't want him ever to return. He completed three and a half years at Catholic St. Luke's College, described as a short distance from Portland. He dreamed of going to graduate school and becoming a history professor. Instead, Francine Whiting summoned him home because his mother was dying. Francine asked him to take over the grill temporarily from the ailing manager. With no money to fulfill his academic dream, he later settled permanently behind the laminated counter facing regular customers on their chosen stools. Wobbly booths with cigarette-burned tables round out the hash house's setting. Francine dangles the bait of Miles's eventual ownership of the business. Then she keeps him in harness to the grill, exercising power and control.

As a hired hand, Miles is a blue-collar character, though he possesses a college education. He's even tempered and good hearted. When Buster—an alcoholic cook—goes on a lengthy bender, Miles welcomes him back with no questions asked. To his mother-in-law Bea, Miles is not only the "nicest, saddest man in all Empire Falls" but also "so good-natured that not even being married to her daughter, Janine, had ruined him." Bea's commentary on her daughter represents a running source of humor in *Empire Falls*. To Janine, however, Miles, "the human rut," inspired thoughts of self-annihilation. Janine is a more complex character than she appears at first. Empire Falls, the grill, middle age, and two decades of marriage to the passive Miles leave her craving for more out of life. Yet even after their divorce she respects Miles's broad decency.

Janine invests her longing for excitement in the grill's most buffoonish patron. Walt Comeau owns the town's fitness club. It's a business that presages Empire Falls' eventual shift toward a service economy. Janine exercises rigorously at the fitness club and makes protein shakes in the Fox's Den. She forgoes Sunday Mass for her new devotion to physical fitness. Walt slaps down large bills for minor charges at the Empire Grill. He wears tight shirts to accentuate his abs. He constantly challenges Miles to arm wrestling. Comeau drives a van with "The Silver Fox" emblazoned above the grill. He boasts a vanity plate "Foxy 1." Comeau looks as if he's in his midforties. Janine will be shocked by his actual age when they go for a marriage license. It marks the beginning of her disillusionment with Walt and the end of her "stair master journey."

Empire Falls swells with many deftly drawn major characters. Place and character interpenetrate, to rephrase what Russo has argued. In this sense, Russo's long involved novel, at its core, transmutes Empire Falls into Winesburg, Ohio, a place-based story of the "quick and the dead," to quote the King James Bible.

To expand Russo's portfolio of major characters, we might ask, why does Miles stay in Empire Falls living in his two-room apartment above the diner after his divorce from Janine? First, he loves "Tick" (Christina), his sixteen-year-old daughter. She is emotionally closer to Miles than to Janine. Father and daughter, for example, have a game they play called "Empire Moments." The two scour the townscape in search of malapropisms: "No Trespassing Without Permission," for instance. Tick heaps all the blame on her mother for upending a twenty-year marriage. She refuses to meet Walt Comeau. When Janine proposes that Tick enroll in modeling classes, "she sneers that maybe she would, after her lobotomy." Her response "pissed off Janine even before she looked up the word 'lobotomy.'"

In addition to Tick, Miles is the caregiver of sorts for his father, a character partly modeled on Russo's Jimmy Russo. Now seventy years of age, the rascally, ill-kempt Max Roby spends his summers Down East slapping paint heedlessly on the seasonal homes of wealthy "Mass holes." He escapes to Key West in winter. As father and husband, Max amounted to a cipher. He remained in Florida

THE MILL TOWN IN TURMOIL

while his wife lay on her deathbed. Max now lives in Empire Towers, senior citizen apartments, and spends afternoons at Callahan's Bar. Hard pressed for money, he scrounges and steals from Miles. Tick sometimes tries to correct her grandfather's slovenliness. "His father, Miles had long suspected, was basically a lower primate. He enjoyed being groomed." Max is a colorful scoundrel in the novel. In his most adventurous caper, he takes off for Key West with the senile pastor of St. Catherine's Catholic Church, who has ripped open envelopes with Sunday contributions.

Miles is seemingly bound to Empire Falls by another family obligation: his younger brother, David, a recovering alcoholic. He seriously injured an arm when he totaled his truck after a hunting/snowmobiling trip with friends. David had consumed booze and drugs. He was fortunate to lose only partial use of one arm. Nine years younger than Miles, David spent a semester at the Maine Culinary Institute. He initiates Chinese, Italian, and Mexican nights at the grill. He serves food with a contemporary flair: "Twice-Cooked Noodles with Scallops in Hoisin Sauce," for example, and shrimp flautas on Mexican night. The students and faculty from Fairhaven College are attracted to the diner for its distinctive combination of a "retro" authentic mill-town setting with nouvelle ethnic food. The appeal of David's cuisine signifies that, like the fitness club, Empire Falls' future resides in a postindustrial world. The grill regularly keeps a waiting list, and Walt Comeau suggests that Miles should add an *e* to its name.

Russo never misses an opportunity to spoof academics, as if it is some kind of payback for his purgatory writing a doctoral dissertation on the immortal Charles Brockden Brown. Charlene Gardiner has worked in the grill for twenty years. She is three years older than Miles; he still possesses something of his high school crush on her. She has taken David as a lover, after three failed marriages. Charlene serves as the earthy voice of worldly experience in the grill. She takes the measure of her new customers: "despite their carefully trimmed beards, their pressed chinos and tweed jackets, college professors tipped in the same fashion as other men—according to cup size."

David wants to increase the grill's profitability by selling beer and wine. Miles needs Francine Whiting's permission. At the "Annual State of the Grill" meeting, an artifice for Francine to perpetuate her power and control, David urges his brother to ask for her consent. In this meeting across the bridge, the reader confronts the reason why Whiting keeps Miles on a string, and his mother before that.

A crucial flashback to when Miles is nine years old provides context for the dynamics of the annual meeting. His attractive thirty-year-old mother, Grace, who works in the office of the Empire Shirt Factory, announces that the two of them are going on vacation to Martha's Vineyard. (Grace's name is rather heavy handed, given her life-altering fall into temptation.) Once they arrive, Miles notices that his mother appears to be looking for someone. At dinner in a restaurant, a man stops by their table and Grace invites him to join them. His name is "Charlie Mayne." What the reader knows quickly—that it's C. B. Whiting—Miles will not discover until decades later. White-haired, hollow-chested, spindly legged Charlie becomes their vacation companion, at dinner, on the beach, and for a tour of the island in his sports car. Once Miles is asleep, Grace slips off for an all-night rendezvous with Charlie. For this single transgression she will interiorize a scarlet letter. That is to say, Grace's fall and its aftermath, in which she is thrown in the moral shade for life, has nothing to do with Nathaniel Hawthorne's Puritan ancestors. Her New England conscience, a generation older than contemporary Empire Falls, rests on geologic strata of Catholic guilt. Indeed, within the novel, Russo offers a kind of excavation of traditional Catholicism and its diminution in the mill town, represented by St. Catherine's sparse Sunday attendance and its badly peeling paint.

To return to the flashback, the lovers' talk of escaping to Mexico dissolves when Charlie plans to leave behind his partially paralyzed daughter Cindy, who is Miles's age. It offends Grace's moral sensibility. Moreover, she's pregnant with David and already afflicted with morning sickness. Grace's idyll on Martha's Vineyard has ended. There will be no exit from Empire Falls, the failing mill, or the self-absorbed Max Roby.

The high drama in the small mill town grows darker, principally in the course of the flashbacks. Consider what happens to Grace after she comes back to Empire Falls. On a sunny Saturday afternoon in August, she dons a dark funeral dress. She has already donated to Goodwill the white dress she wore at Martha's Vineyard. Grace and Miles walk to St. Catherine's for confession. His mother "looked like a woman marching to her own execution." She hopes to draw the young priest to hear her confession. Instead, unyielding Father Tom slides open the confessional window. He dispenses torture, not mercy. His absolution apparently depends on another confession as penance: Grace must tell Francine Whiting of her mortal sin and seek forgiveness. After Sunday Mass, Grace crosses the iron bridge, turns into the hacienda estate, and meets Francine in the gazebo.

Charlie is then exiled to Mexico under the fiction that he runs a factory there. Francine consolidates her control of the Whiting empire and of the town. Grace attends Mass every day. Her guilt has not gone into remission. Its strain lays waste to her youthful beauty. As she approaches middle age, her appearance is "ghostlike." By then she has lost her job.

Francine sells the textile mill and shirt factory to a multinational company. Pay cuts and longer hours are extracted from workers. Still, after a year the mills close. Their machinery is sent off to Georgia and the Dominican Republic. Grace searches for a job. But Empire Falls descends into a postindustrial wasteland with a plummeting population and a battered town center.

Russo skillfully juxtaposes grim Hawthorne-like flashbacks recast in a Catholic moral universe with the abundant humor in a contemporary shriveled mill town. Such a melding of past and present, tragedy and comedy, set in a speck on the map, represents a major achievement. One additional flashback rounds out the background to Miles's annual meeting with Francine. It also underscores the depths of his mother's guilt and the cynicism of Whiting's manipulation of Miles over the years.

Francine falls and breaks her hip. Through a Boston lawyer, she advertises locally for someone to assist her. Francine succeeds in her apparent strategy to ensnare Grace. Francine pays her what amounts to just enough to live on. Once Francine heals, she keeps Grace on to help her with disabled Cindy, who was born on the same day as Miles. As a child, the official story goes, she was struck and dragged by a green Pontiac. Authorities never located the vehicle, and one is skeptical of Francine's version of events. The accident resulted in a broken pelvis, crushed legs, and a head injury that left Cindy in a temporary coma. Cindy has been in love with Miles all of her life. Twice she has attempted suicide by slashing her wrists. She has also spent time at Maine's Psychiatric Hospital in Augusta.

If one pulls the thread of the preceding history, others spring loose. Francine can congratulate herself that she gave her betrayer a job in Empire Falls when none were available. She refers to Grace patronizingly as "dear girl." After several years, she tells Grace, "I've grown fond of you, dear girl." But such rare affection in Mrs. Whiting is not unalloyed. Francine exploits what she knows is Grace's unremitting guilt. Cindy and Grace draw emotionally close in the absence of any parental love. In this way, Grace serves, instrumentally, as a connection to Miles. She throws herself into life at the hacienda, neglecting her young son David. Cindy's isolation at school breaks Grace's heart. At home she catechizes Miles with respect to Cindy: "We have a duty in this world, Miles. You see that, don't you? We have a moral duty?" When Cindy has no prom date, Miles asks her. But duty ends there, as Miles goes off to St. Luke's and Cindy to Bowdoin.

Once Francine calls Miles home and installs him in the Empire Grill, she has no interest apparently other than to have the business flounder and the building deteriorate around him. The grill serves simply as a means of compelling Miles to see that marriage to Cindy is the rational course of action, not to mention his duty. Thus, as with the employment of his mother, the grill serves as a way to persuade Miles of where his self-interest and moral responsibility reside. The annual meeting is a contest that Miles has lost before he throws his first pitch.

Miles drives across the bridge in his ten-year-old Jetta and parks in front of the hacienda. He spies Cindy's Lincoln with its handicapped license plate. She greets him at the door with her aluminum walker. Her neediness soon discomforts Miles. "I'm not sorry about your divorce," Cindy confesses. "It gives me a slender thread of hope." She continues shamelessly, "I still love you, Miles." Lithium has modulated whatever goes haywire in her brain, but it hasn't diminished her unrequited passion for Miles. This assault on Miles's guilt—his sense of duty, which derives from his mother and his Catholic conscience—serves as a prologue to Francine Whiting's offensive against him.

He meets her in the gazebo. She refers to him as "dear boy," infantilizing him the way she treated his mother and Charlie Whiting. On some level, perhaps, Miles suspects her end game because he's the only person in Empire Falls who argues with her. She is a force in town whose physical appearance stands out like the hacienda: stylishly coiffed hair, a "tweed jacket and moleskin slacks smartly tailored, her wrists alive with jewelry, not scar tissue." This last reference captures the irony of mother and daughter. Empire Falls' all-powerful matriarch bears the burden for a largely helpless middle-aged daughter. As the mill workers put it, the situation "went to prove . . . that God didn't play favorites."

Not surprisingly, Francine has no interest in discussing the grill. The talk turns to marriage. Whiting explains why she thinks Miles married Janine. He loved Charlene, but he feared marrying Cindy "because you were certain those were your mother's wishes." Janine was a compromise; in fact, Whiting suggests, Miles's whole life has been a search for the middle ground. Now that he is single again, another compromise presents itself. He can make amends and listen to his mother's voice, "the one that accuses you of selfishness, of not thinking of others . . . like poor crippled Cindy Whiting." Of course, given his mother's lifelong guilt, one might argue that she attempted to use Miles as part of her own moral reckoning. Whiting will later tell Miles that marriage to Cindy will leave him financially comfortable, with money to send Tick to college. Her appeals to conscience and self-interest are as nicely tailored as the cut of her clothes. The diner never rises to the level of Whiting's slightest interest.

Miles returns to the hacienda and invites Cindy to the high school home-coming football game. The rivalry between Empire Falls and Fairhaven has lessened. The former's student body has diminished with the town's popula-tion. Based on enrollment, the high school's sports teams have fallen from class "A" to "B," with "C" in sight. Fairhaven still has two mills operating, though in peril, as well as Fairhaven College. Empire Falls has lost competitive parity with its longtime rival. The plight of the high school and the presence of Empire Towers for senior citizens distills the essence of the former mill town's demo-graphic crisis, and of Maine's as a whole.

Janine and Cindy both make conspicuous entrances at the game. The former arrives late, so that she can strut into the grandstand making a show of her new figure. (She has just discovered, however, that Walt Comeau's age is actually sixty!) Cindy hobbles into the game with a cane in one hand and Miles's arm in the other. Their appearance and labored climb into the grandstand forms something of a spectacle for the fans. Nothing Mrs. Whiting said seems to have prompted Miles's invitation to Cindy. Rather, it recalls the prom; his mother's old call to "duty" seems to explain Miles's impulse. But the relationship comes to a dead end after the game.

Miles stirs from his passivity, his "rut," toward the last part of the novel. He walks to the end of the grill's counter, finally engages Walt Comeau in arm wrestling, and slams him so hard that the Silver Fox is hospitalized. He suffers a broken arm and a concussion. Janine's reaction to Miles's outburst captures Russo's sharp wit: "It was just like him, she said, to finally go and do something interesting after she divorced him."

Miles's assault on his longtime irritant precedes his final explosive meeting with Francine Whiting. He unearths why his mother wore a shroud through life like the Maine Puritan preacher reimagined in Hawthorne's "The Minister's Black Veil." The *Empire Gazette* runs a series on "The Way We Were." It publishes a picture of the shirt factory's office staff in the 1960s. His mother is looking at a man with a white beard. Miles studies the photograph. The bearded figure is Charlie Mayne—C. B. Whiting. Miles thinks back to the aftermath of Martha's Vineyard—how they went to confession on Saturday and after Mass the next day he secretly followed his mother and saw her cross the bridge. She turned into the hacienda's yard.

Miles silently fixates on the narrative of his mother's life. While he scrapes decades of paint from St. Catherine's exterior, his mind labors over the layers of guilt and shame that burdened Grace's life. He thinks of Father Tom ad-ministering a life sentence of guilt. Then Miles quits painting, never to return to the church.

Seemingly emancipated from St. Catherine's, which merges with Sacre Coeur, the durable French parish, Miles declares his independence from the grill and Mrs. Whiting. When he goes to tell her she'll have to find someone else to manage the place, Whiting claws back, claiming that she paid his mother's medical expenses and secretly gave her money for his college tuition. Attempting to maintain her power over him, Whiting asserts, "Did I not offer her every opportunity for the expiation and redemption you Catholics are forever going on and on about?" Miles counters that Whiting trafficked in "retribution," not redemption. Whiting, of course, will not easily relinquish her power and control.

Miles, David, and Bea have joined to open up a restaurant in Callahan's, using an old kitchen from which her late husband once served lunch. Even before Miles had informed Whiting that he was leaving the grill, she knew of plans for Callahan's. A local cop on the Whiting payroll serves as her spy. Two state inspectors arrive and find Callahan's kitchen filled with code violations. Then Bea receives a generous purchase offer from a Boston lawyer. She's sixty years old and has been working in the bar for forty years. The money would ease retirement. But in a principled stand against the lady behind the curtain, she refuses to sell. Mrs. Whiting's power and control over Empire Falls and its people dissolves as she liquidates all she owns in the town, including valuable land for development along the Knox River.

Russo draws on the experience of midcoast Maine, especially his own Camden, to portray the post-Whiting, postindustrial landscape that reshapes Empire Falls' economy. A brewpub is scheduled to open, significantly, on July 4. A credit card company spends millions renovating the mill for a call center. The shirt factory has been transformed into "an indoor mini-mall." Houses in Empire Falls that have long begged for buyers begin to sell. And St. Catherine's? The place where Grace poured out her prayer will be converted into tri-level condos. Miles, like Russo himself, is under no illusion that the new prosperity will accrue primarily to Empire Falls' locals. He suggests that his brother talks "like a real booster" about the changes in the mill town. If there were a sequel to *Empire Falls*, former mill workers would not possess the skills to prosper in the town's new service economy. They also would be unable to afford living in their houses or the community where they were born.[26]

The novel ends with a flashback, a sprint to the finish line characteristic of other Russo works. He adds to the unity of sprawling *Empire Falls* by gathering all the balls he has kept aloft over hundreds of pages. Twenty-three years earlier, when C. B. is summoned home from exile in Mexico, he leaves behind a second family. One reason he likes living in Mexico, we surmise, is that he doesn't feel as physically small among the people. His limousine stops in Fairhaven so that he can purchase a gun. He intends to kill Francine with one shot, make it back to Boston, and fly to Mexico. His plans go badly awry, like so much of his life.

Cindy greets him. He thought she was still in the psychiatric ward. As one has suspected, her life was not ruined by a green Pontiac; that's what Francine told the police. Fuming from a clash with her, C. B. had raced to the garage, "gunned" his car before the door opened fully, and dragged his daughter into the street. Cindy's presence before her father represents only one life that C. B. has destroyed, for an emaciated Grace, once his true love, stands outside the patio door with Francine. His wife is now the more attractive of the two women. It is all too much for C. B., always the weak "Charlie" before Francine. In the gazebo, C. B. plants the bullet he intended for her brain in his own temple.

That is where Francine dies as well. Russo switches back briefly to the present to dispatch her. The winter has been so fierce in central Maine that on April 1 cars in Empire Falls sport red flags on their antennas so that they could be identified amid mounds of snow. Then a week of unusually mild weather across the area melts the snowpack too quickly. The Knox River swells above flood stage. Francine feels invulnerable in her gazebo, apparently forgetting the dynamiting of the Robideaux Blight. She is swept away. Ten feet of water inundates Empire Falls, but the town has been cleansed of the last of the Whitings. As for Cindy, she has returned to Augusta's psychiatric hospital. Russo has executed an artful act of literary jugglery.

With the exception of the young local policeman who attends a bizarre sexual fraternity party in Orono and an abandoned, deranged boy who shoots up the high school, Russo masterfully handles the many moving parts of a powerful and frequently humorous novel. Not surprisingly, *Empire Falls* received prominent, glowing reviews. Two appeared in the *New York Times*. The first praised Russo for, among other things, transforming "Empire Falls into a setting of a rich, humorous, elegantly constructed novel." The second enthused, "Russo's command of his story is unerring, but his manner is so unassuming that his mastery is easy to miss. He satisfies every expectation without lapsing into predictability."[27]

Two other reviews suggest, perhaps, why *Empire Falls* deserved the Pulitzer Prize. The *Washington Post* reviewer singled out how "Russo layers tangled relationships into a richly satisfying portrait of a man [Miles] within a defining community." For *Kirkus Reviews*, *Empire Falls* represented "the crowning achievement of Russo's remarkable career."[28]

There were negative assessments as well. One of the most critical appeared in *The Economist*: "Disappointingly, Mr. Russo returns to the same lunch counter banter in the same knock-off of Gloversville . . . that fills out three of his four previous novels." The reviewer praised the "sweeping prologue" but concluded that "readers are likely to flip through the rest of the novel wondering what went wrong."[29] Yet as a place, Empire Falls, Maine, emerges as far from a simple reproduction of Russo's earlier fictional worlds.

MONICA WOOD AND THE PAPER MILL TOWN

Monica Wood is perhaps the most admired contemporary writer within the state of Maine. Her memoir, *When We Were the Kennedys* (2012), even outsold *Harry Potter* at Portland's major bookstore. It became the store's all-time best-seller and won the May Sarton Award for Memoir.[30] By taking note of this success within the state, I do not mean to suggest that Wood is a local color writer. Her most recent novel, *The One-in-a-Million Boy* (2016), has been translated into twenty languages.[31] Set in Portland, with familiar local references, the city is nevertheless not central to the novel's plot. Wood's most place-bound Maine books, the memoir and *Ernie's Ark* (2002), a collection of stories that cohere around the characters of a working-class community under duress, situate her writing within the world that constitutes her narrative of origins.

Wood was born in Mexico, Maine, in 1954. Its population stood at just over five thousand six years later. Rumford, twice Mexico's size, occupied the bank directly across the Androscoggin River. The hulking Oxford Paper Company dominated both towns through its physical footprint and its standing as the economic engine of Rumford and Mexico.

Wood's parents were devout Irish-Catholic immigrants from Prince Edward Island. For most of his thirty-seven years at the mill (1926–1963), Wood's father worked as what was called "a scaler."[32] He met trucks as they arrived all day, measured their logs, and determined where the drivers would unload their haul. After three decades, he was promoted to foreman, which required him to leave the United Pulp and Papermakers Union.

Wood has described her father as a great storyteller. In fact, she suggests that her fiction incubated from what she first heard as a child. "My father had a lilting brogue and beautiful grammar," she recalls; "the notion that stories had to be told in a certain way was something I learned early." She also absorbed the "long, melodramatic, novelistic ballads" that her father sang.[33]

Tragically, he died of a sudden heart attack at the age of fifty-seven, the wrenching starting point for *When We Were the Kennedys*. He left behind a wife and five children, who ranged in age from their twenties to three girls in grade school, one of whom was mentally disabled. An older sister, who taught high school English and lived at home, and her mother's brother, the Catholic priest known as Father Bob, helped fill part of the emotional void created by the death of Wood's father.

Monica was nine years old when her father died. In her memoir, she re-creates the secure, familiar working-class world of her youth, though labor strife sometimes upended the punch-the-clock rhythm of life in Mexico-Rumford. The Woods lived on the third floor of a triple-decker. Monica attended a French-Catholic school until the eighth grade. Then she enrolled at the local public high school, where her sister became one of her teachers.

Father Bob encouraged his niece to choose a Jesuit school for college. She was admitted to Georgetown University, a galaxy away from a small mill town in western Maine. Her initial reaction is telling: She thinks of her best friend, Denise Vaillancourt, in "Worcester, Massachusetts, moving into a dorm at Assumption College, a place where kids like us belong."[34] After the jarring encounter with her new world, Wood apparently thrived at Georgetown. She graduated in 1976 with a degree in English.

Following Georgetown, Wood worked for eight years as a guidance counselor at Westbrook High School in southern Maine. She began to write seriously around the age of thirty. Formal writing instruction consisted of a two-week course for beginners that she took in Portland. She lauds the instructor who taught her "the nuts-and-bolts of technique."[35]

Wood began publishing stories in her thirties. She also wrote nonfiction and undertook editing to augment family income. Her husband was from Rumford, and he taught at Southern Maine Technical College (later Community College). They lived in Portland. Faber and Faber published her first novel, *Secret Language*, in 1993. It is partly set in Maine. Ballantine released a paperback in 2001. Chronicle published *My Only Story* a year earlier. The novel takes place in Massachusetts and was a finalist for the Kate Chopin Literary Award. Critics were taking notice of Wood.

Perhaps her most popular Maine work of fiction, *Ernie's Ark*, appeared in 2001 from Chronicle. A paperback edition soon followed and then went into a third reprinting. Diverse Maine locales adopted *Ernie's Ark* for the "One Book, One Community" reading and discussion series. The collection of stories was also a Book Sense Top Ten Pick for July/August 2001.[36] It is important to note that between these works of fiction Wood began publishing books for writers based on her own experience.

To date Wood has published two more novels, which testify to her growing reputation. *Any Bitter Thing* (Chronicle, 2005; Ballantine, 2006) spent twenty-one weeks on the American Booksellers Association extended bestseller list. The Ballantine paperback was reprinted six times. The novel is set in Maine, with some scenes in Portland, but the plot could unwind anywhere. Given her polished writing and her stories that transcend the particular, it is not surprising that Wood received the guarantee of wide international translation in advance of her most recent novel.

Of her two Maine-centered books, *Ernie's Ark* precedes *When We Were the Kennedys* by more than a decade. But it is helpful to discuss the memoir first to understand Mexico, representative of many Maine paper mill towns before the fall. Taken together, *When We Were the Kennedys* and *Ernie's Ark* cross genres to create the most perceptive and realistic literary representation of a Maine paper mill town that we have.

Wood's memoir is a product of both research and recall. It's also a stylish literary work, which is to say that she is a novelist by trade and we can't simply expect Wood to imaginatively disarm because she switches genres. *When We Were the Kennedys*, for all of its factual basis, displays Wood's formidable novelistic skill: to draw characters, use dialogue, turn a phrase, and spin out a good "yarn" with a narrative arc. All of this is to suggest that literary memoir and fiction occupy a continuum. Novels are usually rooted in research and fact; writers' memoirs are typically shaped by imagination and literary skill. In Wood's case, she embraces the challenging task of re-creating her world primarily from when she was nine years old.

One of the achievements of *When We Were the Kennedys* is how Wood captures the physical presence of the Oxford Paper Mill, which dwarfs Mexico and Rumford. The book's prologue represents the mill as a kind of cathedral, visible from all points in town, dedicated to work and family prosperity: "The Oxford Paper Company, that boiling hulk on the riverbank, the great equalizer that took our fathers from us every day and eight hours later gave them back, in an unceasing loop of shift work."[37] Like her father, men spend their working lives in the mill, as do many sons (like Wood's brother) and grandsons. By the standards of rural Maine, the mill pays good union-negotiated wages. Wives don't have to work, unless they choose to, typically to support large (Catholic) families. Mrs. Vaillancourt, the mother of Wood's best friend Denise, performs piecework at home, sewing shoes.

Young Monica and the townspeople employ a significant diminutive for the massive mill: the "'Oxford,' we chummily called it, as if it were our friend."[38] Indeed, the mill assumes the attributes of a character in many of the memoir's passages. Consider how Wood imagines her father's personification of the Oxford. He had a kind of love affair with the mill. She prefers "to think that . . . Dad saw the mill . . . as a living being, a bestower of pride and bounty, real as a father: benevolent, trustworthy, unfailingly present."[39]

The school curriculum in Mexico, and apparently in Rumford as well, institutionalizes a heroic narrative of the town's visionary patriarch. Wood re-creates how her fourth-grade nun enthusiastically told the story. She does so deploying her own imagination and literary flair. Hugh J. Chisholm, a Scottish Canadian and a businessman in Portland, arrived in Rumford on a snow-driven day in December 1882. He rode in a sleigh until he heard the "remarkable thundering" of a river. "Out of the sleigh he climbed, his eyebrows grizzled with hoarfrost. He shivered inside his coat, ran a glove along the country-bred nose of his borrowed horse, slipped the beast a sugar cube for its trouble."[40]

Sister, with a wave of her hand, christened Chisholm a Catholic—like "all" great explorers. He stared down the 108 feet of falls cascading in only half a mile: "The sun-spangled water ribboning between Mexico and Rumford existed mostly unseen and unknown, a geysering thunder already changing shape in Hugh's thrumming mind." From this foundational moment, "standing on high like God at the beginning of the world," the dreamer and doer Chisholm built his paper empire mill by mill.[41] On the banks of the Androscoggin, the complex came to manufacture everything from bags to envelopes to newsprint.

In Wood's account, Sister's origin narrative thrills fourth graders at a moment when papermaking rides high in the saddle, untroubled by serious foreign competition. The memoirist, knowing what arrives after the fall, summons a world of security and prosperity that is clearly legible on Mexico's main street. The sidewalks boast banks, churches, shops, and a bowling alley. The schools overflow with "smart, ambitious" children who will enter the mill or seek their fortunes by moving away.[42] Over the town, smokestacks pump out plumes of steam and sulfur, the smell of cooking cabbage, not long ago a paper mill town's proclamation of prosperity. Before his early death, Wood's father embodies Mexico's good times. He buys a new car every year. It's no Ford or Chevy, but a Pontiac and then a Chrysler—not the typical working man's transportation.

Of course, prosperity bred indifference to the plight of the Androscoggin, "our lifeblood river."[43] Hugh Chisholm poured as much toxic waste into the river as planning he put into his manufacturing empire. This chapter, however, was not part of Sister's heroic narrative. Wood recalls how the Androscoggin's "banks [were] lined with ailing willows, houses disfigured with curdled paint, rooftops and window panes and flapping laundry blackened by pulp . . . [and the] legendary river scummed with yellow foam and burping up bloated fish."[44] It is doubtful that anyone seriously considered the river's condition in 1963. The Androscoggin surged through Mexico-Rumford, shoring up mill expansion and buoying Main Street prosperity.

Wood describes the different groups that were drawn to Mexico by jobs. They included Irish, Italians, Lithuanians, Scots, French Canadians, and Prince Edward Islanders. Apparently the town was free of ethnic tensions; at least Wood doesn't take note of any. Perhaps common blue-collar work muted ethnic differences. Maybe union membership underwrote solidarity that cut across ethnic loyalties. The principal conflict in *When We Were the Kennedys* involves a brief wildcat strike and then a much longer walkout. Bill Chisholm, grandson of the founder, comes to town to explain management's position via the local radio station. The strike lasts six and a half weeks. Looking back from the crow's nest of the present, Wood discerns the origins of a much later conflict than what she saw as a young grade schooler during Mexico's glory days: the rise of global corporations and the gradual loss of jobs as papermaking inexorably goes the way of textiles and shoes. *Ernie's Ark* fills in part of that story.

The "Abbott Falls" of *Ernie's Ark* began as a literary composite of three mill towns that Wood knew well because of personal connections—Mexico, Westbrook, and Jay.[45] Wood's reference to Jay, where her brother lived and worked, is telling. In the late 1980s, Jay experienced a bitter sixteen-month strike that closely resembles what happens in Abbott Falls—except for different endings. A character in *Ernie's Ark* observes, "There had been some long violent paper strikes back in the eighties that were supposed to teach us once and for all who we were messing with." The Jay strike was Maine's most turbulent of the final Reagan years; it proved disastrous for the union.

A mill town in western Maine on the Androscoggin and not far from Mexico, Jay went through an upheaval that constituted a different order of union/management conflict from any unrest Wood had seen growing up. It received statewide coverage and even attracted reporters from the *New York Times* and *Washington Post*. The strike lasted from the summer of 1987 to the fall of 1988.[46] The Jay strikers resisted the same changes that antagonize Abbott Falls' papermakers: the elimination of double pay for Sundays and holidays and changes to work rules, including "job combining," which would scrap 178 workers. In both Jay and Abbott Falls, strikes lead to violence, vandalism, scabs, and "super-scabs" (union men who cross the picket line). Unlike in Abbott Falls, the Jay strike ended in calamity for the union. After sixteen months, the union called a halt to the strike. But more than a thousand replacement workers now ran the mill. The more than twelve hundred members of the union local had lost their jobs.[47] Some would only be called back as needed. International Paper had broken the local. Like the Jay strike, the fictional version permanently fractures families and leaves lasting tears in the community's social fabric. In contrast to Jay, however, Abbott Falls' fourteen-month strike ends with the union triumphant, and the reader puzzled, perhaps, by such a reversal of papermaking's trajectory.

Wood takes pride in her background as the daughter of a working-class family from a blue-collar town. She is also sympathetic to the union. But she is not a proletarian writer. One can't classify *Ernie's Ark* as a protest novel. Rather, as she has described her focus, "the book is not about the political ramifications of a strike; it's about life behind and beyond and between and inside the strike."[48] In one of the finest chapters in *Ernie's Ark*, Wood shifts the point of view to first-person singular. She skillfully portrays the CEO of the Atlantic Pulp and Paper Company to articulate how he is whipsawed between competing pressures and not a one-dimensional enemy of labor.

With the exception of the Manhattan CEO, *Ernie's Ark* is a collection of stories about different characters who are residents of a mill community in crisis. Fewer than two hundred pages in the length, the collection doesn't possess *Empire Falls'* sweep. Four of the nine stories were previously published, which explains some narrative overlap in places. Chapters devoted to Ernie Whitten and his ark bracket the collection and, along with the striking community's travails, give the book unity.

Ernie Whitten spent his life in the mill as a pipe fitter. He was three weeks short of retirement with a pension when the union went on strike. He never considers crossing the picket line despite the exorbitant price he may pay for adhering to union solidarity. He suffers the humiliation of standing in the unemployment line, with notorious town "shirkers," to collect a check.

Along with the potential loss of his pension, Ernie faces a graver life-altering crisis: His wife Marie lies in Western Maine General Hospital, nearly forty miles away, dying of cancer. Ernie's world has revolved around Marie and the mill. She worked three days a week in the library; she also frequented local concerts and art exhibits. These activities suggest her difference from the practical-minded Ernie. "You always were such a philistine," Marie tells him from her hospital bed. In an alternative weekly newspaper in the hospital's lobby, Ernie learns of an art competition. It will be held at leafy Blaine

College near the hospital. This discovery sets in motion events that inspire Ernie to build a large ark in his small yard and to enter it, through a photograph, in the art competition.

The ark as a symbol can be interpreted, and overinterpreted, in varied ways. Wood has expressed some hesitancy about her handling of the ark: "I hope I was careful enough not to get carried away with symbolism."[49] Yet the bulky ark stands primed to provoke readers' imaginations. Perhaps, as a gift to Marie, it reflects Ernie's sudden artistic awakening. He has only fashioned practical things for her: the sunporch, a remodeled bathroom, boxes for birds, and planters. As its scale emerges, the ark serves as something of a parallel to the outsized mill. Except for the ark, and its biblical resonance, religion is totally absent from the collection. As a religious symbol the ark seems associated with Marie's impending death and a faith that she will make a spiritual journey to a new life. One could continue investing, and overinvesting, in the ark's meaning.

Marie comes home from the hospital, rests in the sunporch, and watches Ernie working tirelessly. The neighbors complain about the banging into the night, the bright lights that illuminate his work, and the structure's code violations. Dan Little visits Ernie three times. He is a striking electrician from the mill who works part-time as a town-building inspector. He first thinks that the strike has knocked Ernie off kilter. He never submits a written complaint against him. His neighbors' gripes mystify Ernie. He scans his surroundings and "all he saw were FOR SALE signs yellow from disuse, and the sagging rooftops of his neighbors' houses, and their shades drawn against the sulphurous smell of betrayal." The streetscape reflects the town's fall from prosperity. Indeed, the very name of the town, "Abbott Falls," is a complete thought, like Russo's "Empire Falls," that ironically foretells the town's future.[50]

Ernie works in his paper mill clothes, "a grass-colored gabardine shirt and pants." By the time Dan Little returns for the third time, Ernie has finished the ark. Little carries a camera to document the illegal structure. But Ernie asks him to photograph a Noah's-ark-like staged scene for the art contest. Two chickadees perch on the ark; Ernie helps Marie lumber from the sunporch to his creation with her small dog trailing behind. He carries Marie (what's left of her) up the plank. Ernie needs another dog to make a group of twos. It just so happens that Little travels with a female Labrador retriever that he acquired from the pound on the day of his divorce. He lends her to the setting and snaps a picture.

Ernie doesn't win the contest—not the one at the college or the other with life. If the Bible-like final scene represents a prayer for Marie's survival, God doesn't listen. Still, in the ark Ernie has created an artistic-religious object for

Marie before she dies. Moreover, the ark resurfaces in a salvific way at the end of the collection.

Of the nine stories in *Ernie's Ark*, the second, "At the Mercy," is the most surprising and artistically sophisticated. Wood shifts to the first-person point of view. And the narrator is none other than Henry John McCoy, CEO of the Manhattan-based Atlantic Pulp and Paper Corporation, the owner of five mills. McCoy travels north with his troubled twenty-six-year-old daughter. A Harvard graduate, Emily has dropped out of a doctoral program in psychology. A long-term relationship has just dissolved, and she is still furious with her father because he did not return from a Tokyo business trip when her mother, his ex-wife, died. Emily also holds her father responsible for the prolonged strike in Abbott Falls. She views him as a paleo-capitalist, and, ignoring her upbringing, she thinks of privilege as a kind of hate crime. Emily demands that her father "interrogate" assumptions while she reveals blind spots of her own. In other words, the story has a dual focus on father and daughter; in this contest of sorts, she can't win. To put it another way, Wood presents a surprisingly sympathetic portrait of the striking paper mill's corporate power broker. He emerges less potent than the workers think.

McCoy and Emily drive from Manhattan in his "shark-colored Mercedes" with "PAPRMKR" for a license plate. Ostensibly they are on a trip to admire the fall foliage, but Emily has other plans. Her constant reference to her father as "Daddy" amounts to a giveaway. As he notes, she hasn't called him that since she was a child.

Father and daughter engage in banter, which reveals that McCoy has a monopoly on family wit, as well as papermaking. When Emily claims she protested the Vietnam War, McCoy has a quick response: "By hanging a banner from your dorm room on Harvard Square?" As Emily reads difficult contemporary poetry, her father pushes back, holding a brief for poems that rhyme. "I hate you, Daddy," Emily snaps. "Well there's something," McCoy parries his daughter. "There's a word I understand."

Much of McCoy's wit, his impatience with his daughter's self-absorption, and his preoccupation with the strike course through the story in the form of an interior monologue. The trip with a daughter deaf to his problems represents a nuisance. "I've got a paper mill famously on strike; a fleet of overpaid lawyers getting their intestines rearranged by a couple of crew-cut federal-type mediators in cheesy suits; a cabal of accountants secretly floating trial balloons to South African buyers; and a squadron of attorneys sifting every United States labor case since 1870." McCoy wants to sell the mill. Yet eight months into the strike he first has to decide what to do with seven hundred replacement workers and "stay out of jail in the meanwhile."

McCoy and Emily stop for lunch in a greasy-spoon restaurant. He leaves a healthy tip. Once again Emily pounces on him for not interrogating his assumptions. She accuses him of patronizing the waitress. But perhaps his generosity has something to do with his social background. We learn that he grew up in a working-class Irish-Catholic family in a town not unlike Abbott Falls. Emily, the dropout psychologist, has long told her father that he is burdened with Irish-Catholic guilt. He thinks humorously that his parents must have done "a pirouette in their two-for-one grave" when he bought the Mercedes. Now, at age forty-nine, he's a corporate head trying to fend off the forces buffeting American capitalism, not work off childhood guilt.

After lunch, Emily asks to drive, and, in control of the Mercedes, she pursues her single-minded scheme to a frightening climax. She heads to Abbott Falls while he dozes. He awakens as they are about to drive into a nightmare. She approaches the picketers at the mill gate. McCoy challenges his daughter's uninterrogated assumptions about the strikers. He begins pointing to the men: "He bought your braces. The one right next to him paid for your voice lessons. His son footed the bill for Harvard."

The strikers see the Mercedes and are enraged by the license plate. They are the real papermakers. They hurl curses and then surround the car. A bat dents the hood and then smashes a headlight. McCoy is convinced that the strikers mistake Emily for his girlfriend. They pound the roof, trunk, and sides of the car. The confrontation terrifies Emily, so much so that she can't start the car. Finally, they make their escape to New Hampshire. Emily reveals that the trip was her psychiatrist's idea. With her mother dead and her boyfriend gone, she confesses, "I'm in trouble, Henry, and you're all I've got." The shift in how she refers to McCoy suggests how Emily reaches out to her father as a friend, rather than reducing him to a capitalist toady. All McCoy can promise his daughter is a good dinner, as he puzzles over how to respond and at the same time resolve the strike that has him in its talons.

Part of the power of "At the Mercy" derives from its placement in *Ernie's Ark*. By positioning the story immediately after a quiet, poignant depiction of a paper mill worker facing a double tragedy, Wood enhances the portraits of both Ernie and McCoy. The shift in point of view, the humor, and the realistic violence in "At the Mercy" put the reader on notice of Wood's range as a writer in the collection.

Not all of *Ernie's Ark*'s stories deal directly with community or the strike. One about Dan Little, however, captures another side of the violence that McCoy and Emily experienced. It also shows what happens to a super-scab in a union-defined community. Loyalty to fellow workers transcends kinship.

After meeting building-inspector Little in the opening story, we then encounter him as the first-person narrator of a family crisis. At dusk on a grey day, in the strike's ninth month, he drives down Main Street and takes the measure of mill and town. The former "looked like a ruined picnic, a sorry brick blanket at the deep center of the valley." Businesses show telltale signs of poor balance sheets: "a missing letter at Dave's Diner, and at Shower of Flowers . . . the storefront featured nothing but a few carnations headed for some lucky bastard's cut-rate casket." Still reeling from his divorce, the town's decline, and the strike's duration, Dan's disconsolation deepens. His younger brother's betrayal and its effects on the family tip despondency into depression. Timmy, who Dan practically raised after their father died, crossed the picket four months into the strike.

Dan recalls the night when Timmy told the family. McCoy's face flashed on television as a reporter interviewed him with a Manhattan skyscraper in the background. Timmy offered that the CEO had shareholders to consider. The word stunned Dan. He remembers that "in the entire history of our family I don't think the word *shareholders* had ever come up in conversation." After two years in the mill, Timmy announces that he's shedding the union's shackles. Knowing Dan has the closest relationship with their brother, Elaine appeals to him to dissuade Timmy. "Union's like family," Dan pleads with his twenty-year-old brother. "You stick with them even if they're wrong." "Which they're not," oldest brother Roy, president of the local, chimes in. When Timmy raises McCoy's "capital" investment, Dan loses it. "Suddenly I was yelling my head off, fists raised." He had to be restrained.

But Timmy persists because he's earning $18 an hour and sees no equivalent job possibilities in Abbott Falls or nearby. He joins the scabs from Georgia, who march "in and out of the mill with a police escort like they were visiting royalty." For his annual $38,000, Timmy pays an exorbitant price in return. The family renounces him. Timmy's nieces and nephews are told to forget him, to ignore him on the street for having broken ranks with the union and betraying generations of Littles.

Then union members harass him. Someone spray-paints "SUPERSCAB" on his landlady's stairs and hedge. His truck's tires are slashed, and he finds that his cat has been killed. For his local equivalent of Adam's fall, Timmy is not only cast out of his family but also driven from Abbott Falls.

On the one hand, "The Temperature of Desire" is a sensitive story told through Dan Little's remembrance of an older brother's devotion to fatherless Timmy as he grew from childhood through adolescence. On the other, the story, written during an era of de-unionization, captures both the moral back-bone of unionism and the resort to rough justice on members who sell out la-bor's fight. When the union loses a legal challenge to scab workers, the picketers rise up in fury, as Dan recalls: "We tore over the gate for the final shift, singing and hollering and picking up anything we could find—bats, branches, nails and rocks," as the National Guard stood by. Imprinted in Dan's memory, never to be dislodged, the moment "electrified" him. He felt his body "thudding with a terrible pulsating current of fury, a solidarity the like of which I had not felt in eight months, and it thrilled me and scared me as I rounded the corner to the north gate with the bellowing throng."

As Wood takes us back and forth from factory gate to family life, French names surface from time to time. The seventh-grade English teacher is Mrs. Theriault; her husband serves as the local's treasurer. Meghan Bouvier is "Mrs. T's" most beautiful student. On Main Street we find Laverdiere's Drug Store and Melanie Bouchard's School of Dance. Despite these hints, and the strong Franco-American presence in Maine paper mill towns (including her Mexico), Wood imagines Abbott Falls as an ethnic-free community. Perhaps she wanted to avoid particularizing her stories to preempt critics and readers from pigeon-holing *Ernie's Ark* as "Maine" fiction.

In the strike's fourteenth month, McCoy sells the mill to a global South African company. Improbably, perhaps, the new ownership agrees to pay back wages and restore pensions and seniority. In the contemporaneous context of Maine papermaking, which Wood knew only too well when she wrote *Ernie's Ark*, the implication might be that the company seeks to buy peace before the erosion of jobs will begin. Either way, the strike has been momentous for Abbott Falls. Families, the community, and local collective memory have been altered for a generation or more.

At the end of the collection, we circle back to Ernie and the ark, this time with his son. Forty-three-year-old James lives in California, which underscores the emotional distance between father and son. We first meet James when he re-turns to Abbott Falls for Marie's funeral. After high school he had fled the town for college at Berkeley. His parents knew their only child would settle perma-nently in California. A software consultant about to divorce, he's the father of a rebellious daughter who goes off to Alaska with her barhopping, guitar-playing boyfriend. In a sense, she is to James what he is to his parents—complete op-posites. James asks his soon-to-be-ex-wife to accompany him to the funeral, attempting to obscure from his father the collapse of his marriage. Karen agrees; she was always fond of Marie, remembering her birthday when James was always too busy with clients. Yet before she died, Marie (and then Ernie) knew the state of their son's marriage, as Karen's phone calls to her had changed.

For James, the funeral "would simply have to be gotten through"; he and his father have never had any common ground for conversation. Marie appears to have been a buffer, keeper of a kind of emotional truce between father and son. With mourners surrounding them, Ernie and James are shielded from sustained interaction. He does take note of the ark, and Ernie simply explains that it was an artistic gift to Marie.

Five months after the funeral, when the strike is settled, James has business in Portland, and he plans a two-day visit to Abbott Falls. Anxiety grips Ernie. Two days represents a long time to fill in silences, given Marie's absence. Ernie lists some potential discussion topics on a note card. In the end, the ark saves them. Small animals have found a home in the ark; it has weathered, and standing water is taking its toll. James and Ernie decide to pass time repairing the ark—and their relationship in the process. Through "her" artistic object, it seems, Marie has intervened to mend the bond between her husband and son.

Ernie's Ark was republished as a Ballantine paperback in 2002 and reprinted three years later. Though it gained a solid readership, especially, but not exclusively, in Maine, *Ernie's Ark* was not as widely reviewed as Wood's later books. *Publishers Weekly* singled out how Wood did "a remarkable job of illuminating the characters' inner lives[,] skillfully layering their brief but complex stories with humor, empathy, and melancholy." The *Chicago Tribune* argued, "The character-study aspect of *Ernie's Ark* is its strong suit."[51]

In 2015, Wood adapted *Ernie's Ark* for Portland Stage Company.[52] The play, *Papermaker*, was so popular that its run had to be extended. The stage performance renewed Maine interest in the collection of stories. Within the state, *Ernie's Ark* has perhaps achieved acclaim equal to *The Country of the Pointed Firs*. Especially when read in conjunction with *When We Were the Kennedys*, *Ernie's Ark* offers a realistic, humane, and gracefully written story of globalization's challenge to an industry where many Mainers had found well-paying union work.

EPILOGUE

Let us return to the questions about Maine place-based fiction that I posed in the prologue by drawing on the novels that have been discussed in detail. Does *The Country of the Pointed Firs* belong, as Willa Cather argued, and as some feminists claim, in the front ranks of American literature? Or is the novel a major-minor work? Recall how Jewett began *Pointed Firs* as installments in the *Atlantic*, with no intention of publishing a book. After the novella appeared, Jewett continued to write and publish Dunnet Landing stories. Three were posthumously inserted into the original text, one of which Jewett left unfinished. Moreover, the strongest story, "The Foreigner" (1900), was left out. The whole literary production of *Pointed Firs* that comes down to us is marred by posthumous revisions, a major exclusion, and a disrupted narrative chronology.

Yet the novella also displays some of Jewett's finest understated writing. It offers evocative descriptions of changing coastal nature across the summer season, excellent characterization, affecting self-contained short stories (perhaps her real métier), and her strongest expression of imaginative realism. Nevertheless, it is difficult to consider *Pointed Firs* more than a major-minor contribution to American literature. Still, Jewett's best book remains a *major* book about Maine as a place at a particular moment in time. But does it endure as *the great* Maine novel the way it is often represented?

To begin addressing that question, one might ask: Did Jewett exert influence over subsequent Maine novelists? As the first major literary novelist after Jewett, Mary Ellen Chase acknowledged that she wrote under her predecessor's long shadow. Chase's work, however, reveals little, if any, influence of Jewett and her imaginative realism. Producing her best Maine work during the Depression, Chase writes as a caustic realist about coastal Maine's century of decline and the baleful effects of summer people, who recolonize seaside communities in a kind of throwback to when the state remained a District of Massachusetts. For Ruth Moore, the ultimate anti-Jewett (before Carolyn Chute), *Pointed Firs* represented no literary lodestone for writing about islanders facing the Depression's onslaught. Of course, there is a counterargument to this literary history. Namely, Jewett's voice and form are so distinctive that later writers, by necessity, had to secure their own footing. Yet another way of putting this point: Jewett's imaginative realism, however original, didn't speak to subsequent Maine writers' creative needs and historical moments.

As a posthumously revised novella, *Pointed Firs* is far less developed than Maine's leading literary novels—say, *Silas Crockett*, *Spoonhandle*, *The Burgess Boys*, and *Empire Falls*. This study's prologue and chapters underscore how Maine is an expansive, diverse state. No single literary work can profess to plot its real and imagined territory. Thus, rather than a single work, it is more persuasive to think of multiple "great" Maine novels.[1]

The women authors who dominate *Hidden Places* raise several issues. Within local color or regional writing, mostly feminist critics have examined the countercultural world of women that is particularly pronounced in *Pointed Firs*. They have focused on female writing between 1880 and 1920. The work of women writers examined in this study falls beyond those decades and the prominence of the local color school. The many novels discussed in this study disclose no significant deployment of a counterculture defined by gender. Rather, some writers in *Hidden Places* create exceptionally strong, resilient women characters: most conspicuously Chase's Sarah and Mary Peters, as well as Abigail and Solace Crockett, along with Moore's Josie Turner and Sarah Comey.

The relationship of gender to geography presents a thorny problem. There is no question that, from Jewett to Monica Wood, women writers show a strong attachment to Maine places as grounded and conceptual terrain. Perhaps they didn't fear being labeled local colorists or regional writers. Or perhaps Maine has long possessed abundant national cultural capital as a place of rocky coastline, rugged mountains, summer dreams, and artistic inspiration. Also, the state as a cultural repository extends back to antebellum Portland writers who were national contributors to fashioning the Yankee character as a fixture in the American imagination.

Those writers included Seba Smith, John Neal, and Ann Stephens. Their fiction did not focus on Portland. But in his guidebook of 1874, *Portland Illustrated*, Neal made a suggestive observation: "That Portland has never had justice, nor indeed, anything like justice done to her, begins to be felt and acknowledged by pleasure seekers and the great business world."[2] He might have added writers like himself and his contemporaries.

Aside from some crime writers, Portland has not incubated major place-based novelists. In fact, the city has had a fraught relationship with the rest of Maine ever since it was stripped of its standing as the state capital in 1832. In a heavily rural state, Portland—double the size of the next largest city—does not seem to be part of the "real" Maine. Lacking the waterpower of other Maine places, Portland was never a heavy manufacturing city like Lewiston, Biddeford, or Waterville. It has deindustrialized at a faster pace than those communities. Portland's real and imagined geography distances the city from the rest of Maine and has only grown more entrenched as fancy restaurants, expensive condos, homeless people, and African immigrants have become familiar parts of the city's streetscapes. In stark contrast to overwhelmingly white Maine, people of color make up 16 percent of Portland's population of 66,650.[3] Portland has come to represent the "anti-Maine"; it belongs to Greater Boston. The state's population center has failed to produce a governor in more than a generation. Not surprisingly, gubernatorial party nominees from Portland are simply to be avoided, like black flies in May.

Among the writers we have discussed, Cathie Pelletier perhaps best captures the tension between Portland and rural Mainers. The conflict between the McKinnons of Mattagash and the Ivys from Portland propels her early novels. Pearl McKinnon, who leaves Mattagash for Portland at the age of eighteen, marries an undertaker and raises a scoundrel of a son. She pays a price for leaving Mattagash. Her entire family remains on edge when the Ivys visit Mattagash. To the locals, they are city slickers, not down-to-earth rural folk.

Carolyn Chute, in a more limited way, also exploits Portland as the anti-Maine. It's the place where Lucien Letourneau goes on a drunken whoring binge. Portland serves as a nerve center of the state welfare apparatus whose potential intrusion into his personal life Beal Bean resists to the point of his self-destruction. Then there are the newcomers to Egypt who commute to Portland. From their houses to their cars, urban interlopers represent a counterculture to the Beans' world and Miracle City's residents.

With Portland as a cultural outlier, this study has examined how authors of the state's best place-based fiction use their grounded knowledge and literary imaginations to evoke many "real" Maine places. As the state map suggests, Maine is too large a lump of earth to "take in" any other way.

NOTES

PROLOGUE

1. Nathaniel Hawthorne, quoted in Joseph A. Conforti, *Imagining New England: Explorations of Regional Identity from the Pilgrims to the Mid-Twentieth Century* (Chapel Hill: University of North Carolina Press, 2001), 2.

2. Wesley McNair, *Mapping the Heart: Reflections on Place and Poetry* (Pittsburgh: Carnegie Mellon University Press, 2003), 18. See also Wesley McNair, ed., *The Quotable Moose: A Contemporary Maine Reader* (Hanover, NH: University Press of New England, 1994), ix.

3. Ardis Cameron, *Radicals of the Worst Sort: Laboring Women in Lawrence, Massachusetts, 1860–1912* (Urbana: University of Illinois Press, 1993), 6. Kent C. Ryden comes close to the view of place I am describing. See *Mapping the Invisible Landscape: Folklore, Writing, and the Sense of Place* (Iowa City: University of Iowa Press, 1993). See also Ryden, "Region, Place, and Resistance in Northern New England Writing," *Colby Quarterly* (March, 2003): 109–20. On above-ground archeology, see Thomas J. Schlereth, *Cultural History and Material Culture* (Charlottesville: University of Virginia Press, 1992), 183.

4. Judith Fetterley and Marjorie Pryse, *Writing Out of Place: Regionalism, Women, and American Literary Culture* (Urbana: University of Illinois Press, 2003), 11.

CHAPTER 1

1. Mary Ellen Chase, "Sarah Orne Jewett as a Social Historian," in *Appreciation of Sarah Orne Jewett*, ed. Richard Cary (Waterville, ME: Colby College Press, 1973), 182.

2. Jack Morgan and Louis Renza, *The Irish Stories of Sarah Orne Jewett* (Carbondale: University of Southern Illinois Press, 1990), 36.

3. Michael Davitt Bell, ed., *Jewett: Novels and Stories* (New York: Library of America, 1994). All text quotations of Jewett's work are from this edition. The publication of Jewett's most significant work in the prestigious Library of America was part of a reassessment of her place in American literature. See, for example, Margaret Roman, *Sarah Orne Jewett: Reconstructing Gender* (Tuscaloosa: University of Alabama Press, 1992); Paula Blanchard, *Sarah Orne Jewett: Her World and Her Work*, Radcliffe Biography Series (New York: Perseus, 1994); and Karen L. Kilcup and Thomas S. Edwards, eds., *Jewett and Her Contemporaries: Reshaping the Canon* (Gainesville: University of Florida Press, 1999). Other important works are Sarah Way Sherman, *Sarah Orne Jewett: An American Persephone* (Durham: University of New Hampshire Press, 1989), and Gwen L. Nagel, ed., *Critical Essays on Sarah Orne Jewett* (Boston: G. K. Hall, 1984).

4. Blanchard, *Sarah Orne Jewett* is the best biography. I have drawn on her early chapters for some of the biographical background. See also Elizabeth Silverthorne, *Sarah Orne Jewett: A Writer's Life* (Woodstock, NY: Overlook Press, 1993).

5. Blanchard, *Sarah Orne Jewett*, 153. Two collections of letters document the women's emotional bonds. See Annie Fields, ed., *Letters of Sarah Orne Jewett* (Boston: Houghton Mifflin, 1911), and Richard Cary, ed., *Sarah Orne Jewett Letters*, rev. ed. (Waterville, ME: Colby College Press, 1967).

6. The quotation is from a compelling dissent from feminist readings of Jewett. See Richard H. Brodhead, "Jewett, Regionalism, and Writing as Women's Work," in Brodhead, *Cultures of Letters: Scenes of Reading and Writing in Nineteenth-Century America* (Chicago: University of Chicago Press, 1993), 143. Brodhead was responding in part to Sherman's *Sarah Orne Jewett* and Josephine Donovan's *New England Local Color Literature: A Woman's Tradition* (New York: Frederick Ungar, 1983). Donovan's feminist reading of Jewett did not elevate her above the local color school. See also Donovan, *Sarah Orne Jewett* (New York: Frederick Ungar, 1980). For a response to Brodhead, see Judith Fetterley and Marjorie Pryse, *Writing Out of Place: Regionalism, Women, and American Literary Culture* (Urbana: University of Illinois Press, 2003). They mount a detailed critical case for the importance of women's regional writing against the school of local color academics. See also Stuart Burrows, "Rethinking Regionalism: Sarah Orne Jewett's Mental Landscapes," *Journal of Nineteenth-Century Americanists* (Fall 2017): 341–59.

7. Blanchard, *Sarah Orne Jewett*, xvi–xvii.

8. Richard Cary, "The Uncollected Short Stories of Sarah Orne Jewett," in *Appreciation of Sarah Orne Jewett*, ed. Richard Cary (Waterville, ME: Colby College Press, 1973), 264. For online access to Jewett's works as well as to Jewett criticism, consult her site at Coe College: http://www.public.coe.edu/~theller/soj/sj-index.htm.

9. Jewett to Fields, October 12, 1890, in *Letters of Jewett*, ed. Annie Fields (Boston: Houghton Mifflin, 1911), 165.

10. Donovan, *New England Local Color Literature*, 100; Donovan, "Sarah Orne Jewett's Critical Theory: Notes towards a Feminine Literary Mode," in *Critical Essays*, ed. Gwen L. Nagel, 216.

11. Jewett to Andress Floyd, November 22, 1894, in *Jewett Letters*, ed. Richard Cary, 91; Jewett to Fields, October 12, 1890, in Fields, *Letters*, 165; Donovan, *New England Local Color Literature*, 102–3; and Donovan, "Jewett's Critical Theory," 216–17.

12. Blanchard, *Sarah Orne Jewett*, 84.

13. Brodhead, "Jewett, Regionalism, and Woman's Work," 118.

14. Preface to 1877 edition of *Deephaven*.

15. Jewett interview with *Boston Journal* (no date) quoted in Cary, *Letters of Jewett*, 16; Jewett, preface to 1893 edition of *Deephaven*, 3.

16. Jewett, preface to 1893 edition, 3; Blanchard, *Sarah Orne Jewett*, 86–87. On portrayals of the Yankee, see Joseph A. Conforti, *Imagining New England: Explorations of Regional Identity from the Pilgrims to the Mid-Twentieth Century* (Chapel Hill: University of North Carolina Press, 2001), 150–71.

17. Ellery Sedgwick, *The Atlantic Monthly, 1857–1909: Yankee Humanism in High Tide and Ebb* (Amherst: University of Massachusetts Press, 1994).

18. Richard H. Brodhead, "The Reading of Regions," in Brodhead, *Cultures of Letters: Scenes of Reading and Writing in Nineteenth-Century America* (Chicago: University of Chicago Press, 1993), 133.

19. *The Country of the Pointed Firs*, 484.

20. Howells, "Miss Jewett's *Deephaven*," *Atlantic Monthly* (June 1877): 759; *New York Times*, April 28, 1877, Supplement, 8. These and other reviews are available at the Sarah Orne Jewett Text Project located at Coe College in Iowa. On Whittier, see his complete letter in Blanchard, *Sarah Orne Jewett*, 112. Cary, *Appreciation of Jewett*, ix–x, also has a brief review of critical responses to *Deephaven*.

21. Conforti, *Imagining New England*, 234–48. See also Sarah L. Giffen and Kevin Murphy, eds., *A Noble and Dignified Stream: The Piscataqua Region in the Colonial Revival, 1860–1930* (York, ME: Old York Historical Society, 1992). Jewett, preface to the 1893 edition of *Deephaven*.

22. Quoted in Rebecca Wall Nail, "'Where Every Prospect Pleases': Sarah Orne Jewett, and the Importance of Place," in *Critical Essays*, ed. Gwen L. Nagel, 145.

23. Quoted in Blanchard, *Sarah Orne Jewett*, 274.

24. Jewett to Mrs. Henry Whitman, September 8, 1895, in Fields, *Letters*, 114–15.

25. Blanchard, *Sarah Orne Jewett*, 277. For a compelling portrait of a small Maine coastal town of this era (1894–1904), see Lura Beam, *A Maine Hamlet* (1957; repr., Gardiner, ME: Tilbury House, 2004).

26. Sarah Orne Jewett, *The Country of the Pointed Firs and Other Stories*, with a preface by Willa Cather (Boston: Houghton Mifflin, 1925). The Anchor paperback of this edition (first published in 1956) is a reprint of Cather's edition and may be the most widely read.

27. For a suggestive, even brilliant, discussion of Jewett, Homer, and John Marin, see Barton L. St. Armand, "Jewett and Marin: The Inner Vision," in Cary, *Appreciation of Jewett*, 297–305.

28. Jewett to Arthur Stead, February 25, 1895, quoted in Nail, "Where Every Prospect Pleases," 145. Nail offers a brief discussion of seasonality in Jewett's work.

29. Dona Brown, *Inventing New England: Regional Tourism in the Nineteenth Century* (Washington, DC: Smithsonian, 1995), 138–42, 155–57.

30. Blanchard, *Sarah Orne Jewett*, 72–74.

31. Cary, *Appreciation of Jewett*, xi. Cary quotes from some of the glowing reviews of *Pointed Firs*.

32. The reviews Cary cites, and eight more that are positive to enthusiastic, can be found at http://www.public.coe.edu/~theller/soj/sj-index.htm.

CHAPTER 2

1. Sarah Orne Jewett, *The Country of the Pointed Firs and Other Stories*, with a preface by Willa Cather (Boston: Houghton Mifflin, 1925), *The Country of the Pointed Firs* preface, n.p. For an overview of important American novels, see Lawrence Buell, *The Dream of the Great American Novel* (Cambridge, MA: Harvard University Press, 2014).

2. I am well aware that Marine painter George Savary Wasson published two earlier well-received works of fiction that focused on Maine's southern coast and the local dialect: *Cap'n Simeon's Store* (1903) and *The Green Shay* (1905).

3. Gladys Hasty Carroll, *As the Earth Turns* (1933; repr., Nobleboro, ME: Blackberry Books, 1995). This edition contains a helpful preface with biographical information.

4. Mary Ellen Chase, *A Goodly Heritage* (New York: Henry Holt, 1932), 11–12. Within a year this memoir had gone through three printings.

5. Population figures are based on federal censuses.

6. There are three short biographical studies of Chase, none of which is adequate. Two appear to be self-published. Elienne Squire's *A Lantern in the Wind: A Life of Mary Ellen Chase* (Santa Barbara, CA: Fithian Press, 1995) is the weakest of the three. The brief personal biography *Feminist Convert: A Portrait of Mary Ellen Chase* (Santa Barbara, CA: John Daniel, 1988) was written by Evelyn Hyman Chase, the second wife of Mary Ellen's younger brother. Mrs. Chase conducted extensive research but provides no documentation. She never establishes that Chase was a feminist. Perry D. Westbrook's *Mary Ellen Chase* (New York: Twayne, 1964) is intended primarily as an introduction for undergraduates. It briefly discusses all of Chase's works and sometimes offers important insights.

7. Mary Ellen Chase, *A Goodly Fellowship* (New York: Macmillan, 1939; pbk. edition 1960), 3. Squire, in *A Lantern in the Wind*, claims (24) that Chase's father was an alcoholic but offers no evidence. In Chase's third memoir, *A White Gate* (New York: W. W. Norton, 1954), her father is very nearly missing from her account of growing up.

8. Chase details the hardships of teaching in these schools in *A Goodly Fellowship*, ch. 2.

9. Chase, *A Goodly Fellowship* (chs. 3–11) covers these years of her life. Chase, *Feminist Convert*, is helpful on these years, citing much correspondence,

10. Chase, *A Goodly Fellowship*, ch. 10; Chase, *Feminist Convert*, 91.

11. See Squire, *Lantern in the Wind* (57) for a revealing entry in her diary.

12. Chase, *A Goodly Heritage*, 4.

13. The Petit Manan account is related by Chase, *Feminist Convert*, 135–36.

14. Mary Ellen Chase, "My Novels about Maine," *Colby Library Quarterly* (March 1962), 15.

15. Westbrook, in *Mary Ellen Chase* (157), makes the point about eccentrics.

16. Chase, *A Goodly Heritage*, 216.

17. Chase, "My Novels about Maine," 16.

18. The word is used liberally in *Mary Peters* (1934, repr., Yarmouth, ME: Islandport Press, 2005).

19. Chase, "My Novels about Maine," 17–18.

20. Chase, *A Goodly Heritage*, 15.

21. See, for example, Pamela J. Belanger, *Inventing Acadia: Artists and Tourists at Mount Desert* (Rockland, ME: The Farnsworth Art Museum, 1999).

22. Joseph A. Conforti, *Imagining New England: Explorations of Regional Identity from the Pilgrims to the Mid-Twentieth Century* (Chapel Hill: University of North Carolina Press, 2001), 230–31.

23. R. G. F. Candage, *Historical Sketches of Blue Hill* (1886–1907; repr., Blue Hill, ME: Blue Hill Historical Society, 2000).

24. Chase, "My Novels about Maine," 18.

25. Chase, *Feminist Convert*, 130. See also the numerous bestseller lists in Mary Ellen Chase, "Scrapbook, 1934–1936," Maine Women Writers Collection (University of New England), Box 4. This and other scrapbooks were begun by her English publisher and apparently completed by her, most likely with assistance. The scrapbooks include many reviews, advertisements, and notices of talks.

26. *New York Herald Tribune*, September 30, 1934, Review Sunday Books, 3; *Saturday Review of Literature*, November 9, 1935, 17; *Boston Globe*, n.d., n.p.; *San Francisco Chronicle*, September 23, 1934; and *London Daily Mail*, February 1934, n.p. These and many other reviews are in the Chase "Scrapbook, 1934–1936."

27. Edward Weeks, *Atlantic Monthly*, November 1934. This review, without page numbers, is in the Chase "Scrapbook, 1934–1936." A copy, without page numbers, is reprinted in Chase, *Feminist Convert*, 102–3.

28. For a detailed portrait of Jonathan Fisher and his Blue Hill world, see Kevin D. Murphy, *Jonathan Fisher of Blue Hill: Commerce, Culture, and Community on the Eastern Frontier* (Amherst: University of Massachusetts Press, 2010). Also see Mary Ellen Chase, *Jonathan Fisher, Maine Parson, 1768–1847* (New York: Macmillan, 1948).

29. See W. Jeffrey Bolster, *The Mortal Sea: Fishing in the Age of Sail* (Cambridge, MA: Harvard University Press, 2012), 208–9.

30. Ibid., 7.

31. These lists are collected in the Chase Scrapbook, *"Silas Crockett* 1936," Chase papers, Maine Women Writers Collection (University of New England), Box 5.

32. All quotations of reviews are from ibid.

33. Ibid.

34. Ibid.

35. Chase, "Any State with Noble History as Maine's Cherishes Her Past," Portland, Maine, *Sunday Press Herald* (August 30, 1936), ibid.

36. Chase, *Windswept* (1941; repr. Yarmouth, ME: Islandport Press, 2005), xv.

37. Chase, "My Novels about Maine," 19; Mary Ellen Chase, *The Edge of Darkness* (New York: W. W. Norton, 1957).

CHAPTER 3

1. Philip W. Conklin, *Islands in Time: A Natural and Cultural History of the Islands in the Gulf of Maine* (Rockland, ME: Island Institute and Down East Books, 1999), 17.

2. Herman Melville, *Moby-Dick* (1851; repr., New York: Bantam Books, 1981), 67.

3. Elisabeth Ogilvie, *My World Is an Island* (1950; repr., Camden, ME: Down East Books, 1990). For biographical information, I have drawn on her obituary in the *New York Times*. See "Elisabeth Ogilvie, 89, Maine Author," *New York Times,* April 14, 2006, 8.

4. Elisabeth Ogilvie, *High Tide at Noon* (1944; repr., Camden, ME: Down East Books, 1971).

5. "Elisabeth Ogilvie," *New York Times*, 8.

6. Sanford Phippen, ed. *High Clouds Soaring, Storms Driving Low: The Letters of Ruth Moore* (Nobleboro, ME: Blackberry Press, 1992), 453.

7. Ruth Moore, *The Weir* (1943: repr., Nobleboro, ME: Blackberry Books, 1986). I have used the editions of Moore's novels that are most available, though all are out of print.

8. For biographical information, I have used editor Sanford Phippen's detailed introduction to *The Letters of Ruth Moore*, i–x, and Jennifer Craig Pixley's informative and well-researched "Homesick for That Place: Ruth Moore Writes about Maine," 1–13, available at https://swhplibrary.net/digitalarchive/items/show/8485.

9. Quoted in Phippen, *The Letters of Ruth Moore*, iii. See also Pixley, "Homesick for That Place," 3.

10. Pixley interviewed Moore's sister in 1996. See "Homesick for That Place," 2. Betty Holmes Baldwin, who had boarded with the Moores, claims that her aunt lent the money for college; see also Phippen, *Letters of Ruth Moore*, 467.

11. Moore to Philip Moore, May 1936, 20; Moore to Lovina Moore, November 6, 1943, 146; and Moore to Lovina Moore, October 6, 1944, 174, in Phippen, *Letters of Ruth Moore*.

12. Pixley interviewed family members after Ruth's death. See "Homesick for That Place," 5–6, for an excellent discussion of the Moore-Mayo relationship.

13. Moore to Lovina Moore, March 15, 1943, in Phippen, *Letters of Ruth Moore*, 140.

14. Moore was interviewed by the *Maine Sunday Telegraph* and *Sunday Press Herald*. See "Spoonhandle Comes Back to Maine," October 5, 1947, "Spoonhandle

Clippings," Box 4, Folder 197, Moore papers, Maine Women Writers Collection (University of New England). All citations of reviews, publicity material, and newspaper articles are in the Moore papers at the University of New England, unless otherwise noted.

15. From an interview with the *Bangor Daily News*, quoted in Phippen, *Letters of Ruth Moore*, 493.

16. Ibid.

17. *Publishers Weekly*, March 13, 1943; Polly Street to Moore, January 20, 1943; and *"Retail Bookseller* Editor's Choice," February 1943. All of these citations are drawn from "The Weir Scrapbook, 1943," Box 4, Folder 193, Moore papers. Many of the reviews were collected by a service for the publisher. None have page numbers.

18. *Boston Globe*, April 11, 1943; *New York Herald Tribune*, March 14, 1943; and the *New York Times* citation quoted in the Moore papers, Box 4, Folder 194.

19. *Boston Post*, March 7, 1943; *San Francisco Chronicle*, April 8, 1943; *Springfield Massachusetts Union*, April 5, 1943; *New York World Telegraph*, March 19, 1943; and *New Yorker*, n.d., Moore papers, Box 4, Folders 193–94.

20. Chase to Polly Street, February 26, 1943, Moore papers, Folder 194. Morrow's quotation, undoubtedly written by Chase and dated March 13, 1943, is also in Folder 194.

21. Quoted in Joseph A. Conforti, *Imagining New England: Explorations of Regional Identity from the Pilgrims to the Mid-Twentieth Century* (Chapel Hill: University of North Carolina Press, 2001), 283.

22. Publication information and publicity material are in "Spoonhandle Scrapbook 1946," Moore papers, Box 58, Folder 195.

23. Numerous bestseller lists may be found in ibid.

24. Dorothy Canfield, "Book of the Month Club News," July 1946, in ibid.

25. *New York Herald Tribune*, June 16, 1946, "Spoonhandle Scrapbook."

26. *Philadelphia Inquirer*, June 15, 1946; for a critic's complaint about too many characters, see *New York Sun*, June 12, 1946. Both reviews are in the "Spoonhandle Scrapbook."

27. *New York Times*, June 16, 1946; *New York Sun*, June 12, 1946, "Spoonhandle Scrapbook."

28. *Hartford, Connecticut, Times*, June 15, 1946; *Times Literary Supplement*, September 25, 1948, "Spoonhandle Scrapbook."

29. *Chicago Tribune*, June 17, 1946, "Spoonhandle Scrapbook."

30. "Candlemas Bay Scrapbook, 1951," Moore papers, Box 7, Folders 201, 202.

CHAPTER 4

1. The best source of biographical information on Williams is by his wife: Florence Tapley Williams, "About Ben Ames Williams," *Colby Library Quarterly* (September 1963): 261–77. She quotes extensively from personal material that Williams was compiling for a

memoir. See also the remembrance of Williams by his son, Ben Ames Williams Jr., "House United," *Colby Library Quarterly* (December 1973): 179–90. Outside of reviews, critical commentary on Williams's work is spotty. See Charles C. Baldwin, "Ben Ames Williams," in *The Men Who Make Our Novels* (New York: Dodd, Mead, 1925), 578–83; Joseph B. Yokelson, "Ben Ames Williams: Pastoral Moralist," *Colby Library Quarterly* (September 1963): 278–93; Richard Cary, "Ben Ames Williams and Robert H. Davis," *Colby Library Quarterly* (September 1963): 302–35; Richard Cary, "Ben Ames Williams: The Apprentice Years," *Colby Library Quarterly* (September 1972): 586–99; Jane Carr, "Williams, Ben Ames, 1889–1953 Writer," in *The New Encyclopedia of Southern Culture*, 18 vols., 9 literature, ed. Thomas E. Inge (Chapel Hill: University of North Carolina Press, 2006), 463–64; and Jim Booth, "Ben Ames Williams's *The Strange Woman* as Art and Commerce," *The New Southern Gentleman* (blog), http://www.newsoutherngentleman.wordpress.com (October 5, 2014), 3–5.

2. Williams, "About Ben Ames Williams," 269.

3. Ibid., 274.

4. The novel has been reprinted by the local historical society, which praises Williams's research and fidelity to the facts. See the introductory notes to Ben Ames Williams, *Come Spring* (1940; repr., Union, ME: Union Historical Society, 2000).

5. The best short introduction to lumbering is Lawrence C. Allin and Richard W. Judd, "Creating Maine's Resource Economy, 1783–1861," in *Maine: The Pine Tree State: From Prehistory to the Present* (Orono: University of Maine Press, 1995), 265–73. The key section is written by Judd. See also David C. Smith, *A History of Lumbering in Maine, 1861–1960* (Orono: University of Maine Press, 1961).

6. Ben Ames Williams, *The Strange Woman* (Boston: Houghton Mifflin, 1941), acknowledgment.

7. Williams, "About Ben Ames Williams," 274.

8. Henry David Thoreau, *The Maine Woods* (1864; repr. New York: Penguin Books, 1988), 111. In *American Canopy: Trees, Forests, and the Making of a Nation* (New York: Scribner, 2012), Eric Rutkow argues that as early as 1839 New York replaced Maine "as the nation's premier supplier of timber" (108).

9. John Ford's great film, *Stagecoach*, lost. See Booth, "*The Strange Woman* as Art and Commerce," who claims (2) that *Gone with the Wind*, the novel published in 1936, heavily influenced *The Strange Woman*. In 1947, Williams published his *Gone with the Wind*, titled *House Divided*; at 1,515 pages, it was four hundred pages longer than Margaret Mitchell's tome, and it was clearly sympathetic toward "the lost cause."

10. *New York Times*, September 21, 1941; *Saturday Review of Literature*, September 20, 1941; *New Yorker*, September 20, 1941; and *Booklist*, September 21, 1941.

11. Elizabeth Coatsworth, *Personal Geography: Almost an Autobiography* (1976; repr., Woodstock, VT: Countryman Press, 1994), 5.

12. Ibid., 109.

13. Ibid., 147.

14. I have used the widely available paperback edition: *The Enchanted: An Incredible Tale* (1951; repr., New York: Avon Books, 1968).

15. *New York Times*, April 12, 1953.

16. Herman Melville, *Moby-Dick* (1851; repr., New York: Bantam Books, 1981), 60.

17. Thoreau, *The Maine Woods*, 86.

18. *New York Times*, July 1951; *Library Journal*, August 1951; *Christian Science Monitor*, May 10, 1951; and *Kirkus Reviews*, May 1951.

19. Elizabeth Jane Coatsworth, *Silky: An Incredible Tale* (New York: Pantheon Books, 1953).

20. Elizabeth Jane Coatsworth, *Mountain Bride: An Incredible Tale* (New York: Pantheon Books, 1954).

21. Biographical information on Pelletier is based on many revealing interviews with newspapers and online journals. I have also read numerous interviews in "Cathie Pelletier, Correspondence, Reviews, Tours, and Clippings," Maine Women Writers Collection (University of New England), Box 13. The quotation is from John Egerton, "Finding Her Literary Voice in the South," https://chapter16.org/finding-her-literary-voice-in-the-south/.

22. Egerton, "Finding Her Literary Voice."

23. Cathie Pelletier, *The Funeral Makers* (New York: Macmillan, 1986); Cathie Pelletier, *Once upon a Time on the Banks* (New York: Viking Penguin, 1989); Cathie Pelletier, *The Weight of Winter* (New York: Viking Penguin, 1991). For the last, I have used a handsome, readily available reprint. See Cathie Pelletier, *The Weight of Winter* (Napier, IL: Sourcebooks Landmarks, 2014).

24. Edgerton, "Finding Her Literary Voice"; Bob Keyes, "Home Is Where the Art Is for Cathie Pelletier," https://www.pressherald.com/2013/06/30/home-is-where-the-art-is_2013-06-30/.

25. Edgerton, "Finding Her Literary Voice"; Keyes, "Home Is Where the Art Is for Cathie Pelletier."

26. Randy Rudder, "Cathie Pelletier: How I Write," https://www.writermag.com/writing-inspiration/author-interviews/how-i-write-cathie-pelletier/.

27. Rudder, "Cathie Pelletier"; Keyes, "Home Is Where the Art Is for Cathie Pelletier."

28. Rudder, "Cathie Pelletier."

29. Keyes, "Home Is Where the Art Is for Cathie Pelletier."

30. Steve Geck, [untitled interview with Cathie Pelletier], January 22, 2013, 11, https://www.shelf-awareness.com/issue.html?issue=1911#m18655.

31. Ibid., 14.

32. Jon Halvorsen, "Tears and Laughter in a Tiny Maine Town," *Maine Sunday Telegram*, May 4, 1986, 47A; "Correspondence, Reviews, Tours, and Clippings," Pelletier papers, Box 13, Folder 7.

33. On the Aroostook War, a helpful essay is Howard Jones's "Anglo Phobia and the Aroostook War," *New England Quarterly* 48, no. 4 (December 1975): 519–33.

34. On Philip Booth, see his poem "Maine" in *The Islanders* (New York: Viking Press, 1961), 52.

35. *New York Times Book Review*, June 1, 1986; copy in Pelletier papers, Box 13, Folder 7.

36. *Kirkus Reviews*, May 29, 1986, http://www.kirkusreviews.com/book-reviews/cathie-pelletier-3/the-funeral-makers/.

37. Fannie Flagg, "Wedding Chaos," *New York Times Book Review*, October 22, 1989, 21; Howard Frank Mosher, *Washington Post*, November 19, 1989, Book World, 9; *Los Angeles Times*, November 3, 1989, Pelletier papers, Box 13, Folder 11.

38. "Sunday People," *Boston Herald*, February 23, 1992, 6–8; *Booklist*, October 15, 1991, 408. Pelletier papers, Box 13, Folders 20, 17, respectively.

CHAPTER 5

1. The best biographical information on Carolyn Chute comes from interviews. See especially Mary Battiata, "Carolyn Chute, Voice of Poverty," *Washington Post*, February 10, 1985, http://www.washingtonpost.com/archive/lifestyle/1985/02/10/carolyn-chute-voice-of-poverty/93827a1b-86b4-4088-8d95-a44bd37c3fb7/?utm_term=.1c62d8f9869c. See also Ellen Lesser, "An Interview with Carolyn Chute," *New England Review and Bread Loaf Quarterly* (Winter 1985): 158–77. The following local newspaper stories may be found in the Alphabetical File, Carolyn Chute papers, Maine Women Writers' Collection (University of New England): John Rolfe, "Fame Lets Her Fingers Fall on First Novel," *Maine Sunday Telegram*, December 16, 1984, 56A, Folder 1; Peter Morelli, "Writing for Life Often a Struggle," *Portland Evening Express*, September 9, 1984, n.p., Folder 1; Peter Morelli, "Chute to Settle in Parsonsfield," April 27, 1985, 1, Folder 2. All reviews and related material are from the Chute papers at University of New England, unless otherwise noted.

2. Gail Caldwell, "Carolyn Chute of Gorham, Maine: From Back Road to Literary Success," *Boston Globe Magazine*, March 24, 1985, n.p.; and David Walker, "Pondering the Beans," *Maine Sunday Telegram*, March 10, 1985, 36A, Chute papers, Folder 2.

3. Rolfe, "Fame Lets Her Fingers Fall," 56A; Bertha Harris, "Holy Beauty or Degradation," *New York Times Book Review*, January 13, 1985.

4. See, for example, Morelli, "Writing for Life."

5. Harris, "Holy Beauty or Degradation," for both quotations.

6. Battiata, "Carolyn Chute, Voice of Poverty."

7. Battiata, "Carolyn Chute, Voice of Poverty"; Lucia Greene Connolly, "Readers Do Care a Hill of Beans about Carolyn Chute," *People Magazine*, March 25, 1985, 129–31, Chute papers, Folder 2.

8. Battiata, "Carolyn Chute, Voice of Poverty."

9. This unattributed saying used to be heard occasionally when I first came to Maine more than thirty years ago.

10. Harris, "Holy Beauty or Degradation." She was one of many who brought up the comparison to Faulkner and Caldwell.

11. See Holly Larson, "Teaching White Trash Literature," *Teaching College Literature*, http://teachingcollegelit.com/tcl/?page_id=1270.

12. See Nancy Isenberg, *White Trash: The 400-Year Untold History of Class in America* (New York: Penguin, 2016), esp. 150. Isenberg also has a short, insightful discussion of *The Beans* (292–94).

13. Chute is quoted in "UMF Professor Removes Lobster from Her Plates," *Portland Press Herald*, July 2, 1988, Chute papers, Folder 7.

14. Battiata, "Carolyn Chute, Voice of Poverty."

15. Tyler is cited in James R. Thompson, "Carolyn Chute and Joy Williams: Alternate Voices of Rage," in *Constructing the Eighties*, ed. Walter Gruzweig, Roberta Maierhofer, and Adi Wimmerweig (Tubingen, Germany: G. Narr, 1992), 211.

16. Morelli, "Chute to Settle in Parsonsfield."

17. Lee Rove, "First Novels, Literary Boston," *Boston Magazine*, March 1985, 81–82; Dayle Muth, "No Sign of Deliverance in Egypt, Maine," *Christian Science Monitor*, February 8, 1985, 27; Bruce DaSilva, "First Novel Fine Sketch of Poor Folk," *Hartford, Connecticut, Courant*, January 2, 1985, B1. Copies of these and other reviews are in the Chute papers, Folders 1, 2. The *Chicago Tribune* is quoted in Battiata, "Carolyn Chute, Voice of Poverty."

18. Harris, "Holy Beauty or Degradation," 6.

19. Carolyn Chute, *The Beans of Egypt, Maine* (New York: Grove Press, 1995), "Postscript to the Finished Version," 271.

20. Ibid., 273, 275, 277.

21. Carolyn Chute, "The Other Maine," in *The Quotable Moose: A Contemporary Maine Reader*, ed. Wesley McNair (Hanover, NH: University Press of New England, 1994), 229–31.

22. Cathie Pelletier, "Carolyn Chute's Maine Characters Live Again," *Atlanta Journal Constitution*, June 5, 1988, n.p.; Clarence Major, "Making What Passes for Love," *New York Times Book Review*, July 7, 1988, 9; and Will Haygood, "Carolyn Chute: Speaking for Maine's Voiceless," *Boston Globe*, January 21, 1988, 37–38, Chute papers, Folder 3.

23. Elliott Krieger, "Chute's Rural Maine: Poverty as Freak Show," *Providence Sunday Journal*, May 22, 1988, I7, Chute papers, Folder 3.

24. "Author of the Week: Carolyn Chute," *The Week*, November 14, 2008, http://theweek.com/articles/510832/author-week-carolyn-chute.

25. Greg Gadberry, "Poor People Richly Portrayed," *Maine Sunday Telegram*, January 9, 1994, 2E, Chute papers, Folder 5.

26. Chute interview with Emily Burnham, *Bangor Daily News*, November 7, 2008, http://bangordailynews.com/2008/11/07/living/on-living-off-the-grid/.

27. Carolyn Chute, *Treat Us Like Dogs and We Will Become Wolves* (New York: Grove Press, 2014), and Carolyn Chute, *The School on Heart's Content Road* (New York: Grove Press, 2009).

CHAPTER 6

1. See the chart "How Do Mainers Identify Their Ancestry," *Maine Sunday Telegram*, October 8, 2017, A10.

2. Ibid.

3. Gerard J. Brault, *The French-Canadian Heritage in New England* (Hanover, NH: University Press of New England, 1986), 262; and Yves Frenette, "Franco-American Literature," in *The Encyclopedia of New England Culture*, ed. Burt Feintuch and David H. Watters (New Haven, CT: Yale University Press, 2005), 985–86.

4. The best biographical information is by Jim Bishop, in the introduction to the reissue of *Papa Martel: A Novel in Ten Parts* (1961; repr. Orono: University of Maine Press, 2003), ix–xvii. All of my citations are for this edition. The quotation is from Julianna L'Heureux, "Meeting Writer Gerard Robichaud," http://www.mainewriter.com/articles/Meeting-Gerard-Robichaud.htm. L'Heureux also reviewed *Papa Martel* for the *Portland Press Herald*, http://www.mainewriter.com/articles/Papa-Martel.htm.

5. Daniel Hartill, "Still Writing at 98," *Lewiston Sun Journal*, September 12, 2006, B1–2.

6. I am drawing on an excellent case study of Lewiston in Mark Paul Richard, *Loyal but French: The Negotiation of Identity by French-Canadians in the United States* (East Lansing: Michigan State University Press, 2008).

7. Ibid., 119.

8. *Loyal but French* employs this distinction between acculturation and assimilation, which harks back to sociologist Milton Gordon, *Assimilation in American Life: The Role of Race, Religion, and National Origins* (New York: Oxford University Press, 1964).

9. L'Heureux, "Meeting Writer Gerard Robichaud."

10. Quoted in Laura Fecych Sprague, ed., *The Mirror of Maine: One Hundred Distinguished Books That Reveal the History of the State and the Lives of Its People* (Orono: University of Maine Press, 2000), 116.

11. http://www.kirkusreviews.com/book-reviews/gerard-robichaud/papa-martel/.

12. Ariel Levy, "Elizabeth Strout's Long Homecoming," *New Yorker*, May 1, 2017, 22. This is the longest and most helpful essay-interview that provides biographical detail.

13. Ibid., 24.

14. Ibid., 23.

15. Ibid., 22.

16. Ibid., 23.

17. Evan Kerr, "Local Somalis Cheer Elizabeth Strout's *The Burgess Boys'* Focus on Hate Crimes," Minnesota Public Radio News (April 10, 2014), http://www.mprnews.org/story/2014/04/09/elizabeth-strout-book-burgess-boys.

18. Elizabeth Strout, *Amy and Isabelle* (1998; repr., New York: Vintage, 2000). I am quoting from this paperback reprint.

19. Elizabeth Strout, *The Burgess Boys* (2013; repr., New York: Random House, 2014). I am quoting from this paperback reprint.

20. Dylan Foley, "Elizabeth Strout on *The Burgess Boys*," *Chicago Tribune*, March 23, 2013, http://www.chicagotribune.com/lifestyles/books/ct-prj-0324-elizabeth-strout-20130323-story.html; Levy, "Elizabeth Strout's Long Homecoming," 25; Kerr, "Local Somalis Cheer."

21. Kerr, "Local Somalis Cheer."

22. The demographics are discussed in Andrea Voyer, *Strangers and Neighbors: Multiculturalism, Conflict, and Community in America* (New York: Cambridge University Press, 2013), 25–27.

23. Ibid., 19–21.

24. The letter is reprinted in ibid., 1–2.

25. Pam Belluck, "Mixed Welcome as Somalis Settle in a Maine City," *New York Times*, October 15, 2002, http://www.nytimes.com/2002/10/15/us/mixed-welcome-as-somalis-settle-in-a-maine-city.html.

26. Voyer, *Strangers and Neighbors*, 3.

27. Katie Zezima, "A Lone Man's Stunt Raises Broader Issues," *New York Times*, September 5, 2006, https://www.nytimes.com/2006/09/05/us/05maine.html?pagewanted=all.

28. Levy, "Elizabeth Strout's Long Homecoming," 26.

29. On the Bantu, see Catherine Besteman, *Making Refuges: Somali Bantu Refugees and Lewiston, Maine* (Durham, NC: Duke University Press, 2016).

30. The new rally actually drew only about 150 people. See Zezima, "A Lone Man's Stunt." Strout takes the first rally and transfers it to the second incident.

31. Foley, "Elizabeth Strout on *The Burgess Boys*."

32. *New York Times Sunday Book Review*, April 26, 2003. This review, and thirteen more, something of a cross section of critics' responses to *The Burgess Boys*, may be found at the Literary Hub, https://bookmarks.reviews/reviews/the-burgess-boys/.

33. *New York Times*, March 27, 2013, Literary Hub.

34. *Washington Post*, March 19, 2013, Literary Hub.

35. *Los Angeles Times*, April 5, 2013, Literary Hub.

36. Kerr, "Local Somalis Cheer."

CHAPTER 7

1. Among the most helpful interviews are Robert Birnbaum, "Richard Russo," *Identity Theory*, June 16, 2001, http://www.identitytheory.com/richard-russo/; Mel Gussow, "Writing a Novel in the Deli, Making Revisions in the Bar," *New York Times*, August 29, 2001, Arts, 1, 4; and Ray Routhier, "For Pulitzer Prize–Winning Portland Author Richard Russo, the Story Starts at Home," *Portland, Maine, Press Herald*, February 21, 2016, http://www.pressherald.com/2016/02/21/for-pulitzer-prize-winning

-portland-author-richard-russo-the-story-starts-at-home/. For a helpful introduction to Russo and his works that is aimed at undergraduates, see Kathleen Morgan Drowne, *Understanding Richard Russo* (Columbia: University of South Carolina Press, 2014), as well as Russo, *Elsewhere: A Memoir* (New York: Alfred A. Knopf, 2012).

2. Russo, *Elsewhere*, 6; Richard Russo, *Empire Falls* (New York: Alfred A. Knopf, 2001). Drowne, *Understanding Richard Russo*, 3–13, also offers background information.

3. Russo, *Elsewhere*, 7, 85–86.

4. Ibid., 7–13, 37.

5. Ibid., 43, 86.

6. Ibid., 85.

7. Gussow, "Writing a Novel in the Deli," 4.

8. Ibid.

9. Quoted in Drowne, *Understanding Richard Russo*, 4.

10. Russo, *Elsewhere*, 87.

11. Ibid., 92.

12. Birnbaum, "Richard Russo."

13. Ibid.

14. Routhier, "For Pulitzer Prize–Winning Portland Author." *Interventions: A Novella & Three Stories* (Camden, ME: Down East Books, 2012) is about a middle-aged midcoast real estate agent dealing with a recent cancer diagnosis and other personal problems.

15. Drowne, *Understanding Richard Russo*, 10.

16. Ibid., 12.

17. Routhier, "For Pulitzer Prize–Winning Portland Author"; Richard Russo, *Mohawk* (New York: Vintage Books, 1986).

18. Richard Russo, "Location, Location, Location: Defining Character through Place," in *Creating Fiction*, ed. Julie Checkoway (Cincinnati, OH: Story Press, 1999), 68. See also essays in Richard Russo, *The Destiny Thief: Essays on Writing, Writers, and Life* (New York: Knopf, 2018).

19. Drowne, *Understanding Richard Russo*, 19.

20. Richard Russo, *Straight Man* (New York: Vintage Books, 1997).

21. Drowne, *Understanding Richard Russo*, notes his admiration for Steinbeck (11, 301).

22. Russo, "Location, Location, Location," 72.

23. Gussow, "Writing a Novel in the Deli," 1.

24. Ibid., 4.

25. Birnbaum, "Richard Russo."

26. See Russo's comments in ibid.

27. Janet Maslin, "Turning against the Tide," *New York Times*, May 10, 2001; and A. O. Scott, "Townies," *New York Times*, June 24, 2001.

28. Dan Cryer, "Through the Mill," *Washington Post*, May 27, 2001, https://www.washingtonpost.com/archive/entertainment/books/2001/05/27/through-the

-mill/208f98b9-3103-40d7-ab1b-1d73e7979c3b/?utm_term=.45de5c12f9d7; https://www.kirkusreviews.com/book-reviews/richard-russo/empire-falls/.

29. *The Economist* review is quoted in Drowne, *Understanding Richard Russo*, 78. She says that the novel was not "universally well received." What novel is, one might ask?

30. Bob Keyes, "Monica Wood Keeps It Close to Home," *Portland Press Herald*, May 11, 2014, http://www.pressherald.com/2014/05/11/monica_Wood_keeps_it_close_to_home_/.

31. See Wood's website: http://www.monicawood.com/back.html.

32. Monica Wood, *When We Were the Kennedys: A Memoir from Mexico, Maine* (2012; repr., New York: Mariner Books, 2013), 106.

33. www.monicawood.com.

34. Wood, *When We Were the Kennedys*, 193.

35. "Monica Wood: Book Sense Favorite for Her Fiction," https://www.bookweb.org/news/monica-wood-book-sense-favorite-her-fiction-shares-ideas-craft-writing-latest-book-sense-pick.

36. See http://monicawood.com/erniesark.html.

37. Wood, *When We Were the Kennedys*, xviii.

38. Ibid.

39. Ibid., 109.

40. Ibid., 59. For insight into Wood's writing of the memoir, see "Monica Wood: Up in Mexico," *The Writer*, http://www.writermag.com/2014/01/01/monica-wood-mexico/.

41. Wood, *When We Were the Kennedys*, 60.

42. Ibid., 62.

43. Ibid., 105.

44. Ibid.

45. See "A Conversation with Monica Wood," in Monica Wood, *Ernie's Ark* (2002; repr., New York: Ballantine Books, 2005), n.p.

46. See, for example, "Paper Mill Strike Sharply Divides Tiny Maine Town," *Washington Post*, September 7, 1987; and "Maine Paper Mill Workers End Bitter 16-Month Strike," *New York Times*, October 11, 1988, 16A.

47. Ibid.

48. Wood, "A Conversation with Monica Wood."

49. Ibid.

50. Richard Russo points this out about *Empire Falls*. See Gussow, "Writing a Novel in the Deli," 4.

51. http://www.publishersweekly.com/pw/print/20020506/36613-fiction-notes.html; Steve Greenlee, "Life and Times in Monica Wood's Abbott Falls," *Chicago Tribune*, June 19, 2002, http://articles.chicagotribune.com/2002-06-19/features/0206190045_1_paper-mill-anger-intruder.

52. Tom Porter, "Life in the Shadow of a Maine Paper Mill: 'Papermaker' Explores Culture Clash," *Maine Public*, April 10, 2015, http://mainepublic.org/post/life-shadow

-maine-paper-mill-papermaker-explores-culture-clash; Keys, "Monica Wood Keeps It Close to Home." There is also much information about the play in Wood's uncataloged papers at the Maine Women Writers Collection (University of New England).

EPILOGUE

1. Lawrence Buell makes a similar argument for American literature in *The Dream of the Great American Novel* (Cambridge, MA: Harvard University Press, 2014).

2. Kent Ryden, "Writing Portland: Literature and the Production of Place," in *Creating Portland: History and Place in Northern New England*, ed. Joseph A. Conforti (Durham: University of New Hampshire Press, 2005), 178. I'm indebted to Ryden for his helpful analysis. See also Lawrence Buell, *New England Literary Culture: From Revolution through Renaissance* (New York: Cambridge University Press, 1986), 29–30.

3. "Largest [Police] Recruit Class in 2 Decades," *Portland Press Herald*, August 4, 2018, 8A.

INDEX